Praise for *Archangel*

"Satisfying and complex . . . a eulogy for the now demoralized and splintered [environmental] movement."
—*Outside*

"As taut and expressive as a violin string, this is an outstandingly intelligent and significant novel."
—*Booklist*

"*Archangel* captures both a timeless mystery and a timely issue: the invisible bonds between place and personality, between the physical landscape in which we live and the landscape of our hearts."
—Christopher Manes, author of *Green Rage*

"A wonderful literary adventure novel, squarely in the tradition of *Deliverance* and *Legends of the Fall*."
—Howard Frank Mosher

"With devastating precision . . . this politically and emotionally charged story . . . will pique the interest of all working people."
—*Business Ethics*, Minneapolis

"A superior adventure novel, written with skill and nuance."
—*Dallas Morning News*

"Watkins, whose muscular prose has been likened to that of Ernest Hemingway . . . captures the rhythms of the Maine woods. . . . This engaging amalgam of *Deliverance, The Monkey Wrench Gang, Walden,* and the Old Testament is a great read."
—*Yale Magazine*

"A thinking man's action story . . . dynamic and violent, yet oddly tender in its narrative details . . . *Archangel* will rush you to its conclusion and outfox you as you go."
—*San Diego Union-Tribune*

"Clean and lucid . . . the prose precisely evokes the beauty of the woods. . . . The writing soars above the genre."
—*The Providence Sunday Journal*

"Reviewers have already likened Watkins . . . to Hemingway, and the . . . comparison is an apt one."
—*The Hartford Courant*

"The reader will have to resist the temptation to be rushed by the powerful pull of the narrative and linger on the beautifully expressed observations which fill almost every page."
—*The Times*, London

A R C H A N G E L

PAUL WATKINS

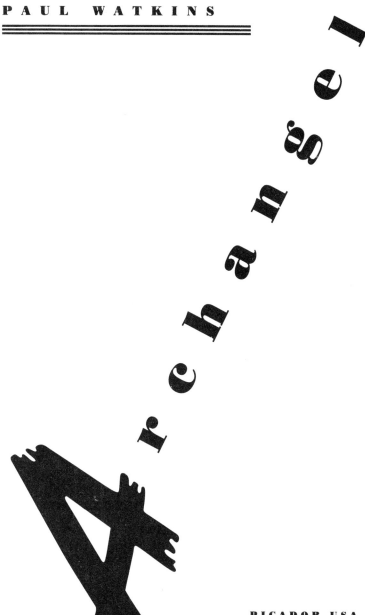

Archangel

PICADOR USA

NEW YORK

Picador® is a U.S. registered trademark and is used by St. Martin's Press under license from Pan Books Limited.

Library of Congress Cataloging-in-Publication Data

Watkins, Paul.
    Archangel / Paul Watkins.
       p.   cm.
    ISBN 0-312-15055-5
    I. Title.
  PS3573.A844A89   1997
  813'.54—dc20   96-33271
                                   CIP

First published in the United States of America by Random House

First Picador USA Edition: January 1997

10 9 8 7 6 5 4 3 2 1

For my brother, Clive

The author would like to thank
Leita Hamill, Jon Karp, Amanda
Urban, CRW, the Seltzers, Barry and Dini
Goldsmith, Tom Perry, Jean-Isabel
McNutt, Peddie and Lawrenceville
for their help and support in putting
together this book.

"Let us cross over the river and rest in the shade of the trees."

Stonewall Jackson,

Army of the Confederate States of America.

Last words. Chancellorsville, 1863.

ARCHANGEL

Twice in his life he prayed to God, and both times he left it too late. It was a December evening in the north Maine woods. The trees dissolved to coal-black silhouettes. Jonah Mackenzie stood alone and knee-deep in the snow, half-deaf from the rattling hum of his chain saw as he cut down a tree for his woodpile. Fat, damp flakes of snow fell around him. They settled on his short-cropped grizzled hair and melted on the warm skin of his neck. They filled in his footprints on the wandering path that led out to his truck.

Mackenzie raised his head, feeling sweat run fresh tracks down his face. He saw the Dog Star in the periwinkle sky. At the same time, a huge bird sliced the air above him, gliding without sound across the treetops. Its tip feathers spread like the fingers of a human hand. A bald eagle. He knew they hunted at dusk.

It was dangerous for one man to be out in the forest alone. Dangerous to be cutting down a tree in which the sap might have frozen. But Mackenzie was embarrassed not to have laid in a woodpile until now, which was why he had waited until the loggers went home. After all, he thought, it would look bad if the owner of the logging company hadn't completed a job that everyone else had taken care of weeks before. It would look even worse because he had only just inherited the Mackenzie Company. People were already saying that he couldn't keep up. Couldn't fill his father's shoes. The population of Abenaki Junction seemed to have a personal stake in watching the son of the wealthiest man in the region run his father's company into the ground. It had become Mackenzie's goal to disappoint them.

He sawed a wedge from the trunk so that the tree would fall away from him. The vibrations numbed his arms and scuttled ticklish across his ribs. A spray of sawdust, like chips of bone in the gathering night, fell at the base of the tree. He walked to the other side of the pine, raising his knees to clear the level of snow. His hands were slick with sweat inside his leather gloves. He pulled the trigger of the chain saw and its growling putter rose to a snarl as the blade ate into the tree.

Mackenzie heard the familiar groaning crack of the tree as it began to fall. Instinctively, he breathed in to shout "Coming down!" but remembered his solitude before the words formed in his mouth. At the same time, another realization came to him: the tree was not falling as it should. A shadow passed across the navy-blue sky. As Mackenzie jumped back, the deep snow caught his heels and sent him down. He saw the tree toppling. Saw the needly branches swishing through the air and the trunk pale and ragged at its chain-sawed base. He waved his arms as he fell and his gloves flew away like sloughed-off layers of skin. It seemed to him he had all the time in the world to know what was about to happen.

The tree fell across his left leg. Mackenzie clearly heard the bone snap just below the knee and felt the earth shudder as the trunk smashed into the ground. Pine needles rained down on him. At first the twisting crunch of bone shocked him into silence, but at last the scream came, climbing the the bands of his windpipe. It was shrill and hideous and raced through the forest until Mackenzie felt the burn of empty lungs. The sound trailed away. Slowly he brought his hands to his face and clawed his fingers down his cheeks, trying to wake himself in case this might have been a dream. He smelled the sap of the fallen tree, which stuck like glue to his palms. His stomach clenched, waiting for the pain to reach him. For now there were only strange bolts of shivering that rode up his leg into his buttocks and clambered up the joints of his spine.

It was dark. Beyond the trees, Mackenzie could just make out the road where his truck was parked. He knew that no cars would pass this way tonight. This was a logging road and it was Friday. No one would drive into these woods until Monday. There was no sense crying for help. It was a quarter of a mile to the main road and then three miles to town from there. In what seemed to Mackenzie to be the first clear thought to run through his head since the tree fell, he realized that he would freeze to death before his wife, Alicia, even considered him overdue. She would assume that he'd stopped at the Loon's Watch bar for a drink on his way home. She wouldn't miss him until midnight, and even then she wouldn't call the bar. Alicia wouldn't embarrass him that way. Instead, she would lie in bed and grow impatient. When he tiptoed in late and lay down beside her, she would turn away from him so that he was left to stare at her pale and freckled back. By now she would have let down her hair, the way she did every night. By day she kept it in a ponytail, clipped with a silver barrette. It was very fine hair, dark the way Asian hair is dark, and when the light caught it, the strands shone steely blue. He had known since before they were married that he could not live without her. With equal certainty, he knew that Alicia would manage in his absence. She would mourn, but she would not be the husk that her departure would make of him. Thinking this now made him determined to survive.

He sat up, using his hands as much as he could so as not to put pressure on his pinned leg. His hands sank into the snow until they reached the ground, where he could feel the frozen pine needles from previous years carpeting the soil. His other leg was tucked up toward his chest, clear of the trunk and cramped from the awkward position. Now the babble of his nerves was dying down. Soon the pain would focus.

His hand crept past branches and along the wool of his trousers. He reached past his knee to the frayed threads of torn cloth. Then his fingers snagged on something. It felt like broken glass. He realized it was bone, and jerked his hand back. New sweat broke out all over his body and nausea like a bubble of foul air swelled in his belly. His fingers brushed against the chain saw, which had fallen to the ground blade-first and now jutted from the snow like a stubbed Excalibur.

In panic, Mackenzie dug around the area where his leg was stuck, scooping out snow and throwing it over his shoulder. His fingernails became packed with bark where he'd scraped them against the trunk. But after a few minutes of this, he realized that he couldn't dig his way out. The trunk had slammed his leg down to the ground, and the ground was frozen. He tried to ease himself backward. Electric jolts jumped from his leg, sparked across his ribs and showered down the side of his head.

At last the pain was coming. It moved in twisting, knifelike cuts along his flesh. The cold had reached him, too. He could no longer feel the toes of his good leg. Slowly he began to understand what he would have to do. The knowledge took its time, pushing through the veils of disbelief. He knew he couldn't wait. If he did, he might not be able to go through with it. The indecision would kill him.

Mackenzie didn't pause to brace himself or cry or think about the future. He snapped a finger-thick branch off the tree, set it between his teeth and bit down. Then he grabbed the chain saw, heaved it out of the snow and pulled the starting cord. It coughed once and he pulled again and it started. When he set the blade in motion, ice and dirt thrashed at his face.

He cut off his left leg two inches below the knee. The blade slipped quickly through his bone and skin, vibrating along the length of his body. He bit down on the stick and howled. His back teeth cracked from the pressure. Then the saw struck the ground and he let go of the trigger. The motor stalled out and it was quiet again.

Mackenzie was beyond the point of crying. Any sound at all seemed useless to him now. He eased himself back from the trunk and used his heavy bridle-leather belt to make a tourniquet. Then he began to crawl as fast as he could toward his truck, elbow over elbow, hands knotted into fists, sinking into the snow. The pain was growing, taking shape. Heat and cold flashed at the place where his leg had been severed. Mackenzie looked back to see the bloody skid of his wound and the shreds of cloth from his trousers. The space where his leg should have been seemed to shudder with emptiness.

He reached the truck. It looked huge from where he lay. He clambered up the side until he reached the door handle, and when the door opened he swung back with it, dragging the stump of bone along the ground. He climbed into the cab, smelling the plastic of the seats and the coffee he had bought at the Four Seasons diner on his way out of town. The styrofoam cup rested on the dashboard. The coffee was cold and muddy-looking in the sharp yellow glare of the overhead light.

He couldn't find his keys. He slapped at the left chest pocket of his Filson hunting coat, where he normally kept them. He slapped harder, as if to jolt the keys into existence, but the pocket was empty. His hands clawed across his trouser pockets. Change rattled onto the floor. A handkerchief wafted into the dark. The keys had fallen from his pocket and lay somewhere out there in the snow. He'd never find them now.

Mackenzie heard the tiny patter of his blood dripping on the plastic floor mat. The muscles had spasmed. The blood flow was light. In every moment of stillness, shock draped itself around him, layer by paper-thin layer. He knew he had to keep moving. He drank the cold coffee, tasting its bitterness in the corners of his mouth, then crushed the styrofoam cup into squeaky chips and threw it outside. He took a flashlight out of the glove compartment and eased himself down from the truck. He started crawling along the road, over the snow-padded gravel. The moon came out from behind the shredded clouds and he caught sight of his own warped reflection in the funhouse mirrors of the frozen puddles.

He begged himself to rest. Fatigue purred in his head and slowed him down. When he felt it taking over, he grabbed snow and rubbed the gritty crystals hard against his face. Sometimes the stub of bone scraped on the ground. It sent the same rude shiver through him as nails scraped across a blackboard. Mackenzie followed the strange valleys of his own tire tracks until he reached the main road. He had no sense of time passing.

He propped himself against a speed-limit sign in the slush at the side of the road. Then he waited for someone to come, listening above the waterfall noise of the wind through the pines for the grumble of an engine. The cold walked up to him and sat down beside him and laid its hands on his goose-bumped flesh. Soon he was shivering out of control. He began to think he might have preferred to stay in the woods instead of lying there like some possum, road-killed on the verge.

Twenty minutes later, when he heard a truck coming, his hands were so numb that he couldn't switch on the flashlight. The high-beams of the truck burned through the forest and splashed across the road. Suddenly Mackenzie was trapped in their fire. It was too small for a logging truck. Too big for a jeep. He raised the light and waved his ice-cut hands and shouted.

The machine slowed. Its gears downshifted. Mackenzie could see the red-and-white sign of the Sparks and Loftus Dairy.

It was Barnaby Sparks in the truck, returning from Skowhegan after dropping off milk at the dairy. He was drinking from an old army canteen into which he had poured cream and vodka and coffee liqueur to make himself a White Russian cocktail. When he saw the man, he stamped on the brakes, which squealed as they brought the heavy Mercedes truck to a stop. He could make no sense of it—a man out here in the middle of the night. In a panic, he wondered if it might be a police trap, to catch him driving-while-intoxicated again. He opened the window and threw out the canteen. Then he reached into his pocket and ate a roll of mints, gouging them from the packet into his mouth one after another with his thumb, hoping to hide the smell of alcohol. He crunched them and swallowed the gritty fragments. They went down his throat like pieces of broken china.

Mackenzie heard a door open. Boots thumped the road as the driver jumped down. "By Jesus, what's going on?" asked Sparks. He moved with the same heavy plod as his cows.

"It's me," Mackenzie said. "I'm all fucked up," he whispered.

"What are you doing?" Sparks's thin face crumpled as he recognized Mackenzie. In the headlights' glare, Sparks's tight blond and receding curls made a fuzzy halo around his ears.

Mackenzie lowered his gaze to where his leg had been. "Look what I had to do," he said. The bone glimmered green-white and the torn skin was so pale it looked like carved alabaster.

Sparks fainted. His eyes rolled back into his head until they looked like two peeled hard-boiled eggs. He pitched facedown into the snow.

"No!" Mackenzie bashed Sparks on his springy-haired head with the flashlight. "I didn't come all this way to die at a road sign. Not with you lying there right in front of me. No!"

After a minute, Sparks raised his head. His eyebrows were crusted with snow. When it looked as if he might pass out again, Mackenzie hooked his finger under Sparks's jaw and kept it there, sunk deep into the man's throat, until his fluttering consciousness returned. "I swear to God," growled Mackenzie, "that I will take you with me you goddamned milkman if you don't get us both back to town."

"By Jesus," Sparks said, as he dragged Mackenzie to the truck, hands tucked under the man's armpits, "I never seen anything like it. There I was and here you are and the leg and, by Jesus, I can't even say."

Mackenzie smelled the sour milk on Sparks's hands and the syrupy sweetness of the White Russian on his breath. The whole truck carried a yogurtlike sourness to it, which caused people in town to hold their breath in the gust of wind whenever the truck rumbled past.

"OK," Sparks announced when he had them both in the truck. "OK," he said again, and slapped the large black ring of the steering wheel, a confused look on his face, as if he had suddenly forgotten how to drive.

"Look, Barnaby." Mackenzie's jaw trembled with the cold. "After you get me to a doctor, can you go up the logging road until you find my truck?"

"Yes." Sparks nodded, bracing himself, hands clasped on the wheel, but still unsure how to set the truck in motion.

"And can you get my leg and bring it back?"

"By Jesus," said Sparks, and fainted again. His head cracked down on the steering wheel.

As soon as Mackenzie realized what had happened, he reached across and grabbed the white cloth of Sparks's overalls at the back of the neck and heaved the man across his lap. Then Mackenzie shoved Sparks headfirst into the passenger-side seat well and slid himself across to the driver's seat. With his good leg, he revved the engine high in neutral, then slipped it into drive. As Mackenzie rode into town, he gripped the wheel to fend off the pain that mauled him each time the truck bounced over a pothole. Nausea churned his stomach, hoisting the cold coffee into the back of his throat.

Then, for the first time in his life, Mackenzie began to pray. He prayed to stay alive, clouding the windshield with his breath.

Sparks groaned in the seat well. The first lights of houses slid past.

At last Mackenzie felt shock overtake him. His nerves retreated deep inside. The outside world was vanishing like smoke. He stopped at the Four Seasons diner, its windows blurred with condensation and the shapes of people at their tables more ghostlike than real.

Mackenzie could go no farther. He lowered his head onto the silver half-moon bar of the horn. As his muscles relaxed, the weight of his skull set the horn's long wail sounding across the town and out into the hills around Abenaki Junction. It was the last thing he remembered from that night.

He would not pray again for many years. Not until the moment of his death.

A decade passed before Mackenzie's chain-saw dreams finally left him alone. It was as if his debt to them had at last been paid and they evaporated into the same red cloud of thought in which they had been born.

Sometimes he would wake in the night and feel the leg in its casing of dull pain. He would place his hands down hard, fingers spread, on the place where the leg should have been, and touch nothing but the wool of the blanket and the hard mattress underneath. But he could feel it, as if the leg existed on another plane of being and would always be there, even though he could not see or touch it, or walk without the heavy plastic limb which he placed at his bedside each night, sock and boot attached, its colored plastic chosen to match the opalescent chalkiness of his other leg. He strapped on this prosthesis every morning with the same unthinking precision with which he strapped on his belt and shaved and brushed his hair.

He didn't worry anymore about what people thought of him, the way he had in the first struggling years of running the company. Now people stood in awe of Jonah Mackenzie, believing that a man who had done this much damage to himself and survived would be left alone by bad luck and disaster from then on. So far, it seemed to be true. Since he had turned to clear-cutting the forest, his profits were far greater than his father's had been. Mackenzie's whole life had been shoved into the same charmed and half-real world that his old leg seemed to inhabit.

This all changed one morning in early June, when Victor Coltrane arrived at the Mackenzie mill, bringing news of a death in the forest. Coltrane was Mackenzie's company foreman. He had been around since the days of Mackenzie's father. Mackenzie watched him coming down the corridor. He saw the hard sinews of muscle wrapped around Coltrane's arms and the way he wore his shoulder blades like medieval armor on his back. His neck and legs seemed built to take the shock of a danger that hadn't yet arrived.

Mackenzie sensed disaster coming, the way he recognized miniature tornadoes of dust in the millyard as signs of an approaching storm. Coltrane stopped in the doorway to Mackenzie's office. The knit of Coltrane's sleeveless sweater expanded and contracted across his chest as he caught his breath. For a moment, the two men just looked at each other, one standing and the other sitting behind his custom-made black-cherry desk, its wood dark amber and glowing.

Then Coltrane spoke. "Get down to the car," he said. "Something terrible has happened."

Without a word, Mackenzie stood, picked his black-and-red plaid jacket off a wooden peg and put it on. Then he took up his walking stick, its top a plum-sized ball of walrus ivory, and, stiff-legged, followed Coltrane out of the office. People turned to watch them go, secretaries and mill workers and a man who'd come to restock the Coca-Cola machine. Mackenzie did not return their stares.

On his way to see the accident, Jonah Mackenzie caught a glimpse of his own reflection in the Range Rover's window. He raised one hand and touched the mirror image of his eye. It bothered him, but he didn't know why. Then he focused past his face to the ranks of young pine trees that grew beside the road. The pines had been planted in such straight lines that the empty avenues between them seemed to race away like frightened animals. Mackenzie vaguely recalled what this place had looked like before he clear-cut the land, not unlike when the French and English settlers used the gently sloping ground on the banks of Pogansett Lake as a place to trade with the Abenaki Indians. Guns, knives, beads, pots and pans for beaver and muskrat pelts. Mackenzie's family had been here since 1790, almost as long as the town. His ancestors had helped to drive out the Indians once and for all. Mackenzie used to tell Alicia, who quietly endured his repetition, that if it weren't for him Abenaki Junction would be swallowed by the forest. The scouting vines and sapling trees would spread their stubborn tangles through abandoned buildings, across the rusty railroad tracks and down the potholed main street until nothing remained of the town.

On any other day, to see the landscape ordered in this way would have filled Mackenzie with a calm that moved like sleep through his nerves. Tabula Rasa, he thought. Clean Slate. Sweep the forest aside and start again with himself as supreme architect. Tabula Rasa. He loved the way those Latin words rolled off his tongue. The finality of it. The absoluteness. Its purity was almost sexual. The trees in their planted rows appeared to rise in obedience to him. He thought how much he had changed since leaving Yale thirty years before and returning to the north Maine woods to work for his father. He had found himself in the middle of a war against the other logging operations—Deschamps, Mottet, Ruger. The Mackenzies had outlasted them all. It was also a war against faulty machinery, against dishonest employees and wasted time. Once a month Mackenzie went through a day with a stopwatch, marking down whatever he did at fifteen-minute intervals, to see if he was working as efficiently as he could. It was also a war against the forest for taking his leg and leaving him to pace through his life with a cripple's awkward gait. It would not end until each thing that grew in the wilderness and could be useful to man was spread out in vast, worshipful columns around the town of Abenaki Junction.

As Coltrane drove, he told as much as he knew. Some loggers had been cutting into trees just south of the Canadian Atlantic Railroad. The chain saw being used by a young man named James Pfeiffer had snapped its blade, which whipped back in Pfeiffer's face and killed him outright. Pfeiffer had come to Abenaki Junction a year ago. Before that, he had worked on a fishing boat out of Newport, Rhode Island. As soon as he made enough money, Pfeiffer had planned to go back to the coast and buy a boat of his own. Mackenzie had liked the boy. He spoke softly and straightforwardly. He wished it could have been someone else, if it had to be anyone at all. There had been accidents before at the company, but never an on-the-job death. A placard on the gates of the Mackenzie Company listed the number of days without an accident. Mackenzie went out each morning to slide the black numbers into place. Today it had been 137. As soon as we get to the mill, Mackenzie thought, I'll take down the placard and wait a while before putting it back up. Of all the bad-publicity ways to go, Mackenzie thought. Killed by a goddamned chain saw.

Chain saw. The words interrupted his thoughts. Chain saw. Chain saw. They repeated in his head as if he had never heard them before. Once more he felt the buzz of the blade through his leg. He closed his eyes and gritted his teeth.

Coltrane turned off the road and the Range Rover began moving along a gravel track that led up to the Algonquin Wilderness. Mackenzie had just purchased logging rights for 50,000 acres from the government. By the time the news was made public, the clear-cutting had already begun. He had nine months to finish the job, after which the area would be declared a permanent wilderness preserve. Mackenzie thought the idea was ludicrous. By the time I've finished with the Algonquin, he told himself, there won't be any wilderness left to preserve. But the price is good. Timber's good. I'd be a fool to turn down the offer. Someone else would take it instead. Some of the forest had never been cut. It had that rare name "old growth" attached to it, which struck Mackenzie as a challenge he could not turn down. He thought the idea of old growth was stupid. The Forestry Service would replant the area and in twenty years the land would be ready for cutting again. "If anybody needs a better reason than that," Mackenzie had told his wife, "they can go to hell and I'll join them there at my convenience."

Mackenzie set his hand on Coltrane's shoulder. "Why are we going so slow?"

"Man's already dead." The car bounced over potholes filled with the cream-colored water of dissolved clay. The puddles exploded across the Range Rover's hunter-green cowlings. Coltrane kept his eyes on the road, but the muscles stayed tensed along his shoulders, where Mackenzie's hand had settled like a crow.

In the distance, almost lost among the pines, Mackenzie could see a dozen of his loggers in their yellow hard hats and blaze-orange of vests, a letter *M* stamped in red on the backs. They clustered around a clearing, where sawdust powdered the ground. Parked on a dirt road across from the accident was a paramedic truck. Its flashing lights were off, the cargo doors shut. The driver, a man named Twitch Duvall, stood beside the body. He was called Twitch because he never sat still. He wore the blue-and-white jacket of the paramedic unit, and under it the white apron of his other job as manager of the Fresh Time Supermarket. Duvall was wringing his hands, as if squeezing water from a sponge.

Seeing this useless gesture gave Mackenzie his first clear message of the death. Before that, he had refused to believe it completely. To watch Twitch just standing there made Mackenzie furious. The Range Rover had barely come to a stop when Mackenzie swung open the door and climbed down, tottering on his good leg until he'd regained his balance. He felt the urgency of standing in front of someone badly hurt. He wanted to rush in, stop the pain and yell at his loggers to do something. But before he could speak, Mackenzie had a sudden and horrible vision—that it was not himself coming to see the dead man but the dead man rushing down to meet him, cackling and bloody through the trees. He reached out to take hold of Coltrane's arm for support, but the vision went away and Mackenzie's arm slipped back to his side.

As Coltrane began to wade through the crowd, the loggers stepped away from him as if in a well-orchestrated dance. No one had ever thought Coltrane would become a foreman. He had never been one to give orders. But this was precisely why Mackenzie had hired him: so he could give all the orders himself. Coltrane's rank had set him apart from the people who were once his closest friends.

As soon as Mackenzie saw Pfeiffer's body, his anger at Twitch Duvall disappeared. At least, the excuse for it did. The anger itself left a residue, which would oblige Mackenzie to become enraged at something else in order for him to leave it behind. There was nothing to be done for James Pfeiffer, no thread of life remaining by which to pull the young man back from death. Death had arrived completely and taken everything. The yellow-painted, black-oil-smudged chain saw lay almost on top of the corpse. The broken chain-link blade was lodged in Pfeiffer's face under a ragged flap of skin, and tangled in the flaked bone of his burst skull. The blade had woven like an iron snake through his hair and across the ground. One of his eyes remained open, peering suspiciously, as if Pfeiffer still needed some visible sign before his soul could abandon his body.

Mackenzie knew at once that even though jokes had been made about what happened to him, the peg-leg gibes that he allowed because he had invented them, there would never be jokes about this. The spilled-blood curiosity left him so quickly that he suddenly forgot what this curiosity felt like, even though he had been filled with it only a few seconds before. Instead, he felt suddenly cold, as if his flesh were no more than cheesecloth and the wind was blowing clean through him. It was a chill so deep that for a moment Mackenzie felt the terror of his own life slipping through the soft gauze of his flesh. He could not bring himself to believe that only a shell remained of James Pfeiffer, something to be hustled underground and remembered from now on in fading photographs.

The stares of the loggers had turned toward Mackenzie. They waited for some words to release them from their spell, for his voice to rise above the muttering.

Mackenzie breathed in deeply, summoning courage, not daring to show fear. "Twitch!" he shouted.

Twitch Duvall stepped forward. "Yes, Mr. Mackenzie?"

"Bring this poor man down the hill," was all Mackenzie said. He did not know where the body should be taken after that, but it did not matter. All he had to do was give the one command and everyone was suddenly in motion, the body in its stillness strangely distant from them now. Twitch carefully removed the saw blade from Pfeiffer's face. Then the men took off their belts and slid them gently under the corpse. They all lifted at once and carried Pfeiffer to a flatbed truck on which there was a crane for raising logs.

It was evening now. The air had filled with the tiny silver parachutes of dandelion seeds, blown in from the valley beyond. From a nearby tree, a bald eagle beat its massive wings and soared up toward the granite skull of Seneca Mountain.

The distant but fast-approaching sound of a police siren came from the main road. A minute later, the police car arrived, bouncing and sliding up the hill, its red and blue lights flashing. The car skidded to a stop in the chalky mud and Marcus Dodge climbed out. Dodge stood six feet three inches tall. He had short blond hair, a straight nose and eyes the brown-green color of old bronze. He was the only policeman in Abenaki Junction, and driving the only police car. They had never needed more than Marcus Dodge to keep the peace. His family had been in these woods even longer than Mackenzie's, and the way Dodge moved and spoke and thought were so much a part of the town that he never had to raise his voice to anyone, or ask twice for a thing to be done. He turned off the siren, but left the red lights flashing. They made a quiet, whirring noise.

The loggers stopped their talking. They waited to see what Dodge would do. Before he could speak, another car appeared at the end of the dirt road. It was a red Volkswagen Bug, chrome fender pimpled with rust. Mackenzie felt his heart clench like a fist. The outlet for his anger had arrived. It was Madeleine Cody in that car. Editor of the *Forest Sentinel*. Environmental activist, she called herself. Mackenzie considered Madeleine and her watchdog newspaper his own personal plague of locusts. He could not deny that she was very intelligent and pretty and full of potential. But Madeleine was the kind of person who needed to be told these things, and by someone she trusted to know. And the only person in this town who could say them to her and be believed, thought Mackenzie, is me. This was one of his greatest weapons in their private battle. Another was that she reminded him of his wife. Both Madeleine and Alicia had a sense of fair play that made them helpless against anything that was not fair. Mackenzie had been biding his time with Madeleine. He waited for her to tire out and move on. But his patience was wearing thin. If she didn't pack up soon, he would make her go, the same way he had finished the owners of those other logging companies.

For a while after *Forest Sentinel* started up, Mackenzie had thought the paper would fold by itself. Nobody seemed to be reading it. Then he realized that people were reading *Forest Sentinel*, they just never read it around him. He marveled at the way Madeleine wrote the paper and distributed it and solicited advertising all by herself. Although he would never have said it to her face, Mackenzie thought she was the hardest-working woman he had ever met. He had watched her grow up in Abenaki Junction, and the day she left for the University of Maine at Orono on a full scholarship to study journalism, Mackenzie doubted he would ever see her again. He was surprised when she returned four years later, having given up offers from newspapers all over the country. Madeleine had chosen to start her own paper. When Mackenzie found out what kind of paper it was to be, he felt an irritation that had never quite left him alone since.

As the Volkswagen approached, Dodge sensed the tension in the air. Some of it came from himself. He was in love with Madeleine and had been for years, as much as anyone could be from a distance and with no way to tell her how he felt. He knew what she thought of him and what he stood for. To Madeleine, he was the two-dimensional image of everything she fought against. The law that protected Mackenzie. Dodge wished he could tell her how much he despised the old man. He saw Jonah Mackenzie as a ravenous, grabbing giant, whose sense of law and fairness was loud and blustering until things went against him. Then he would turn around and cheat until he won. Getting what he wanted had become like a drug for Mackenzie, and he couldn't do without it. Dodge never said any of this. He kept his opinions to himself. His job demanded it. The way he felt about Madeleine had gotten in the way of every relationship he'd tried to have, and sometimes he resented her for it, out of frustration more than logic.

The Volkswagen skidded on the gravel. Then came the bone-crack sound of the emergency brake being applied. The puttering engine coughed and quit. Madeleine jumped out. She carried a camera slung around her neck, and an old leather mailbag, in which, he knew, she kept a tape recorder and notebook. Madeleine was thirty-two years old. She wore her cedar-colored hair pulled back with a rubber band. Not even one of those glittery bands made for the purpose, Mackenzie noted. An actual rubber band. Each detail of her existence seemed designed to piss him off. Her beauty taunted him, especially her eyes, which were a shiny mahogany brown. He knew that she had been an athlete in college, and even though it had been several years since then, her body still carried the same compact muscularity. Her skin stayed pale, even in the summer, but her cheeks were brushed rosy in the cool air. "How is he?" she shouted, and ran toward the flatbed where Pfeiffer lay, his head covered by an orange vest. She had not taken the time to put on her boots, and her feet, in sandals, looked naked next to the heavy, boot-clad feet of the loggers.

"James Pfeiffer is dead, Madeleine." It was Mackenzie who spoke. He sounded paternal and impatient.

Madeleine stopped in front of the body. Pfeiffer's blood-spattered hands hung down off the flatbed, the cuffs of his work jacket dark with old sweat. For a moment, it looked as if she might raise the orange vest to see the corpse's face, as if she didn't trust Mackenzie's word. The chill wind raised goose bumps on her naked forearms and batted at the baggy sleeves of her T-shirt. She hesitated in front of the body.

In that moment of hesitation, Mackenzie felt sure she would not look, and in not looking would show herself to be weak in front of the loggers.

Madeleine raised the cloth and stared stone-faced at the wreckage of Pfeiffer's head. Then she set it down, the bloody fabric molding against the wounds like a cast. She turned to face the crowd, but her eyes were aimed at Mackenzie. "Mr. Mackenzie." They had always been cordial to each other, but it was a brittle, flinty politeness that held more hostility than any insults that could pass between them. "You've got your men working double shifts, haven't you?"

"They get paid double. I don't hear any complaints. It's not against the law to be in a rush. Most people spend their lives rushing around. You, for example."

"The reason you're in such a hurry is because you're afraid someone will come along and find a way to stop what you're doing here."

"Not legally, dear. And not at all if I can help it."

Madeleine unshouldered the bag and the camera. She let them dangle on their straps until they touched the ground and then she let them go. "Why can't you admit the importance of this being the last area . . ."

"Area of old growth in the northeast." Mackenzie droned out the words. "Yes, I've heard all that. I've read it in your paper and seen it on your posters. I bought the right to cut here from the government. If you don't agree with it, take the matter up with Uncle Sam." Mackenzie began walking toward her, his cane digging deep into the pine-needled ground.

"Are you trying to make some connection between this accident and my purchasing the land? Because if you are, well, say it right here in front of all these people. I'm interested to hear it. Is there some cosmic force at work here that I'm not aware of?"

"I'm suggesting that you are cutting this timber so quickly to get as much as you can in the nine-month time limit, that you might be over-working your crews."

Dodge watched all of this closely. He saw Mackenzie and Mad-eleine as two different species, a cobra and a mongoose, ingrained with such instinctive mutual dislike that they seemed destined to clash whenever they crossed paths. To him, there was something deadly in the way they sidestepped around each other, as if waiting for one badly timed blink before rushing in to attack.

"Who says I'm overworking my crews?" asked Mackenzie. "Just you?"

"I've heard it in town." She glanced at the crowd. "From your own loggers."

"Who? Give me their names!" Mackenzie glared for a second at the logging crew, hunting for a guilty face. He didn't doubt there had been complaints. He had ordered Coltrane to push the crews hard while they cleared out the wilderness.

"You know damn well I won't tell you who they are." Madeleine gathered up her camera and bag, as if Mackenzie meant to smash them with his jabbing cane and heavy-treading artificial leg.

You're pretty when you're indignant, Mackenzie wanted to say. But he could not afford to admire her just now. "Of course you won't tell me. Journalistic integrity and all that stuff. Still, it does hurt your credibility a little." He looked around at the loggers, a half-smile on his face, mocking her.

Some of the loggers half-smiled back. Others glanced down at the chafed toes of their boots. Many loggers did agree that the land should not be clear-cut. When Mackenzie was not around, they would talk among themselves about the days when Jonah Macken-zie's father, Abraham, had run his business without leveling the forests. Sustainable yield. No one could even say those words in Mackenzie's presence and think that his job was still safe. Not even Coltrane. After what had happened to the last foreman, especially not Coltrane. The only person who dared was Madeleine. For this, the loggers respected her.

"Will somebody tell me what happened?" Madeleine looked around, asking them with her eyes to break Mackenzie's grip on their silence.

"Accident," Mackenzie told her. "Appears to be. You'll just have to let Dodge here do his investigation. Then you can find out along with the rest of us."

Dodge looked up at the mention of his name. He had been sitting in the car and smoking a cigarette, preparing himself to look at what had happened to Pfeiffer. He had met Pfeiffer's family when the boy first came to town. The father was wiry and weatherbeaten, his jaw permanently set from years of hard physical work. The mother seemed nervous to have her son live so far from home. And James Pfeiffer himself had seemed a little ill at ease. He kept looking around as if to see the huge waves of the Atlantic pounding on a beach nearby. But he had settled in all right. The boy could have made a career of it, if he had lived a little longer.

Mackenzie shuffled a little closer to Madeleine. He ran his fingers through his dry gray hair in gesture of losing his patience. "Please don't make me remind you that this is private property."

Madeleine turned to Dodge. "Do you mind if I take a picture?"

Dodge met her gaze. He thought of all the things he would say to her if he could, and if he thought it would do any good. But he just lifted one hand and let it drop on the open car door to show it was all right.

While Madeleine took pictures, Mackenzie drilled a stare so hard into Coltrane that the man looked up from his boots. "Drive me home," Mackenzie said, and threw him the Range Rover keys. Then he turned to the crowd. "As soon as Dodge is finished with you," he called to the loggers, "go home and take the day off." He turned to leave and then turned back. "With pay." He didn't pause to see if any signs of gratitude flashed across their faces. He didn't want their gratitude now. He would claim it at some later date. It was like paying insurance, and given for the same reason he handed out free turkeys at Thanksgiving and Christmas trees at Christmas, and paid for the annual Fourth of July fireworks display. Everyone in town owed Jonah Mackenzie something, even if it was just gratitude. And in return he owed them nothing, which was as he wanted it. Everyone except Madeleine, anyway.

A storm was coming. Rain from the north in a gray stampede. Its dampness sifted through the air.

Coltrane drove Mackenzie down the hill. "Now then," said Mackenzie, "what the hell happened up there?"

"We could talk about this later, if you want."

So it's as bad as that, thought Mackenzie. He slapped his thigh pocket and felt the squared-off edges of his notebook. He pulled it out and removed a tiny pencil from its spine. On one of the delicate blue pages he wrote "James Pfeiffer." He always carried his notebook with him, and always in the same pocket. Several times a day, he would slap his thigh pocket to see that the notebook was there, then the left chest pocket of his coat to check his wallet and finally a gentler tap across his right shirt pocket, where he kept his glasses until the moment when, every night, he set them on his bedside table. It gave him peace of mind to know what belonged where, the same for people as for things. "Just go ahead and tell me," he said.

"Well, it was an accident . . ."

Mackenzie didn't let Coltrane finish the sentence. "So that's all there is to it?" Mackenzie kept his pencil poised above the notepaper.

"No, sir. The chain bust because the saw was no good. It was one of those old saws that should have been replaced at the end of last year's cutting season."

"So why wasn't it?" Mackenzie noticed the clot of mud that had fallen from Coltrane's boots onto the seat-well carpeting.

"You told me not to, sir. I still have the memorandum. You told me to string out the machinery until it fell apart. Which it just did. Sir."

Mackenzie sat back. His lips puckered as he sucked at his teeth, deep in thought. "Fuck," he said, after a minute, as if it had taken him this long just to choose the right word.

"If Dodge has the chain saw analyzed by an expert, he'll be told that it was unsafe equipment. And if Pfeiffer's family finds out about that . . ."

"They'll sue me."

"They'll want some kind of restitution, anyway." Coltrane wiped his hand across his stubbled chin, trying to find a gentle way of agreeing. He could think of other families in town, who, if they heard that one of their own had been killed by unsafe equipment, would load up their guns and come hunting for Jonah Mackenzie. He didn't know about Pfeiffer's family. They were from the coast and he had no idea about those people.

At that moment, Madeleine's red Volkswagen overtook them on their way into town. Mackenzie looked down at her pale hands gripping the steering wheel. She had undone her ponytail and her hair streamed behind her in the breeze.

Mackenzie would regret closing down Madeleine's newspaper. He admired her stubbornness, even when it worked against him. He wanted to protect her, even when he had to protect himself against the things that she had done. Mackenzie wished she could have come to work at the mill instead of making things difficult for him every chance she got. When she was a teenager, she had stood in single protest outside his logging company gates, with a sign condemning his first clear-cut operation. The sign was made of plywood, with STOP CLEAR-CUTTING in fuzzy-edged, black spray-painted capital letters. The sign was too heavy for her to hold up for more than a few minutes at a time. She leaned against the fence, coughing in the dust that logging trucks kicked up as they rumbled into the mill. Mackenzie once sent out some lunch to her on a tray, but she refused it, just as he would have done if he had been in her shoes.

Despite her hostility toward him, Mackenzie could not help his affection for her. Mackenzie had no children, and Madeleine was the age his own child would have been if things had gone differently.

The Volkswagen passed by, its engine puttering with the same persistent energy that Madeleine herself seemed to possess.

Mackenzie thought about the other newspapers that would be calling soon—*The Skowhegan Times* and *The Down East Gazette,* based over in Greenville. He thought of them smacking their lips at the scandal. The Forestry Safety Commission would demand a report, too. They would send investigators to check every machine in his mill, every chain saw, every truck. The Pfeiffer family would have to be taken care of. There would be a burial. A memorial service organized. He would shake hands and make a speech and politely refuse the Spam-and-mayonnaise sandwiches with the crusts cut off. Even if the news of the unsafe chain saw never leaked out, Mackenzie knew he would still be blamed by the family. He would be blamed because there always had to be someone to blame. Mackenzie thought of time moving ahead without mercy for James Pfeiffer, already chipping away at the memory that remained of him in other people's minds.

"If we can just make it through these months ahead," Mackenzie said, as much to himself as to the silent man who rode with him, "we'll be all right. Better than all right." At that moment, he caught sight again of his reflection in the car's window. He shuddered. Suddenly he remembered why it bothered him so much. The warped image reminded him of the night he cut off his leg. He had stared at his pain-twisted face in the moonlit frozen puddles on the road as he waited to die or be saved.

Long after dark, Mackenzie sat in his office. Floodlights illuminated the lumberyard. They gave a shine like snow to the corrugated iron rooftops. Grit left over from the winter still pebbled the roads. With one more season, the old Victorian houses on Main Street had sunk deeper into the ground. Their roofs were bowed like the backs of beaten horses and the porches tipped forward, as if they meant to dump their cargo of paint-chipped Adirondack chairs onto the front lawns.

Mackenzie laid his hands on the lime-green blotter on his desk and felt the paper drink sweat from his palms. Dodge would follow through with the investigation. No sense praying that he wouldn't. I have to find a way out, thought Mackenzie. Make it look like someone else's fault.

He picked up the phone and called Coltrane. Told him to come back to the mill. Then he went down to the storeroom, where spare chain-saw blades and hammers and boxes of nails were piled so high that he could not see the walls. He felt uneasy in the quiet. For Mackenzie, the mill was a place of noise and motion always bordering on chaos. It haunted him to be here when the place was closed. When he returned to his desk, carrying the thing he needed from the storeroom, Coltrane had already arrived. Mackenzie stashed it in his desk drawer and waved Coltrane into his office.

Coltrane stood in front of him, arms folded, long back arched with age. Coltrane hadn't sounded sleepy when Mackenzie called. He knew I would call, thought Mackenzie. Knew I wouldn't leave this mess to sort itself out. That this wouldn't be a night for dreaming.

"Coffee?" asked Mackenzie.

Coltrane shook his head. There was no time for small talk and caffeine.

"Mr. Coltrane," he said. Mackenzie always used last names at the mill. The fact that the workday was over made no difference to him. The mill itself demanded such formality. "Go ahead and sit." Mackenzie waved at a chair.

"I'll stay on my feet." Coltrane's windburned forehead reflected the lights in the office.

"Chances are that it will come out about the chain saw being— being—" He didn't want to say "defective."

"Worn out," Coltrane said. "In need of replacement." He was poker-faced, all emotion hidden somewhere behind the Maginot Line of his skull.

"Exactly. It could destroy the whole company." This was the first time he had actually said the words, and hearing them now made him realize how true they were. "I'm way in debt from buying the Algonquin rights. I couldn't handle a lawsuit. Not the kind that could come from a man dying."

"I don't know how the money works that far up the ladder."

"Well, I'm telling you. And I'm telling you this, too. If this company goes down, the whole town goes with it. The mill is the town and everything else is servicing the people who work for the mill. Can you imagine what this place would look like if all those jobs suddenly vanished?" Mackenzie didn't pause. It wasn't a question to answer. "We have to do something to take people's minds off the condition of the chain saws."

"How are you going to do that without breaking the law?"

"Whose law?" Mackenzie raised his hands and let them slap down on the blotter. "Look, this was an accident. That's all it was. And I'll take care of Pfeiffer's family. But I don't want some lawyer getting fat off what was only an unfortunate mistake."

"So what are you going to do?"

Now Mackenzie slid open the drawer of his desk, slowly, ceremoniously. He took out a finger-thick, ten-inch bridging nail. There had been a whole case of them down in the basement, left over from some repairs done to the mill five years before. "All you have to do is hammer this into the tree at the place where Pfeiffer's chainsawing ended. Make sure the metal is gashed with a file or something and people will blame it on that. They'll call it somebody's prank. Or terrorism. Or the work of one of those radical, environmental, dirt-eating, tree-kissing druids that Madeleine wishes we'd all turn into. And in return you save the lifeblood of this town."

"I'm not doing that, Mr. Mackenzie." There was no hesitation in his voice.

"It would only take you ten minutes!" Mackenzie rolled the nail between his palms. It was cold and dull and gray.

"Time isn't what it's about." Mackenzie honestly believes what he's saying, thought Coltrane and shook his head slowly in amazement.

"You'd be an unsung hero, Coltrane. It requires courage." Mackenzie set the nail down within the man's reach. "Not to do this— well, it's almost the opposite of courage, isn't it? A person could almost call it cowardice." He knew he had to be careful with this word. It carried the same power to insult as the abrupt shoves he had seen start fights in bars.

"The cowardice, sir, is that I'm not quitting the company." Coltrane ran his hand over the smoothness of his head. His sled-dog eyes blinked shut for a moment and he whispered, "Christ."

"If you don't want to do it, Coltrane, then don't. I don't need you to quit. I won't fire you, either. I just need you to keep your mouth shut. Can you do that much?" Mackenzie waited long enough to breathe in once, then said again, "Can you?"

"I think I'm going home now, Mr. Mackenzie. Pretend I'm having a bad dream."

"Good." So it is a night for dreaming, after all, he thought. "I'll see you tomorrow."

Coltrane shut the door and found himself alone among the empty desks of the main workroom. The place smelled of old cigarettes. Coltrane was thinking how unfair it seemed that he felt like a crook when all he would do was stay silent. He hadn't done anything wrong, except to do nothing at all. He marveled at how unruffled Mackenzie had seemed. So convinced of what he was doing. That was Mackenzie's power in this town. He ruled by foregone conclusion.

Mackenzie waited until the sound of Coltrane's car had faded away down the road. Then he stood up to leave. As he was pulling on his frayed canvas jacket, he saw a movement outside the gates. At first, Mackenzie thought it might be the wind twisting up another cyclone of dust to warn of the approaching storm. Then a figure stepped from the curtain of black and into the glare of the floodlights.

Mackenzie knew he was being watched. He turned off the light in his office, realizing that his had been the only light in the building. Darkness swept around him. He crept close to the window.

Mackenzie saw the figure was a woman, dressed too warmly for this night. She wore red galoshes instead of the rubber-and-leather Sorrell boots that people wore all year round in Abenaki Junction. She wore a ratty World War II sheepskin flying jacket, torn to fluffy shreds across her back, and on her head a Russian-looking rabbit-fur hat, pulled down until it almost covered her eyes. It was clothing for the February days when people could not raise their heads to stare into the wind without their eyelashes becoming mascaraed with ice. She looked like a ghost from the winter.

She wore one more thing, and it was from this that Mackenzie recognized her: a large Big Ben alarm clock with two bells on the top and a black face with white-painted numbers. A length of rope was looped around each bell so that she could wear the clock around her neck. She'd worn that Big Ben for almost as long as Mackenzie had known her, which was all his life. She was Mary Frobisher. Mary the Clock.

Mackenzie thought back to when they were children and Mary used to go around with a tin of Crayola crayons—seventy-two in each green-and-yellow box—scribbling illegible fragments of poetry on every smooth-barked tree and sidewalk she could find. He recalled the gradually changing rainbow of quotations across town as Mary went through her crayons.

She was the first girl he loved, or thought he did when he thought he knew what love was. She showed him affection that neither his parents nor the others his own age could seem to find inside themselves. Mackenzie saw himself and Mary as outcasts in the town, cast out for different reasons, she for her eccentricity and he because he was the son of the wealthiest and most-feared man in the region. But what made them separate from others did not matter. What mattered was that this loneliness brought them together. He loved the smooth sweep of her hips under her flower-patterned dresses. He loved her fine-boned ankles and wrists. And he loved the way she spoke to him, in a language that he could never completely understand, in pictures that would come clear only after hours of thinking. The treadmill of her logic was different and it was this that he called beauty, more than the texture of her skin or the hair so dark it seemed like an absence of light.

He recalled the rudeness that was heaped on her by the other children, because she dealt none of it back. She seemed to have misplaced the capacity for lashing out that preserved an ordinary child. Whenever Mackenzie thought about this, Mary's face appeared to him like a hologram, green and shimmering. As they grew older, she remained happy in a childlike way when others her own age had discovered the trendy gloominess of adolescence. The first rumors of her mental instability began to spread. Mackenzie stood by her, against the wishes of his parents, perhaps simply *because* it was against their wishes.

When he told his father that he thought he might be in love with Mary, his father raised his hand as if to strike him, wide-eyed outrage on his face. "She's out of her goddamned mind!" his father had yelled. "And there isn't anyone who can save her from that. Not you or anyone. Now you can pour your feelings and your loyalty into that woman and it will never be enough because she don't even know what you're doing. Is that what you want, boy? A fight you can't win?" His father walked to the stone mantelpiece, on which he kept a crystal decanter of scotch. He poured some into a tumbler and handed it to Mackenzie. "I see things clearly and I know you don't right now. Here." The amber liquid rocked in the heavy glass. "Put a fire in your heart."

For Mackenzie, this offering was the rarest and most sought-after gesture that could come from his father. It was the offer of comradeship. The bridging of the gulf between them. But it was only there if Mackenzie accepted the glass, and accepted that his father was right. There could be no hesitation, and the offer might never come again. Not in his father's lifetime. He was that kind of man.

Mackenzie had gone out with Mary later that night, thinking he would make a break with her but not knowing how it could be done. He ended up making love to her on a blanket thrown across the scattered sawdust of the Mackenzie mill's cutting-room floor, the smell of oil and pine sap in the air. She never spoke the whole time. It seemed to him she never closed her eyes. They blazed at him with the same puzzle of emotion that made up the riddles of her speech.

She was seventeen then, and he was twenty-one. Mackenzie's father would have killed him if he'd known.

When Mary left town shortly after her eighteenth birthday to attend a special school in Portland, Mackenzie thought he would never see her again. She had little reason to stay. Too many others had driven away to the south, been swallowed up in the trees that crowded down to the road. They simply disappeared. But when Mary returned six months later, carrying her infant son and refusing to name the father, Mackenzie watched Abenaki Junction turn into an echo chamber. Rumors traveled like wind through laundry hung out to dry, through open windows and across the shingled rooftops.

Mackenzie's fear that the child was theirs began in him like the drawn-out ringing echo of struck crystal and never lessened in intensity. He didn't dare to ask, telling himself that if the child did belong to both of them, Mary would let him know. But he didn't believe it. What Mary did and didn't do followed no corridor of logic that anyone else could hope to understand.

Mary's insanity began to seem obvious to Mackenzie. Or perhaps, he thought, I am just seeing it the way others always have. It was as if a spell had finally been broken, and what had made them separate from parents and friends now drove them apart from each other. The possibility of staying together was suddenly both unthinkable and absurdly out of reach. But the worry never left him that the child could be his, too. No amount of distance could change that. He never told a soul about it, not even his wife, Alicia, whom he married three years later. Mackenzie often thought about the strange hand he had been dealt, with no child from his marriage and the possibility of a child that would never know its father's name.

What might have been a tolerated life for Mary the Clock—the shack she lived in, the food she bought more for the color of its packaging than for what was inside, the out-of-season clothes she wore— was not tolerated in her young son. Abenaki Junction lost patience with her eccentricity. The boy was taken away at the age of nine months and put in foster care, while Mackenzie stood by feeling sick and helpless and a coward.

Mary began to wander the streets again, just as she had done with her crayons a decade before. The crayons never reappeared. Instead, she took to wearing her Big Ben clock. People said it seemed to be there to replace the tiny heartbeat of her son. It served as proof of insanity to those who had judged her an unfit mother.

Twenty years later, Mary's son had come back. Now his name was Wilbur Hazard. He arrived almost penniless, wearing a glossy black leather jacket and thin-soled, shiny-buckled shoes, walking with a shuffle that made him seem always on the verge of stumbling. People said he wouldn't last a week. A year and then two years later, they were still saying it. In time, he put away the leather jacket. The shoes wore out on the grit-strewn sidewalks and he replaced them with the heavy boots that the local men wore. And like the local men, he wedged a baseball cap onto his head and kept it there. He was blending in. Soon the only mysterious thing about him became the reason for his being there. Having learned about his past, by all the reasoning of every gossiped word in town, he should have moved on. But he stayed. Wilbur Hazard made few acquaintances and no friends at all. It was as if he and his mother had barricaded themselves into a private other world. He fixed up Mary's house, and with money from his job as a cook at the Four Seasons diner, he bought her new clothes. He earned the two of them an almost respectable but stony silent place among the comfortably sane of Abenaki Junction.

Mackenzie had not spoken more than a few words to Mary in years, and had never spoken to Hazard at all. Mackenzie tried not to stare at the young man when the two of them passed on the street. He waited for some jolt of recognition, a ghost of his own younger self in the man's face, or the stare that confirmed what he feared. Mackenzie knew exactly what would happen to him in this town if it turned out to be true about Hazard and if the truth ever became public knowledge. He knew how people thought. They would fasten the story to him like a limpet and it would undo every fragment of respect they had for him. This was Mackenzie's oldest nightmare, rising from the deep water of his memory but never quite reaching the surface.

Mary stood at the wire-mesh gates, penned in by the floodlights' glare. She shook the heavy lock and chain that secured the gate. Her mouth formed words, but Mackenzie, cloaked in the dark of his office, could not hear what she was saying. He waited until the small and tottering figure vanished into the night. Then he took up the nail, fetched a hammer, got in his car and drove out to the woods.

With the first hammer blow against the bridge nail, Mackenzie recoiled at the noise. He stood very still in the darkness, trying to hear above the sound of his own heavy breathing. He switched on a flashlight and hammered at the nail until its head was flat with the bark. Then he pinched a fingerful of dirt, spat in it and rubbed the mud over the steel to camouflage it. As he rubbed, he saw the nailhead turning red-brown. He had picked up the soil stained with Pfeiffer's blood. Mackenzie took out a handkerchief, wiped his hands clean, and slipped a long rat-tail file into the cut made by Pfeiffer's chain saw. He slid the file in until it reached the nail. Then he filed a short jagged rip into the shaft.

Finally he stood back, sweat sticking his shirt to his chest. He shined the flashlight on the place where the nailhead lay embedded in the tree trunk. He could barely see it. He turned to leave, and shuddered. It was too quiet here. Quiet the way it would be now at the house of James Pfeiffer, with the silence that filled all houses of the dead.

Marcus Dodge stood in a meat freezer at the Fresh Time Supermarket, looking at the corpse of James Pfeiffer. The freezer was the only place where Pfeiffer's body could be stored for now. The nearest mortuary was a hundred miles to the south in Skowhegan, and it was too late to drive that far. The Pfeiffer family had been notified, but an autopsy would have to be performed before the remains could be released for burial. Dodge felt the unraveling of his heart in search of sympathy, but this dead thing already looked so different from the way Pfeiffer had been in his life that Dodge couldn't tell whether he ought to feel ashamed to cry or ashamed not to.

A sliver of condensation rose from Pfeiffer's barely parted lips. It occurred to Dodge that there might still be some life in the body, but he quickly put that aside. Dodge had hardly known Pfeiffer. He had only one clear recollection of the boy, from sometime earlier in the year, when the snow was still on the ground. Dodge had been sitting with Coltrane in the Four Seasons diner. The sound of laughter across the room distracted Dodge. He focused past Coltrane's shoulder to the source. It was Pfeiffer, laughing either at his own joke or at someone else's. He sat at a table full of other loggers, broad shoulders in faded shirts. Pfeiffer rocked back and opened his mouth as he laughed, showing his strong white teeth. Dodge's mind had made an unexpected Polaroid of that moment, and stored it away in his brain.

Twitch Duvall stood next to Dodge in the freezer. He wore a thing like a shower cap, required for all employees who went into the frozen-meat section. Twitch tried to make Dodge wear a shower cap, but Dodge took the puffy pale-green thing and popped it onto the head of a cardboard cutout of a woman advertising oven cleaner.

Twitch's breath was visible in the stale damp air. "Now, you just make damn sure nobody hears that you're keeping this guy in my supermarket." Twitch edged over to the body. He pattered his fingers on the bib of his starched and bloodstained apron. The raggedness of Pfeiffer's wounds had no visible effect on Duvall, as if the sight of supermarket butchery had long ago numbed him to this.

Dodge made no comment about Pfeiffer. He kept his feelings to himself. He knelt down next to the corpse, which lay stretched across two pallets, six inches off the wet concrete floor. For a while, the still-warm body had steamed in the steel-walled room, but Pfeiffer was cold now, and felt clammy to the touch in the way only refrigerated meat can feel. Dodge noticed the whiteness of the dead man's fingernails, and how black the dirt seemed under their tips. It made him clench his own hands into fists and jam them deep into his pockets, as if the paleness of death might be contagious. He walked over to a side of beef and sat down on it. The dull white armorplating of fat across the carcass was tattooed with blue USDA stamps. Dodge smoothed his hands across his face, feeling the skull beneath the skin.

"Are you all right, Marcus?" Twitch sat down next to him on the carcass. The bones creaked under his weight.

"Just give me a minute," said Dodge.

Twitch stood and opened the freezer door. Condensation billowed across the floor. "Well, I don't see as why you got to stare at that body anymore, anyways. It ain't nothing now." He walked out into the musty stockroom and the door clunked shut behind him.

Dodge took out his notebook and began to write. His report on the accident was due first thing tomorrow. He had only written three words when the door swung open again. Dodge sighed and looked up, ready to tell Twitch to leave him alone a while longer. But it wasn't Twitch. It was Madeleine. "Oh!" said Dodge, unable to hide his surprise. He stood up from his beef-carcass seat.

Madeleine walked into the room. Heat seeped like smoke from her clothes, as if her whole body were smoldering. "I'm doing a story on the accident," she told him. Her voice was too loud in the cramped space of the freezer.

"I know," Dodge answered quietly. The cold was getting to him, seeping through each layer of his clothes, but now he felt sweat on his forehead. Sometimes it made him nervous to be stuck alone with Madeleine, even if he longed for her company. He found conversation with her difficult. Not because he had nothing to say. It was because of all the things he wanted to tell her but did not dare. He was afraid the words would slip out, and he would look worse than a fool.

She looked down at the body for a few seconds. Her eyes slowly narrowed and she pressed her lips together.

Dodge could tell she was holding her breath. He had done the same when he first walked in. But now all the smells of the meat locker had soaked into his lungs and he could not tell one scent of death from another.

Madeleine turned to him. "So what do you think? Are the Pfeiffers going to sue Mackenzie? Is Mackenzie going to settle out of court?"

None of this had occurred to Dodge yet. In time it would, but not now, when the body was just growing cold. "I wish you wouldn't say things like that at times like this," he said.

Madeleine knew it was inappropriate, but she couldn't help herself.

She never could. If she thought something, she almost always said it without thinking of the consequences. "I'm sorry," she said, and genuinely did regret the remarks. But even as she apologized, she knew she would say the same thing again if she had the moment to live over. "Has anybody checked the chain saw? Was it working all right?"

"I'll get to it." Just now, Dodge could not look her in the eye. He looked past her to Pfeiffer's body. He had seen plenty of corpses, but mostly they were old people. People about whom you could say "They had a good run" and not think that their passing was a tragedy. But about a death like this he could find no words of consolation. There was nothing to do but feel sick about the waste.

"You're really casual about this, aren't you?" Just then, Madeleine felt no reverence for the dead. There was too much that she wanted to know. Suspicions crowded her head. "Are you even going to have an investigation? Or has Mackenzie taken care of that, too?" She knew Dodge was the last person who could be bullied into something by Mackenzie, but she wanted to make Dodge angry. She wanted to punch a hole through his calm, and at the same time, she wished she could find that same calm in herself.

He looked at her and shook his head. He was not angry or disgusted. He knew Madeleine well. They had grown up together. He knew what she was trying to do and how she never could sit still or keep her mouth shut when she ought to. He accepted it, just as he had been forced long ago to accept the whole impossibility of any future they might have together.

"Nothing ever gets to you, does it?" she asked.

"It's not like that, Madeleine." Dodge closed his notebook and slotted it into his pocket. He had to leave now. He could no longer stand the cold.

"Then how is it?" she asked. She was so frustrated at him that for once she found herself at a loss for words.

"Nothing ever gets to me in front of you." He walked past her, resting his hand on her shoulder as he squeezed between her and a hanging side of beef. He drank in the smell of her cologne and the leather of her satchel and the faint clean smell of shampoo.

Madeleine said nothing to him as he left. To her, Dodge was the enemy. He had been ever since he became a policeman. She had to keep reminding herself that nothing would change that. As soon as he was gone, she sat down on the beef carcass where Dodge had been sitting when she walked in. She stared at the body of James Pfeiffer and after a minute she began to cry.

Even in the cool air, Dodge felt heat wrap around him. It was deep in the night. Loons wailed out on the lake. Dodge had grown up believing the Abenaki Indian legend—that the noise of the loons was really the voices of the dead calling to their loved ones from the spirit world. The sound made better sense in legend than in truth. Dodge walked away down the road. He moved with the unconscious rhythm of a long-distance runner, as if he could keep going for the rest of his life and never tire, drawing footprint rings around the world. He kept thinking of James Pfeiffer. The great fragility of flesh. The swindle of dying too young. But in that freezer room, with everything around him dead except that woman, Dodge had never felt so close to life.

CHAPTER 3

*T*wenty miles to the north, Adam Gabriel was moving through the forest. He walked alone through the trackless thickets of pine, past nameless lakes and shimmering groves of white birch. He was thinking about what he planned to do in the days ahead, and how he stood a chance of being killed. It was not fear that reached him now, but loneliness. To keep himself company, he sang:

> "Get out the way for old man Tucker,
>   He's too late to get his supper.
>   Supper's over and breakfast's cooking,
>   Old man Tucker just stand there looking."

The song did not cheer him up, the way it had done when he was a child and he had shouted the first line when he walked home through these woods after a day of fishing or climbing Seneca Mountain. It was a song that all his friends used to know, and if one person heard another singing it, they would join in. He remembered his relief when someone in the distance would sing out the rest of the song. He wondered where those friends were now, and whether he would be fighting against them in the days to come.

Gabriel sang until the words made no sense to him anymore. After three days in the woods, he needed to hear the sound of a human voice, even if it was his own. He needed the rhythm of the words to keep himself moving, because hunger had made him weak. It had pushed his senses beyond the confines of his body. It seemed to him that he could feel the stones and branches in his path before he touched them. His canteen, which he had filled from a stream that morning, was almost empty now.

Gabriel was tall and strong without looking muscular. His hair, which he combed straight back on his head, was dark brown with threads of coppery-red bleached in by the sun. His lips were full and chapped and sometimes he ran his tongue over them to moisten the dried skin. His heavy canvas shirt and trousers were dirty from living in the woods. Mud and pine needles had lodged in the laces of his boots.

Returning here alone and after so much time had brought his life full circle. Everything he had done and what he had become all boiled down to these past few days, from the time he had set out into the wilderness from the side of a highway in Canada, smuggling himself across the border. He knew about the sale of the Algonquin and had watched from a distance as environmental groups petitioned against it. He read their well-tuned arguments. He watched them fail and move on to other sales of wilderness land, just as they had many times before. When the Algonquin sale went through, he decided he would have to come here himself and put things right once and for all. Gabriel's family had been gone from Abenaki Junction for many years, ever since his father was fired as foreman of the Mackenzie Company for complaining about the clear-cutting. But Gabriel still knew Jonah Mackenzie well enough to understand that no amount of reasoning would change the old man's mind about clear-cutting the wilderness. Other methods were required. The more he thought about this, the more extreme his plans became.

When Gabriel took off his canvas backpack to rest, he saw an arch of sweat darkening the cloth between the straps. He had been sweating so much that he'd lost track of where his skin ended and his soggy clothes began. When the clothes dried, the salt tie-dyed them with white powder. It had been a hot day, even under the canopy of trees, where the still air filled his lungs with the fragrance of earth and pine needles and the faint sweetness of white birch. In places, the pines grew so thick that nothing but poisonous amanita mushrooms grew between the trees. When he came to the stands of birch, the bony pillars seemed to shift around him.

The only thing Gabriel had now to guide himself with was a compass. There were no paths except the narrow trails of moose and deer, which he followed when he grew too tired to make paths of his own through the face-scratching branches of pine. Every hour, he took out his compass and took a bearing. Then he began walking again. Often there were mountains in the way. He climbed them, feeling the ascent in his calves and his thighs, leaning into the slope so that his face was no more than a couple of feet from the path. His arms went numb from the digging pack straps. When he reached the stony skull of the mountain crest, he would stop, let his pack slip from his shoulders and sit down on it to rest. Blueberries grew among the ripples of the rock and he would pick as many as he could, the pale-blue and the dark-blue, almost black berries disappearing without inspection into his mouth. He would crush them with his tongue and swallow, feeling the sugar jump through his body.

It was dusk before he even realized it was growing dark. The light had faded so gently that he'd barely noticed it. The first stars popped out of the blue. He walked on a while longer, seeing color fade from the trees until he was in a world of black and white and the navy of the sky. He began to stumble on roots. Then he knew it was time to stop.

Gabriel found a patch of soft earth. He walked around the place where he would put his tent, the way a dog circles the ground it chooses for a bed. When his tent was pitched, he cut a two-inch-deep hole into the trunk of a birch tree. As the sap started to run, he folded a piece of birch bark into a tube and set it in the hole to act as a funnel. Then he pulled the lace from one of his boots and tied a blue-and-white-speckled enamel mug to the tree to catch the dripping sap. He touched his finger to the drop-by-drop trickle and brushed the clear liquid across his lips, tasting the sweet pepperiness of the sap. He checked that the mug was secure and crawled inside his tent.

The night brought silence, except for wind moving like a scavenger around the trunks of trees. Inside his tent, he felt the quiet cup itself around him. He switched on his angle-headed flashlight. It had a red filter over the bulb to help him keep his night vision. He rooted in his pack, taking out the plastic-bagged bundle containing his clean clothes, smelling the perfume of detergent from a Laundromat in Thunder Bay, Ontario, where he'd washed them a week ago. At the bottom of the pack was a tan canvas holster. From it, Gabriel pulled an old Webley revolver. Its blue-black, hexagonal barrel showed him back the red light of the bulb. There were no bullets in the gun now. He kept those in an airtight plastic tub, which was itself wrapped in plastic. He was careful with the bullets: they were .455 caliber, which was hard to find, and he could not afford to go buying handgun ammunition now. Suspicion would follow him out of the shop. He put the gun away and sniffed the oil on the tips of his fingers. Each time he brought out the gun and looked at it, he felt reminded of how far he was beyond the point of turning back.

The last thing he looked at from his pack was his wallet. It was made of black nylon with a Velcro closing strap. From it, he pulled his American driver's license and social security card. It was a New Jersey license, with a red band across the top that said *Operator.* The name on the license was Adam Gabriel. The first name was his, but not the second. He had been given the forged document six weeks before, out in Idaho.

Gabriel switched off the flashlight and lay down in his tent. He looked out through the mosquito-netted opening. A meteor shower cut arcs above the trees. He imagined the night as black paint on the glass vault of the sky, the meteors scratches across it, showing the sunlight beyond. "Get out the way for old man Tucker," he whispered. Then he stayed silent, as he used to do, but not even his daydreams called back.

One year and six months earlier, Adam Gabriel had bailed out of an F-14 jet fighter at three thousand feet over the Iraqi desert. He had been flying bomber escort from the USS *Pendleton.*

Gabriel was banking to cover a second run over the city. As he turned, he saw tracer fire like huge pearl necklaces moving slowly through the sky. Parts of the city were burning. He could make out sections of road in the downtown area, where a number of the bombs had fallen. These smooth paths vanished into shadow-filled craters. Rubble lay in giant crumbs across the streets.

He was leveling out of the turn when he heard a slamming noise from somewhere behind him and to the right. It was exactly the same sound that the kitchen door in his parents' house used to make when someone swung it shut. For a moment, the noise stunned him. Then he waited for the first sign of damage—lights on the instrument panel, or no response from the controls. His mind clattered through the bail-out procedure. There had been no missile-tracking alarm. No hurricane blast of air through the cockpit, as he'd been taught to expect when the canopy shattered. No desperate bleep from any of the aircraft sensors. He banked slowly through a second turn. Then the fuel warning light went on.

Gabriel radioed that his plane was hit, but he did not know how badly. Sweat from his upper lip smeared on the helmet microphone. He called into the dark that if his engine began to fail, he would try to land his plane at one of the supply runways in Kuwait. If he could not make it that far, he knew he would have to bail out over Iraqi territory.

He disengaged from the bombers and headed for the nearest runway. Another fighter accompanied him, piloted by a lieutenant named Casper Wright. Flying from the aircraft carrier to their rendezvous with the bombers, Wright's plane had banked with him, in and out of turns, as if the two machines were joined by invisible wires.

Wright reminded Gabriel to tighten all his straps as hard as he could take it and to prepare his cockpit for bailout. It was a comfort to hear Wright's voice. Wright was from Tallahassee, Florida. Gabriel could make out the Panhandle twang in his voice. Gabriel's mind still plodded back and forth along the question of what could have hit him. He had seen no tracer fire. There had been only one slamming noise, not several. He knew what the other pilots would say when they heard he had been brought down. They would say he had lost out to the Golden BB, one stray unaimed bullet wandering through the sky.

All through training and all the way out to the Gulf, Gabriel had worried that he might not behave correctly if something went wrong in the air. He'd been taught the procedures. It was not about that. He was afraid that dread would cloud his mind. But now here he was, the fuel alarm flashing tiny rubies in his eyes, and his thoughts were as clear as they had ever been.

Gabriel played the game of placing odds on his chances of making it home. He wrote them on the notepad that was strapped to his right knee. He played the game to concentrate his thoughts, in case panic reared up and caught him by surprise.

Wright asked him to check the fuel gauge. The reading was lower now. Gabriel realized he would probably never find out what had caused the damage. He tried to remember how much he had been told these planes cost. Gabriel was surprised to feel embarrassed at having been brought down. He had not expected this emotion. Then he wondered if his own negligence had put him in the line of fire.

He was losing altitude now. He looked up and saw the belly of Wright's jet, set against the navy-blue night sky. A web of stars fanned out around the plane. The yellow-orange exhaust flame was like a comet, chasing and always just about to catch the F-14.

Gabriel told Wright he was going to have to bail out and asked if he knew whether they were over Allied territory yet.

Wright said, "Not yet." They were near the Kuwaiti oil fields, which were just inside Iraqi lines. That area was expected to be a heavy combat zone as soon as the land assault began. Wright was quiet for a minute, his voice replaced by the soft rush of static in Gabriel's headset. Then Wright said he would radio in the coordinates of the bailout and would make sure a rescue helicopter was deployed immediately. He told Gabriel to lie low and get his distress beacon going as soon as he hit the ground. Gabriel knew all this. He knew what he would do and what Wright would do, because they had all been trained in it until the moves were chiseled into their minds like some kind of genetic coding.

Gabriel's fuel marker bounced off zero. He could feel the power fail, the smooth rush of the jet becoming choked. Any second now, the engine would die. Then the plane would move into a free fall.

Wright said he would see him real soon.

"Thank you," Gabriel said. Then he switched off the intercom. He checked his straps again, breathing as slowly as he could in the last few seconds before bailout. He looked down and saw dozens of fires burning in the dark. The flames were thick and yellow-orange, obscured by coal-black smoke. Gabriel knew the wellheads had been blown and the oil was burning out of control. He knew this meant that the Iraqis might have pulled back, leaving the burning wells for the Americans to deal with. The plane shuddered slightly, and then a steady tone from the fuel-tank warning system reached his ears, like the sound of a TV station when the programs are finished for the night. With the first cough of the dying engine's thunder, Gabriel blew the cockpit canopy. Cool desert night air rushed around him.

The nose of the F-14 dipped. The horizon rushed over Gabriel's head and out of sight. He closed the visor on his helmet.

He fired the bailout charge. His blood drained from his skull with the roughness of sand and slammed into his feet. The visor shattered as something smashed against it and in the fraction of a second that he could keep his eyes open, Gabriel saw the plane hurtling away from him. The heat of the jet's engine surrounded his face, stabbing through the broken visor. It felt as if his flesh would melt like wax. Then the heat was gone and only the pain of having been scorched remained on his face. His flameproof Nomex suit and gloves protected the rest of his body. He was upside down and then right side up. Blood zigzagged across his face. He could feel wind chilling the blood across his forehead. He didn't know how badly he'd been cut.

Gabriel cartwheeled through the air. The chair rockets that had launched him from the plane still hissed. Then the rockets quit and he found himself surrounded by nothing but the sound of rushing wind. Gradually his head stopped spinning. He understood that he was falling sideways.

The chutes popped and jolted him upright. He felt a tug in his neck. Blood plowed into his head. He was blacking out.

Suddenly the ground was very close. Gabriel did not know if he had fainted. The desert filed away beneath him. He could see the ripples of dunes and cracks where the sand had blown away, exposing hard-packed earth. The oil-well fires blazed in the distance.

The chair straps were bands of pain across his shoulders and stomach, digging into his flesh. Dizziness rocked in his skull and he wondered if he had been badly hurt. The cuts sent pain in streaks across his face. His burned flesh felt tight and stretched across his cheekbones.

Gabriel looked out into the dark, hoping to see where his plane had landed. But he saw nothing, and he knew that since the plane had no fuel in it, the jet might not burn, leaving no smoke to trace. It would not leave the enemy anything to follow, either. He had seen no vehicles on his way down, no towns or roads. Just desert. Wright would have called in his position by now. He was grateful for Wright's company. A daydream sputtered through Gabriel's head of himself going to visit Wright when they both reached home again. He imagined a house surrounded by palm trees and cypresses draped in Spanish moss. Strange to be thinking this, Gabriel thought, while I'm drifting through space like sad old Major Tom.

The ground climbed up to meet him. The snakes of wind-rippled dunes. He smelled the earth now, the heaviness of it. The chill of the Arabian night against his face.

He wondered if he was going to die. He felt strangely calm about it, as if the outcome had been decided long before and he was only going through the motions.

The earth seemed to rise, gaping like shark jaws.

The jolt of landing slammed Gabriel facedown. He felt grit in his eyes and his mouth and up his nose and then he felt nothing. He did not even have the time to wonder if he were dead.

Dawn woke him. The first thing he saw was grains of sand a few inches from his face. The top of the jet seat had prevented him from being plunged into the dune, where he would have suffocated. He crunched sand between his teeth when he bit down. Some of the grains were in his eyes and he wiped them away with his aching fingers. They ached as if he had arthritis. He was aching all over. Each joint seemed to have been prised apart and popped back together. He could feel bruises where the straps had held him in place, down around his shoulders and across his waist. They would be the kinds of purple ones that take months to go away. When Gabriel twisted his head to one side, nerves in his spine cracked in sparks of pain across his shoulders and down into his arms.

He released his straps and crawled slowly out from under the chair.

The hugeness of the desert sky hung over him. He had never seen anything like it. Stars reached from one end of the horizon to the other. All his life until now there had been a jagged line of trees to mark the distance of his sight. He knew that soon the sun would rear up from the dunes and scorch this place. Gabriel took a deep breath and coughed at the dead-fireworks stench that came from the underside of his seat. The bailout rockets had blackened his boots and melted the rubber soles. From where he stood, he could not see the oil fires, but their smoke massed in the sky like the iron-gray clouds of an approaching hurricane. Through breaks in the darkness, Gabriel could see the silhouetted outlines of skyscrapers—the blacked-out towers of Kuwait City.

The sun came up angry from the desert. He walked up to the highest point in the dunes and squinted off toward the horizon, turning himself slowly around in the sand, hunting for signs of life. Before him lay what he imagined hell must look like: vicious bolts of flame shot from spigots where the oil wellheads had been. Already the pale sand was a slick creosote black. There was no sky. There was only the smoke. He could smell it, vaguely sweet and sickly. It felt as if drops of the oil were condensing in his lungs.

Gabriel wondered how long he had been unconscious. He worried that the rescue helicopters might have been out looking for him but had given up when they found no distress-beacon signal. As quickly as he could, he set up the distress beacon, the TACBE, which would connect him with any AWAC planes flying over the area. It was a small metal box with a long aerial and a stand to keep the unit upright. There were two settings for the TACBE, one which would make the unit function as a long-range beacon, and another which would put him in touch with any aircraft in the immediate vicinity. He had been told that once he turned it on, he would be in touch with an AWAC within fifteen seconds. He pulled the long-range tab and heard the swishing sound as the unit engaged.

"Hello, AWAC," he called into the microphone. I am F-15 down, over." Then he said it again. "I am F-15 down, over. Can you hear me? Over." He talked into the machine for fifteen minutes and then switched it off. The battery was good for only twenty-four hours, so he decided he would turn it on and off every fifteen minutes. The routine would keep him busy. He worried about the Iraqis homing in on his signal.

Gabriel dug a hole in the sand under his chair and crawled into the space. Every fifteen minutes, he reached his arm out into the skin-prickling sun and turned the beacon's on/off switch and called into the microphone. "I am F-15 down, over. Can you hear me? Over."

He heard big guns firing in the distance. Several times, he heard the sound of jets but could not see them. Once he made out the thin profile of a helicopter, appearing and disappearing through the smoke. It wasn't close enough to see him. On the morning of the next day, Gabriel saw the red light die on the TACBE's battery pack.

Loneliness clamped down on him. Gabriel crawled out from under his chair and shielded his eyes from the sun. He knew he'd have to start walking toward Kuwait City, through the oil fields. He set out immediately, knowing that, without food or water, the longer he waited, the weaker he would become. As he walked, he heard a distant rumbling like thunder. First Gabriel thought it was close by and then it seemed to have disappeared altogether. Wind was carrying the sound. As he came closer to the oil fields, he realized it was the sound of the fires, roaring open furnaces incinerating the sky.

The burned rubber on his boots picked up sand until it looked as if the soles were made of the tiny grains. It was harder to walk. Gabriel wound his silk scarf around his mouth and nose. He normally wore it to stop his neck from chafing as he looked constantly from side to side in the cockpit of his plane.

All day he walked toward the fires. They were much farther away than he had thought. Gradually the ground turned black, each grain of sand caught in a sphere of oil. When he looked behind him he could see his own footprints, white like bone and trailing off in a drunken-looking line into the dunes. Scrub brush had become fans of shining black like coral.

Kuwait was vast and silent on the horizon. Gabriel began to feel as if he were the last person left on the planet. It was harder to breathe. He ran his fingers through his hair and the strands were thick with tar. His overalls were as black as the sand. Burning drops of it collected in the corners of his eyes.

The sun went down, bloody through the smoke. Gabriel walked all night, sometimes so close to the fires that he could feel their heat. They glimmered off the low-hanging clouds and by this light he saw old corpses that had been lying there for days. They were sculpture-like now, all features slathered into anonymity by oil.

When the first smudges of dawn filtered yellow through the smoke, Gabriel found himself to the east of Kuwait City. He crossed a deserted highway and saw the ocean in the distance. By ten in the morning he had reached the sea. But it was not the sea. It was oil. The slugglish-arcing waves that slopped up on the black beach were black and the seaweed was a fringe of black at the edge of the waves. Hideously dying cormorants tried to swim in the sea, their wings like black knife blades now, and useless. Turtles like half-constructed toys lay tangled in weeds and oil at the high-tide line or crawled blind and mostly dead onto the black sand and vomited oil and tried to blink the oil from their eyes. The crabs still scuttled on the sand, but they were black and dying. He could smell the rotting fish. Their bodies were gleaming bumps in the slick black water. It was black as far as Gabriel could see. Everything that had lived on the beach or swum in the ocean here was dying or dead. Gabriel moved in a trance along the beach toward the city. He was overcome with horror. He looked down at himself and saw that he had become the same greasy obsid-ian black as everything else. He rolled up his sleeve and the skin underneath seemed so pale that he barely recognized it as his own.

This entire land had been visited by the devil, Gabriel thought—not a mansized, horned devil who bothered to torment one soul at a time, but a devil who hated all men and the world and was killing every-thing at once.

These pictures would never leave Gabriel. They would not leave anyone who had seen the oil fires in Kuwait. They would be carried as communal scars by people like him who would never meet again and never return to the desert.

At the outskirts of the city, Gabriel saw more bodies lying on the roads. One man's eyes had been pecked by birds, and the sockets were dried brown-red caves. Gabriel walked into a house whose front door had been kicked in. The hinges were wrenched half out of the wall. It occurred to him only as he walked through the doorway that the place could have been booby-trapped. He walked over broken glass in his melted-sole shoes and went straight to the kitchen sink, stumbling in the blue-gray moonlight that had found its way through the oil clouds now that the wind was blowing the smoke out across the desert. He held his head under the tap and turned on the faucet. He stayed, neck painfully contorted, and waited, feeling his open mouth dry up in the cold night air. After a minute, he realized there would be no water. He turned on all the faucets in the house, but there was no water anywhere. It was the same in several other houses. All empty. All ransacked. Things too big to steal heaved out of windows or bludgeoned with gun butts.

As he crossed one street, he saw a body lying in the road. It was a soldier in desert camouflage, tans and yellows and greens, none of which hid the corpse in the moonlight. Instead the blurred lines of color seemed to hover around him, like static. Gabriel walked up to him. The man was not as badly coated with oil as the other bodies had been. The dry air had pinched the skin around the corpse's face and dimpled the tips of his fingers. At first, Gabriel could see no wound. Then he turned the man over, the body stiff and strangely light, so that when he tipped over onto his face, his open arms made him seem as if he were falling from a great height and trying to slow himself down. A huge hole had been blown through the man's back. The combat jacket was shredded and bloody around the wound. It looked as if he had exploded from the inside. Stubs of broken rib jutted from the skin. Gabriel did not feel nausea or sadness. The man had been dead too long. Too little remained that he could recognize and pity. The corpse was only a thing now, its teeth bared in hostility against what it once had been. Gabriel took the canteen from the soldier's belt, splashed a little of the water onto his palm and sniffed and then tasted it. Then he drank. At first, his throat was so cramped from dust and oil that he could not swallow. But he forced the water down. The greasy bitterness of the oil stayed in his spit long after the canteen was empty.

In the soldier's side pack, he found an ID card written in Arabic and a mess tin. He opened the tin, slicked fingers slipping over the aluminum lid. It was filled with olives in a paste that looked red in the moonlight. Gabriel sniffed at it and the spices made his eyes water. He ate some of the olives and his mouth caught fire from the chili paste. He knew what it was. Harisa. There was no water to wash it down. His lips buzzed painful and raw. He puffed to cool them down.

But he was too hungry to stop eating and he finished what was in the mess tin, squatting with his back to the body, looking up and down the silent street in the dingy light.

He kept moving. Now that he had reached the city and found it empty, he no longer knew where he was going. Gunshots sounded in the distance. They echoed across the thousands of broken windows and blast-chipped white walls. Now and then Gabriel came to a road and could see the desert. The nuclear mushroom clouds of burning oil merged in the sky, snuffing out stars as the wind changed direction.

Gabriel walked past the zoo. The animals had been set loose. A hippopotamus walked by him down a sidestreet, swinging its head from side to side. Three giraffes ran, hooves clattering through a park and away down a road lined with burned-out businesses. An elephant walked slowly down the street, knocked softly on each door with its trunk. Gabriel wondered if it was part of some trick that the elephant had learned at the zoo, some man-taught ritual.

Black rain fell on the city. Only pale and darkening shadows remained of places where cars had stood. Gabriel left his footprints in the empty streets, and when he turned to look at them, he had the feeling that he had walked into a parallel universe, where images remained like photographic negatives, all the light in them reversed.

It was getting bright. Now that the dawn was finally arriving, Gabriel dreaded its approach. He had grown used to the night, which he felt convinced had lasted longer than half a dozen nights, and his watch and his eyes had conspired to cheat him of the daytime in between. With oil sweat-welded to his clothes and body and smeared obscenely in his hair, it was as if he had become a part of the darkness and he would never find his way back into the light. He felt pushed past the brink of his own sanity, and knew that even if he made his way to safety, a part of him would always be out there among the oil fires, lost in an atrocity of pollution and waste.

He had stopped in a doorway to rest. He sat on his haunches, arms resting on his elbows. The dawn was gray around him. The colors had not yet returned.

A window above his head burst into slivers and it seemed to Gabriel that the sound of the gunshot came afterward. Glass like hardened rain fell on his head and stuck in his hair. At first he just sat there, looking to see who had fired the shot. Then he scrambled through the doorway and into the house. As he ducked inside, another bullet zipped along the wall, tearing the wallpaper as if a knife had been drawn across it. The bullet vanished into the plaster, leaving a scorch mark. He ran through rooms, jumped over a bed and through a bathroom, and as he ran he heard a strange and muffled engine outside the building. Then voices. Then the thump of footsteps in the house. He heard Arabic being shouted. It sounded as if they were calling to him.

He wished he had a gun, at least to take one of them with him. But the pilots had been cautioned against carrying sidearms because if they were shot down over enemy territory, it gave the people who found them an excuse to open fire.

Gabriel ran into a room and there was no way out. Even the window was too small. It was a child's room, with posters of cartoon figures on the wall.

I'm going to die, he thought. They're going to kill me. The knowledge came to him as an absolute fact. There wasn't even a tremor of doubt. When he had thought about death before, he had always imagined it coming in a sheet of fire as his jet exploded, or the screaming free fall of a pilot whose chute has failed to open. But not this. Not dying in some child's room in an empty chair with his pockets picked, being left to rot like the dead man in the street.

He turned. They would catch him in the hallway. They would shoot him in the chest with their burp guns. He saw it so clearly that it was as if he had already been killed. There was no use running. The hallway or in here. Same difference. He raised his hands and stood there in the dark room, waiting to die and wishing only for it to be over quickly.

The men rushed past the hallway. They were not talking now. He heard the rustle of their clothing and the soft pad of their boots on the carpeted floors. Gabriel knew they were on either side. Any second now, they'll fill the hallway with bullets and rush me, he thought. Or throw a grenade. Just get it over with, he thought.

A head wrapped in a wool cap jabbed around the corner and swung back again. More whispers. Arguing. Then a voice called to Gabriel in Arabic. But it was bad Arabic, as if someone who didn't know how to speak the language were reading it off a phonetically spelled flash card.

Gabriel breathed in slowly, the first threads of hope returning cool into his lungs. "Hello," he said. His voice was thin and he barely recognized it.

"Identify yourself!" shouted a voice in the corridor. It was a nervous voice. Jumpy.

Now Gabriel was more afraid than he had been before. To be killed now. By my own people. By this man behind the jumpy voice. He told them who he was. "I was shot down on the other side of the oil fields. I think two days ago. I can't even remember anymore."

The head appeared again. It didn't disappear immediately. Instead, the body followed it, hunchbacked under ammunition belts and an assault pack. "What base are you off?"

"A carrier. The *Pendleton*."

"Are you hurt?"

"I'm hungry."

The man started walking toward him. He was carrying an assault rifle with a huge infrared scope attached. "You're fucking lucky, Mister. I don't know how the hell I missed you with that first shot."

Gabriel kept his hands in the air. "Who are you guys? What's going on? How come there's only you?"

The man was close to him now. He wore an American flag around his neck. The red and white bars twisted like Christmas candy canes under the desert camouflage. The man raised and lowered his hand to show Gabriel he did not need to keep his arms in the air any longer.

"So who are you guys?" Gabriel asked again.

"We're kind of an advance unit. That's about all we can tell you." The man stepped closer. He sniffed. "Did you get burned or something? You smell like gasoline."

"Oil," Gabriel said. He smelled Juicy Fruit gum on the man's breath.

They led him outside to where three other men were waiting. They crouched in doorways and peered around through their infrared scopes. Parked in the street was a vehicle that looked to Gabriel like a dune buggy. It was all pipes and fat-treaded tires. Gear hung in string bags from the frame. The engine was hooded to muffle the sound. He thought these men must be Delta Force. Or Seals. He knew there was no point in asking.

They put him in the buggy and drove him out of the city, keeping clear of the highways, until they reached a radio post set up in a drained swimming pool on the property of a grand house that had been burned and blown up. Its roof had caved in and the protruding metal beams of the roof structure reminded Gabriel of the dead man's ribs sticking from the cavern of his wound. A Hessian net had been strung over the swimming pool and the radio satellite dish was hidden in the landscaped bushes nearby. A generator puttered next to it.

None of the men wore any insignia. They seemed only half-aware of his presence. Some were American and some were Arab. Stacks of guns lay in the basin-smooth corners of the room they had created. Lantern light glimmered off the turquoise-blue walls.

A man threw him some camouflage clothes. They were the American pattern, browns and yellows in irregular splotches. The men watched him as he changed, snorting as the paleness of his skin revealed itself against his painted hands and face.

"You look like you took a bath in the stuff, bubba." The man had sat down at his field desk. He had a flat, midwestern voice. When Gabriel didn't answer, the man pointed to a canvas-backed chair on the other side of the desk. "Why don't you tell us exactly what happened to you?"

Gabriel quit the Air Force soon after returning to America. The work it had taken him to become a pilot and the ambition and the pride he had felt in it seemed suddenly to belong to someone else. It wasn't even something he could understand anymore. In its place was all the horror of the oil fields. The wreckage it made of the land. He began to see the same destruction everywhere, in the forests and the rivers and the air. It was not happening with the same intensity that he had seen in Kuwait. At home, the damage was more gradual, which made it seem all the more sinister.

His life started to take on a different purpose, one that he would never have considered before. He wondered if it had something to do with how close he had come to dying. He had heard about people who had been changed suddenly and permanently at the point of almost losing their lives. He could not trace his feelings to their source, the way his old self would have done, analyzing and rethinking until all facets of the issue were laid bare. All Gabriel could do was act on them. Not long afterward, he joined his first environmental activist group. He quickly used up his savings and his patience in peaceful protests. He attended meetings where philosophical discussions dragged on into the night. He stood on street corners and handed out leaflets to people who glanced at the words, crumpled the paper and threw the leaflets into the nearest garbage can.

Then Gabriel heard about a man named Hannibal Swain, who operated a group out in the Gros Ventre Range in Wyoming. He heard them referred to as environmental terrorists. Others called them radicals. Extremists. There seemed to be any number of names given to this group, which specialized in the spiking of trees and the disabling of heavy logging and road-building machinery. They were the only ones Gabriel had heard of who had actually stopped logging projects from going through.

In his frustration, Gabriel traveled out to Wyoming. For a while, he found it impossible to contact Swain's people. He began to wonder whether they were just a myth. But in the end, they were the ones who found him.

He had been with the group only two months when Hannibal Swain came to the restaurant in Jackson Hole called the Peppermill, where Gabriel had a daytime job. Swain was the man's real name, unlike others in the group, who had chosen to give false names. The best camouflage, Swain had said, was not to hide at all. So far, at least, it had worked. Swain sat down at a table. When Gabriel came with the menu, feeling the veins in his neck thump with worry at the sight of the man, Swain told him, "Meet me out front at the end of your shift." Swain had watery blue eyes, and the sun had withered his skin so that he seemed to be a decade older than he was. His blond mustache looked like threads of straw. Swain handed back the menu and stood up to leave.

Gabriel knew that something terrible was about to happen. Only two days before, they had spiked three hundred trees and were just finishing up when a logging patrol heard the dull sound of their copper-headed hammers. The patrol came charging through the woods and ran right past where Gabriel lay, covered with the earth he had thrown over himself. He realized then that he could not have been what he was now without first having been a soldier for the other side. None of the group had been caught that day, but they all knew it was only a matter of time.

After the shift, Gabriel walked out of the restaurant into the glare of late-afternoon sun. He moved past the huge arch of elk horns at the entrance to the town square and found Swain sitting in a pickup at the corner. One arm, wrapped in the faded indigo of a jeans jacket, hung out of the window and down the glossy, tomato-red door of the truck.

"Get in," Swain said, and rapped his knuckles on the door.

They drove out of town and over the pass into Idaho. Swain didn't speak. For a long time, Gabriel waited to be told what was going on. He knew what a risk Swain had taken to meet him in broad daylight. To Gabriel, Swain was a man who often took big risks, but never without reason. Swain allowed no more drama into his life than he had to. He didn't spend his time in philosophical discussions about whether he was breaking the law. If the subject ever did come up, it was in hope that the laws would be changed and that their work would eventually become redundant.

They passed through smoke from a burning leaf pile in someone's garden. For a moment, as the smoke stung Gabriel's eyes, he heard again the roar of blazing oil spigots. Then suddenly it was gone.

After an hour, they pulled up outside the Painted Apple Ranch Café in Victor. The dust of the parking lot blew past them. The rolling plains of Idaho reached out to the horizon. It was more than just a different state. It looked like a different country from the forested hills they had been in only a short while before.

"I'm about to get arrested," Swain said in a deadpan voice, as if he had been saying it to himself all the way over the pass. He didn't look at Gabriel as he spoke. He had his gaze fixed on the giant red-apple sign of the café. "Federal agents have traced me to the last spiking we did in the Gros Ventre Range. Traced me and all but one person in the group." Swain swung his head wearily to face Gabriel. "And you're it. And you have to get out of here now."

Gabriel said nothing. The shock had silenced him.

Swain settled back in his seat. He seemed calmer now that he had told the news. Resigned to it. "You weren't on the Feds' list. A friend of mine found out. He tried to warn me about the others, but it's too late."

"How did my name get left off the list?" Gabriel asked.

"There used to be someone in the group before you arrived. He disappeared one day without saying good-bye. It's not the first time that's happened. He looked like he could take care of himself. I didn't think too much about it." Swain passed his callused fingertips across his chin, rustling the bristles. "But I guess he was working for the police. That's what I was told. He got the names of everyone in the group at the time. You weren't with us yet."

"I should go home and get my stuff."

"No, you shouldn't go home. You should get the hell out of here before they start making arrests and another member of the group gives up your name."

"But they wouldn't do that."

"You never know what people will do." It was hot in the truck. The windshield seemed to magnify the sun. The dusty air gave no relief. "You can't stay here. You'll have to go south or east or up to Canada."

"But how much good can I do on my own?"

"There is one place where one person could get something done, but it's on the other side of the country." Then Swain told Gabriel about the Algonquin and how it was due to be cleared.

As Gabriel listened, he felt pressure building in his head. It pushed at his eyes from behind. He had not told Swain about growing up in Abenaki Junction, or that his father had been fired by Mackenzie.

"It's a long shot," Swain said.

"I'll do it," Gabriel told him. He explained that he had grown up there.

Swain got out of the truck. His chisel-toe boots stirred the dust. He had to move around. Nervous energy was sparking inside him. "When's the last time you were there?"

"It's been years."

"Where are your parents now?"

"Oh." Gabriel shook his head. "My father died in a car crash a year after we left. He sailed over a bump on a dirt road and hit a telephone pole. It split the car in half. The police said there was no explanation for the accident."

"Maybe it was suicide."

"Maybe so," said Gabriel. You never did soften your words, did you? he thought "Mackenzie made it so that my dad couldn't find work with any of the other logging companies. I think that part of it broke him."

"And your mother?"

"She runs a bed-and-breakfast in Stonington, Connecticut. She's never been back to Abenaki Junction either. She won't even say the name."

"In some ways, that's good. They won't be looking for you. But still, you'll probably be caught," Swain said. "If you believe in luck, you can bet you used up all you've got right here."

Gabriel didn't answer.

Swain pulled off his cowboy boot and shook out a pebble. "I'm driving east tomorrow. It would be too dangerous for you to come with me, but I could drop off some supplies for you, if I get that far, and if you tell me where to go."

Gabriel gave Swain the directions, using an AAA road chart and then drawing his own map for the last mile. He chose a safe place in the ruins of a cabin down by Pogansett Lake. He hoped the old house was still there.

"Good enough." Swain pulled on his boot again. His jeans were tattered at the cuffs.

"Where are you going from there?"

"Washington. I'll turn myself in after I've talked to the press. I figure it's where I can do the most good before they shut me away."

Gabriel thought about the Navajo Indians, who were imprisoned by the whites and died in a very short time. It wasn't the prison that killed them. It was the idea of not being free, so alien to them that they could not survive it. Swain might be the same way, thought Gabriel, and suddenly he knew he would never see the man again.

"I have to go now." Swain walked back to his truck and climbed inside.

"Why don't you run?" asked Gabriel. "You don't have to turn yourself in."

Swain lowered his head slowly until it was resting on the steering wheel. "The truth is I am tired. I'm all tired out. My luck is all gone. And the most good I can do now is hope the newspapers will print what I say in the courtroom. I'll still go to jail, of course. I never tried to pretend I wasn't a criminal. But you know"—he raised his head from the steering wheel—"I believe that history will absolve us. The same way it absolved the people who ran the Underground Railroad to free the slaves in the Civil War. Or the people who blew up Zyklon-B gas chambers in Germany in World War Two." He had one last thing to say: "You'll be on familiar ground in the Algonquin. You must be careful. No fight is more vicious than the one for your home ground. They'll fight you with everything they've got. They'll kill you if they think they can get away with it. And the question you have to ask yourself is whether you are prepared to kill them. It's all about knowing how far you are prepared to go. And don't expect people to understand why you would risk your life for a bunch of trees. If you have to explain to them why the wilderness is important, with all the information that's out there, they're already part of the problem. The time for reasoning is past. But you have to be careful not to lose your humanity in all of this. What use is it to fight for humanity if you lose your own in the process?" Swain started the engine. He reached into the glove compartment, took from it a small manila envelope and flipped it to Gabriel. "It's forged ID. Driver's license. Social security card. Everyone in the group has a set of these. Do you have any money?"

Gabriel tapped his belt buckle. It was a money belt. He had $2,200 in rolled-up hundreds inside. He opened his mouth, but Swain spoke first.

"You trying to think of a way to say good-bye?" He had to shout over the rumble of the engine.

Gabriel nodded.

"Well, I guess we just did." Swain smiled. He nodded one last time, lips pressed tight together. Then he knocked the truck into gear and drove out of the parking lot.

Gabriel watched the truck until it vanished into the hills. For a while he could hear the whine of its engine as it changed gears. Then that faded, too. That afternoon, Gabriel hitched a ride up into Canada. Then he took a series of buses across the Trans-Canada Highway.

Now that Gabriel had arrived in the Algonquin, the more he thought about stopping the clear-cutting, the more of a long shot it seemed. He knew he was walking toward a conflict in which there could be no middle ground. To prepare for it, he had stored away a vast reservoir of strength, a cavern deep inside himself, packed to its stalagtite rafters with weapons for the war. He knew he would probably be caught and what would happen to him then, but it was as Swain had said—the time for reasoning was past. After all he had been through already, Gabriel did not know how much of his humanity he had left, but he was in too deep to care.

When Mackenzie saw Marcus Dodge walking across the compound toward the company office, he knew something had gone terribly wrong.

Dodge strode up the stairs and into Mackenzie's office without knocking. He held something behind his back. People in the work-room outside Mackenzie's office could see what Dodge was holding. They kept their eyes fixed at the level of his black gun belt, with its spare flat-headed bullets in loops along the small of his back, the handcuffs in their pouch and the slot for his nightstick, which he had left down in the car. Mackenzie saw mixtures of shock and fear and puzzlement on the faces of his employees. He did not have time to wonder what this new disaster could be. All he felt was the onset of dread.

Dodge swung his arm around and held out the bridge nail. "I dug this out of the tree."

Oh, thank God, thought Mackenzie. Nothing's gone wrong after all. In fact, it's all going according to plan.

Dodge set the spike down on the desk. It was the same color as a galvanized tin bucket. The head of the spike was as thick as a man's thumb and had been dented with the half-moon shapes of hammer blows. Dodge pointed to a shiny gash in the nail. "This here's where the chain saw struck it."

Mackenzie stared at the nail. He imagined the news spreading through Abenaki Junction like a drug through blood. No stopping it now, he thought. No, by God. Now this thing has a life of its own. It left him with a feeling of being swept downstream by a great river, and no way to pull himself out.

"It's a killing, Mr. Mackenzie. This morning it was just a death and now it's a killing." Dodge picked up the nail and set it down a little closer to Mackenzie. "You got any ideas who could have done it?"

It sounded to Mackenzie like an accusation. Perhaps Coltrane had talked. It was just a question, he told himself, trying to stay calm. A question Dodge had to ask anyway. After a minute of quiet, with no other sound but the creaking of Dodge's leather belt as the man shifted from one foot to the other, Mackenzie stood, leaning hard on his desk to hoist himself upright. "I have no idea who could have done this." For the first time, he looked Dodge in the eye. "Ten thousand dollars for information that leads to an arrest."

"Ten thousand." Dodge scratched the back of his neck, a look of disagreement on his face. "That could cause more trouble than we've got already."

"Well, that's what I'm offering. I'll post the reward. Spread the news around." Mackenzie kept his eye fixed on Dodge, trying to detect any sign of suspicion. But he didn't see Dodge. Instead, the ripped face of James Pfeiffer appeared behind Mackenzie's eyes, blinding him to everything outside. The face was gray like dirty snow, and cold and bloated with death. Get away from me, Mackenzie thought. Get the hell back in your grave.

Deep in the night, an old black bear came to the place where James Pfeiffer had died. It was following the scent of blood. The bear did not walk up the long dirt road from town, or across the wreckage of the clear-cut ground beyond the road. It arrived through the forest. The long pine branches slipped against its fur.

The northern lights glimmered like abalone shell. There was no moon. All the stars were clear. When it reached the clearing, the bear crouched down. With its black bayonet claws, it dug into the earth and sawdust where Pfeiffer had fallen. It sniffed the bloodstained dirt, then swung its head away and snorted and breathed in clean air.

After a minute, the bear slipped back into the woods. Meshed branches cut out the stars and the sky until there was nothing but blackness. The bear groped its way past trees, claws brushing through the combs of pine needles, feeling the dark the way the blind feel the absence of light.

Gabriel crawled out of his tent. It was six-thirty in the morning. He had been dreaming of the Gulf again. He kept waiting for the dream to lose its sharpness and take on the blurred edges of every other repeating dream he had experienced. But the oil fields were like nothing he had ever seen before. He was thankful that the rising sun had snuffed out his sleep, dappling the shadows of birch leaves on his tent.

In the mornings, he always felt hope. There was something about starting out that made him believe all he had set out to do was possible. The rain and the darkness made him cynical, but today there was none of that and, as he looked up through the trees, Gabriel could see only the vault of blue sky. Days like this, he felt the preciousness of his solitude.

He dropped the tent and packed it. Then he sat on his rucksack and ate the blueberries he had saved from the day before. They were cold, and the cold took their sweetness away. He had almost a cupful of the birch sap in his tin mug. He made a wooden peg from some deadfall birch and stuck it into the hole he had cut the night before. The peg fit tightly and stopped the flow. He pulled on his boots, feeling pain in the curve of his spine as he hunched over.

Gabriel poured the birch sap into a mess tin and set it on his hand-sized Trioxane stove. The sap was only a little thicker than water. He lit one of the Trioxane cubes and set it on the stove. Soon it was wrapped in a salty blue flame and the bitter smoke made Gabriel go and sit down a few paces away. After twenty minutes, when the Trioxane cube had burned out, Gabriel lifted the mess tin from the stove and waved his hand through the steam above the liquid in the mug. The sap had darkened and the level had dropped by two-thirds. He took a handful of blueberries and stirred them into the syrup. Then from his pocket he took another handful of pale, spaghettilike strands and stirred them in, too. The strands were cambium, the soft inner bark of a birch tree that he had found the day before. The tree had grown on rocky ground and the wind had recently tipped it over. The leaves on its branches were still green. From another pocket, he pulled the black crumbs of some rock tripe that he had scraped off a boulder at the top of the last mountain and stirred it all together in the mess tin. The rock tripe turned the stew into a kind of jelly and gave it a bitter taste, which the sap just barely covered. The sap was sweet and spicy, like maple syrup with a small amount of licorice thrown in.

Until now, all Gabriel had eaten for three days was blueberries and raspberries. His daydreams of food had grown so intense that they seemed to appear in front of him. He would be walking along and see a plate of roast potatoes set out on the path, or a glass of milk perched on a branch above his head. His hunger had become more than an annoyance. He began to feel his strength fade after only an hour of walking. From the crests of mountains he had seen lakes where he could have fished and maybe pulled a few landlocked salmon or trout, but the lakes were not on his route. The amount of energy he would have spent getting to them was more than the journey was worth.

Gabriel didn't know how many days he had been walking. Five. Maybe six. The leather and canvas with which he surrounded himself had drunk up so much of his sweat that it was as if they had become a part of him. The trappings of his other life became clumsy ornaments of comfort. He had been worried about returning to this other world, afraid of having lost the instincts that he needed to survive there, but the longer he spent in the wilderness, the less he wanted to return to that other place. He felt as if he were metamorphosing. Soon the change would be complete.

When Gabriel had finished his meal, he heaved on his pack. The arches of his feet were bars of pain. He stood still for a minute, waiting for some sign or thought to shove him into motion. But no sign came, and his thoughts were fluttering like moths inside his head from lack of food. He forced himself to start moving. Ahead on the path, a strangely luminous image of a Granny Smith apple was resting against the tree trunk. "Go away," he said, and walked through the image as it disappeared.

After three hours, he came to the base of a mountain. The slope was steep and he had to ease the pack straps off his shoulders one at a time as he walked, holding them away from the skin around his collarbone because they had rubbed his flesh raw. One more day of this and his shoulders would start to bleed. Already the toes of his socks were red from blisters that had burst. He took them off every night and threw them to the other side of the tent because he did not want to look at them.

There would be blueberries on the top of the mountain, he told himself. There had been some on every other mountaintop, and the raspberries grew in the valleys. He knew where to look for them, was able to spot the exact lush green of raspberry leaves and the smaller, more brittle, brown-tinged blueberry bushes that grew in crevices in the rock.

He looked around for water. He had an instinct for that, too, now. He could smell the dampness in the air whenever he came close to a spring. But there was nothing for him here. The air was thin and empty. The clouds were like rippled sand. Stratocumulus. He knew it might rain tonight. He was thinking how gloomy it would be to set up a tent alone and in the rain, when he heard a sound come from beyond the mountain. It was a wail, a huge mournful noise that echoed through the trees. At first it startled him. Then he knew what it was. The train. The only train to run through these woods. The Canadian Atlantic express. Then he knew that this was Seneca Mountain he had been climbing. Abenaki Junction lay only two miles beyond the other side.

He used his last reserves of energy to climb the rest of the way, hand over hand up the steep slope, until he reached the bald, rocky outcrop of the summit. He scrambled past the clots of blueberries bubbling up out of each hollow in the stone until he could see across the valley of the Algonquin Wilderness. Far below was Pogansett Lake, and there was the train, trailing the sound of its thunder, crossing the bridge, the whistle blowing again as it slowed to pass through Abenaki Junction. He could see the white church tower and faded-shingle rooftops and the road that looped down from Canada. Gabriel had not risked taking that road because of the border guards there. The sound of the whistle faded. The murmur of the wind returned.

Until now, his eye had been following the train, but now he saw the clear-cut everywhere, patching the wilderness like a checkerboard. Here and there, one pine tree stood alone in the middle of the emptied ground, left by the loggers to seed the area with pine cones. The dirt tracks of new logging roads unzipped the forest. Gabriel's thoughts began to jumble as the endless destruction piled up in his head. He thought of the animals who would no longer be able to move through the forest because they could not cross open ground. He thought of birds and animals and plants that depended on the types of trees that would not be resown by the loggers. He thought of the soil, which would dry up and be washed into the streams, killing the fish and the eggs they laid. The infinitely complicated balance of life that man had not yet understood, or had chosen to ignore. He thought about what Swain had said, how some people would not comprehend why he might put himself at risk to stop this damage. He didn't own the land. No invading army had come to take control. They would see it simply as business. Jobs. The making of money. Even his old self might have questioned why he would fight for an ideal that he did not fully understand. But the way Gabriel thought now, that was the best reason of all.

As he stared at the ruined landscape, a familiar anger spread like wings inside him, but this time it was worse. He started running down the mountain.

"It's blood money, Jonah." Alicia Mackenzie sat on the couch in the living room. She picked at the fuzz balls on her sweater. She glanced at her husband and thought, Does this town have to become a slaughterhouse before you realize what you have just done? But she kept silent. There were ways to argue with him, and this was not one of them. As soon as he felt threatened, he would go down into the bunkers of his stubbornness and refuse to be budged. It was some vicious instinct left over from the time of his ancestors, when the solution to all threats was violence.

"What?" Mackenzie held a newspaper in front of his face. It was the latest copy of the *Forest Sentinel*. He found he couldn't concentrate on the headline about Pfeiffer's death. I know what it says anyway, he thought. He refused to lower the paper, not wanting to catch Alicia's eye and have her beauty muddle his thoughts. She was younger than Mackenzie by five years, but looked more like ten years younger. She wore thick glasses and people rarely noticed her eyes. Growing older had not worried her. She seemed more curious about it than afraid.

"Is it wise to have offered so much money for the information about whoever nailed the tree? It will make people crazy. People will kill for it."

"Dodge said something like that."

"Well, maybe you should listen to him. He's no fool."

"If they find who did it, the money will be well spent." He wheezed at her in exasperation.

"Blood money brings blood."

He wished she would not use that word. Blood. Alicia knew him better than anyone. Mackenzie sipped at his coffee. He had tried to quit drinking it, because it gave him headaches at the base of his skull. But Mackenzie had been drinking coffee for too long to think of how he might live any other way. He liked the ceremony—the daily measuring of beans, the way the coffee grinder motored across the counter as if it meant to hurl itself off the edge.

"With that much cash at stake," he said, "at least they'll know I cared enough to make the offer."

Alicia looked away, not agreeing but not wanting to fight, either. "I still can't quite believe that James Pfeiffer has passed away. To think that's he's already been gone several days."

"How time flies when you're dead." Mackenzie rustled the paper, turning the pages, still unable to focus.

"Why say a thing like that? I hope to God no one overhears you when you get into one of your moods."

Mackenzie grunted. Just then he felt angry at Pfeiffer for dying. He didn't care how little sense that made. He was angry the same way he had been angry with himself when the tree fell on him. It was clumsy to die. Clumsiness had cost him his leg. In his heart, Mackenzie had no sympathy for Pfeiffer, just as he had none for himself. And he was angry to be keeping yet another secret from Alicia. It was never so simple as just being able to forget them. Hoarding these secrets required concentration. If he let his attention slip, even for a moment, the secrets might reappear into the light of day and there would be no way to answer for them. It wouldn't matter if she agreed that spiking the tree was the best thing to do. It was simply wrong.

Mackenzie had never heard a bad word spoken about Alicia. People trusted her to bank their money, look after their pets when they were in the hospital and check in on their houses. Mackenzie could hardly believe the number and assortment of keys on Alicia's key ring. She had keys to half the homes in Abenaki Junction. It seemed to Mackenzie that Alicia had spent her entire life in the service of other people. She was their confidante and caretaker. She knew almost every secret in the town. Few changes occurred without Alicia's being consulted. The town had forged an emotional dependence on Alicia that Mackenzie felt sure could never be replaced by someone else.

That, thought Mackenzie, is genuine power. Then he thought about his own power in the town. It seemed more heavy-handed. More obvious. More the way of a man. And he knew his way bought him enemies, while her methods never brought a ripple to the surface of the calm she carried with her. "Can Coltrane be trusted?" he asked her suddenly.

"Trusted? Well, good Lord, yes. Your father trusted him, and as far as I know your father trusted almost no one. Why are you asking that? Are you thinking that he might have spiked the tree?"

Mackenzie grunted. It worried him that he did not have anything on Coltrane, the way he did on most people. After the tree-spiking, it seemed more as if Coltrane had something on him. This was a new sensation for Mackenzie, heavy and sharp in his stomach, as if he had swallowed a piece of glass. He had a bad feeling that Coltrane was going to play a larger role in his life than he had ever wanted him to. Mackenzie drank more coffee and felt pain like a fist clenching around his brain.

Alicia laughed at him. "You trust Coltrane more than you trust yourself."

Mackenzie tried to get himself annoyed, but he realized she was right. He looked at her while she absentmindedly picked at her sweater. Mackenzie thought how similar she looked to when he first realized he loved her, back in their college days, sitting just as she was now and picking at the white chenille patch on his dark-blue varsity lacrosse sweater. But her absentmindedness was only a veil. Alicia always knew more than she seemed to know. It was the only thing about her that Mackenzie had never truly figured out. He felt fortunate that morning. If Alicia believed Coltrane was trustworthy, then he believed it too. He began to feel that his plan would work out. The small discomforts of his life seemed far away.

Alicia looked up at him and smiled.

He smiled back and looked away, embarrassed for a moment at how clearly she could see the desire in his face.

"I'm glad to see you reading the *Forest Sentinel*," she said. "At least now you'll know what they're talking about."

"I was reading it"—he folded the paper and let it drop to the floor—"because this is the final issue."

Alicia's eyebrows bobbed with surprise. "How do you mean?"

"I'm working on a little plan."

"When are you not? But what exactly do you mean, Jonah?" She knew even as she asked the question that if he had not told her outright, he would not tell her at all. Once he had decided to be secretive about something, no amount of badgering could prize it out of him, and he enjoyed watching all attempts fail.

"You'll see soon enough," he told her. "I'm just waiting for the right moment to spring the trap."

"Don't for God's sake bully her, Jonah. That's one thing you can't do with Madeleine. It would backfire in your face."

"I think that now might be a good time for her to move on."

"Good for you, maybe."

"She's to blame for Pfeiffer's death as much as if she hammered the nail in herself."

"That's ridiculous, Jonah, and you know it."

"Sooner or later, people will see it that way." I just bet ten thousand dollars on it, he thought.

"Be fair, Jonah. That's all I'm asking. She's not like the people you're used to dealing with. You can't just go in and trade body blows with her until one of you drops dead. It's precisely where you think you're strongest that you'll find out you're not." Alicia sensed that he was digging in again, so she changed the subject. "Pfeiffer's funeral is coming up," Alicia said. "You'll have to say something."

"I'll tell them what they want to hear. Nobody ever remembers what gets said at a time like that anyway."

"As long as you mean what you say, that will be enough. You must take care of that family. Be good to them."

"I will," he said. "I love you." Mackenzie spoke without thinking whether Alicia would want to hear that now. He thought of what she'd said about Madeleine and the Pfeiffers. He loved her for her purity of vision, but he knew he could not hold to it himself. She has that luxury, Mackenzie told himself, of being able to say what should happen in a perfect world. She never had to learn to fight dirty, the way I did. He knew how much Alicia would despise what had been done. God, he thought, it's hard to keep the fighting clean.

As Dodge drove his patrol car down the long dirt road to Coltrane's farm, the horrible daydream passed through his head that he might already be too late. He felt sure that whoever had spiked that tree would have come across Coltrane's property. If Coltrane had stumbled onto the intruder, he might have gotten himself killed. And his wife, Clara, too. He stamped on the accelerator, sending grit and pebbles ricocheting off his muffler pipe. The tall grass in the ditches was spotted with purple chicory flowers and black-eyed Susans. Their colors were so bright they made him dizzy.

At the end of the valley, he could see Coltrane's faded red barn. The grain silo was stooping to one side, as if trying to get a peek down the chimney of Coltrane's house. The farm had fallen partly into disrepair since Coltrane took on the job of company foreman. Before that, he had managed to keep some crops going. Now all he had was a cornfield.

On most occasions, Dodge liked coming out here. It was a peaceful valley and he never went away from Coltrane's without some pie or a dozen eggs or a bottle of the maple syrup that Coltrane boiled down every spring. He thought about blueberry pie, the berries picked off the mountainside by Coltrane's wife. He knew the way she used her thumb to brush the berries into her palm and the red-speckled enamel bowl in which she brought them home. Clara took a pleasure in the simplicity of her life, while people in town stormed through their days in a fury of conflict and control. From living so close to the land all this time, the Coltranes had realized something that could not be put into words. You could tell it just by looking at them. It was a kind of innocence, but one which came only after years of quiet reflection. Maybe that was it, Dodge thought. The Coltranes just took time to think. Dodge drove into the black-muddy farmyard and cut his engine. Worry sent the blood thumping in his temples. The barn towered above him, shaving the late-afternoon sun from the roof of Coltrane's house. "Please don't let them be dead," he said to himself.

Coltrane's two dogs, Tucker and Bugs, apricot-colored muddles of collie and shepherd, came running from the shadow of the barn and barked until they recognized him. They sniffed his hand and smudged their wet noses up against his palm, tails wagging furiously. Then they wandered back into the shade and flopped down in the straw-covered dirt.

Dodge stood in the silence of the barnyard, slowly wiping his dog-sniffed hand on his shirt. He did not trust the quiet. He pulled the revolver from his belt and glanced at the cylinder to see if it was loaded. The dull gray of bullets nested in the shiny blue-black steel. "Hello?" called Dodge. His voice seemed to sink into the dust and bleached planks of the farmhouse. His imagination swam with blood.

Just then, there was a movement in the barn. Dodge raised the revolver and cocked the hammer, not caring who it was who walked out of the shadows, as long as he had the person in the fat sights of his gun.

Coltrane appeared. He wore faded canvas work clothes. His many pockets were always filled with wrenches and screwdrivers and bits of leftover sandwiches. The sun had rubbed itself into his skin, so that even in winter his cheeks were the cheerful red of McIntosh apples.

Dodge lowered his arm, uncocked the hammer and set the gun

back in his belt. He breathed deeply. The sour barnyard smell filled his lungs.

Coltrane nodded hello. "Who'd you think it was going to be?"

"I thought . . ." He did not want to say what he had thought. "I came to tell you I found a bridge nail hammered into that tree, Victor."

So Mackenzie did the job himself, thought Coltrane. He wanted to tell Dodge the truth, but he was afraid of Mackenzie, so he said nothing and felt sick.

"I know you said you had seen Wilbur Hazard cutting across your land and going up into the trees lately . . ."

"Oh, I don't suppose it's him," said Coltrane. Out of nervousness, he began emptying his pockets, inspecting bits of crumpled paper and coins and putting them away again.

"But we should check. I'll be back later to see if he comes by again."

Coltrane looked behind him, as if he'd heard a voice from somewhere else. "Last murder here was over seventy years ago."

"When Dabney Hanks came home from being overseas a year, fighting in World War One." Dodge knew the story by heart.

The fact was they both knew the story, but still took pleasure in the telling. It wasn't so much the importance of the story as it was two men reminding each other of what they shared. And the laughter or the knowing looks that came of it were like secret handshakes in a brotherhood. It was a thing that anchored them to Abenaki Junction and the land around it. To understand the story of Dabney Hanks and the reasons it continued to echo through the town was to understand the town itself, what its people feared and what made them proud, and why the death of James Pfeiffer had sent a tremor through them which would never disappear, and would soon be a legend of its own.

"Dabney comes home," Coltrane continued, "and finds his wife gives birth to a son that wasn't theirs."

Dodge nodded. "So he goes right over to the man he knows is the father."

"That was Andy Truitt." Coltrane raised a finger.

"And he shoots him with the same rifle that he's been using to pick off Germans over in France." Dodge nailed the story shut, and both men stood frowning for a few seconds afterward, as the memory receded into the darkness of their minds.

Coltrane started walking back toward the screened front door of his house. He was desperate to lead the subject away from Pfeiffer and the spiked tree. I can hardly stand to keep quiet about it, he thought, but I know I can't look Marcus Dodge in the face and lie and be believed. "Now, would you like a nice piece of Clara's blueberry pie?" he asked hopefully. "The berries were on the bush but three hours ago."

Dodge saw again the gentle rolling of the berries between Clara's fingers as they fell into the bowl. He saw the faint purple stain on her fingertips. Ten minutes later, he was finishing his second piece of pie. The full force of the summer seemed stored in each fragile berry.

The three of them sat at the kitchen table, Clara with flour still on her apron and dusted across her hands and in her hair. She'd had three sons and three daughters, all of them grown now and moved away. Her body had given with the work, so that the angle of her bones was gentler in the curving of her skin. She kept her hair long and braided and the gray in the braids was silver shiny and did not hold the brittleness of age. Often she raised her fingers to her mouth, as if embarrassed at how time had creased her lips.

Looking at her from the corner of his eye, Dodge wanted to tell her how beautiful she was. She seemed the kind of woman who had never heard those words from anyone. As he stared, he realized suddenly that the almost sensual rhythm he felt when he came to this valley was her doing. Victor was a part of it, but he did not create it. It streamed from this woman in the calmness of her gaze and the way she took from the land without taking more than she needed.

"Nice to see you, Marcus," she told Dodge as he and Coltrane walked outside. She laid her hand on his shoulder.

Dodge smiled and said nothing. He rested his hand briefly on hers, then brought it down from his shoulder and let go and was in great confusion at how difficult the letting go had been. Dodge prayed that Coltrane had not known what he was feeling. Nothing had been said, no gaze too long, no touch that needed explanation. But it did not seem possible to Dodge that Clara had not sensed the powerful swing in Dodge's heart. It seemed to exist in some uncalibrated energy, sparkling through the air around them.

They were back out in the sharp light of late afternoon. Suddenly, Coltrane wheeled and faced him.

In the moment of his wheeling, Dodge felt dread pass through him like a shadow. Fearing that Coltrane knew about his thoughts. Oh, God, here it comes, thought Dodge.

"Pfeiffer," Coltrane said. It was only the one word. He blurted it out, half hoping Dodge would force the truth from him.

But Dodge only nodded. He felt lightheaded with relief that this had nothing to do with Clara.

Coltrane waved his hand toward the ridge that separated his land from the Algonquin. "Mackenzie ought not to be cutting it down. I mean, he's not even thinning it. He's destroying it."

"I don't know, Victor." Dodge shrugged. "Mackenzie paid for it."

"But I'm saying it shouldn't be for sale."

"I don't know, Victor." Dodge said again. Mackenzie's clearing of the Algonquin seemed to Dodge more like a force of nature than any logging enterprise. There was nothing to do but endure it.

Coltrane gave Dodge a crooked smile. The guilt of Coltrane's silence was like acid in his stomach. "You come around again," he said.

Dodge drove away, scattering chickens, careful not to kick up gravel with his tires. Bugs and Tucker chased the car as far as the road, then stopped and drank from a puddle. As Dodge made his way back to town, he thought of the investigation. Now while others could move on with their lives, it became Dodge's job to shuffle through the past, intruding into people's memories like someone who wears muddy boots into a tidy house. Part of him wanted to call it an accident and let the dead man lie buried in peace. But there would be no calm in Abenaki Junction until this was solved. No calm.

Still dazed and angry at the sight of the clear-cut land, Gabriel followed the trail that led down from the mountain. He reached Pogansett Lake and peeled off his clothes. Dried sweat was gritty on his skin. He walked through black flakes of dead leaves at the water's edge and let himself fall into the tea-brown water. It was cool but not cold. Clutched in Gabriel's hand was a razor. He had no mirror, so he shaved by feel, dragging the blade across his skin and following it with the tips of his fingers to see if any stubble remained. The razor was half-blunt and hurt when he shaved his upper lip. His eyes teared with the jabbing, pulling pain. It was strange to have smooth cheeks again. He ducked his head underwater and ran his fingers through his hair. Gabriel's memories of this lake were still clear in his mind. He remembered riding out with his father in the predawn fog to go fishing. He had sat bundled in his parka, watching the V of their motorboat's wake in the glassy water. Then, later, he had sat for hours watching the yellow and orange bobber on his fishing line, waiting for it to jerk beneath the surface. He had seen eighteen-wheeler trucks drive out across the ice in wintertime and felt his hair freeze in the wind blowing down from the north. Leg-thick icicles hung off the narrow river bridge, sometimes reaching the surface of the frozen water and forming bars like a gate across the river. He had been woken in the middle of the night by the gunfire sound of ice cracking on the lake, signaling the approach of spring. Now, as Gabriel raised his head from the brown water, he caught sight of the bony ridge of Seneca Mountain and beyond it the purple hills of Canada. Heat haze blurred the distant trees. It looked as if the mountains were smoldering.

For Gabriel, this place had lived so long as holy ground inside his head that it was hard at first for him to believe that he had actually returned and was not passing through it in the fog of some daydream. Unlike most places remembered from childhood, which might appear absurdly small when revisited as an adult, this wilderness had lost none of its vastness. He knew that in its shadowy cloisters of trees were places where no person had ever been before, where people could be lost for days and bears skulked in the hollows or sunned themselves on the bare rocks of Seneca's crest. He was as awed and humbled by it now as he had ever been. It was not a mass of living things. It seemed to have, instead, a single collective life of its own.

He combed his hair and changed into the clean clothes that he had wrapped in newspaper in his pack. He wore his father's old Filson cruiser jacket, heavy wool in a black-and-gray plaid, and khaki trousers with a double thickness of cloth from the knee up. These had also belonged to his father. It used to take him a year to wear out the trousers and he never wore out the Filson. Gabriel stashed his pack and strapped on his money belt.

He walked the tracks into town, using a long stride to tread along the deep-cracked wooden spacers. Here and there beside the rails were piles of bolts for fastening the lengths of track together, left behind by the work crews. He crossed the narrow bridge, black paint chipped away to the brown antirust coat underneath. The builder's plaque was still there—McClintock and Marshall 1931—not yet prized off for somebody's collection.

A white-and-green-trimmed cabin stood just back from the tracks. Gabriel knew that it belonged to a family called Booth. His father had been friends with the Booths. Mr. Booth always flew an American flag on the flagpole whenever he was home. No flag was there today.

Gabriel walked past the ruins of the cabin where he had told Swain to cache the materials. For now, he did not check the cache, in case the place had already been discovered and was being watched.

Gabriel passed the first few houses. Mutt dogs on rope leashes barked at him and wagged their curled-over tails. Behind the garages, Gabriel saw snowmobiles set up on cinder blocks for the summer and huge piles of wood sheltered from rain under blue tarpaulins. Most of the houses needed a new coat of paint. The winters had bleached their colors away.

The Four Seasons diner was a short distance from the place where the VIA tracks ran through town. By the time Gabriel reached it, he was carrying his jacket because of the heat of the day. The food at the Four Seasons had never been his favorite, but Gabriel had been thinking about it for so long now that he kept having to swallow the saliva that welled up in his mouth as he walked toward the brown-and-yellow building with its potholed parking lot just now emptying of lunch-hour customers. Dusty-booted workers clomped down the steps of the diner, fitting on their baseball caps. They climbed into their trucks, some of them with suspensions that jacked the chassis far off the ground. The men wore beat-up jeans, wallet marks faded into the back pockets. Some had clip-on suspenders to hold up their trousers. They wore T-shirts or flannel. All of them had caps, greasy-brimmed and perched high on their heads. Their faces were deep-creased from hard work and living outside. These men reminded Gabriel of old pictures of his father, black-and-white shots of a man leaning on his chain saw and standing next to a pile of fresh-cut logs. In later pictures, after Jonah Mackenzie had fired him and the family had moved to New Jersey, Gabriel's father's face had changed. His father never fitted into the suit that the pharmaceutical company made him wear to work. Gabriel had once walked into his parents' bedroom and seen his father dressed in his old logging gear, standing in front of the mirror. His father was embarrassed, and quickly pulled off the jacket. One of the buttons came loose and he scrambled to pick it up as the button rolled toward Gabriel's feet. That was the last time he ever saw his father in those clothes.

When Gabriel walked through the door, only a family of Quebecois tourists remained in the Four Seasons. The man and woman leaned across the table toward each other, whispering in French. Their two children, both girls, were playing ticktacktoe with a purple crayon on a paper place mat. They all wore the clothes of city people, fashionably fragile against the coarse cloth of the Abenaki Junctioners. Gabriel sat with his back to the wood-veneer paneling. An electric clock hummed on the wall above him. Arranged around the clock were gold-painted flowers and a plastic cherub with a featureless face.

At first, Gabriel was worried that someone would recognize him. He tried not to catch anyone's eye. After a few minutes, he settled into his chair and reassured himself by counting off the years that he'd been gone. He had changed too much since then for his face to be familiar, but he still felt a part of this town. Time had no bearing on how strongly bound to it he was. He ordered a salad and a bowl of soup and a ham-and-Swiss omelet and some french fries. It was a lot of food, but the waitress didn't blink at it. All she said was, "It might take a minute." She wore white nurse's shoes and an apron over a pink dress. She poured him a cup of coffee and dropped two tubs of half-and-half on the table.

Gabriel had picked up a free copy of the *Forest Sentinel* from a stack at the door. He saw it was a local publication, but he had never heard of it before. The headlines announced the closing of Mackenzie's purchase of the logging rights to the Algonquin. There was no shock, only the dullness of confirmation. There was also a story of a logger who had been killed in an accident that may have been caused by a nail being driven into a tree. Gabriel set the paper down. Without thinking, he began smoothing his hand across the print, as if to rub the words away. His palm came away sooty with newsprint. Somebody's started already, and didn't mark the trees that had been spiked. That might have ruined everything. He realized then that he was shaking, maybe to have come this far for nothing. But until he found out for sure, he knew he had to continue as he had planned, so he flipped to the back of the paper and looked through the Help Wanted section.

Short-order cook at the Four Seasons.
Experience preferred.

Line Walker for the Railroad. Must be Good
Physical Shape. Potential.

Subject for Experimental Weight-Loss Program.
Work at Home! Good Pay!

One by one, Gabriel weighed the jobs in his head. With a french fry dunked in ketchup, he drew a line through the cook and the weight-loss program, wondering how much weight he had already lost these past few days in the woods. The cook's job was no good. It would keep him tied down too much of the time. This left the line-walker job. He wasn't even sure what that meant, but if it was the only job available, he knew he'd have to take it. And before anything else, he had to find a place to live.

His coffee shuddered as a logging truck approached. Then the whole restaurant shook when the huge machine rolled past. The minor earthquake reminded Gabriel of the times when his parents had brought him to this diner. He recalled the way his father greeted everyone and then walked from table to table having private, muttered conversations. His mother talked with the waitresses, who stood with one hip cocked and heavy coffeepots gripped tightly in their hands. Gabriel had felt safe here. Everyone knew them in town. He had not known how fragile all this was until it ended. The truck drove on down the road, leaving behind a screen of khaki dust which painted the cars and the houses. He wished he could start up a conversation with one of these people. Just to talk after his days of quiet. But these conversations, which had seemed so simple before, had become dangerous now. It was his silence which would keep him company in the days and weeks ahead.

Gabriel couldn't finish everything he had ordered. After days of hardly eating, the saltiness of the ham was almost too much for him. The flavors of the spices jumped like sparks in his mouth. And the news of James Pfeiffer had tied a knot in his stomach. He had the waitress wrap the rest of his french fries in foil and he took them with him. As he left the restaurant, he paused on the stairs that led down to the parking lot. He saw a woman walking on the other side of the street. She carried a camera and a leather satchel. When she saw Gabriel, she paused. Instinctively, Gabriel stared down at his boots. It was not the sidelong glance of someone finding him attractive. It was a look of suspicion. The woman walked on down the street, and after a few seconds Gabriel felt his heartbeat return to normal. He looked out past the houses at the Algonquin forest. It was a green ocean, with Seneca Mountain rising from it in a sawtooth ridge of pines. Then, on the breeze, Gabriel heard the whine of chain saws from deep inside the forest. There was no time for considering the odds. No time even to think. He would just have to begin, and not weigh the cost of it on some quivering scales in his imagination. The cost would show itself in time, and either he would stand it or he would not.

It was Madeleine who had seen Gabriel as he walked out of the diner. He had made her suspicious because he was dressed like a local, and she didn't recognize him. But then Madeleine convinced herself that he must be some young truck driver passing through. She told herself not to be so mistrusting of people, but it was in her nature and she knew she couldn't change it.

Gabriel stood looking down Main Street. Bright, powdery light sparkled off grit in the road. It seemed like the end of the world. He walked for a few minutes, until he was standing in front of the house where he had spent the first sixteen years of his life. The sun was hidden behind its chimney and threw bolts of gold across the shingle roof and into the sky. A FOR RENT sign hung on the door. The house was still painted red, although its color was faded now and in places the white undercoat showed through. The porch sagged like every other porch in town. The house seemed to have exhaled and forgotten to breathe in. He was sad that the house had fallen so badly into disrepair. He thought of how hard his parents had worked to keep it up. The flowerbeds his mother had planted in the garden were gone now, and it had obviously been years since anyone replaced the damaged cedar shingles on the roof, the way his father had done every spring, the new wood dappling the roof until it faded silvery like the rest. The garden had become a cemetery of old lawnmowers and car fenders, bedsprings and busted chairs, and car engines gouged from their chassis and a truck filled so full with old magazines that anyone who opened its door would be buried under a yellow avalanche of *National Geographics*.

A man walked out onto the porch. He stood in the shadows, as if frightened of the light. He wore brown trousers with clip-on suspenders over a thin white T-shirt. He had hemmed the trousers himself. Pink thread inched across the brown polyester. "You come about the room?" He let the last word trail in a Down East drawl.

"The room," Gabriel echoed. "Yes." It was not the same man who had bought the house from his parents. Gabriel wondered how many times it had been sold since then.

The man stepped into the light, squinting through round-framed glasses, his mouth crooked with the effort. His neck was deep-trenched with age and reddened from the sun. It had the tough, grooved dullness of elephant hide. Gabriel recognized him now. Booker Lazarus. He was famous in Abenaki Junction. Lazarus used to live in a cabin on the outskirts of town, collecting junk from the dump and selling it to tourists as antiques. The wooden fence in front of the cabin had been a barricade of hubcaps, chrome-plated bull's-eyes winking at people who drove past. Now, scanning the junk heap, it seemed to Gabriel that Lazarus had scaled down his operations.

Lazarus clumped down the steps and shuffled toward Gabriel through the dust. "I don't recognize you, boy." He pulled at his earlobe and edged closer, as if he might recognize Gabriel through smell if not by sight.

"No, sir." Gabriel felt relieved. If Lazarus, the nosiest man in town, didn't recognize him, then perhaps nobody would. Gabriel searched each pale trench of Lazarus's leathery neck where the sun had not reached, the moon-surface of his nose and his pendulous earlobes. The old man's hazelnut eyes were almost lost in the pouchy skin of his face.

"It's the bottom floor that's for rent. I got antiques stored up-stairs." Lazarus waved his hand at the dusty windows on the second floor. "Things too valuable to be leaving them outside. I used to have more. Lots more. And you know what happened? I'll tell you what happened to my antiques. They took them away. Council did. Two hundred thousand dollars' worth. Council, with that old bastard Jonah Mackenzie leading the pack. Said it was a health hazard. Said it was ugly and ruining the tourist trade. What tourist trade? I don't know. I tell you, those fuckers." He smacked his lips on the curse. They were honey in the old man's mouth. "I was going to retire on that money. Go to Florida and buy a condo in Delray Beach. But now look. I'm up here where I always been and I'm not leaving here before I die." The way Lazarus saw it, they had condemned him to death. Condemned him to the ache in his joints when the winter clamped down on the north like the hatch on a submarine. To eucalyptus-smelling liniments and everything gone fuzzy in the distance as his eyes gave up on him like binoculars going slowly out of focus. To the fact that he had to work as the bartender at the Loon's Watch bar when he would have preferred to be one of its customers. It had gotten so that Lazarus blamed the people of Abenaki Junction for the very fact of his old age, as if the pile of blunt-bladed lawnmowers and beat-up refrigerators and all things broken and rusted would have guaranteed him eternal youth.

"Fuck!" he would say as he sat in the bathtub and watched the ripples of sound fan out from his ivory-haired chest.

"Fuck!" He shouted it in his sleep and woke himself up. The value of his treasures had exploded in his head and come to rest in the rafters of financial possibility.

"Fuck!" He wrapped his lips around the curse and spat it out like the brown juice of Red Man plug tobacco and found it pleasant. Lazarus wondered where his antiques were now. They wouldn't tell him. They just showed up with Dumpsters and piled the stuff in, a job that took two days. He wanted to kill them, but all he did was learn to swear. He had written to the television program *Focus America,* hoping they might do an exposé. "But the bastards didn't write back!" he told his friend Benny Mott. Told him so many times that Mott asked Lazarus please to shut his face about it.

"Bastards!" Lazarus was too old to make war on Abenaki Junction anywhere but in his head. He saved a special place of rage for Jonah Mackenzie, head of the council in the year they removed his antiques, and on whose shoulders Lazarus had heaped the blame.

Every year since then, Lazarus had watched the steely-skied approach of winter riding like a cavalry charge down from the north. He stuck holiday brochures of palm trees and beaches on his refrigerator door, and tortured himself with dreams of coconuts and sand the texture of flour between his toes, the way he'd heard it was on the beaches of Tulum in Mexico.

Lazarus told all this to Gabriel, keeping him trapped on the saddlebacked porch for over an hour. But he was grateful for the listener. He knocked thirty dollars off the rent, which put it down to $220 a month.

Gabriel paid the first two months in advance in crumpled hundred-dollar bills. After Lazarus had gone back to the small shack he owned at the other edge of town, Gabriel wandered through the house. He walked into the pool of sunlight bleeding through the kitchen window. He remembered the space, the precise feeling of enclosure within its walls. But the rest—the bare floors that he had known only under carpeting, the light fixtures now only bulbs like upside-down mushrooms growing from the ceiling, the dust, the dump-scavenged furniture—none of this sent any pulse of familiarity through his blood.

The staircase to the second story was blocked by a door that had been sealed with a heavy bronze padlock. Gabriel's bedroom was where the old den had been. He sat on an old bed frame, springs tracking his movements with squeaks and groans, even when he breathed. The tinsel from some ancient Christmas party still hung in the corner of the room. It was no party that he could recall. Besides, he thought, my mother would have taken down all the tinsel. The Christmas parties he remembered were surrounded by the stabbing cold of winter in northern Maine. One Christmas Eve, he went to scatter salt on the sidewalk outside too soon after taking a shower. By the time he returned to the house, his hair had frozen almost solid and felt brittle on his head like threads of glass. The stars were sharper in the winter night, and the northern lights, like the rosy wings of angels, billowed in the sky. Added to the rumble of the logging trucks was the high-pitched whine of snowmobiles, laying their wide, ribbed tracks through the snow.

Now dust filtered a khaki light through the old window blinds. The room was warm and musty, and for a moment seemed less real to Gabriel than these powerfully returning pictures of his past. For a long time after that, he sat very still in the old house, until the medicine-bottle blue of twilight sky pressed hard against the windows and the trees outside faded, becoming two-dimensional in the dark. Quietly he sang to himself, just to hear a human voice, while the ghost of his childhood ran laughing from room to empty room.

"What job?"

Benny Mott squinted at Gabriel. He pulled on his oil-splattered signal-orange raincoat and sat down in his Putt-Putt machine.

As Gabriel stood there, the Putt-Putt's engine burbled quietly, like something blowing bubbles underwater. Mott was hump-shouldered like an ox. Age had crumpled his skin. His hands were so muscular and worn that the fingerprints had almost disappeared. He scowled without meaning to. He had never married, and years of living alone had left him without the desire ever to comb his hair or talk much or be polite when he did talk. Mott had been working so long on the railroad that he smelled like the railroad—of iron, rust and oil.

"The job in the paper."

Gabriel could tell the man wanted to leave. It was only five in the morning, and the first brass blades of sunlight were stabbing through the trees. But that was when Booker Lazarus had told him to show up if he wanted to catch Mott. Even at five, he had arrived only just in time, running across the tracks toward the depot building and waving his arms like a madman.

Mott stared for a second, judging him. Then he cut the Putt-Putt's engine. "You want that job? How bad do you want it?" He continued to stare, gathering the details of Gabriel's face. He had been given complete control over the hiring of his replacement. Mott guessed that this was because the comptroller in St. Johns couldn't be bothered to come down here and do the job himself.

"Well, I want the job pretty badly," Gabriel said. He knew he was being judged and that once this man had made up his mind, there would be no way to change it. So Gabriel spoke carefully, like someone trying to guess a secret password.

"A lot of people want it." Mott didn't recognize the face, which was good, since he couldn't think of anyone in town who deserved his job. Ever since the order came to retire, Mott had been leaving earlier and earlier each morning and coming out of the woods at dark to avoid anyone trying to find him. He knew someone must have tipped this man off. Probably that old fathead Booker Lazarus, he thought. "It's long hours," he said. "The pay is pretty much shit."

"I figured it would be."

"I'm retiring. The railroad's making me retire, now that I'm sixty-five. Sixty-five," Mott said again, as if amazed to have grown old so fast.

"Yes, sir." Gabriel was beginning to understand the old man's hostility. "I imagine you must want to be sure about who takes over the job."

"Damn right!" Mott's eyes opened wide. "It's not just any old job."

"I'll tell you what, sir . . ."

"Mott." He did not reach out his hand to shake.

"You could take me out and if you don't like the way I work, you can just take me back again. Or I'll walk back. And I'll be on my way. You don't have to sign me up. Just see how I do."

Mott chewed at the inside of his mouth, worried that he might be falling for some kind of trick. But if it was a trick, he couldn't see how it worked. A smile crept into the corner of Mott's mouth. He tried to wipe it away with his knuckles as if it were a crumb of food. "I guess I could do that. Nothing to lose by it, I guess." He started the motor again. "Get in!" he shouted to Gabriel over the rattle and hum of the Putt-Putt. "There's just about room for two!"

They motored out of town. Inside the Putt-Putt, Gabriel smelled gasoline and cigarettes. Soon they had passed the last shacks of old railway storage sheds, the roofs fallen in and fuzzy green with rot. They watched the pines shuffle past, half-deaf from the rapid-fire flatulence of the motor.

The Putt-Putt was a small, diesel-powered cross between a car and a go-cart, designed to fit on the rails of a train track. It had first been manufactured in the 1950s by the Bradford Supply Company in Augusta, Georgia. Very few of them remained. Trucks had taken their place, made with retractable wheels that converted the truck from road to rail use at the flip of a switch. A pin could be fitted into the steering column so that the truck would only run in a straight line, which kept it on the rails. Mott had seen these trucks as they motored past on official business. They were painted yellow, and looked like giant hornets as they barreled down the tracks. He wasn't jealous about not having one. Instead, he considered it part of his job to wrestle with the temperamental Putt-Putt.

For eighteen years, Benny Mott had been riding up and down the tracks five days a week, checking for rail-tie spikes that had come loose or for wooden spreaders that were disintegrating. Sometimes a trainman would call in and say he had hit a moose. Then Mott would go out in the Putt-Putt and either cut up the moose to feed himself over the winter or dump a bag of quicklime on the carcass if it had been dead too long. The animal would disappear under a cloud of the white-dust and in two weeks there would be nothing left except bones and fur. Sometimes he rode back into Abenaki Junction with one giant bloody moose flank sticking out of either Putt-Putt door. There wasn't room for much in the Putt-Putt. With the hammers and draw pinchers for removing nails, and spare nails, and spray-paint cans for marking up the ruined tracks, Mott could barely fit his body into the cab.

As long as he kept the tracks in good repair, no one minded what he did when he was out in the Putt-Putt. Some days, he would park the Putt-Putt out on the tracks beyond the town, careful to have filed a Track Occupancy Permit with the main office in St. Johns, and sit by the rails picking berries or writing a letter to his brother, who was a halibut fisherman in Alaska. Mott had a recurring dream: that the Canadians changed their train schedule and didn't let him know. In the dream, he met an eighty-car freight train coming toward him around a corner at sixty miles an hour. It was driven by the man who had been working the train for as long as Mott had been working the rails. His name was Alain Labouchere. They had waved and smiled to each other almost every day for eighteen years, but they had never met.

Sometimes Mott would take a break from his work and walk into the woods to sit on a soft bed of pine needles. He liked to read novels. He listened to books on tape on a Walkman. He read the newspaper. He studied encyclopedias of plants and wandered through the forest identifying species: Mott knew the peace of the North Woods. He thought of other people, ones who found happiness in jobs in which they were left alone as long as the job got done. He knew their vast contentment, untroubled by cravings for fame, or the blood-boiling Great Causes of the world. He knew these people, like himself, were the watchers and the thoughtful ones. They had learned not to be in the race.

But Mott was tired now. His body had begun to creak. He had worked long enough to earn himself a pension that, with the wages he'd made as a hunting and fishing guide in the fall and winter months, would allow him to retire. It was a sacred thing, this handing down of the job, and he wanted Gabriel to know that.

Gabriel sat awkwardly in a too-small orange raincoat Mott had lent him. He squinted through the scratched Plexiglas of the Putt-Putt's windshield like an old man peering through cataracts. He wanted to get a closer look at Mott, as if to see what he himself might become if he remained in this job as long as Mott. But they were sitting too close together, so Gabriel settled for a flicker of his eye across Mott's creviced skin.

Mott had already decided to give Gabriel the job, but he did not want to say so yet. He made the decision because it seemed right to give this post to a stranger, just as he had been a stranger to the town when he had arrived eighteen years before. There was so much to learn, and the best way to learn it all was from scratch.

Since no one had ever taken over from him before, Mott did not know what to say. At first, he had wanted to tell Gabriel everything, more than just the routine skills of track maintainance and bridge inspection and the filling out of Track Occupancy Permits. He wanted to share each reflex of his body that knew the lay of the tracks and what to look for in the clouds to tell the weather and the wind and how he had once caught sight of a bird that maybe was an eagle but he swore looked more like a man with wings. Mott had seen some things in these woods that he could not explain and because they were not explainable, he had kept them to himself. All of it would soon belong to Gabriel, in the same way it had belonged to no one but Mott until now.

Mott stopped himself from saying all of this. It occurred to him that maybe this special knowledge wasn't meant to be shared. Then the pleasure of Gabriel's life, and the calm and the peace of the woods, would be his own and not borrowed from Mott. Mott decided he would teach only the bare minimum to Gabriel. Enough to keep him safe and do the job.

Trees stooped over the tracks, as if to get a better look at the new man in the Putt-Putt. Silver lakes winked through the barricades of pine. As they rounded each curve in the track, voices in Mott's head babbled like a guide rushing through a tour, giving the names of these lakes, names he himself had given because they had no other. He pointed out half-hidden paths that led to patches of treeless ground where raspberries lit up in the sun like Christmas ornaments, and where the almost-black blueberries were so fat they made their branches sag.

Mott was desperate to tell. He'd never had such trouble keeping quiet. It seemed to him to be the only time in his life when he'd ever had anything truly worthwhile to share. Years before, he had tried to share what he knew, going down to the Loon's Watch and telling about how he had followed a moose trail to a secret lake and seen the cloven moose prints in the mud at the edge of the water. Or how he'd seen a bear rolling in the blueberries, the pads of his paws smudged purple with the juice. Or how twenty loons had appeared from the flat stillness of a lake in total silence and just as silently disappeared again. He would see a dullness in the eyes of people who heard him tell his stories. They had seen these things themselves, or things like them, and it had left them unimpressed. To them, these pictures carried no weight. But they had impressed Mott deeply, and they were all that he had to offer, so in time he began to grow quiet. People left him alone, and he would go and sit in silence with Lazarus on his porch, watching the man drain another bottle of sticky Manischewitz wine.

Mott thought maybe someday in the future, after Gabriel had been working awhile, the two of them would meet and talk about the wilderness. But for now it seemed to Mott as if this one act of silence was the noblest thing he'd ever do, and his choice was clear and right.

≡

James Pfeiffer's memorial service was exactly as Mackenzie had imagined. The family drove up from Rhode Island, along with a truckload of huge and cold-eyed fishermen, who seemed to be looking for an excuse to slaughter everyone in Abenaki Junction by way of retribution. The whole town turned out. The crustless sandwiches had the dry and pasty texture that Mackenzie had come to associate with all funerals. There was a great sameness to these occasions, with never anything to say that could reach through the veils of grief and touch the people mourning. The Pfeiffers stayed quarantined inside their misery. As he sat in the church and heard brave words from the line of dark-suited friends, Mackenzie felt impatient to get on with his own life.

Pfeiffer had been buried on the coast the day before. It was a private gathering at a place called Monhegan Bluffs, on Block Island. Now his grave had earth piled on it in the shape of an upturned rowboat, with a white wooden cross at the head. This would be replaced in a few days by an engraved black tombstone. Mackenzie had ordered it himself.

Mackenzie felt a muffled heaviness surround him as he spoke from his stock of benevolent phrases about this young man he had rarely seen, apart from every Friday at the lunchtime handing out of paychecks. Afterward, Mackenzie moved from one cluster of people to another on his way out of the Abenaki Junction Methodist Church, walking as quickly as he could without appearing impolite, shaking hands and looking down at his shoes because he had run out of words.

Later, in a back room of the church, Mackenzie met with Mr. and Mrs. Pfeiffer. The man was named Joseph and he never did catch the wife's name. Joseph Pfeiffer was thin and sunburned, with hollow cheeks and a look of seriousness, which, Mackenzie could see from the wrinkles on his face, was always there and not just because of the funeral. Mrs. Pfeiffer's blank expression told Mackenzie that the shock of her son's death had not yet reached her. She was drifting through a gray and hovering uncertainty, while her body prepared for the truth to sink in.

He had already told them how sorry he was. There was nothing more to say. Mackenzie felt himself choking. He wanted to run out of the room and vanish into the woods and be alone. But he had one thing left to do. He reached into the inside pocket of his suit jacket and pulled out an envelope. In it was five thousand dollars in hundred-dollar bills. "The insurance should kick in within a few weeks," he said. "Your son was fully covered. Everyone who works for me is covered."

Joseph Pfeiffer nodded.

Mackenzie continued, "Here's a little something extra." He set the envelope down. Of course, he wanted to say, it can't take the place . . . He couldn't even finish the thought. He knew what he was doing with this money. The envelope sat there on a table. Take it, he thought. Take the damn money.

"We don't need it," said Joseph Pfeiffer. He looked at Mackenzie with his watery blue eyes. He knew what that money was.

Suddenly Mrs. Pfeiffer seemed to wake from her trance. Her eyes were clear and focused. She picked up the money and put it in the pocket of her coat. She said nothing.

And then Mackenzie knew that she had granted him no easing of his guilt, which the money was supposed to bring. She was just taking the money and letting him know that nothing had changed because of his donation.

"I really am sorry," he said, almost indignantly, as if all that they had been thinking had in fact been said out loud. "I know what a waste it is!" He had never felt so powerless before. And suddenly tears were running down Mackenzie's face. They caught him by surprise. "I can't undo what's done! Don't you think I would if I could?" And he would have done, if there had been a way, because sitting there in the presence of these two people whose lives were now shattered beyond repair, Mackenzie saw the point at which his endless struggle for the company turned to gibberish. In a while, he would go back to the struggle, and it would be no less important when he did. But for now, the weight of the Pfeiffers' grief had tipped the scales of what was most sacred to Mackenzie, and he could do nothing about it. These moments of revelation came rarely to Mackenzie, and when they did he had no idea how to use them. They were like strange offerings, whose meaning he could barely grasp. The only thing he knew how to do was let them pass, like the skull-cleaving pain of a migraine.

Mrs. Pfeiffer stood. "Thank you," she said, and as she walked out of the room, she rested her hand for a brief moment on Mackenzie's shoulder.

Mackenzie's head hung down, as if the strength had been drained from his body, siphoned through the woman's fingertips.

The Pfeiffers walked into the main room of the church.

After a moment, Mackenzie stood and walked out the back door into the parking lot. He made his way to the Range Rover and climbed inside. He jerked his tie loose so he could breathe again, then pulled out onto the road, past the black funeral-procession cars and the drivers in dark suits, all of them dramatically overweight, leaning on the hoods and smoking cigarettes.

As the Range Rover pulled off the paved road and onto the dirt track that led to the mill, Mackenzie could see three eighteen-wheeler flatbed trucks waiting at the gates. They were due to pick up lumber and bring it down to Portland for sale. "What the hell's going on?" he shouted. The mill was short-staffed that afternoon because of the service, but not enough to stop a few trucks being loaded. He cut alongside them, taking the Range Rover across the patch of grass that separated the mill fence and the road. Chicory flowers became tangled in the bumper and the radiator grille. Mackenzie looked up at the drivers, who leaned out of the cabs of their trucks, eyebrows raised with curiosity.

Madeleine stood at the gates, blocking the trucks from entering. She held up a sign that said, in stenciled black letters spray-painted onto a white board, STOP CLEAR-CUTTING THE WILDERNESS.

Mackenzie stamped on the brakes, trenching the grass with his tires. He picked up his car phone and tapped in the number for the police station; then he sat back with the receiver hooked under his chin while he undid his seat belt. "Is that you, Marcus?"

"Yes, Jonah." Dodge's voice was tolerant and precise.

"Look, we have a problem here at the mill."

"What kind of problem?" There was the sound of paper rustling.

"Madeleine's here again with one of her billboards."

The paper stopped rustling. "Oh." Dodge's voice sounded suddenly tired.

"Yes, I'm afraid so." Mackenzie pitied Dodge just then. "I have three logging trucks that need to be loaded and sent down to Portland by sunset. Someone's going to have to come out here and move her."

"I'll be there in five minutes," Dodge said and hung up.

Mackenzie put down the phone and climbed out of the car. He walked toward Madeleine, swishing his feet through the tall grass.

Madeleine always seemed to make her signs too heavy. She was straining to hold this one up. No one had asked her to move. The mill workers were so used to her protests by now that they just tried to carry on around her as best they could. Mackenzie had never pressed charges, because that was what she wanted him to do. He just waited until she got tired and walked home. She had a paper to run, after all.

Mackenzie ignored Madeleine, who watched him closely as he went past. Stop this, he wanted to tell her. You're that child I used to know. The one with the Donald Duck barrette in her hair. It was so much easier to be angry at her when she was not around. Then she became abstract to Mackenzie. Something to be disposed of. But here, in front of her, he was reminded of the past they had in common in this town, which dulled his best war instincts. "Coltrane!" he shouted into the shadows of the mill house.

Coltrane came jogging out.

"Do you have the lumber ready to load?" Mackenzie plucked the carnation from his buttonhole and threw it in the ditch. He felt uneasy to be so smartly dressed in front of Coltrane. His best funeral clothes.

"It's ready." Coltrane looked uncertainly over at Madeleine. He hoped Mackenzie wouldn't see the cooler of water that he had brought out to Madeleine half an hour earlier.

"Tell those truckers to drive in," said Mackenzie. "Start the loading."

"What about Madeleine?" Coltrane asked quietly. He felt awkward to be talking about her as if she weren't standing right next to them.

Mackenzie turned to Madeleine. Today you went too far, he thought. Today was the end of James Pfeiffer and today is the beginning of the end of your little newspaper. "Why don't we talk this over?" he asked her.

"I'd be happy to." Madeleine was immediately suspicious.

"Will you meet me for dinner? I think that would be better than standing here in the dust and trying to have a conversation."

Madeleine stood in silence for a moment, trying to figure him out. "All right," she said slowly.

"I'll pick you up from your house at six o'clock." He didn't smile or say good-bye. He wheeled around and walked across the mill yard to his office, leaving the business to Coltrane.

Coltrane shrugged. "It does look like you'll have to move, ma'am."

Wearily, Madeleine put down her sign. "When are you ever going to go on strike?" she asked him. "What is it going to take?"

Before Coltrane could answer, a police car pulled up beside them. Madeleine waited for Dodge to fine her fifty dollars for the repeat offense of illegally parking her car on the logging road, and then follow her as she drove home. Just as he had done dozens of times before. In the past, she had found it hard to dislike Dodge. She wished they weren't separated by ideals. There were times she had even imagined a future between them. But lately, with her work against the Mackenzie Company having less and less effect, she found herself becoming bitter.

Dodge always dreaded these moments. "Please, Madeleine," he said, getting out of the car. "You're going to have to leave."

She looked at the car and the lights bolted to the roof and then at Dodge's uniform, at the black gun belt at his waist, and suddenly she was furious with him. It was the residue of all the times she had swallowed her anger because he had just been doing his job. The law sheltered Mackenzie's interests like a huge iron umbrella, obediently held in place by Dodge. Now, when she thought of it that way, she found herself unable to hold back her rage. "I'm not going anywhere. Not this time."

Dodge sighed and scratched at the corner of his eye. "Why not, when every other time you went home?"

"Because this is different. This is the Algonquin that he's shipping out truckload by truckload. Doesn't it make you sick? You'd be lying if you said it didn't."

"Madeleine, please." He raised his hands a few inches and let them fall again to his sides. "You are blocking a place of business."

"Jesus!" she screamed and threw the sign to the ground, breaking it. "All right, go ahead and arrest me!"

"Please don't make me do that." He saw the loggers watching him. He knew they couldn't hear what he was saying above the noise of the forklift trucks. But they could guess. As soon as he caught their eyes, they turned away.

"If you don't want to do it, why don't you just go away?"

Dodge had never heard so much anger in her voice. "You're under arrest," he said, and heard his own anger like barbs on each word he spoke. She had no right to make life so difficult for him, when all he was doing was upholding the law. He took her by the arm and led her to the back door of the police car. He read her the Miranda and by the time he had finished, angry tears were running down her face. But even in the middle of his anger, he kept thinking back to a time one winter when he had driven her home from picketing Mackenzie's mill and she had invited him in for some soup. He recalled that she had been wearing red mittens. They kept her from fastening the safety belt. He had to reach across and do it for her. The smell of her body so close went through him like electricity. Then later, at the house, he remembered watching her bend over the stove to taste the soup with a wooden spoon, holding back her hair with one hand. That was when I fell in love with you, he thought. He rested his hand on her head to stop her banging it on the door frame as she climbed into the back of the car.

"I can't believe you're doing this." Madeleine's fingers locked onto the iron grille that separated the front seat from the back. "You're letting Mackenzie get away with this. You of all people, Marcus Dodge."

"Why me of all people?" He pulled the car out onto the road.

"Because you're smart enough to see what's going on."

Suddenly he swerved the car onto the grassy verge, jammed it into park and twisted around to face her. "What do you think I am? Your goddamned punching bag, just because I wear a uniform?"

"You know," she said, her voice slick with disgust, "I used to like you. I don't know why, but I did."

For a moment, Dodge seemed to be frozen. Then the muscles in his jaw clenched and unclenched. He swung open the door and got out and started walking down the road.

Madeleine opened her own door, climbed out and stood beside the car, watching the tiny plumes of dust kicked up by Dodge's boots on the road. "Where are you going?"

He didn't answer. He was muttering to himself in words she couldn't understand.

"Are you just going to leave me here?" she shouted.

Then Dodge stopped. He bent down, picked a handful of pebbles off the road and began throwing them one by one into the trees. "You liked me?" he called back, without looking at her. When he had thrown all the pebbles, he took off his police cap and threw it on the ground. "You liked me?" He picked up the cap and jammed it on his head. The black visor was filmed with dust.

"Yes," she said uncertainly. "I liked you. So what?"

"After all these years, that's the best you can do?" He started walking toward her, but not in a threatening way. He only looked resigned, as if he knew that what he was saying did not make total sense. At least, it made sense, but only to him, and he had just realized that she would never understand. All the words he had kept bottled inside because the time never came for saying them. He had waited too long. He knew that now. And even if he had not waited, the time would never have been right. Dodge reached where she stood. He wiped the sweat off his face. "Just forget it," he said. He moved to get inside the car.

She held onto his arm and stopped him. "I don't want to forget it. I want to know what you're talking about. Why are you so angry because I said I liked you?"

"Because." He did not want to say what he was thinking. Somehow to have held it secret kept alive in him all the dreams he'd had of them together. But it was too late for that now. "Because I loved you," he said slowly. "I loved you for as long as I could remember. I never did not like you. Do you understand? I loved you." Dodge made sure she heard he was speaking in the past tense. "But I don't anymore. You don't have to worry."

She stared at him wide-eyed. "You loved me? When?"

"All the fucking time." Dodge sat behind the wheel and revved the engine.

She walked around to the front-seat passenger side and climbed in. "I wish you'd mentioned it before."

"After you saying you liked me, I'm glad as hell I didn't tell you anything."

"So why say it now?" She wanted to touch him. To run her fingertips across his face. She had to stop herself from doing it. The movement seemed so out of place. A minute before, she had hated this man. She could not understand what she was feeling.

"Don't you think," asked Dodge, "that if Mackenzie was half a step outside the law, I'd put him in cuffs and throw him in the holding cell? Do you think I enjoyed arresting you? Do you think I enjoy seeing the Algonquin getting butchered? Didn't I grow up in it just as much as you did? More, I think. But do you expect me not to uphold a law just because I don't agree with it? The next day, someone might decide to throw a rock through your window because they don't like something you're doing. And if I don't happen to mind what they did, do you expect me to do nothing about it?" Dodge knew it sounded like a speech. It was a speech. He had told her all these things a hundred times inside his head. He didn't wait for her to answer. He knocked the car into drive and took her home. He didn't expect her to apologize. He didn't know what she would do, and even though his curiosity jabbed at him to look, he made no attempt to catch her eye. He felt better now. Saying what he had said to her seemed to put his daydreams of a life with her permanently out of reach.

Madeleine folded her arms and looked out the window, but she was thinking so hard that she saw nothing. It was the first time Dodge had spoken to her like that. She had not known he thought about these things, and she knew she had misjudged him. But she was not surprised. She often misjudged those around her. She didn't have an instinct for understanding people, the way she understood ideas. From then on, she would see Dodge differently. She had chosen, until then, to forget that they had grown up together in this town. Both had stayed when they could have abandoned Abenaki Junction and Maine and these forests. Most people their age had already gone and they did not come back. They left it behind like a dream that made no sense. She and Dodge were closer than she had ever wanted to admit, but Madeleine had needed him to be the enemy. The man behind the uniform. Not like Mackenzie. Someone her own age. Of her own generation, who had chosen to follow the path of everything she hated. That kind of enemy. But after what Dodge had just said, Madeleine could no longer see him as the polar opposite of all that she called passion in herself. She did not have the courage to say any of this out loud. She only half understood her own thoughts about Dodge, and what she had come to realize in these past few minutes both frightened and confused her.

Dodge dropped Madeleine off at her house. He had to get straight over to Coltrane's farm, in case Hazard used that trail again.

Madeleine watched through the lace curtains as the police car drove away. She had often been told that Dodge would make a good companion for her. That was the difficulty with being a single woman in a town as small as Abenaki Junction. Everybody had something to tell her about the way her life was supposed to be going. Mostly they were kind words. Sometimes the kind people were too kind, ready to say what they knew she wanted to hear. She found this a comfort at first. Then one day in the bread aisle of the Fresh Time Supermarket, Alicia Mackenzie bumped her shopping cart into Madeleine's. She had been trying to avoid two boys who were using the aisle as a runway for their skateboards. In the conversation that followed, Alicia said something Madeleine would never forget: "You'd better make sure you don't fall so deeply in love with some idea that there's nothing left over for the people around you. I've done that myself enough times."

Madeleine knew that Alicia had not come cheaply by this knowledge. She could see it in Alicia's strained and permanent squint. Over the years, she had taken on the weatherbeaten look that many women in town carried around their eyes and tight-lipped mouths, the same winter-punished look that was on the houses where they lived. It was not enough to stop Alicia from being pretty, but enough that people who saw her thought she must once have been truly beautiful. Alicia had made her a gift of this knowledge that had cost perhaps years off her life in anger and confusion, even though she never let it show in public.

Madeleine let the curtain fall. She turned away from the window

and was met with the static-charged emptiness of her house. She
always had a feeling of helplessness when Dodge drove her home. She
had to keep reminding herself that each article, each arrest stockpiled
against Mackenzie. She was afraid that if she even thought about
giving up, it would already be too late. It's like the fable of the
tortoise and the hare, she thought. I am the tortoise. I will win in the
end.

It was twilight. Dodge walked down the dusty road that bordered
Coltrane's chest-high crop of corn. The woods rose up in front of
him. His instincts told him to turn back. The dark hollows of the
Algonquin called out a warning, which Dodge could not hear or see
but which he felt like a vibration in his bones.

He stopped at Coltrane's house to ask for directions.

"Look, why don't you just come in for dinner instead?" Coltrane
asked him. He set his hand on Dodge's shoulder, to guide the man
inside.

"Can't do it, Victor. But thank you, anyway." Dodge smelled the
warm, dry sweetness of baking bread.

Coltrane's hand slipped from Dodge's shoulder. He aimed a finger
at the deer trail that Hazard followed on his way into the woods.
"Don't stay out there long."

The ridge of the hill had sunk into darkness before Dodge reached
the trees. This ridge marked the border of the Algonquin. Beyond it,
everything was wilderness. Even local hunters, who had been tramp-
ing through those woods all their lives, sometimes got lost in its thickets. Ever since childhood, he had tried never to go in there alone. In
his dreams, he had watched the Abenaki Indians move from shadow
to shadow in silence so complete it seemed to him he had gone deaf.
Their faces, war-painted half yellow, half black in a vertical division
of their features, appeared and disappeared among the shimmering
birch leaves. Sometimes he had followed them, unable to stop himself,
moving as if hypnotized into the depths of the woods.

Dodge hiked the steep, brown-needled ground to an outcrop of
rock that let him see out over the valley. He settled himself down on
the dry pine needles, resting his back against a tree. Red squirrels
chuntered in the branches. From here the sound of wind blowing

across the lake was deeper, as if the mountains beyond them had come alive and were breathing from the granite vaults of their lungs. Sounds of Coltrane's tractor reached him over the purplish tops of the cornfield. The faded red paint of Coltrane's barn looked bloody in the sunlight. He wished Coltrane were up here with him now. The two of them could stop each other's imagination from bubbling over into nightmare.

Dodge's gun belt was digging into him, so he took it off and laid it at his feet. The buckle was shiny silver. He didn't want Hazard catching sight of any metal winking in the sun. He sprinkled pine needles on the belt, which reminded him of sprinkling rosemary into a stew. He wondered how it would be to question Hazard. He felt uneasy about the man. Hazard always seemed to be heading someplace in a hurry, with his long and loping stride. Always on the dark side of the street, always almost out of sight down some alley or halfway through some door. Dodge had never seen Hazard smile. All that Hazard's face seemed to show was a failing containment of rage.

Long shadows reached across the valley. The loggers had finished for the day and the air seemed strangely empty without the sound of chain saws. The afternoon sun was fading. As it dipped behind the ridge of a hill, all the colors suddenly changed. The cornstalks turned from emerald to the dull green of live bamboo. A chill rose from the ground.

Down at Coltrane's farm, a screen door clacked against its frame. Coltrane walked across the yard and got into his car. He drove up the dusty road, headlights flicking on as he approached the highway. Then he turned toward town and was gone. Dodge knew where he was headed. The same place he went every night. To the Loon's Watch for a beer.

It was seven o'clock. He wondered how much longer he should wait. His calves kept falling asleep. When he tried to rub the pins and needles from his skin, his nerves fizzed as if his veins were filled with seltzer. His toes felt like bees jammed into the ends of his socks, buzzing to get out. He raised himself up slowly and had to lean against the tree to avoid falling over. He heard a branch snap down the hill, and for a fragment of a second his mind told him to ignore it. He leaned slightly forward, careful not to make a sound, and saw the head of a man at the bottom of the steep slope. The man climbed the hill at an angle, first in one direction, then another, zigzagging his way up.

It was Hazard. He walked with his head down, a black nylon rucksack on his back. It was the kind of sack that children used to carry their books to school.

Dodge slipped around the other side of the tree. He had lost sight of Hazard, but could tell from the footsteps that he was still approaching.

Then Hazard came into view. He stopped to pull off his navy-blue baseball cap and press the sleeve of his red-and-black checked hunting jacket against his forehead. Then he stuffed his cap back on and kept walking.

Dodge made himself thin behind the trunk of the pine. He saw no sign of a weapon.

Hazard was walking toward him now, up the slight incline, head still down as if to pull the weight of his rucksack from its slump against his spine.

Dodge pressed his hands against his trouser pockets to soak up the sweat that had gathered on them like a slick of oil. Then he stepped out from behind the tree. He moved so quietly that Hazard didn't notice. Dodge raised his hands up to rest against his gun belt and remembered suddenly that it was not there.

Hazard looked up. There had been no sound from Dodge. Instinct had jangled Hazard's nerves. As soon as he caught sight of the man, he leaped off the ground as if his legs were loaded springs. "Jesus Christ," Hazard shouted, "you scared the hell out of me!"

" 'Evening," said Dodge.

Hazard stepped backward, then tripped and landed on the roots of a pine that bubbled up from the ground like snakes. He jumped to his feet. "What do you want from me?"

"It's Marcus Dodge," he said. Then he added, "With the police," to show that this was business. Dodge saw the fear in Hazard's face and his own worry began to diminish. "I've been looking to talk to you," he said.

"What do you want?" Hazard squinted at the darkening branches to see if Dodge was alone.

"Would you mind now if I took a look in your pack?" Dodge did not step toward the man. Instead, he just held out his hand.

"What for? I'm not doing anything."

Dodge saw no more need to be polite. "Just stand right where you are and take off your pack." He watched Hazard's features blurring in the dusk. In a couple of minutes, the colors of his clothing would vanish in the purple light.

Hazard's foot brushed against something on the ground. When he glanced down, he saw Dodge's gun belt, the buckle still sprinkled with needles.

The two men faced each other. For a second, Dodge's confidence stumbled.

Hazard noticed it. His lips twitched. Then he exploded into movement. He shoved past Dodge and sprinted into the forest. He just seemed to disappear.

By the time Dodge had lunged for his gun belt, Hazard was already ten paces ahead, swerving between the trees. Dodge ran after him, his chest burning even after the first few paces. He tried to buckle the gun belt as he moved, but gave up and kept it knotted in his fist. "You stand your ground, God damn you!" he shouted at the blur in front of him. He could hear Hazard's breathing and the stamp of his feet on the uneven ground. "What the hell's your mother going to do without you?"

Hazard's head snapped back as he ran. As his dark eyes caught the light, they looked like pools of mercury.

Dodge was gaining on Hazard. He reached out his hand toward Hazard's hair. He imagined its stringiness in the grip of his hand. Hazard rushed ahead suddenly. He moved even faster, as if all his running until then had been at a casual pace.

Dodge couldn't keep up. His lungs seemed filled with sand. He knew his strength was leaving him. His face was scratched by the pine branches. Pine sap stuck to his hands from fending off trees like a football player fending off tackles. Dodge felt the heaviness of his limbs as he lost speed. Then he stopped and bent over, gasping and angry with himself for having taken off his gun belt. Over the thunder of his breathing, he heard Hazard's footsteps fading away into the darkness of the Algonquin. More than darkness. It was like the inside of a sealed coffin.

Dodge hiked out of the woods, stumbling against tree trunks. When he reached the lane that ran between Coltrane's fields, he turned to look at the Algonquin ridge. It was like a tidal wave of ink rising silently above him and about to drown the valley in darkness. He pitied Hazard being in there now. The Algonquin had swallowed him up. Dodge walked back to Coltrane's farmyard. The breeze-shifted corn muttered on either side of him. Coltrane's two dogs barked at his heels until he was close to his car. The curtain of night-fall billowed behind him, and against all the scoffing reason in his head, Dodge could not help quickening his pace.

He sat quietly for a moment in the car, which he had parked at the end of the road. He would have to go in after Hazard, but first he was going to find Coltrane at the Loon's Watch and ask for his help. Coltrane knew these woods better than anyone. As Dodge pulled out onto the road, he looked back over his shoulder. The valley had become a lake of blindness. The only sign of life was a light in Coltrane's house, a floating cube of amber in the dark.

*W*hen Mackenzie stopped at Madeleine's house to pick her up for dinner, he shut down his last nagging feelings of affection. In his mind now was the clamp-jawed coldness he had once felt years before, when he had finished off a deer that he had hit with his car. It was lying in the road, bloody at the mouth and staring at him in the bleached glare of the car headlights. He thought he must have looked a bit like this himself that time he crawled out of the woods. Mackenzie had taken an old entrenching shovel from the trunk of his car, kept there for digging himself out of the snow. He killed the deer with three hard swings of the sharp edge of the shovel, splitting its skull. He then dragged the animal to the ditch and rolled it in. It was a distasteful job, but it had to be done. He felt that way again now. He hoped it would be quick. He hoped to keep the fighting clean.

"We are thorns in each other's sides, aren't we?" he asked Madeleine, once he'd pulled the Range Rover out onto the road.

Madeleine studied his sun-crumpled face, the coarse hair and the way the white shirt dug like a garrote into his creased neck. She had never seen him this close before and was unable to recall when she had last felt so uncomfortable. She knew this had to be one of his schemes, but she couldn't figure out what it was. "Where are we going?" she asked.

"To the Woodcutter's Lodge." Mackenzie kept his eyes on the slick black road ahead.

"I could have walked, you know. It's only at the edge of town." She thought how every word that passed between her and Mackenzie became a calculated move. She hated herself for being this way around him, but Mackenzie himself was the archduke of calculation.

"Well, I thought we might do things in style for once. Besides"—he rapped a knuckle against his artificial leg—"I'm not as fast on my feet as I used to be."

"I thought that the lodge had officially closed down. I mean I thought it was just a meeting hall now."

"It would have closed down if it weren't for me."

"It smells so funny in there." The place always had a musty reek of wood fire and tobacco and leather and brass polish and the sweat of men.

"It's a man's club. At least it used to be. All women think men's clubs smell funny. To men, it's a comfortable smell."

And you want me to feel as uncomfortable as possible, she thought. "Why did you ask to have this dinner?"

"I came to offer you an olive branch." Mackenzie smiled. He had choreographed the whole evening, which would end, perfectly and on time, with closing down the *Forest Sentinel*.

Mackenzie leaned into the steering wheel as he twisted it arm over arm into the parking lot of the Woodcutter's Lodge. As he climbed out of the Range Rover, he looked at the huge door of the lodge and wondered how many hundreds of times he had walked through it. He had been coming here all his life, brought by his father to the annual meetings of the logging company heads. He recalled the massive fires in the fieldstone fireplaces at either end of the hall and the harsh tobacco smoke and the knuckle-bunching handshakes of the logger barons. Now its main room was used for dances and flea markets. But the back part of the building was reserved for the members-only Loggers' Club, and there was only one member now and that was

Mackenzie. The caretaker, an old Welshman named Paul, kept this part of the hall locked up until Mackenzie called. Crowded onto its walls were the paintings and smoke-blackened prize antler racks that had once been spread across the entire hall. The paintings were of presidents—Washington, Jefferson, Andrew Jackson, Lincoln, Grant. The Washington portrait was painted by Gilbert Stuart. The most famous thing about the Loggers' Club had been that if a call ever came through to speak with one of its members, Paul would say the member was at the club, but could not be reached just then. Not for any reason, not for bribes or favors or threats. This used to mean, for the shadowy and secret-living members of the club, that they always had an alibi. Sometimes it was even called the Alibi Club. But it had been years since the last time Paul had given an alibi. To Mackenzie, the club was more the vapor of ghosts than anything real, a place where he had two whole legs again and could drink all night and never be hungover in the morning. His youth was locked somewhere inside these walls. He felt the slight melancholy of memories he could not share because they would not be understood except by his old friends who had come and gone from here. Now they stared out through the fading photographs of old club-member reunions. One day, he thought, I will be in there as well.

As Madeleine walked up to the door of the hall, she paused to wait for Mackenzie, whose stiff-legged shuffle slowed him down. She felt the muscles tighten around her temples. The windowless door carried no sign, but the push-plate and handle were shining more like gold than brass. It was only in the last ten years that the club had allowed women to enter the dining room. Before that, they had been made to wait in the foyer. It was Alicia who had forced Mackenzie to change the rule, and it had taken her five years before he finally gave way.

Paul came to the door. Age had made his eyes watery and bowed his back and crooked his once-strong hands. He wore a plain blue double-breasted suit with gold buttons, each stamped with the emblem of an ax splitting a log. He took Mackenzie's coat and then Madeleine's, laying them across his arm as he walked them into the foyer.

"Good evening, Paul," she said and watched the faintest smile appear on his face. She wondered what had led him to this place,

what he had left behind, and why he was content to live in such loneliness, the caretaker of a club with a membership of one.

They walked across the black-and-white parquet floor, footsteps
echoing, to a room whose walls were duck-egg blue. In the corner
stood a table with a backgammon board inlaid into the wood. Ivory
counter pieces were stacked on either side. Several current newspapers were laid out on a large table at the back of the room. Mackenzie picked two chairs close together beneath the portrait of
U. S. Grant. He settled in the body-polished leather as if his imprint
had long ago been set into its burgundy hide. The horsehair stuffing
rustled. His artificial leg stuck out stiffly in front of him, until he
hooked his hand under the knee and bent it into a sitting position.
Then Mackenzie pressed a brass button bolted to the table next to
him. There was no sound that either of them could hear, but a
moment later, Paul appeared. He stopped a few paces short of where
they sat. Mackenzie ordered two Tanqueray and tonics. "Paul's
specialty," he explained. "Along with the occasional dangerous
margarita. You don't mind trying it, do you?"

"It's your club." She looked around, marveling at the way Mackenzie could continue this tradition purely for himself. The newspapers
that Paul must have known would never be read. The way each
surface had been polished. The way drinks were kept in stock. The
clunking tick of the 1750-dated Thomas Lister grandfather clock in
the corner. And Paul himself, who had kept up Woodcutter's Lodge
in all capacities, from reshingling the roof to baking single soufflés in
its giant ovens, for as long as Madeleine had been alive. Now, face-to-
face with every exclusive and wasteful thing she took pleasure in
despising about Mackenzie, Madeleine could not bring herself to
loathe him altogether. There was something charming about this
bizarre evening out. Mackenzie was the last of his breed and he knew
it, but just as clearly he knew he could not change and he would live
out these rituals until his old heart surrendered to time.

When the drinks arrived, they were half gin and half tonic, served
in tall condensation-beaded glasses. Mackenzie let the taste of juniper
berries roll across his tongue and down his throat. He watched
Madeleine take her first sip, wince at its strength and place the glass
back on the table.

"Is everything all right?" he asked. He wanted her to like the place. Bringing Madeleine here was his way of showing he admired her, even if she was the enemy.

"Everything's fine." Madeleine breathed in the concentrated smell of men. Generations of men. Not the locker-room smell of old sweat, but the dry, honeyed reek of cigars and port and gin and roast beef and cream and coffee and the creaking hide of these chairs, left over from the days when there had been a kind of aristocracy in Abenaki Junction. She had wanted to be angry at Mackenzie, but the old man was impeccably polite. He was famous for his courtesy, particularly to women, even at the moments of his most ruthless hostility. There was no talk of business. He hadn't played the trick of bulldozing through her with strong opinions and a loud voice. She could have fought well against that. But the way this man moved seemed to have no shape or direction. So she found herself wondering whether Mackenzie was in fact naïve, or whether he was making her dance like a puppet, politely giving way and making her advance until she no longer knew where she was.

The quiet of this room surrounded her. Madeleine sat under the stern gaze of the statesmen, who looked at her as much as to say, "What the hell are you doing here?" She found herself listening not to the noise but to the lack of it—the rustle of horsehair stuffing and of matches being struck as Mackenzie lit himself a cigarette. This half silence—it was peculiar to men. If this had been a club for women only, she thought, the quiet would be different.

Paul called them almost in a whisper to the dining room. Then he served them roast beef and boiled new potatoes with string beans. They drank 1968 Haut-Médoc from large crystal glasses. The table at which they sat was long and dark, weighed down with huge silver beakers of water and candleholders and platters of grapes, apples and pears. In the candlelight, these looked more like painted fruit than anything that could ever be tasted. All of the silver was engraved with the log-and-ax crest of the club. The idea of this long table, the only one at which dinner had been served, was that a person could come to the club and never have to worry about eating alone. Mackenzie had always admired this unspoken law, this table that had been built inside the room because it was too big to be brought in from outside. You did not complain here. You did not burden others with your problems. You did not swear and you did not exclude anyone from the conversation. You never ridiculed another member of the club. That was why, in all the years when he had dined elbow to elbow with mill owners who were at war with one another, he had never seen an argument.

Instead of talking business, Mackenzie ran through his reservoir of memories of Madeleine growing up in Abenaki Junction. He did not leave out the recollections of her picketing his mill, or the speeches she had made against him in community meetings. He didn't shy away from them. It was the only way he could think of diffusing any of the anger that had fed off the silence between them for so long.

Madeleine was surprised at how much he recalled, and how generously he brought the memories to life, speaking fondly of her even when she knew her actions had made him furious at the time. For a moment, as Paul placed a bowl of perfect raspberries in front of her, Madeleine forgot about the business of the evening, the olive branch Mackenzie had said he would be offering. She rested one of the berries on her tongue and crushed it against the roof of her mouth. The faint bittersweetness of the fruit snapped her back to a day years before when she had gone berry picking beside the railroad tracks. There were so many berries that she had filled her bucket and then had to collect them in her hat. It was on that day that she had looked down the tracks and seen a black bear rummaging through its own patch of raspberries. She saw the huge pads of its feet and the brown fur on its muzzle. The bear was only a hundred yards away, popping the berries off the bush with its tongue. Madeleine wasn't afraid, although it went against her instincts. When the animal saw her, it also showed no fear. She watched the bear until it had eaten enough. Then it plodded off into the forest. She swallowed and the daydream disappeared.

When the meal was over, Madeleine walked with Mackenzie back into the front room and sat at the backgammon table. Mackenzie cleared his throat, as if to choke down everything that had been said until now. "I'd like to make you an offer that at first might seem a little crazy, but if you think about it, I'm sure you'll see that we can both benefit." He paused to let his words sink in. "I would like to buy the *Forest Sentinel*."

"Oh, really?" Madeleine's own laughter caught her off guard. The worst she had imagined was that Mackenzie would request some kind of interview with her in which he would be guaranteed favorable coverage in the *Forest Sentinel*. But this! She waited for him to smile and show that he was joking.

"I mean to pay very well for it." His words were measured and calm.

"But then what would you do with it?" She held her hands open, waiting for an explanation.

"I'd close it down."

Madeleine nodded slowly and quietly. At least he was being honest. She picked up one of the backgammon pieces and pressed it between her palms. "Mr. Mackenzie."

"Jonah."

"All right. Jonah. You've known me all my life. And you know that for years now I've worked toward setting up an environmental newspaper. How do you expect me just to walk away from it?"

"I'm prepared to pay you thirty thousand dollars. All in cash. All immediately."

The mention of so much money jolted her nerves like caffeine. "The paper's not worth that. Let's not even pretend."

"I'm not pretending. I'm not paying for the paper. I'm paying for you to move it someplace else. That would be part of the agreement. You wouldn't start up another paper within two hundred miles of here." Mackenzie raised his hand as Madeleine's mouth snapped open. "Please let me finish. This paper is worth about ten thousand dollars. Tops. That's for everything. The rent on the building, the deposit, all the equipment. Not even ten. And I'm even happy to let you keep your equipment. You could start up another paper in a much bigger way with this money. You know that's true. I know it must leave a bad taste in your mouth to have me buy you out. You might feel as if you are compromising your values. But it's a compromise that can serve you much better in the long run than you are serving yourself at the moment. If you look at this realistically . . ." He let his words trail into silence. He had said what he had to say.

For Madeleine, everything took on the clumsy and ponderous movements of being chased in a nightmare. "You just want me out of your hair."

"Exactly."

"Well, Jonah, I don't mean to flatter myself, but what have I done to get in your hair so badly that you'd pay that kind of money to have me out? If you adopted some ecologically sound measures—sustainable yield, for example—I think my paper would actually help you, not hurt."

"It's just a chance I'm not prepared to take." Mackenzie slapped his hands wearily on the arms of his chair. "Look around. I'm all that's left. Why should I trust anything except my own instincts? And what about you, Madeleine? What do you trust except the world of your ideals?"

Madeleine was about to talk back, to say anything that would refute his point. But Mackenzie was right. Beyond the world of her ideals, everything was crooked with doubt.

"You see it all," he said, "through the world of that camera you're always carrying around. A neatly bracketed world which you only have to see the way you want to see. You can't just live off ideals."

Watch me, she wanted to say. "But what if I don't accept?" she asked him. She waited for him to take off the gloves of his politeness. She gave him every opportunity.

What if? he thought. He looked at Madeleine and thought, I'll sweep you away until every trace of you is gone, the same way I'll do to that damn forest, whether you like it or not. Tabula rasa.

"What if I don't accept?" Madeleine asked again, suspicious of Mackenzie's silence and the menacing drowsiness that seemed to wash across his face while he sat there deep in thought.

"Well." He rolled his neck as if there were a crick in his spine. "I hope it won't come to that. It isn't in my nature to offer compromises, but if we can handle this like civilized people, I'm all for that."

"Yes." Madeleine leaned across the table and tapped the backgammon chip in time with her words. "But what if I don't sell? Just tell me that much." She realized even as she said this that she might have to sell, if not to Mackenzie then to someone else. The *Forest Sentinel* had been so close to going under for so long now that Madeleine had forgotten what it was like to live any other way.

"If you don't accept my offer, then you'll probably save me some money." Mackenzie was staring right at her and through her.

"That sounds like a threat." Here it comes at last, she thought. The sweetness of the raspberries bubbled sickly and acidic into her throat.

"Not at all. Please don't think me so clumsy. I say you'll save me money because your newspaper will fold. You just aren't printing enough copies. More important, people aren't reading it. Sure, they take it home from the pile in the supermarket. Then they use it as kindling to start their fires. Madeleine, I have to speak bluntly. It's not just the paper. It's you. There's nothing for you in Abenaki Junction."

"It's not true!" she snapped.

"Well, I'm glad to hear it." He did not believe her and he let his voice show it. "But you have to know when to quit." Mackenzie saw a tired look come into Madeleine's eyes. All evening, it seemed to him, they had been shining and now they were suddenly dull. This was when he knew that he would get what he wanted. Not now, perhaps. But the process had begun. He jammed his thumb against the brass nipple button on the table, as if to mark the last period on what he had to say.

When Paul arrived, Mackenzie ordered a coffee and a cigar. He knew Madeleine wouldn't want one, so he didn't bother to ask. The cigars were Cuban, Punch and Monte Cristos, smuggled into the country and sent to him each year by an old college acquaintance named Sal Ungaro, whose line of work kept changing and always seemed to go against the law. Mackenzie clipped the end of the cigar with a cigar cutter and then lit the cigar, rolling the end around through the match flame that Paul held out to him in order to get an even burn. Then he sat back and looked at Madeleine, the strong tobacco smoothing out his thoughts.

Madeleine felt the quiet that had suddenly come between them. It circled and was menacing, swimming like a shark from room to room.

Mackenzie broke the quiet. "Did you enjoy the roast beef?"

Madeleine could feel it in a knot in her stomach. She almost never ate red meat anymore. "I thought it was a little rare, actually."

"Usually is."

"I think I should be getting home, Jonah. Thank you for dinner."

Mackenzie nodded slowly, puffing on the cigar. "You'll forgive me if I don't get up. My leg and all."

"Of course. Will you be coming back to town now?"

"No," Mackenzie held up his half-finished cigar. "Can't rush one of these. Paul will drive you home. I'll just sit here until he gets back. I'll keep that offer open for a while."

"All right," she said. "Thank you again for the dinner. I didn't expect to enjoy myself, but I sort of did." She shrugged. "I guess I couldn't help myself."

"Well, thank you for coming," he told her. After she had gone, Mackenzie sat in his chair and smoked the cigar down almost to his fingers. Then he walked out of the hall and stood looking at the stars.

While the Range Rover drove through the dark, Madeleine noticed that the lights were on in the house Booker Lazarus was putting up for rent. She wondered who was new in town.

Mackenzie's words tumbled in her head. She knew she would not sleep tonight. She leaned over and spoke quietly in Paul's ear. "Would you mind dropping me off at my office just here? There's some work I need to catch up on."

"Yes, of course." Paul stopped the car and let her out. He waited until she had opened the office door and turned and waved to him. Then he drove back to the lodge.

The *Forest Sentinel* was in a newly built, prefabricated structure near the center of town. The walls were thin and the building reminded Madeleine of a trailer put up on a construction site. It was all she could afford for now. The office was only two rooms, busy with computers and corkboards scaled with notes. The back room had cutting boards set out along the walls and a light table for viewing photo negatives. Even when the office was quiet, everything seemed to be in constant motion, down to the speckled pattern on the carpeting.

Madeleine sat at her desk and picked up a blue pencil. Then she began editing a piece she had written the day before about the interdependence between pine and white birch trees, and asking loggers to reseed areas with both species instead of just with pines. She had been working a few minutes when she heard a knock on the door.

Through the rippled glass door, she saw the pink smudge of a face.

"It's open," Madeleine called out. She wondered who it could be this time of night. Most people went to bed early in Abenaki Junction.

The door opened. It was Alicia. She closed the door quickly behind her. She looked a little pale. "I've been thinking about you this evening. Asking myself how things went with you and Jonah."

At first, Madeleine didn't answer. She couldn't understand why Alicia was here. Why she hadn't even said hello and why she didn't just ask her husband about the evening when he came home. But Madeleine trusted Alicia, even if she didn't understand the meaning of her visit. "He said I was a thorn in his side."

Alicia nodded. "You're supposed to be a thorn in his side, Madeleine. The fact that he says it is proof that you're doing your job." She walked over to the desk. "May I sit down?"

Madeleine waved her hand at the chair on the other side of the desk.

"He'd kill me if he found out I was here."

Madeleine understood the risk Alicia took in coming. If Mackenzie knew, he would be furious. Her gaze traveled to the glass door, as if expecting to see Mackenzie's face materialize.

"He wants to shut you down, you know."

"Yes, I know." It crossed her mind that Alicia might be working with Mackenzie, but she knew that Alicia would never do something so underhanded. It wasn't in her nature.

"He means to do it." Alicia stared at Madeleine, as if trying to say more with her eyes than with her words.

Madeleine tapped her pencil on the desk, beating out a rhythm in her head while she debated whether to say what she was thinking. "I feel strange saying this to you about your husband, but I kept waiting for him to threaten me. That's what I would have expected from him. I mean, he has this reputation of being so ruthless. It only made sense that he would have threatened me. But he didn't. He was actually kind of charming."

"He is whatever he needs to be to get the job done. If threatening you would have worked, you would have been threatened. But think about it. What puts you most off balance? The fact that he's nice to you. Even if you aren't going to sell the paper, at least he made you consider it."

"How do you know I considered it?"

"Didn't you?"

Madeleine puffed her cheeks. "It was a fortune he offered me."

"A fortune to you or a fortune to him?"

Madeleine shrugged. "You already know the answer to that. You seem to have a better idea than I do about how this stuff works. All I do is write the paper. I never really was much good at business."

"Well, you have to be able to do both."

"Why are you telling me all this?" Madeleine sat back. "Why should I believe you?"

Alicia sighed and nodded. It was a fair question. "I'm not trying to help you so that I can help him. It's not like that at all. He's still my husband and I still love him. I'm just trying to stop this from turning into a war. I've lived through too many already. All those other logging companies that Jonah shut down one after the other. That went on for years. I just don't think I could stand to live through it again. And the other reason I'm here now is that I respect the work you're doing. I know it isn't easy. I know how much of an uphill struggle it's been. I wish I didn't have to come here in the middle of the night to say this, but now seems to be the right time. I just wanted to tell you to be careful."

"The truth is, I'm scared of him. You look in his face and you see he could do anything."

Alicia leaned across and tapped her fingernails gently on the desk. "But so could you, and I think he knows that."

"What do you want me to do?"

"I didn't come here to tell you what to do. But I won't stand by and watch him bully you, Madeleine. Just be careful. He feels threatened by you, in a way that he never was before. And when he is threatened, he is dangerous." Alicia had said what she came to say. "I have to get home." She left without saying good-bye.

It was only then that Madeleine realized she was shaking. In her mind, all the civility and gentleness of the evening had inverted into something hideous and brutal. She told herself she should be happy. The tortoise was winning the race. But at that moment, all she felt was alone and frightened about what would happen next.

odge burst into the Loon's Watch bar. The local pair of bar-
stool residents turned to look at him—Frampton and Barnegat,
both bleary-eyed from alcohol. Dodge scanned the room until he saw
Coltrane sitting in the corner. Then he walked across, as calmly as he
could so as not to draw attention.

Coltrane's table had a video game built into it. There was only one
video table at the Loon's Watch, and Coltrane claimed it whenever he
walked in. The surface of this table was a plastic screen, scratched
into opaqueness by beer mugs. Underneath, the video game acted
itself out in awkward microdot spasms. It was an old game, the late-
seventies graphics clumsy. The sound effects were tiny grunts and
squeaks. On a level below the table was a slot for putting money in
and red buttons for firing at the aliens.

"I found him," said Dodge. His cheeks were burnished from the
cold.

Coltrane wasn't listening. He had wiped the beer sweat from the tabletop and stuck a quarter into the video game. He jabbed at the red FIRE button, killing aliens for three minutes until they shot him down with their grunting, squeaking spaceships. At last, Coltrane looked up at Dodge, radish-faced from the effort. "I can't do this stupid game."

Dodge sat down. "I think I found our guy," he said again.

Coltrane had pulled another quarter from his pocket. He was about to fight the aliens again, as if to kill them off forever, but Dodge's words snapped him out of it. "What did you just say?"

"It's like we thought. Wilbur Hazard." Dodge lowered his voice. Barnegat and his friend had fallen silent, both doing their best to listen in.

"How come you're so sure?" Coltrane stood. He wished he could tell Dodge the truth, but the job at the mill was the only one he'd ever had. He was five years from retirement. He could not bring himself to throw all that away. Still, he hated himself for being a coward. If there had been no one else in this bar but him, Coltrane would have taken his mug and smashed it through the table screen onto the grunting aliens in their Day-Glo spaceships.

"We need to start now," Dodge said.

"We?" Coltrane's voice rose on the word. "Oh, no. This isn't my job."

"I need your help, Victor. Won't you help me?"

Billy Frampton's large eyes seemed to swivel like radar dishes toward where the two men sat.

"Sit down a minute, Marcus," Coltrane told him. "We need to talk more."

"We have to go now." Dodge's whisper hissed across the table. "Please, Victor. I need your help."

"Let me go tell Mackenzie, at least."

They were facing each other now. The video-game table flashed beneath them.

"All right," said Dodge. "I'll meet you at the station in fifteen minutes." He walked out quickly and the sound of the police car's engine rumbled through the walls of the bar.

Coltrane realized that Barnegat and Frampton were staring at him. Barnegat was a worker at the mill and resented Coltrane's promotion to foreman. He wore a black wool watch cap all year round and sported a stubby mustache, the same color as the cap. He'd grown the mustache because he had been slashed in the face during a knife fight and his upper lip had never healed. Billy Frampton, half-dead and mean, had been retired from logging for almost a decade. He had the sad eyes of a bloodhound and a way of sucking at his teeth whenever he got ready to speak. He wore a dirty toupee that sometimes stayed in his hard hat when he took the hat off his head. Frampton lived in an old shop on the main street. He put curtains in the windows so people couldn't see into his living room, but sometimes he drew them back to let in the light and sat in his rocking chair, watching people watching him.

Suddenly Coltrane had the strange feeling that everything around him had become two-dimensional. But the wilderness outside had three dimensions now. Soon he would be going out there, against every instinct in his body. And then it would be too late forever to tell Dodge that he knew who had spiked the tree. Coltrane walked out of the bar. He kept his eye on the two men, wanting them to know that they were being watched.

By the time Coltrane left the room, sweat was running down Frampton's face. "Goddamn that man," he said. "He can make you think you done something wrong even when you're just sitting there sucking in air." Frampton blinked his eyes very hard when he talked, as if whatever he said was a constant source of amazement to him.

Barnegat didn't answer. He was thinking about the $10,000 reward that Mackenzie had posted. "That Hazard boy is ten thousand dollars' worth of fool running around in the forest," he whispered. "Be a shame to let the bears get him first."

Frampton understood. He had been thinking the same thing. "I'll meet you at the logging road in half an hour." He reached a finger under his toupee and scratched. The furry pancake shifted as if it were alive. "We got to bring guns." He talked too loudly. He had been raised by an uncle named Johann Kaslaka, who had been blown through a hedge by an artillery burst during the invasion of France in 1918. The blast had shattered Kaslaka's eardrums, leaving him mostly deaf, and to compensate, Kaslaka always raised his voice when talking, as if people could hear him as faintly as he heard them. The result of this was that he caused listeners to wince at his lung-emptying shouts, turned heads in every quiet room and so confused the street dogs of Abenaki Junction that they barked at him whenever he walked past. The habit spread to Billy Frampton, who had never lost it, even though he tried.

Barnegat set his hand on Frampton's shoulder. "You're too old for this, Billy."

Frampton stared at the hand until Barnegat took it away. "I ain't too fucking old. I could still pop the eyes out of your head."

"All right, Billy," Barnegat said slowly. "Whatever you say." He was tired of taking orders from Frampton. The old man had nothing left but his foul mouth to exert any kind of authority. Tonight I will teach him some respect, thought Barnegat. "We head straight up the middle to the tracks." He drew a line through a puddle of spilled beer on the bar top to mark the path they would take through the Algonquin.

Lazarus stood in front of them now. He drummed his fingers on the counter, eyebrows raised, asking them without words if they wanted more beer.

Frampton slid the dull gray tankard across the counter. Most nights he drank eleven beers, grimly and steadily. Tonight he had drunk only four. "Goddamnit, old man," he snapped at Lazarus, "how come you're always staring at me as if you're looking for an excuse to bust open my head?"

"Maybe I am," said Lazarus quietly, "and maybe I found one." Then he walked away. He sat at the end of the bar and thought about winter, just to get himself pissed off.

"Hunting season's coming early this year," said Barnegat. "I swear I'm going to tag me some meat before the sun comes up."

When the men tramped out into the dark, Lazarus eased himself off his stool and began to mop down the copper bar top with a chamois cloth. "Do you want another cup of coffee?" he called into the shadows of the room. The bar lights were shining in his face and Lazarus could not see anyone, but he knew a man was there.

At first there was no reply and Lazarus breathed in to ask again, but then the man appeared suddenly, as if walking out of another dimension. It was Gabriel. He had heard everything. He set his coffee cup down on the wet copper of the bar. "What was that all about?" he asked.

Lazarus fetched the coffeepot and poured him some more. The coffee was thick and dark like old motor oil. "They're fixing to kill a man tonight."

Gabriel sipped his coffee and said nothing.

Lazarus fetched a cup and poured out some for himself. "Sometimes I think that people in this town are never more than a dozen words away from killing each other. There's times I look at this town and it seems like the painted backdrop of some movie, and behind it all the claims we make about being civilized don't mean anything. The instincts are still there to make us savages. It don't take much to bring them to the surface."

The bar door swung open and a woman walked in. A gust of cool night air followed her and vanished in the heat of the room. She carried a bulging leather mail satchel and a bundle of papers in her arms. She nodded at Lazarus.

"Hello, Madeleine," said Lazarus. He pulled at one earlobe, as if suddenly self-conscious about the condition of his bar. He began to wash glasses that were already clean.

"I just need some coffee. I'm going to be up all night with this stuff." Madeleine set her bundle on the countertop. The pile slid to one side, fanning the documents like a giant pack of playing cards. From the satchel, she took a small thermos and handed it over to Lazarus.

"Here's another coffee drinker." Lazarus nodded at Gabriel while he rinsed out the thermos. "Seems like nobody ever wants to sleep in this town."

Gabriel had glanced at Madeleine when she walked in, but he had glanced away again. Now he turned to face her. He smiled uncertainly, embarrassed at the forced introduction.

Madeleine stared at him. She did not smile back. She gave him a look that made it clear he was a stranger.

Gabriel peered down into his coffee. He had noticed her intelligent face and the curve of her hips in her jeans, and he did not blame her for staring at him with the narrowed eyes and clenched jaw of someone who is suspicious. In her place, he might have done the same. Gabriel felt a tightness in his chest, and raised his head and saw his own tired eyes in the mirror behind the bar. He thought of all the avenues of possibility that he might once have imagined with this woman, even if it came to nothing more than a glance which showed that they both knew the possibility, no matter that it would remain a dream. He could have none of that now. All need for companionship had been replaced by the fear of discovery. Even if she did want to know, he could tell this woman nothing about who he really was. All he could do was envelop her in lies, and the closer he might come, the more lies he would have to weave around her. And the more he might care about her, the more he would detest himself for lying. He felt the trap in which he'd caught himself. If he liked her, he would not lie to her, and if he didn't lie to her, she would have nothing to do with him.

Gabrel knew what he was. He knew the destruction he would bring to the lives of people in this town. And he knew that the extremity of his beliefs and what he was prepared to do to act them out was only the first step in a long series of steps that he believed in absolutely. He had accepted the price of that, which was to become like a machine. Not feel loneliness. But far away inside himself was the old Gabriel, nameless now, and waiting patiently but always less patiently for the time when the two sides of this man might somehow merge.

Gabriel was in a war. Any other name for it fell short. And part of the war was with himself, to keep in place the mask that he now wore. It seemed a fragile thing, and even the thought of being close to this stranger seemed to Gabriel to reveal in the bar's mirror his old face. He hoped that no one else could see it.

Lazarus filled the thermos with coffee and handed it back to Madeleine, who paid for it with a pocket full of change. Before she turned to leave, she looked at Gabriel again. This time she did smile, but it was a smile that gave nothing away.

When Madeleine had gone, Gabriel gulped down the last of his coffee. He tapped the rim of the cup to show he wanted some more.

Lazarus filled the cup and set the coffeepot down on the counter. The bar-top copper rippled blue from the heat. "You ought not to drink that stuff so late at night."

"I don't sleep much, anyway."

"No," said Lazarus, as if he had known in advance.

Gabriel put a crumpled dollar bill on the counter. There was something in the old man's voice that both bothered and comforted him. There was a softness to the way he spoke which Gabriel had not heard before. It was the first faint offering of acceptance of Gabriel's presence here. But it bothered Gabriel, because Lazarus talked as if he knew more than he was letting on. Maybe Lazarus knew everything. Gabriel glanced up and caught Lazarus's eye, searching for some blink of recognition, but it was too dark to tell. It's just nerves, Gabriel thought to himself. It's just the coffee jabbering in my head. But Gabriel knew it could just as easily have been himself out there in the woods that night and running for his life, instead of that poor man Wilbur Hazard.

"Get home fast," Lazarus told Gabriel as he walked out. "And lock the door and load up your gun if you have one. And make yourself another pot of coffee. It ain't worth sleeping tonight anyway. By the time those boys are finished in the woods, this place will be hell above ground."

≡

Before Coltrane knocked on Mackenzie's door, he sat in his car across the road and smoked a cigarette to calm his nerves. It seemed to be the fastest-burning cigarette he had ever smoked. After only a few puffs, the butt had burned down so low that it looked as if he had made a fire by rubbing his thumb and index finger together. He flicked the cigarette out the window and then walked across the road. He rang the doorbell several times before Alicia let him in.

"I heard you the first time," she said, laughing, but her eyes were serious.

Coltrane breathed in the beeswax-and-lemon smell of polished wood. "Dodge thinks he knows who did it," Coltrane said. "The nail. He thinks he knows."

The expression changed on her face. It was no longer reservedly polite. Now her gaze was fixed. "I'll get Jonah. Please do sit down." She vanished up the stairs.

Coltrane watched her go, silently admiring how out of place her gracefulness appeared in Abenaki Junction. She seemed to him like some rare and tropical plant growing in among the pines.

Mackenzie came down wearing nothing but a towel wrapped around his waist. His skin was red from sitting in a bath. Alicia followed him with a bathrobe, but he shook it off. Steam curled up from his skin.

Coltrane found himself looking down at his shoes in the presence of this mostly naked man.

"Alicia says you found someone." Mackenzie's gray chest hair clung in tight, angry curls to his body. He squinted at Coltrane, asking him without words, What the hell are you talking about?

"Well, Dodge saw him going into the Algonquin this evening. He's going to try to find him and wants me to help."

"Who is it?" Mackenzie was pug-faced with indignation.

"Wilbur Hazard. That city boy."

"Hazard?" Mackenzie looked as if he had bitten into a piece of rotten fruit. "Hazard?" he asked again.

"I came right by to tell you. Tell you both." Coltrane glanced at Alicia, to show he was talking to her as well.

"And Dodge wants you to help?" Mackenzie raked his fingers through his chest hair.

"I'll go in there and *help*." Coltrane stressed the word. He meant, I'll go in there and fuck everything up on purpose, so nobody gets hurt.

"I think Victor needs to set out as soon as he can, dear." Alicia took hold of her husband's arm.

Mackenzie did not answer. He allowed himself to be led away upstairs. It never occurred to him that Alicia might know about him and Mary and the identity of Hazard's father. He had never seen a flicker of suspicion on her face. But if he had looked her in the eye just then, he would have seen from the pity in her expression that she did know. She had known for a long while, and had forgiven him, although it had taken time. It was between him and Mary, this thing that had happened so far in the past. Alicia did not feel a part of it. Emotions had filtered down the way they always do in the end, and it seemed to her that each had made a separate peace. She pitied her husband now, because she knew he would never mention his pain to her and she could never tell him that she knew. Better to let it go. The punishment Mackenzie had dealt himself over the years had been hard enough to bear. No one judged Jonah Mackenzie more harshly than he judged himself, and if he thought she knew, the judgment would only be harsher. She did not want that. Didn't want to hurt him, or for anyone to be hurt by this. In her mind, all debts had been paid. Alicia hoped it wasn't true about Hazard spiking the tree. It would bring scandal to that fractured little family, which deserved it less than others she could name.

Coltrane stood for a moment by himself in the hallway, not sure what to do next. Then he left without saying good-bye. Five minutes later, he met Dodge at the station and the two of them headed for the forest. Coltrane drove. Dodge knew he liked to drive the patrol car, feeling the power of its supercharged engine. So now Dodge sat beside him, slipping new .357 bullets into the chamber of his revolver. At first they didn't speak. Then, a few miles down the road, Coltrane suddenly jerked the steering wheel to one side. The police car swerved onto the shoulder. Gravel and dust kicked up behind them. A truck with a gun rack behind its seat sped past, the driver craning his neck around to see why they had stopped so suddenly.

"This guy could be anywhere in the Algonquin, in places nobody's even seen before. It's crazy going in now. We need to set out in daylight." Coltrane looked out the car window. The darkness seemed almost solid, leaning with force against the glass.

Dodge brushed a hand over the stubble of his end-of-the-day beard. "It probably wouldn't hurt to get some troopers up from Skowhegan to help with the search. I bet they could send us a few."

"No," said Coltrane hurriedly. "We know the Algonquin as well as any logger in the Mackenzie Company. You and I been stalking around there since we were kids. Longer than Hazard, any road. We'll find him. We don't need Skowhegan people for that. Ten men and the bear will hear you coming, but only two and you can come up close for the kill." Coltrane flinched at a sudden and viciously returning memory. It was from years before, when he had shot a bear at a place called the Narrows, where Pogansett Lake flowed into Crescent Pond. The water ran fast there, and bears would sometimes come to scoop fish from the rapids. They were trout mostly, rainbows and browns. What jolted Coltrane was the image of the bear after his first bullet had struck. He shot the animal at fifty yards with a 30-06 hollow-point. The bear rocked from the hit and stood up, furious at the sudden pain. It was five feet tall. The pads of its paws looked to Coltrane like light-brown pillows in the black fluff of its fur. Then the bear looked down at its chest and saw, in the cold air, a jet of vaporized breath coming from the hole punched into its lungs. Coltrane saw all fierceness leave the bear's face. Instead, there seemed to be a look of disappointment. That it had no chance to fight. That whatever had just happened was the end. Coltrane saw the dull downcasting of its eyes. He would never forgive himself for killing that bear. He did not know why. It was hunting season when he shot it. He had a license. It was legal. But this made no difference to the way he felt. The bear had not deserved to die, just as Hazard didn't now. Tears jumped into Coltrane's eyes and he wiped them away fast with his fur-tufted knuckles. He had not cried in years. Please God, he thought, don't let that man get hurt.

"Tomorrow, then," Dodge said with a gravelly voice, "We'll set out at six A.M. to track him down." He knew he couldn't find Hazard on his own, and Coltrane wasn't going anywhere but home. He felt the kind of disappointment in his friend that was so bad he couldn't even mention it.

Coltrane swung the car out onto the road and headed back toward town. It seemed that each joint of his spine was in the grip of a small and angry fist. He knew what Dodge was thinking. The worst thing one man can think of another. The automatic gears changed smoothly as he stepped hard on the pedal. The two men sat in silence. Yellow road dividers slipped away under them like the musical torpedoes of the aliens, born and trapped and dying inside the plastic universe of their game table at the Loon's Watch bar.

Dodge dropped Coltrane off at his house. Then he got back out on the road but did not head for home. He had one more place to go.

He drove to the house of Mary the Clock. He reached the royal-blue door and knocked on it with three heavy thumps of his fist.

"Well, it's Mr. Dodge," said Mary, spying on him through the keyhole. "Mine eyes have seen the glory." Then she opened the door and laughed. Happy to see him. She was still dressed, despite the lateness of the hour. Without inviting him in, she turned and walked back into the house. She moved with the steady poise of a girl who has been taught to walk with a Bible balanced on her head. Her eyelashes were so dark around her green eyes that it looked as if she wore makeup, but she didn't. In a few years, her beauty would leave her. She would still be beautiful, but in the way that people would think of her as old first and beautiful afterward. For now, she kept her beauty in the bright green eyes and unwrinkled smile and the hair that ran halfway down her back. She did not have the leering grin Dodge would have painted on an imagined crazy person. Instead, her smile seemed absentminded, as if she were constantly off visiting happy memories. Dodge wondered sometimes whether people were so busy feeling sorry for Mary that they failed to see she was sorry for them, too. She seemed to hold some precious secret in her mind, something so valuable that even to hold on to it excused her from the logic of the crowd.

Mary walked into the kitchen, which was mostly taken up by a table. It was draped with a red-and-white checked cloth, reminding Dodge of an Italian restaurant. Old Christmas cards still stood propped on a shelf above the fireplace. In the corner he could see the Christmas tree, its needles long since dead and the ornaments dangling on bare branches. Dodge knew it was a fire-code violation and he should have said something, but he let it go. He scanned the walls for signs of positive insanity. Pictures hanging upside down. Backward devil-writing in the dust on the windows. There was none of that.

"Take your place," she told him, and pointed to a metal frame chair with coarse red upholstery. Dodge sat down in it. The chair was narrow and uncomfortable. At the base of its steel-tube legs were holes for attaching it to the ground. There was an ashtray in one of the arms. Suddenly Dodge knew what this was—a chair taken from an airliner. He looked down and saw a printed plastic sign on the chair frame. YOUR LIFE JACKET IS UNDER YOUR SEAT. Dodge could not help bending down to peer under the seat and see if the life jacket was there. It was.

"Would you like a cup of tea?" Mary asked him, holding out an empty cup as if to show that this was where the drink would go. "I'm going to have some."

Dodge snapped upright, dizzy with the rush of blood from his head. "I'm OK for now, thank you." He waited for a moment while the chips of light from his dizziness spun around like bumblebees in flight and then vanished. "Mary, you probably know why I'm here."

"Nope." She smiled vacantly.

"Do you know about your son spiking those trees in the Algonquin?"

"Wilbur works at the restaurant." Mary put on the kettle for tea. "All the livelong day."

"Yes, but he's been going into the woods, Mary. And driving nails into trees, we believe. We told you a man was killed the other day. We came by asking about it. Do you remember?"

"Yes." She spoke as if she couldn't quite be sure. "I want a pony."

"I saw your son running into the woods this evening. He didn't stop when I asked him to."

"Yes." Mary let the word sift into the air as if she were breathing out smoke.

"So is there anything you can tell us that might help? Wilbur's just going to get hurt if he keeps running away." Dodge tapped his fingers lightly on the tablecloth, feeling the hard wood beneath.

"No one would hurt Wilbur." She laughed to show the stupidity of his suggestion. "He said he would come back, but I don't know where from."

"When will he come home?"

"When he's ready." Mary shrugged. "And we must reason not the need." The kettle was boiling now. She started to prepare the tea.

Dodge could not bring himself to be impatient with the woman. He wished he could tell her how much trouble Wilbur was in, but he doubted it would do any good. In the end, he thought, she might be better off not knowing.

Dodge didn't sleep that night. Instead, he stashed himself in a children's playground across the road from Mary's house. There was a swing set in the park, its chains rusted and creaking in the night breeze. Children had not played here in a while. Weeds climbed up through the sand. Dodge smoked a cigarette, hand cupped over the flame to hide it. He knew he had to be patient. Hazard will return, Dodge told himself. It's the nature of the beast.

Barnegat and Frampton met at the logging road. Each carried a rifle. There was no moon, only a vast fan of stars above the trees. The road was a pale river running into the blackness of the forest.

"We split the money in half," announced Frampton. Barnegat said nothing to disagree, so he assumed it was all right. He had spoken only to break the silence, which seemed to pace around them as if it were alive. He knew the woods by day, but it occurred to him only as he stepped creaky-kneed from his car that the wilderness at night was part of a different universe. He thought back to his stool at the bar and the gum-fuzzing beer he had left in his mug, and he wished he hadn't come along. But it was too late now to show fear.

They walked up the road, the sound of their footsteps on the gravel drowning out everything but the running-water murmur of wind through the tops of the pines.

As the minutes went by, they met nothing and felt braver. Their eyes grew used to the dark and now they could make out the individual pines instead of the tarlike wall of night that seemed to rise sheer from the edges of the road.

Frampton held his rifle tight against his chest. The gun was the most valuable thing he owned. It was an antique Winchester 30-30 Goldenboy. For the past three years, he had been paying off the loan he took out to buy it. He saved money by not going to the dentist. Instead, he pulled three of his own rotten teeth with a pliers, having first glued pieces of leather to the gripping steel. Early in the year he had slipped while fly-fishing in felt-soled boots down by the railroad bridge that crossed a corner of Pogansett Lake. He trod between two rocks and fell, twisting his arm, which broke above the elbow. Too angry about the cost of a doctor's bill to feel the pain, Frampton set his own arm right where he stood, waist-deep in the stream, fly rod clamped between his teeth. He still had that fly rod, teeth marks etched into the graphite. He didn't go to a barber, figuring he had little enough hair to worry about anyway. Whenever it grew too long, he would light a candle and burn the ends. Then he would rub out the fire with his clawed fingers. Sometimes when he picked up the Goldenboy he wondered if it had been worth it. As he looked at the polished brass barrel and burnished cherrywood stock, he would remember the foul, metallic smell of his burned hair and the orangy crumbs that clung to his wool clothes like little spiders. "You figure Hazard'll come quietly?" Frampton asked.

"I hope not," Barnegat said. "I hope he puts up a fight, so we can fuck him up and pay him back for Pfeiffer." Barnegat had not liked Pfeiffer and had never spoken to him except with the condescension of an old hand talking to a newcomer. But none of that mattered now.

The two men began to turn their thoughts from money to vengeance. They unshouldered their guns and slid bullets into the breeches. They sensed the particular never-to-be-mentioned thrill of men who feel justified in bringing violence to a weaker enemy. The more they thought of Pfeiffer, the more angry they became. Barnegat had seen the way he died, and Frampton had seen other accidents, which he assembled in his head until they matched the level of atrocity that Barnegat described.

Frampton reached into his pocket and took out a half-crushed packet of Camels. He shook it until a cigarette slid from the end and put it in his mouth. He was just reaching for his lighter when Barnegat slapped the white stick from between his lips.

"I can tell you don't know shit about hunting."

"I been hunting all my life." Frampton talked back with as much bluster as he could manage against a man he almost loved.

"And I seen how much you get each season, too. Alls you do is sit there in the bushes drinking peppermint schnapps and catching cold. That cigarette will show up like a flashlight in the dark." Barnegat ground the fallen cigarette into the road as if it were burning and he needed to put out the fire.

"What do you know about it anyway?" said Frampton, angry to have been humiliated. "I know about killing. I shot a man once. It was the only man I killed in World War Two. I fired at a lot of people, but this one I know I got. It was a German who at first I thought was dead. He was lying in a ditch and he was wounded. All bloody in the legs from some machine-gun burst. He pulled a pistol as I was walking past along a muddy road. I don't know if he meant to shoot me or not. But I saw the gun and I let him have it with my Thompson. Then saw it was no man at all. It was just a kid. Maybe seventeen years old. It was some Waffen SS recruit in dappled sniper camouflage. But I was crazy angry at the time. I ripped the zinc identification disk from around that boy's neck. And I still got it." Frampton reached into his shirt and pulled out the tag, which hung around his neck on an old leather cord. "I went home and put it on before I came out here. I can still read his name: Sebastian Westland." Of all the hauntings he had

brought home from the war, the sight of that young man haunted him
the most. Now Frampton wore the disk as a talisman against the fear
that had clouded his thoughts.

Barnegat snorted. He was fed up with Frampton. His usual eleven
beers made him jovial, but having only four had sharpened his
temper. He had been wondering if there was any way he could get out
of sharing Mackenzie's reward money once they had got hold of
Hazard. That was why Barnegat stayed up front, so he could be the
first to track him down. And he decided that, for Hazard, there would
be no coming quietly. That had been dismissed without discussion.
Both men planned to beat Wilbur Hazard close to death, and then
drag him into town like a shot deer and make sure everyone saw what
vengeance they had taken on the son of Mary the Clock.

They passed the yellow police tape around the place where Pfeiffer
had been killed. It rustled in the breeze as the men moved quickly by.
After an hour, they reached the railroad tracks. They sat down on the
creosote-smelling slabs of the track spacers and rested their guns
against the rails. The sweat began to cool on their backs.

Frampton had given up hope that they would find Hazard. One by
one, he snuffed out the daydreams of all the things he would buy with
his share of the money, far more than his share ever could. The truth
was he cared less about the money than the adventure. Lately, he had
felt himself drifting apart from Barnegat, and he saw it as only a
matter of time before Barnegat's jokes about everyone else in town
would include him. He would be fuel for all Barnegat's private chuck-
ling and then there would be nothing for him but to leave. This walk
in the night had saved him. Even if they came out empty-handed,
Frampton knew they would be brothers again, the way it had been in
the beginning. He needed Barnegat's friendship more than he could
ever admit without ruining it. Frampton had no other friends in town.
Everyone else had grown tired of his drinking and the way it made
him crazy. He wished he were drunk now, as he didn't feel like taking
a swing at Wilbur Hazard, least of all with precious Goldenboy.

It was as if Barnegat had read Frampton's mind. He leaned across
with a pewter drinking flask in his hand.

Frampton took Barnegat's hand in both of his and slapped the back
of Barnegat's palm in thanks. Frampton carefully unscrewed the
pewter cap and let it dangle on its tiny chain. Then he took a slug and

felt the taste of peppermint schnapps run stinging across his tongue. It was like liquid candy cane, and he knew he would need to drink the whole flask and then more if he was to feel the hypnotized rage he needed to face Hazard. At least it might be enough to take the pain of walking from his joints. Frampton had not complained about the length of the walk and the weight of the rifle, but his hipbones were so sore that he doubted whether he'd be able to stand again when they decided to move on. Instead, he'd been worrying about Hazard. He didn't trust Barnegat to be any good in a fight, and he didn't know Hazard well enough to feel sure that two of them against one of him would put the odds in their favor. The son of a crazy lady, he was thinking. I never did like the look of him. Frampton quietly envisioned a massacre, with himself as one of the victims. He stared at his boots and prepared to die.

Barnegat walked to the other side of the tracks. A moment later came the rough sputter of him pissing on the pale stone track bedding. Then the noise stopped. "Hey!" he whispered.

"You get something caught in your fly?" Frampton didn't look up from his boots. He reached across and took another drink of the schnapps.

"It's a light!" Barnegat rasped. "Someone's got a fire going."

Frampton felt his heart jump in his chest. He closed his hands around the dew-smeared stock of his gun, and crawled to where Barnegat crouched.

The fire was a bubble of marmalade light deep in the woods. Trees between the fire and the men seemed to shift in the sway of the flames. Someone stirred the ashes. Sparks rose into the sky.

"We'll make too much noise if both of us go in." Frampton could no longer hide his fear. He rested his forehead on the cold iron of a rail and in his mind he cursed his cowardice.

"I'll go." Barnegat was not afraid. He suddenly felt more brave and ready for a fight than he ever had before. He had no idea where his courage had come from, but suddenly it was there like a transfusion running through him. He fanned his eyes across the cowering man and thought, When this is over, nobody's getting any money except me. And there'll be no more bowing down to you and hearing about how you could pop my eyes out if you wanted to. When we get back to town, things will be different, and they will stay that way. Then he crawled down the embankment, through the oily water in the ditch and into the woods, carrying his rifle in the crook of his elbow.

Wilbur Hazard sat as close to the fire as he could, arms around his knees, rocking slowly back and forth. The cold had sunk into his bones. Beside him was his backpack, in which he carried a hammer, nails, a saw and three glass mason jars. For the past few weeks, he had been sneaking into the Algonquin and cutting down trees to make himself a cabin. He didn't know who the land belonged to. He only knew it wasn't his, and so he had to keep his cabin a secret. That was half the thrill of building it. It would be his hideaway. He had studied a book about cabin building and learned how to notch the logs so they would fit together. Instead of windows, he was going to cut a window space but fill the gap with old mason jars, which he could bring into the woods a few at a time. He would caulk the jars and logs with moss and dirt and pine sap, the way prospectors had done in Alaska in the last century. He had gently lifted the moss from rocks on the crest of Seneca Mountain and set it right side up on the wood so it could continue to grow. For this he used a long-bladed Gerber knife, which he kept in a sheath at his waist. With the Gerber, he could reach into each crevice of the stone. The cabin was three-quarters built. The only thing it didn't have was a door, and the windows still needed a few more jars.

But now that policeman had ruined everything. He had run from Officer Dodge with no sense of where he was going. Only to get away. He wished now that he had stayed, because in the past few minutes of sitting by the fire it had finally occurred to him that Dodge was looking for the tree spiker, not for him. Hazard had first assumed that someone had found the cabin and reported him. He didn't know how he could get himself out of this mess, and he didn't know if they would believe him, even if he told the truth. I'm the son of a lady everyone thinks is crazy, thought Hazard.

In his frustration, he picked up a stick and whacked the fire, sending shreds of ember up into the trees. He raised his head to watch them and saw pine branches shimmering like copper above him. If I could only get to Mr. Mackenzie, he thought, I could explain it to him and he would understand. Mr. Mackenzie is fair. He's a straight dealer. People will do what he says. He had never met Mackenzie before, but knew he was the most influential man in town. This was

Hazard's only plan. As soon as it grew light, he would make his way to the mill and plead his case to the man who had everyone's respect.

He didn't hear Barnegat behind him. All he heard was the thump of the rifle butt striking the back of his head and the pain that closed around his face as if someone had put his hands in front of his eyes. He pitched forward into the fire and embers fell into his mouth.

Then a hand grabbed the material of his coat and yanked him from the blinding light and pain. Hazard smelled the bitter reek of his own torched hair. Burns laid raw his cheeks and lips and forehead. A man was standing over him. Hazard couldn't see who it was, but he could see the raised gun, the brass butt plate aimed at his face. He tried to talk but couldn't. His mouth was filled with blood.

"Time's up," the man said.

Hazard felt the slam of the rifle into his chin and blacked out. He couldn't tell how long. It couldn't have been more than a couple of seconds. When he opened his eyes, he saw he was still by the fire. Scrabbling through Hazard's pain came the knowledge that this man was trying to kill him. He rolled over and began to crawl away. A gurgling moan pushed itself out of his throat. Then his legs were yanked out from under him and his nose hit the dirt and he felt pine needles digging into the opened flesh of his burns.

"I got him!" Barnegat yelled. He dragged Hazard a few feet back toward the fire, then stopped and rolled the man over with his boot. He shoved the barrel of the gun in Hazard's face. "I swear to God, the only thing stopping me from killing you right now is I don't even know what. You even fucking talk to me and I'll shoot you." Then Barnegat undid the top of Hazard's rucksack, which was still strapped to his back, and began to empty out the hammers and small nails and newspaper-wrapped mason jars that Hazard had stored inside. "Look at all this shit!" He smashed the mason jars one after the other on top of Hazard's head, hearing the glass break inside the paper wrapping. "What the hell got into you, boy? Didn't your loopy fucking mama teach you any better? What did Pfeiffer ever do to deserve what you did to him? And worse than that, you could have fucking killed *me*!" He kicked Hazard in the stomach, feeling the man curl up around the blow. Then Barnegat shouldered his rifle, knowing there would be no more trouble from Hazard. He took hold of Hazard's legs and dragged him back toward the tracks.

Frampton stood with his gun ready, wishing now that he had volunteered to go in Barnegat's place.

"Look at this fuck!" Barnegat dragged Hazard the last few feet up the embankment and then dumped him on the tracks. He wiped the sweat off his face. "Fucking short-order cook!" He felt unstoppable. Part of him wished that Frampton would fight him now, because he would kill the old man with his bare hands.

Hazard rose up to his hands and knees. His head lolled down and he spat. His lips moved and he began to whisper.

"He's saying something." Frampton bent down, hands on his knees. "What are you saying, Mister?" He had drunk the last of the schnapps and felt the first flickers of uncontrollable anger igniting in his chest. He wanted to do something he could brag about later.

"I can explain," Hazard whispered. His stomach felt loose and heavy, as if something had ruptured inside him. "It wasn't me. I swear."

"Don't listen to him." Barnegat shoved Frampton out of the way.

"Don't push me!" Frampton walked up close to Barnegat. He had an inkling that Barnegat meant to keep all the reward money, which was what he would have done himself if he could have come up with half an excuse. "Don't you push me, Barnegat!"

Barnegat stared at Frampton. Just give me an excuse, Barnegat was thinking. Just say something and watch what happens, you roly-poly motherfucker.

Hazard rose unsteadily to his feet. He tottered, hands held in front of him because he could barely see from under his swollen eyelids.

Frampton stood before Barnegat a moment longer. His lower lip began to curl. Then he wheeled around and knocked Hazard over with a swipe from his heavy boot.

Hazard rolled down the embankment, the sharp gravel digging into his palms and knees, and splashed into the oily ditch water. For a moment, he just floated. It seemed suddenly clear to him that he would never reach town alive. He had seen the guns they carried. He had heard the anger in their voices. There would never be a chance to explain. He knew that if he didn't run now, he would die. While the two men were still shouting at each other, he slipped as quietly as he could through the reeds. When he reached dry ground, he stood, holding his hand to his stomach, and began to run. The light of his fire still shimmered in the distance. He ran at an angle to the flames, so the two men wouldn't see his silhouette. The looseness in his guts was agony.

It was only a few seconds before Frampton noticed that the water in the ditch seemed much too still. He didn't wait. He lunged down the bank. His hips complained in sharp grinding jabs halfway up his back. The second he landed in the water, he knew that Hazard was gone. He swished his hands through the water and felt nothing but the pine needles that glued themselves to the tops of his hands and his wrists. He thrashed through the reeds and walked onto dry ground, then heard Hazard's footsteps, irregular and plodding in the distance.

"What's going on?" Barnegat called down from the tracks.

Without replying, Frampton ran after Hazard. He knew he could make up for not volunteering earlier and now with Hazard beaten up so badly, there wouldn't be any more fight left in the man.

"What the hell's going on?" Barnegat's voice echoed through the trees.

Frampton sprinted after Hazard's dark and hunchbacked shape. He could hear the pain in Hazard's voice each time he took a breath.

Hazard knew he was being followed, but he couldn't go any faster. There was too much pain.

"Stop," Frampton wheezed at the bobbing shadow ahead of him. "Make it easy on yourself." He was gaining on Hazard now.

The trees were getting thicker. Branches lashed at Hazard's eyes. He heard the old man's whispering close behind. His lungs blazed as if they had been filled with embers. He could not go on.

"Stop." The whisper rushed past Hazard's ears.

And suddenly he did stop. He wheeled around and drew back the heel of his palm and smashed it into Frampton's nose before the old man had time to slow down.

Frampton fell wide-eyed onto his back. He had no idea what had happened. One second he seemed to have Hazard almost in his grasp and suddenly here he was looking up at the blurry sky and blood was leaking down the back of his throat. Over the rattle of his own half-choked breath, he heard Hazard running away.

"Billy?" It was Barnegat. "Billy, where are you?"

Slowly, Frampton raised one hand and touched it to his face. He felt the bulbous lump which had taken the place of his sharp, birdlike nose. He spat blood off his lips and breathed in and howled, "He killed me!"

Barnegat came running. He found Frampton on his back and lifted him into a sitting position.

"He killed me!" Frampton wailed and gripped Barnegat's shoulders, as if they held him at the edge of life itself. He heard the familiar *clink-switch* of a Zippo lighter being opened and struck and then by the oily fire's light he saw Barnegat.

"It's not so bad. I think it's just your nose."

Frampton could smell the metallic peppermint schnapps on Barnegat's breath. "Not bad for you, maybe!"

Barnegat stood over him, staring into the dark. He knew they wouldn't find Hazard now. He imagined hundred-dollar bills sifting through his fingers as if blown by a great wind and fluttering away, completely lost across the wilderness. He had never been so angry and so sick with disappointment. For the first time in his life, he had envisioned money whose earning he could not check off on a watch as hourly wages. Each minute of his normal life had a dollar value. The value climbed with such miserable slowness over the years that he could no longer bear to calculate how much sweat he put into the slow drag of every minute passing. It wasn't even that the money would have changed his life. Ten thousand was a lot, but not enough to let him quit his job. What the money meant to him was the chance to see his life differently, even if only for a while. Now he looked down on half-drunk Frampton and had to stop himself from the short, precise movements of chambering bullets in his gun and blowing off the old man's head.

The next morning, the two men sat in orange plastic chairs at the police station, while Dodge made out his report. Frampton's face was obscured by white bandages. The corners of his eyes showed purple-yellow bruises and his lips were scabbed and split. He also had a hangover. Schnapps always did this to him. He felt as if his brain had been squeezed like a sponge. Barnegat showed no sign of change. His black watch cap was pulled down over his ears. He was gnawing on a toothpick which he had taken from a dispenser at the cash register of the Four Seasons. He switched it violently from one side of his mouth to the other.

"I'm a little stuck here, gentlemen." Dodge's voice was low and even. His patience had worn thin. "You say you went looking for him and *he* ambushed *you*?"

"That's right." Frampton's voice was a plugged nasal hum.

"Why wouldn't he just let you walk by?"

"Because he's crazy. He's a murderer." It hurt Frampton to speak, each word another corkscrew twist into his hungover skull. But he had to talk. It was his fault that Hazard got away, since he'd kicked him into the ditch. The more distance and blame he put between himself and last night, the safer he would feel. "He's Mary's son. What else do you need to know?"

"Shut up, Billy." It was Barnegat.

"You guys found him first, didn't you?" Dodge shoved his typewriter out of the way. He would have to retype the whole report anyway once he found out the truth of what happened. "Did you ask him if he was the one who had spiked the tree?"

"Of course we didn't ask him." Barnegat sat back and thumped his shoulders against the wall.

"So how do you know it was him?"

"Because of all that stuff he was carrying! Because he didn't stop when you told him to!"

"You beat the shit out of him, didn't you?"

"Look what he did to me!" Frampton held his hands up beside his head.

"But only because he thought you were trying to kill him, right?" Dodge leaned forward across the desk. His face was creased with disgust. "Am I right?"

"The way we see it . . ." Frampton moved as if to stand. He felt the time had come to make a speech, although he didn't know what he would say.

"Get out." Dodge heaved his typewriter back to its original position.

Barnegat stood. "What are you going to do?"

"Go in there and find him myself if I have to." Dodge wound a piece of paper into the typewriter. "Do you have any idea how hard that's going to be now?"

"I should get that ten thousand dollars." Barnegat didn't care if it sounded like a threat.

"You should be going to prison for assault, Barnegat. And if Hazard presses charges, you *will* go." Dodge waited calmly for Barnegat's next move.

Barnegat walked out into the dusty parking lot. Frampton shuffled in his footsteps.

Dodge tried to keep typing, but he couldn't see the keys. Instead, all he could see was an image of Wilbur Hazard cowering alone and in pain, out there somewhere in the wilderness.

≡

Wilbur Hazard sat cross-legged on the dirt floor of his half-completed cabin and wept. Sunlight filtering down through the trees made beams through the mason-jar window. His eyes were swollen almost shut and everything he saw was obscured in the mesh of his eyelashes. The pain in his gut was a steady thumping nausea. He knew he needed a doctor. When he ran his nervous fingers across his stomach, he could feel bulges of torn muscle deep under the skin.

Hazard assumed that he had in fact killed Frampton last night. So in his own mind he had become what they already thought he was. He knew he couldn't go back into town. They would be looking for him, and if they hadn't let him talk before, there would be even less chance of that now.

He took the Gerber knife from his belt and in his misery he stabbed it over and over into the dirt. He thought about his mother and wondered if she knew what had happened to him. He thought of all the work it had taken to persuade his foster parents to tell him who she was, and how quietly and deeply disappointed he had been to find a woman so cheerfully lost in a land inside her head. It had taken months before the mother he'd invented for himself, the woman much closer to Alicia Mackenzie—tall and beautiful and sane and respected and loving—flickered and died away and he forced the blankly smiling image of Mary the Clock into her place. Hazard wished he'd never come to Abenaki Junction. The people of the town had never let him be anything but an outsider, and the speed and violence with which they came to hunt for him seemed to Hazard like the acting out of a plan that had been set in motion long ago.

Hazard decided he would wait for dusk, then head along the tracks to the old Booth cabin. He would allow himself to rest there until dark. Then he would sneak the last half mile into town, take his car and drive out and never come back. He kept his savings in bundles of cash in a strongbox in the garage. It would be enough to start again. He wondered how many times in a life a person could start over before he forgot who he was.

artha, the police switchboard operator, unlocked the gun cabinet at the station. She kept the key on a string around her neck, along with a crucifix with tiny rubies in the eyes of the Jesus. She ran her finger along the rank of polished gunstocks until she found what she was looking for. "You said the twelve-gauge, right?"

"Yes, ma'am," said Dodge. He had always been formal with Martha, treating her like a woman much older than himself, even though she was only thirty-five. He pulled two cases of OO shotgun shells from his desk and spilled the cartridges out across his blotter. He began filling his pockets with the copper-ended tubes, hearing the faint rattle of the pellets inside. As Martha walked over to him, carrying the heavy shotgun, Dodge noticed that whenever this two-hundred-and-fifty-pound woman moved forward, she seemed to move sideways as well. Dodge had seen the ten-year shelf-life spongy cakes that Martha ate on her coffee breaks every half hour, and did not feel sorry for the woman as much as he felt sorry for her heart. He imagined the two as separate beings, one trapped inside the other. Dodge knew her heart would give out soon, pop like a cranberry-colored balloon, and then all of Martha would deflate and slide under her desk. Too many cream-filled cupcakes had been eaten. Too much bologna folded into fleshy pink envelopes and swallowed nearly whole.

Mott called her a Happy Stack of Woman. He said that without her to hold the place down, Abenaki Junction would drift away over the hills into Canada.

For a while, Coltrane had taken it on himself to act as her fitness counselor, even though he did no exercise himself. He said she should walk to work every day. She laughed in his face. He wrote her a list of nutritious foods as she sucked the filling out of a Twinkie right before his eyes.

Martha sat back down at her desk. "I swear if you just waited a bit, Hazard would come back to his momma's house." She folded her hands over her stomach. "He can't live out there in the Algonquin."

"I don't know about that, Martha." Dodge set a yellow-and-black box of shotgun shells on his desk and began feeding the shells into his pump shotgun. "People can live out there if they know how."

"He'll come out." Martha tugged open one of her desk drawers. It was filled with individually wrapped Yankee Doodle chocolate cakes. She snatched one, tore off the wrapping with her teeth, and spat it into the garbage can at her feet. Then she crammed the cake into her mouth.

"I should go," Dodge said. Coltrane was waiting for him outside. Dodge felt sure they would find no trace of Hazard. They would walk all day and get nothing but tired.

"That poor woman, Mary." Martha spoke with her mouth full. "All she's been through."

"I don't think she knows what she's been through, Martha." Dodge pulled on his heavy canvas hunting coat, dappled with green and brown splotches of camouflage. He tucked the shotgun under his arm and started to walk out.

"You don't know for sure about Mary," Martha shouted after him. "Nobody does."

Outside, Coltrane was no longer thinking about Mary. He was praying that they would not find Wilbur Hazard. Besides the fact that

Hazard was innocent, Coltrane remembered the first time he had looked Hazard in the eye. It was once when Hazard appeared from his kitchen at the Four Seasons. He had stared at the customers as if someone had called him out there for a fight. Coltrane recalled he had looked down at his western omelet and been scared that this man had cooked his food. Since that day, he knew that if insanity did live in their family, its danger was with Hazard and not with Mary. Coltrane had seen it in Hazard's eyes—cold and sparkling and vicious. As he and Dodge headed out into the woods, Coltrane tried to hide an uneasy creeping sensation that tracked along his spine. It was instinct, telling him to turn back—the warning lights of danger blinking red behind his eyes. But he didn't trust his instincts, and he walked on into the wilderness.

Both men carried Savage shotguns and .357 revolvers. Across their shoulders they had slung canteens. Their pockets were filled with sandwiches and bullets. The men passed the tattered yellow strips of police tape, looped from tree to tree around the place where Pfeiffer had died. Printed on the tape in black letters was POLICE LINE DO NOT CROSS.

A long wail came from the distance. It spread through the trees and the trees echoed back until the whole forest took up this wail and held it, trembling and ringing as if the Algonquin were one vast struck crystal. Then at last the sound began to fade. It was the Canadian VIA train on its way from Montreal to St. Johns. They heard the thunder of its wagons crossing the iron bridge that ran across the Narrows of Pogansett Lake. Sometimes these trains were sixty cars long, pulled by four engines and showing on their doors dozens of railroad company names—Southern, Santa Fe, Solid Gold, Railbox, Canadian National, Ashley, Drew and Northern, the Chessie System, Missouri Pacific, the blue and white of the Bangor and Aroostock Line and the far-from-home banana-yellow cars of the Appalachicola Northern. They shook the ground, made the tracks too hot to touch, and flattened into shiny postage stamps the coins that children placed upon the rails. Then the sound was gone, leaving only the murmur of wind through the tops of the pines.

Dodge and Coltrane walked in silence, sometimes following the trampled broadness of human trails and at others the narrow, branch-crossed paths of deer. Then they came to a stand of white birch. Old bark peeled in scrolls from the trunks. It was like moving in a maze. The thin white birch trees seemed to shift in the corners of their eyes.

"Footprints!" Dodge called back.

Coltrane came running, heart beating faster now. He reached where Dodge was standing and looked down. The earth was damp from a stream trickling out of the rocks and dead leaves. In the mud was the print of a lug-soled boot. The print was fresh, too new even to have been made last night by Barnegat or Frampton.

Coltrane crouched down and set his hand in the mud. He dabbed his fingers in the neat boot print and blurred it. "It guess it must be him," he said. "There's no one else here now."

Dodge raised his head and looked around. Then suddenly his expression changed, as if something were there, circling them, but he could not see it.

"What?" Coltrane yanked his gun out of its holster. He pulled the hammer back. "For Christ's sake, what?" Then suddenly he knew what it was about the place. "This is where we stopped to rest when we carried Gil Kobick down the mountain. After he got attacked by that bear." Coltrane lowered the gun.

"Yes it is," said Dodge. His voice was a murmur. "When Kobick went hunting up on Seneca Ridge. Who was that man who went with him?"

"That was Harry Crowe," said Coltrane. "That Irish guy who used to be in the IRA in the twenties. Guy used to go hunting with some old English service revolver and a rifle. Liked to get in close with that revolver. Said he liked to blur the line between the hunter and the hunted. And Gil Kobick, that clumsy, crooked little money-lending man, had been pestering Harry Crowe to go hunting with him for years. And then finally Crowe agreed. He'd seen the bear earlier in the summer, eating some berries on the ridge."

"I remember when they went into the woods," said Dodge. "Crowe was wearing an old trenchcoat. The one he said he used to wear in Ireland. And there was Kobick with all his spiffy new gear. His boots not even scuffed. They went in on the train tracks and then cut up the side of the hill."

"Yes," said Coltrane, "and that's where Crowe told Kobick he would loop around the other side of the crest and they would meet on the summit. So it meant Kobick was supposed to hang back a little as he made the shorter climb. But that man Kobick . . ."

"That stupid dead man." Dodge remembered the smell of his blood, heavy and metallic.

"He goes racing up the hill to get that bear first and then take the credit for himself. And that was when Crowe said he heard a sound that he mistook for Kobick falling into the bushes. Kind of a thrashing sound. Then he heard that roar and after that . . ."

"Screaming." Dodge's voice was faint and distant. He remembered lying with Coltrane and Crowe on the muddy ground beside this stream, too tired to carry Kobick any farther. And Kobick's body lay there beside them, his stomach open and the ribs all smashed like a flimsy packing crate.

"That screaming," echoed Coltrane. "Crowe pulled out his revolver and dumped his rifle in the bushes, and then he sees the bear standing on top of Kobick. And its ears are all chewed off from being in some old fight. And it's pinning Kobick's arms to the ground and tearing off his scalp. Crowe shoots off some rounds to scare it away, but that bear wasn't afraid."

"That poor dead man." Dodge remembered washing Kobick's blood from his hands at the same stream where he stood now. He remembered how the blood had stuck to his skin and how he scraped it away with his fingernails in the painfully cold water.

"And Crowe stands right up to that bear," said Coltrane, "the way nobody but Harry Crowe could have done, and he shoots that bear right in the face. And there's blood and spit flying out of its mouth and its jaw goes *snap!* Like a whipcrack from the bullet. And then Crowe was out of bullets. So he didn't have a choice but to stand there and stare the bear down. And you remember what Crowe said? He said even shot half to death that bear seemed more alive than he did. It sniffed the air with its ragged, bloody nose, like it was getting Crowe's scent and would come back for him later. And then it ran away. Then Crowe goes running down the side of the mountain. Left Kobick where he lay. Took him two hours to get off that mountain and then he found us."

"And we had to go clambering up this hill in the pitch dark. By the time we got there, he was already dead. But after what that bear did to him, Kobick was better off gone." Dodge saw again the empty eye sockets. The teeth exposed and twisted in different directions.

"Do you remember when we dug his grave?" Coltrane tapped Dodge on the arm. "And Reverend Barnes comes out and tells us we can't do it. But then he gets a look at Kobick and he goes and gets a shovel and helps us dig."

Dodge lowered himself down, knees cracking, and washed his hands in the stream as if they were covered in blood again. "Remember how hard we looked for that bear afterward? And how we spent so much time thinking about that bear, we just ended up giving it that name: No Ears. As if it was one of us."

"I wonder if it died."

"Oh," said Dodge, the cold clamping down on his fingers, "I bet its bones are out here someplace."

"It could be alive," Coltrane said. "A bear is tough to kill."

"Let's not stay here anymore, Victor. Let's keep moving."

They pushed on through the woods, but feeling different now. They stayed closer together and often looked back down the trail as it closed up after them. They put out their guns and kept their fingers straight beside the trigger guards. Neither spoke of being afraid, but now they were hunting Hazard the same as if he'd been that bear.

More prints studded the wet ground around another spring. They scooped some water up to drink, just as they knew Hazard had done.

Earlier, Coltrane's head had been crowded with daydreams, as if his mind had fled from the forest and left the rest of him behind. But now that he had seen the footprints, he'd felt his senses sharpen. The Algonquin had hundreds of sounds and Coltrane heard all of them at once. Each shading of green and brown reached his eyes. Each branch zoomed into perfect focus. Coltrane smelled the still, cool air in the hollows. He thought about how easy it was to hide in the woods. Shadows dappled you into invisibility. You stayed still until each sound and smell became familiar, and the birds started singing again. You gathered the silence around you, becoming a part of the forest.

Late in the afternoon, they came to a new logging road that had been built into the Algonquin. The road had appeared suddenly. The glaring gravel stretched out of sight in both directions. Dodge knelt down and tried to make out any new footprints with the same lug-sole print as the one they had found earlier. They found no more prints, so they crossed the logging road and continued toward the railroad tracks.

When they reached the tracks, it was almost sunset. The rails were shiny where the train's wheels ran regularly across them. The rest was dull and orange with rust. On each creosoted wooden tie was a steel shoe, holding the rail to the ground. The shoes were stamped with the mark of the Lundie patent, with the date 1971. It was too late to walk back through the woods, so Coltrane and Dodge decided they would head along the tracks and into town. Later, they would drive to Coltrane's farm and pick up the patrol car they had left at the trailhead.

Seeing that no one was home at the Booths' cabin, the two men stopped there to rest and eat their sandwiches. Dodge spotted two Adirondack chairs tucked under the porch. They pulled out the chairs, set their guns against the cabin wall and sat looking across the lake. The sky turned purple with the closing in of night.

Coltrane tried to hide his relief at not finding Hazard. But he felt sure they had been close. At some muddy twist in the trail, Hazard had been there, had seen them walking by.

"Maybe we should call Skowhegan tomorrow. Get some more help." Dodge kneaded the joints of his toes.

"We don't need help," Coltrane said, a sandwich bunched in his fist. "Just promise me we aren't going to hurt him."

"Not if we don't have to," Dodge replied. He got up and walked off into the bushes to take a piss.

Coltrane rummaged in his pockets for his pack of Lucky Strikes, then lit one with a matchbook from the Loon's Watch. The bar's logo was a black-and-white loon with red eyes. The locals appreciated that detail, because a loon really did have red eyes, as if the devil had a hand in its creation.

Coltrane heard Dodge behind him. He turned, holding out the red bull's-eyed cigarette pack. "You want one?"

It was not Dodge. The door to the cabin was open and a man stood halfway out.

Coltrane thought it must be Jerry Booth, the owner of the cabin, but the shadows had stolen his face, so he couldn't be sure. Coltrane stood up, composing an apology in his head for making himself comfortable in Mr. Booth's chair. But the man was not standing like the owner of a place in which strangers have appeared. Instead, he clung to the darkness. The air around him seemed to shudder.

The man took a step toward Coltrane. The planks creaked under his feet.

"Hello?" Coltrane tried to say, but only whispered. Then the knowledge reached him in a wave of nausea. He felt dizzy and sick. It was not Booth. It was Hazard. Coltrane lunged toward the place where his shotgun stood balanced against the cabin wall. He grabbed the gun and turned to face the man.

Hazard stood almost on top of him. In his right hand he held a knife. Its blade was double-edged and longer than an outstretched hand.

Coltrane tried to raise the gun and with one vicious shove Hazard wrenched it from him. The gun flew out of Coltrane's grasp and skittered away onto the cabin's front lawn. He felt the sudden coldness in his empty palms.

Hazard's foot slid forward over the rough planking.

With all the strength he had, Coltrane grabbed at Hazard's chest, hands clawed into the rough wool of his coat. He was about to throw his head forward into the man's nose, when suddenly the breath vanished out of his lungs and his head started spinning inside. Coltrane saw the man turn and leap out into the dark, as if the grass were not land but water, and he would disappear beneath it.

Coltrane did not know what had happened to him. His whole body was trembling. He stepped back until he was resting against the wall of the cabin. As long as I'm on my feet, he thought, it cannot be that bad. Then he looked down at the splotches of his hunting-jacket camouflage. There was a small tear in the cloth. The knife blade had cut him. He reached a finger through the tear and felt blood pouring down his stomach. Not just a trickle. It was pouring. The dizziness grew suddenly worse. Coltrane dropped to his knees. He vaguely felt the thud of wood against his joints. His body had become a whirlpool, and he had to try to spin the other way or he would die. He coughed and blood flew from his mouth, spattering the cabin boards.

Hazard felt a sickness at how easily the blade had gone in, as if behind the layer of canvas the man had been made of nothing more than sand. He sprinted across the lawn and up the steep sides of the railway embankment. He kicked through the raspberry canes that grew beside the ties. The knife was still in his hands. He swung his body up and landed on the tracks. Then he began to run, adjusting his stride to the awkward distance between the spacers and the tracks. In a strange, fragmented thought, he wondered why the tracks ahead seemed to vanish in a wall of blackness.

Something burst against his face, and suddenly his nose and teeth and jaw all felt like broken glass.

Dodge was standing on the tracks. He had seen what happened and had been running toward the cabin when he saw Hazard jump from the porch. So Dodge stayed where he was and took the revolver from its holster. An ugly calm hovered in his body as he stood waiting, the checkered grips of the gun digging deep into his palm. He saw the long knife in Hazard's hand. He knew Coltrane would be dead. Dodge had no time to be angry. He raised his revolver, cocked back the hammer and put three rounds into Hazard at a range of fifteen feet.

Hazard's mouth was wide open as if to scream, but he didn't make a sound. His arms spread like bony wings. His legs swung out from under him and his head smacked hard on the ground, teeth cracking as they smashed together. The knife clattered onto the tracks.

Dodge kept the gun aimed at Hazard. Cordite smoke billowed past him. Its smell was bitter in his lungs. He waited for Hazard to move, but in the dark it was as if Hazard had vanished and all that remained of him were crumpled clothes and boots with the leather chafed to suede.

Dodge ran to where Coltrane lay, scrabbling down the gravel embankment, hacking the skin from his palms so they looked as if he had run his hand down a cheese-grater. He dove into the blackness that had sunk down on the cabin.

Coltrane was still on his knees. He kept his hands pressed to the wound. It was difficult to breathe. He thought it would be easier if he could just stand, but he felt too frightened to move. His head was filled with a jumbled desperation to be well again. Not to need help. Not to go to the hospital. Voices in his mind were trying to tell him, in hopeful sputtering broadcasts, that he would need only a few stitches. He would not be sent to the vaporized land of general anesthesia. But the rest of him knew he was at the mercy of whoever would help him, and if no one helped him he would die. Several times, a heaving groan pushed out from deep inside him. It was a sound he did not even know he could make. It did not come from the pain. It came from his great disappointment. The slow, downward glance of knowing that this was the end. I'm like that bear, he thought. The one I should never have killed. I'm paying for that now. It wasn't enough to be sorry.

"Clara," he said. He wanted to talk to her. In his confusion, Coltrane felt as if the distance would not stop his voice from reaching her. "Clara, I'm hurt." He struggled to his feet. It was the hardest, bravest thing he'd ever done. He clenched the skin around his wound and felt only tiredness where he expected to feel pain. He wished there would be pain instead of this dragging fatigue.

A shape lunged from the night. Coltrane wheezed in terror. He thought it was Hazard, come back to finish him off. Coltrane knelt crooked like a hunchback, arm raised in an offering to the blade.

But it was only Dodge, who took Coltrane in his arms and made him sit against the cabin wall. Dodge talked to him and held up fingers, trying to make Coltrane say how many there were, to see if he had drifted into shock. It all seemed impossibly childish to Coltrane. Dodge slapped him in the face. The *pop* of Dodge's palm boxing his ear spread a fuzzy sensation across Coltrane's cheeks and spider-crawled over his head.

Dodge prized away Coltrane's bloody clawed hand and undid his shirt. He took Coltrane's Zippo lighter, struck it and used its flame to see by. Dodge could tell from the tiny bright-red bubbles appearing around the gash that it was a sucking chest wound. He had to cover the hole or Coltrane would drown in his own blood. Dodge ran into the cabin.

Coltrane was trapped in the whirlpool. He could not fight it. The vortex had hold of his heart. He held up the whites of his palms in surrender to the dark angels that seemed to cluster around him.

Dodge reappeared on the porch with a roll of plastic wrap, some electrical tape and a flashlight. He set up the flashlight, whose beam glanced off the rafters of the porch and enclosed them like the dome of a bell jar. Then he laid Coltrane down and bared the man's chest. He set the plastic wrap over the wound. The candy-apple red bubbles pressed up against the clear plastic. He took the roll of black electrical tape and taped the plastic wrap to Coltrane's chest. He knew that Coltrane was going into shock and would die soon if help could not be found.

It was two miles down the tracks to Abenaki Junction. Dodge knew he could not carry Coltrane that far. It was half a mile across the lake, but they had no boat. Dodge did not want to leave Coltrane here. The shock and the night cold would kill him. Then he had an idea and ran around to the back of the house. A canoe was propped against the wall. Under it were paddles and square flotation cushions. He dragged the canoe fifty feet to the water's edge. It slid across the lawn with a gentle whispering sound. He reached the lake. Water rushed into his boots. Then he ran back to the cabin, hooked his hands under Coltrane's armpits and hauled him down to the canoe. Coltrane's heels dragged through the grass, leaving a phosphorescent trail through the dew.

"I'm going to put you in the canoe, Victor. We're going to make you a little chair out of these cushions. Are you listening to me now? Am I getting through to you, Victor?"

Coltrane wasn't listening. He coughed blood into his hand and looked at it. He kept floating in and out of his body, like playing hopscotch in slow motion. One second he was being dragged down to the beach and the next he seemed to be gliding far above the Booths' cabin, where he could see the railroad tracks running through the forest like a river. Then Coltrane tumbled back into his body. He looked out across Pogansett Lake. It was a darkly ruffled plain, which he knew they would never cross before he died. The idea no longer frightened him. It was just a fact.

"You see, Victor?" Dodge set up the floating cushions at the bow, and slapped them like someone fluffing up a pillow. He talked to fill the quiet, as if silence itself would bring death skulking from its hiding place. "I'm making you a chair. Make you comfy for the ride. Can you hear me, Victor?"

Coltrane wanted to speak with Dodge, but whatever strength he had left was not enough to bring the words to his mouth.

Tiny waves patted the shore. They were clotted with dead leaves, which painted Dodge's boots as he shoved the canoe into knee-deep water. He then climbed aboard, grabbed the paddle and dug it into the crow-black lake. As he swung the paddle up and over, he sent a spattering of water across Coltrane's face. They moved slowly out toward the distant lights of Abenaki Junction, which lay like a cluster of fallen and still-burning meteors among the trees on the far shore. Wind blew off the mountain and into their faces. Sweat trickled down the trench of Dodge's spine. With no moon visible, the stars seemed brighter than he had ever seen them before. He could see the silver smoke trail of the Milky Way from one end of the horizon to the other. Even with the pain from the constant shoveling of water to push them forward, Dodge felt amazement out there on the lake.

"You still with me, Victor?" Dodge asked.

"Yes." Coltrane's dried-out mouth opened and closed, as if to drink the droplets that had splashed across his face.

"You stay awake now."

This time, Coltrane only managed to snuffle. He felt more pain in his chest than before. Earlier, the hurt seemed to come from everywhere at once, fanning out through his body like ripples across a pond. But now the wound was calling to him, sending out hard thumping messages through his chest. Then a thought appeared that woke Coltrane from his numbness. "Did he get away?"

"No." Dodge hadn't thought of Hazard since he set out across the lake. After half an hour of paddling, it seemed to him that he could feel each band of tendon, each thread of muscle outlined with pain. He looked up at the moon, just as a chevron of Canada geese passed before it. He heard their distant honking. It reminded him of a story he had read as a child, of a woman who traveled out among the stars, sitting in a chair towed by geese. The illustration showed the same silverplating of moonlight on her face and hair that Dodge saw now on the smooth backs of the geese. He used to send himself to sleep at night imagining himself in the chair and hearing the thrum of beating wings as the geese raised him up through the dark, cloudless sky. It seemed like such a miracle. As the geese passed into the dark over Pogansett Lake, Dodge realized that Coltrane needed the same kind of miracle, something that appeared so out of reach that even to dream of it seemed foolish.

They were close to the town now. Dodge began shouting for help. His voice carried on the lake, amplified among the ranks of pine.

After a few minutes, flashlight beams began to clip across the water. They found Dodge's canoe and clung to it.

He went blind in the glare, but kept paddling toward the harsh silver that splashed at his eyes.

Coltrane had no idea where this light was coming from. He wondered if it might be the angels and he was already dead. The pain had stopped. He could no longer feel the grip of the plastic wrap at every rise and fall of his chest. It wasn't so bad, this business of being dead. He felt only curious about what would happen next.

The bow of the canoe ground against the sand and suddenly people were everywhere. Dodge heard familiar voices, but for now he couldn't place them. He was still too blinded by the glare to see. They dragged the canoe up onto land. Faces zoomed in close out of the night and questions popped in his ears. Dodge did not answer. He was too tired and confused. Strong hands helped him from the boat and walked him over to a picnic table which in daytime had a view of the lake. Dodge realized he had come ashore at the edge of the municipal park, just across the road from the house of Mary the Clock. Dodge looked at the man who was leading him. It was Twitch. He was wearing his paramedic jacket. He asked Dodge what had happened, so Dodge told him.

An ambulance bumped over the curb of the parking lot and drove across the grass to where Coltrane had been laid beside the canoe. Twitch opened Coltrane's shirt. Under the glossy film of plastic wrap, Coltrane's blood was a puddle of neon cherry.

Talking. Everyone seemed to be talking. In each voice was the high-pitched jabber of panic. Wind blew off the lake and slapped waves on the pale sand. Loons grieved out on the water. Children ran past him toward the flashing lights.

Coltrane was placed on a stretcher, strapped to it with orange nylon straps, and carried to the ambulance by five times as many people as were needed to hold the man's weight. Lazarus was there, holding the IV bottle.

Dodge could not see Coltrane's face. He was lost in the crowd.

The ambulance spun its wheels on the grass. It roared into the street, ear-drilling sirens sounding through town, rising and falling.

The children ran after it, until the ambulance gained speed and left them behind, coughing from the exhaust.

Dodge had no idea where they were taking Coltrane. There was no place in town that could handle such an injury. Part of Dodge wanted to get away from the noise, but the rest of him thought he should stay. He told himself there must be more to do, bringing order to the chaos of the crowd. As a policeman, he should be helping. But the chaos belonged to itself and was unstoppable. For a while longer, Dodge just sat there, his sweat growing cold and pasting his shirt to his back with the clamminess of raw meat. No one came to talk to him. They still hovered around the canoe, as if afraid to leave the place.

Dodge got up and walked. He was going to tell Clara what had happened. It was several miles to their house, but he was too dazed to think of anything but walking there. He headed down Main Street. Grit crunched under his boots in the gutters, sand left over from the winter, scattered on the roads to stop people and machines from slipping on the ice. People ran past him toward the park. Some wore windbreakers over their pajamas. Their eyes were fixed on the commotion. When Dodge turned to look, he saw the sabers of flashlights, still feeling their way across the black water. It was as if they were expecting more canoes, a flotilla from the island of the dead.

Dodge moved past the Quonset-hut arcade, where teenagers played out the last of their video games before running over to the park to see what was happening. Past the Ice Cream Shack, its windows plastered with sun-bleached pictures of people holding ice-cream cones and smiling. A boy leaned across the counter and shouted at Dodge, "Where the hell did everybody go?"

Dodge didn't answer. He just pointed, feeling like the Ghost of Christmas Yet to Come. He walked on a ways farther and then somebody called his name. He looked up and saw it was Madeleine. She stood on the porch of her house across the road. She was barefoot and had pulled on some jeans and a sweatshirt. Her hair fell in front of her eyes.

"Where are you going?" she asked him.

"To tell Clara."

"She already knows." Madeleine hugged herself against the chill. She walked down the rickety boards of her porch steps.

There were times Dodge had dreamed of walking up those steps, taking off his boots at the front door and setting them by the fire-place. In the dream, he would strip as he moved up the stairs, draping the banisters with his clothes. He would slide in beside Madeleine and spoon himself into her warm and sleeping body. And even in her sleep, when she felt him there she would move closer to him, and his hand would come around under her arm and cradle the softness of her breast. And he would sleep so deeply that he was afraid he might never wake up. Dodge exhaled suddenly, snuffing out the dream.

"I'll make us some cocoa," she said.

It was the only peace offering she had ever made him. They sat on the porch, holding their steaming drinks and looking out into the dark.

"It'll be hard on the town if Victor dies," Madeleine said.

"I don't think he'll make it." Dodge felt the cramp in his hands being smoothed out by the heat of the mug. "I should go," he told her. "I'm not good company right now."

She took the mug from him and set it on the porch beside her. "I was thinking about what you said in the car the other day. It helped to see things from your point of view. We've known each other for a long time. I think we're closer than we realize."

"I could have told you that a long time ago."

"Then why didn't you?"

"I think you had to see it for yourself. I know you well enough to see you don't take advice if you can help it, especially on how to live your life."

She was looking at him.

He leaned across and kissed her on the cheek. Then he stood and walked down the steps.

"Call me if you need anything," she said.

Dodge walked home through the streets. He didn't know what would come of their meeting and whether he had started something or ruined everything with that one kiss. He couldn't think about that now. At first light, he had to get out to the tracks and find Hazard's body.

Madeleine stayed on the porch. She noticed how quiet it had become. In the night, Abenaki Junction and the Algonquin forest and Pogansett Lake all lost their boundaries and merged. Silence wandered in the streets and through the woods and up into the hills. Then the cold drove her inside.

Hazard lay spreadeagled on the tracks. His consciousness kept ducking into black. He had been shot once in the side of his neck. Another bullet had smashed his cheekbone and exited just under his ear. The third slug had struck him in the left shoulder joint, and he could no longer feel his left arm. Now his heart beat with a strange metallic clanging like hammer strikes inside a fifty-gallon drum. He could not keep his head clear for long enough to know exactly where he was or to realize that he was dying.

When he had reached the Booths' cabin that evening, he'd broken in and lain down on a sagging mattress in a room at the back of the house. Moving through the woods had tired him out. After a few minutes, he'd found enough strength to roll over. The next thing he knew, the two men were on the porch and he had no idea where the daylight had gone. He knew he had to get out of the house or he felt sure he would be caught. He had stabbed Victor Coltrane in what he thought was self-defense. Now he played and replayed the scene in his mind, as if in a fever dream.

A large black bear was walking down the tracks. The fur on the bear's back was shiny and caught a pale silver-blue light, even though there was no moon. The bear crossed over the iron railway bridge, the Narrow River slipping by below. It stopped and raised its head to the breeze, wet nostrils twitching. The bear smelled Hazard's blood. It lost the scent and turned and caught the scent again. Then the bear began to move toward the smell. A moment later it saw the shape of Hazard's body lying in the middle of the tracks. The bear skidded down the gravel embankment to avoid coming at the thing head-on, in case it was not dead. It thrashed through the raspberry bushes that grew thick at the base of the embankment, and then worked its way slowly up until it came to the body. With its nose an inch from Hazard's face, it took in the scent of the man's cooled sweat and blood. The bear rolled Hazard over, shredding his jacket until it reached flesh. Then the bear opened its mouth very slowly and clamped down on Hazard's head.

Hazard smelled the bear's breath. It was musty and foul and clammy warm on his half-open eyes, which he could not close. The truth of what was happening to him flashed briefly in front of him, but he could not bring himself to believe it.

The bear bit down on Hazard's temples and his bullet-broken cheek. Then it began to drag him down the tracks.

Hazard felt the pressure on his head, but the force of it seemed to come from inside his skull, not outside. Saliva ran over his face. Rail ties slid underneath him, bruising his chest. The toes of his boots dragged through the gravel.

The bear dragged Hazard fifty feet and then dropped him. It hooked its paw under Hazard's chest and heaved him up. The man found himself sitting in a slumped-over position. His hands lay useless on the ground in front of him. The bitter, sugary smell of creosoted rail ties reached into him and branched off through his lungs.

One of the rails made a sound like cracking ice. The bear started. From the distance came the rumble of a train.

Hazard did not hear the train. He wondered if perhaps he was still lying on that sagging mattress in the cabin and this was all the jabber of a nightmare. The train's whistle sounded as it passed through Abenaki Junction. It rode with four engines and fifty-five wagons, carrying fuel and liquid nitrogen and boxcars of farm machinery.

The bear stood and followed the whistle's echo across the lake, turning its head slowly as the sound spread out through the trees. The rumble of engines was clearer now. A steady, rising roar. The first gold blast from the train's forward light showed through the trees. The ground beneath the rails began to shake.

The bear loped away down the embankment. Then it stopped. As the beam grew stronger and the earthquake of the train came closer, the bear turned again and ran from the sound and the light.

Hazard's head felt strangely clear. He knew it was the train and that he was on the tracks. The pinging of the rails was almost constant now. He raised his head, rolling his neck to the side away from the bullet wound, and he could see the great eye of the forward light. He felt the rushing wind. The light surrounded him. The beam burned out his sight. The noise hammered through him. Hazard stared at the train with a lopsided glance and howled out the last of his breath.

The lead engine roared around a bend in the tracks. Alain Labouchere, the driver, did not even have time to blow his whistle at what he thought looked like a wounded deer. He ducked his head away from the window, its ironplated grille segmenting his view like the eye of an insect. Labouchere felt a thump as the train slammed into and through the obstacle. Then he was past it. The rails were smooth again, and bright.

Four hours later, Clara Coltrane heard a sound out in the cornfield. She was sitting at the bare-wood kitchen table. The rising sunlight slipped across the walls. She had only just arrived back from the hospital and she was still in shock. Twitch had said he would probably survive. She alternated between convincing herself that if Twitch said this it had to be the truth and not believing anything but the worst.

At first she thought the noise came from the dogs. They were always play-fighting roughly enough to draw a yelp now and then. But this sound was different. There was a shrillness to it. Something wrong in the way it trailed off. Clara waited for another sound, but there was only the breeze, which shuffled through the dust and scattered straw in the barnyard as if it were looking for something.

Clara pulled on Victor's ratty wool vest with the old Indianhead nickel buttons, and walked outside. She called to the dogs. When a minute had gone by and no dogs came, she walked down the dirt road that ran between the fields. She glanced toward the trees, where turkey vultures always circled in the summertime.

A huge shape was climbing the slope toward the canopy of trees. At first, Clara thought it was a man, but the shape was too big. Too dark. It seemed to be more than one thing. Two things joined together. Clara squinted and saw now that it was a bear, a huge bear, and in its clamped-shut jaws was one of the dogs. It was Bugs. She could tell from the white-tipped tail. The bear had Bugs by the neck. The dog's head lolled down and its legs trailed on the ground. Clara could tell the dog's neck was broken.

She let out a long shout. The noise trailed across the field. She knew that bear. Knew from its gnarled ears that this was the same animal that had killed Gil Kobick, the bear people thought was long since dead.

The animal heard her shout and turned. The dog's head swung toward Clara. Its muzzle was crushed and bloody. Then the bear turned again and was gone, merging with the shadows of the trees.

Clara ran back to the house, kicked open the screen door and grabbed Victor's Springfield rifle from its two-pronged iron cradle over the fireplace. Then she ran back out the door. The rifle felt heavy in her fine-boned hands. The bear was gone, but she still fired off a round to chase it away. The concussion left a far-off ringing in her ears and bruised her shoulder. The valley's echo met her with slamming applause. She fired another round and then another, and the valley's thundering ovation did not stop. When all of the bullets were gone and the bright, smoking cartridges lay ejected at her feet, Clara lowered the rifle and stared through the disappearing cordite smoke at the trees. They seemed impenetrable to her, as if the copper-jacketed bullets had just bounced off the solid wall of their trunks.

Then suddenly Clara remembered the other dog, Tucker. Her eyes raced along the rows of corn until she found the broken stalks where the bear had rushed out. As she followed in the bear's path, the corn arched over her. What she found was like a chamber. A space knocked flat and floored with trampled stalks. The walls of this chamber were painted with blood. The floor was paved with fur and gray-white sticks of bone jutting from meat, and here was a white band of tendon and here the bloody mouth and staved-in jaw of something dead. It was Tucker. Clara turned in slow circles in the room of gore. She smelled the vomit reek of the animal's opened stomach. It was her father who had taught her about the power of a bear's jaws, how if a bear was big enough to get its jaws around a man's head, that man was finished. Clara dropped to her knees and dug in the crumbly earth with her hands and with the rifle butt until she had a shallow grave for the dog. Then she buried the animal where she found it. She pressed the soil down with her hands. The imprints of her fingers were like wings on the dark earth.

hat morning, Dodge returned by himself to the tracks. Mist was knee-deep in the tall grass. At first, he could not find Hazard's body. Then he remembered the train. He took off his cap and ran his fingers through his hair, preparing himself for what he was about to see.

Blood lay in shiny buttons on the creosoted wood. Dodge walked up the track and down again, but there was no sign of Hazard. He paused and looked up at the ivory boil of clouds. Far in the sky, he saw a huge bald eagle gliding from one cloud into another, higher than any bird he had ever seen before. Just as he lowered his gaze, he saw Hazard.

The body was tangled in a maple tree, a dozen feet above the ground but almost at a level with the tracks because of the embankment on which they were built. Hazard appeared to be sitting, one arm slung casually across a branch. But when Dodge looked more closely, he could see the man's body was crumpled almost beyond recognition.

The anger that Dodge had felt toward Hazard suddenly slipped away, as if it had never been there. Whatever vengeance might have occurred to Dodge had already been exacted on Hazard's remains.

Dodge climbed the tree. He tried lowering Hazard's body as gently as he could down to the ground. Then he realized that this broken man was beyond all need of gentleness, and pushed the body out. It swished through the bushes and thumped hard against the earth. The corpse was stiff and Dodge carried Hazard in the same sitting position to his car. It took him over an hour and sometimes he just dragged the body. When Dodge rested, he sat with his back to the corpse, trying not to breathe in the faint sweetness of the dead man, but he gave up and breathed it in deeply to make himself used to the smell. He tried not to see the way Hazard's broken bones reshaped the arms and the legs into a warped reflection of what they used to be. The bullet wounds were almost lost among the scrapes and blue-black dents in the flesh.

He finally reached the car, his path through the tall grass made wider by Hazard's clenched body. He thought about piling Hazard into the trunk, but decided to set him in the back seat. Dodge drove quickly into town. He did not look in his rearview mirror at the grotesquely squatting corpse, whose arm reached across the seat and into the air beside Dodge's face.

That afternoon, Dodge received a call from the Skowhegan hospital. Coltrane would recover. Relief edged its way toward him, but he did not trust it. He did not want to kindle hope and have it be snuffed out. After filing Hazard's death reports, Dodge went to Mary's house.

Mary opened the door before he pressed the buzzer. "It doesn't work," she told him. "The buzzer doesn't buzz."

"How are you, Mary?" Dodge stared at her with hollowed-out eyes. The blood had drained from his face. He had not allowed himself the time to dread what he was about to tell her.

She held open the door and aimed a hand into the house. "Come in."

"Mary, I have some bad news." He ducked into the dark cool of the house.

She wandered into the kitchen and put the kettle on the stove. "Tea?"

"It's bad news, Mary. You might want to sit down."

"Oh, sit-down-bad-news. Yes." She heard him but she wasn't listening. "I sent off for a dancing class in the mail."

The kitchen floor was covered with black footprint cut-outs. A dance instruction book lay on the table. Mary danced over to the sink on the black footsteps.

She never could talk in a straight line, Dodge thought. It was like flipping through the channels on a radio station. If he concentrated, Dodge could see how she jumped from one subject to another, but to do this needed the kind of concentration he normally reserved for crossword puzzles. "Mary, it's about Wilbur." Dodge stayed in the living room. Something about the large black footsteps across the kitchen floor made him edgy.

"Wilbur's gone."

"Yes, Mary." Thank God, Dodge thought. Somebody already told her.

"He's gone, gone, gone." She said the words in time to her dance steps around the kitchen.

Say the word, Dodge wanted to tell her. Dead. Say it. Say the word that shows you know I killed him. Or worse, that he was still alive when he took the punch of a few hundred tons of Canadian steel going sixty miles an hour. Dodge hovered in the vast and ugly silence until he could not take it anymore.

"He's gone, but he'll be back soon." She was twirling and dancing.

"No, Mary. Please understand." Dodge was tangled up in his sadness. Poor, beautiful, simple-in-the-head Mary the Clock, he thought. "He's not coming home this time."

"He comes home when he's ready. That's how he likes it."

Dodge nodded, giving up for now. He realized he was crying. He smudged tears on the sleeve of his jacket and looked around the room. The Christmas tree still stood in the corner. Through his blurred vision, the Christmas ornaments sent rainbows through the room.

"Stay for tea," Mary told him, facing out the window. Her voice had suddenly changed. A heaviness passed through it. The truth seemed to be reaching her at last, particle by particle, sifting through her blood. "He wanted to be friends." The cheerful bounce of Mary's voice had disappeared. She stared out the window to her garden, where a row of sunflowers stood heavy-headed under the clear sky.

The black footsteps seemed to shuffle across the floor. Dodge felt himself choking.

"He'll come back," Mary said again. She said it like a threat. Now she turned on him and her face had become something horrible. Snakelike. Turning him to stone.

Late that night, Mackenzie woke suddenly. He lay there for a second, the remains of sleep rising like steam from his body. Then he heard the noise that had woken him. It rose and fell away. The breeze carried it like dust, in tiny cyclones up and down the street. It was a woman's voice, crying out one word over and over into wind. "Wilbur!" the woman called. "Wiiilbuuuur!"

Then Mackenzie knew that it was Mary. He began to sweat. He felt the blame for Hazard's death as much as if he'd been the one who pulled the trigger. No one blamed Dodge. Not even Mackenzie, and he wished he could blame somebody. Instead, there seemed to be a communal sense of guilt that Hazard had never been made welcome in the town. Mackenzie thought of the small kindnesses that had been withheld because Hazard was a stranger and the son of Mary the Clock. Guilt settled on Mackenzie like some kind of poisonous vapor. So now he clung to the only thread of possibility he had left—that Hazard might not have been his son after all. He forced himself to believe it. It was either that or go mad.

"Wiiilbur!" The voice came again.

Mackenzie walked out onto his porch. He stood listening, taunted by the noise.

Mary wandered down the middle of the street, her voice gone hoarse from calling out her dead son's name. She knew the town better by night than she did by day. For many years, she had lived mostly after dark. She thought of the night as a living thing that protected her. Mary had heard what people said about what happened to Wilbur, but the idea of life leaving someone completely made no sense to her.

As she walked past Dodge's house, she saw the man had left his laundry out on the line. She stepped into his yard, took his clothes down and folded them very neatly. Then she set the wooden pegs back in the canvas bag that hung from the weather-greened copper washing line, and set the clothes in a precise pile on his porch, where the dew would not soak them. Then she moved on, calling to Wilbur, while Dodge lay in a sleep like death, moonlight silvering his face.

Then Mary saw Madeleine running toward her. At first, she thought it was a giant bird trying to take off. She saw a lot of things that other people didn't see, like the ghosts of Abenaki Indians, faces yellow and black with warpaint, sliding without sound across the lake in their white birchbark canoes. She once saw a bird with the face of a man, flying above Seneca Mountain. Sometimes, after people had died in the town, she saw them peering through her window. Their mouths moved as if they were speaking, but she couldn't hear a word.

Madeleine had been delivering a new issue of the *Forest Sentinel,* dropping off bundles that had come from the printer that day. It was cold outside and she had the car's heater turned up high. She had brought coffee and doughnuts and smudged the stacks of papers with sugar-greasy fingers. She surfed back and forth along the radio dial, listening to the Quebecois cowboy music. In the past, there had always been something about the empty streets and blacked-out houses that made her feel as if she were taking part in a truly hopeless task. But each new issue made her feel more confident. Each one was a slow step forward. The tortoise and the hare. She kept the image always in her mind.

Madeleine had finished delivering the papers when she heard Mary's voice. She ran out into the street and stopped a few paces short of Mary. "Are you all right?" She spoke to the woman as if she were speaking to a child who had picked up a gun or a knife and didn't know the danger she was in.

"Looking for Wilbur," Mary said.

Madeleine smiled at her gently. She knew she could not leave this woman to walk through the town at night, more of a ghost than the ghost of her dead son. Madeleine took hold of Mary's arm and began to lead her home.

Mary did not protest. The two women walked to Mary's house. The only sounds that passed between them were sighs, one to comfort the other. Madeleine wondered if there might be some simple way of explaining to Mary that her son was dead, some way that no one had tried yet. But if such a way existed, Madeleine didn't know it. As they approached the front gate, Madeleine heard a noise behind her and turned. She thought she saw a shadow darting back into the night. She moved on quickly.

In the house, she helped Mary into bed and then sat down beside her. She took a brush from the bedside table and ran it gently through Mary's hair. Mary bent forward, and Madeleine brushed the hair down the length of her back, smoothing it with her hands after each brush stroke. Mary never made a sound. Madeleine set down the brush and gently eased Mary back until her head was resting on the pillow, then tucked in the sheets around her. Mary gripped the covers to her throat. Madeleine sat beside her until at last Mary's eyes closed. Then she went downstairs and fell asleep at the kitchen table, her head on the red-and-white checked tablecloth.

Jonah Mackenzie stood outside in the shadows. He had watched, still as a heron, barely breathing, as the two women made their slow way down the road and into Mary's house. He had left Alicia sleeping and gone outside to find Mary. Mackenzie didn't know what he would do when he found her. He had hesitated when he at last caught sight of her. It was only a second's hesitation, but then another figure had appeared, some ghoulish thing in white he recognized as Madeleine. So he followed them, footsteps hidden in the breeze. He wished he could have reached Mary first. He wanted to show that he still cared for her, even if this care was drawn from guilt. But now Madeleine had taken away even that small chance. To Mackenzie, she had become a lightning rod for everything that was not right in his life. He swore that he would pay her back for all her small injustices to him. And people won't soon forget it, he thought. What I do to her will echo through this town for generations.

Gabriel checked the cache that Swain had left behind. It contained several thousand ten-inch bridge spike nails, some copper-headed hammers, gloves, paint cans, a grease gun, tubes of grease, a bolt cutter, packets of graphite powder compound, a heavy knife and some tubes of wood glue. There was no note from Swain. No last wishing of good luck. But that was Swain's way. Gabriel was impatient to begin his work, but he knew better than to start before his cover was complete. First, he had to learn the job from Mott, and make sure that his presence in the town no longer drew stares from the locals. He had to structure his new identity around him like a cocoon, until the place where his old self ended and his new self began became lost, even in his own mind. Patience, he told himself. You did not come so far so carefully to commit suicide at the last moment. Swain had warned him that the temptation would be there to rush in before he was ready. That was the mark of an amateur. But every day he waited, huge swaths were being cut through the Algonquin. It took every fragment of discipline that Gabriel owned to wait just a little longer before unleashing himself on the Mackenzie Company.

For the first few days, Mott and Gabriel spent their time close to town. It was the last week of the blackfly season, before the tiny, vicious insects sank back into the swampy ground and stagnant ponds of the Algonquin. Mott taught Gabriel how to inspect the rails, to mark all places where the tracks would need repair by spraying the ties with pink fluorescent paint. Gabriel learned how to hammer rail spikes into the wooden ties, and how to drive the temperamental Putt-Putt. Mott taught him to write up all repair reports as soon as he arrived back in town and then send them to St. Johns first thing the following day. Gabriel learned to keep an eye on his watch, making sure to bring the Putt-Putt back to town before the VIA train was due. Mott explained to him that this was a little like Cinderella getting home from the ball before midnight, except that in this case if Cinderella arrived late she would find herself on the wrong end of a freight train. Mott found this hilarious. He had been saving up the joke for years. Soon Gabriel no longer noticed the rustle of his blaze-orange vest, how it seemed to glow in rainy weather and the way its brightness jabbed at the corners of his eyes whenever he raised an arm or bent down to inspect a rail.

The Abenaki Junction station house had been converted to Mott's repair shop. The building's shuttered windows gave nothing away from the outside. Inside, Mott had created a museum of strangely shaped rocks and animal skulls, moose antlers and wood carvings done by himself on afternoons spent sitting by one of the several bodies of water named Mott Lake. When it came to naming them, he couldn't help himself. Gabriel walked in amazement through the musty waiting room with its church-pew benches and frosted-glass ticket window. TICKETS it read, the word twined with ivy carved into the pane. On every surface were antlers, black and white loon feathers, eagle feathers. In the corner was an old musket Mott had found in a deserted cabin. It was the museum of Mott's life. Gabriel began to see not only what Mott had learned, but also why it was that he stayed silent. He realized the great gift that Mott was making to him, and the only gift Gabriel had to offer in return was not to ask for explanations. Mott cleared out his stuff from the old station house on a Sunday morning when the sky was Carolina blue. He had no idea where he was going to put all his possessions. He would have given them to Gabriel, if Gabriel had asked. Gabriel helped with the packing, gentle with the artifacts, some of which belonged more to their coatings of dust than to what they had been in life.

"You're ready to work on your own now," said Mott. "I'll stop by sometimes to see how you're doing."

Gabriel closed the truck's gate. It made a hollow boom as the latch clicked. Gabriel was sad to lose the old man's company, even though he knew it would be safer that way.

Mott had no experience with good-byes. He just nodded and drove away. Something weighed on his mind. There had been one more reason he agreed to retire. He knew he could have made a stink and stayed on two more years, but there had been rumors, which he was starting to see come true, that the Mackenzie Company was going to cut down the entire Algonquin Wilderness. As first, such a thing seemed impossible to Mott, but he forced himself to realize that with enough time and enough men to work the chain saws, it could be done. And worse, he wouldn't be able to do anything except stand by and watch it happen, because there was bound to be some contract somewhere that gave Mackenzie the right. Mott couldn't bear to see that happen. He hoped Gabriel wouldn't have to watch the Algonquin reduced to a tundra of stumps and plowed ground, which he had seen Mackenzie do before to stretches of wilderness that once had seemed impenetrable. That was another reason he had chosen a stranger: it would hurt less never to have known the place at all.

It reminded Gabriel of his childhood to be woken every morning at five when the house shook and the springs of his saddle-backed bed vibrated as fully loaded logging trucks began to rumble past on their way up to Quebec. Strips of red tape were tied to trunks that hung out over the end of the truck. As each one passed, a spray of dust and pine needles blew up against the porch. Until then, the night was so quiet in Abenaki Junction that sometimes Gabriel would wake and think that he had gone deaf. It was as if everyone had slipped away, as the Abenaki Indians had done more than a century before, without sound and leaving no trace, and knowing they'd never return.

At five-thirty, dressed in soft but heavy canvas clothing, Gabriel would set out from the old red house. He ate breakfast at the Four Seasons, alongside the telephone-line repairman and the loggers. By six-thirty he was out in the Putt-Putt, passing through the steel cage of the McClintock railroad bridge that marked the beginning of the wilderness. Every thousand yards, Gabriel would stop the Putt-Putt and walk back over the track, checking for damage. He carried the spray cans in the pockets of his jacket. The ball bearings rattled inside them as he walked.

At noontime, when he heard the Mackenzie Company horn, like the bellowing of cattle through the woods, he would sit down and pull his sandwiches from their waxed-paper wrapping. He sat on a rail in front of the Putt-Putt, smelling the bitterness of creosoted wood growing warm in the sun. Or he walked some narrow path to the edge of a lake, took off his boots and waded out into the water. He munched on his sandwiches and wiggled his toes in the pale sand.

Chain saws buzzed in the distance. Gabriel could hear their motors powering down as the logger stood back to let the tree fall. It was not until he reached a high point on the track that he could see the clear-cut forest in the thick green of the Algonquin. Each time, when he saw how much land had already been cleared, his stomach toppled and sank.

When a few days had passed, Gabriel knew it was time to begin. It was as if he had been waiting for some signal, some clear order. Now he realized that the order would never come if he did not give it himself. There was no different feeling in his bones. That was the strangeness of it. He felt only the vague and distant vertigo of how much work remained in front of him. It was the time that he most wished he had a partner, someone with whom he could bluff his way out of fear. He missed the company of a woman. He had been without it for a long time, but he knew that starting any kind of intimate relationship now was the worst thing he could do. He could live in the cocoon of his lie, but only if the people around him stayed distant.

The next day, Gabriel ate his breakfast as usual at the Four Seasons. It was easy to tell which of the customers had jobs that kept them outside. They were the ones squinting uncertainly through the windows at the low clouds hanging over Abenaki Junction. The clouds were crystalline bright, which meant rain. The outside workers had brought their foul-weather gear with them, oily blaze-orange raincoats made by Grundig, most so beaten up that the pop snaps had ripped out and the edges of the coats hung in tatters. Gabriel was using rain gear that had been left behind by Mott in the station house. The signal orange had faded to pink. The cloth had been stitched and patched and now even the patches were peeling off, but Gabriel felt more comfortable in it than anything new. It drew less attention to himself.

A few people nodded good morning to him and he nodded back. The waitress knew his name and what he always ate. She poured him his coffee without being asked. Gabriel had lost the tightening of his stomach whenever he walked into the place. At first he had turned heads, as people tried to size him up, but now, as familiarity sank in, they no longer bothered. A few people knew he had taken over from Mott, and asked him how he liked the job. Gabriel was surprised at how little they pried into his business, and they seemed grateful that he did not pry into theirs. They smiled at him as if they knew he meant to stay and now was worth their committing him to memory.

Gabriel was not hungry that morning. He ordered his food out of habit more than appetite. After breakfast, he walked quickly to the station and wrote his report from the day before. He filled out a Track Occupancy Permit and signaled it through. When the permit received clearance, he walked out to the Putt-Putt carrying a green duffel bag. He had gone to the cache the night before and taken what he needed—a hundred nails, some glue, the bolt cutter, a hammer and the knife. As he set out into the Algonquin, the tracks looked wide and empty and the town was still gray with sleep. Gabriel felt the trees close over his head like huge clasping hands. Two miles in, he stopped the Putt-Putt and checked his watch. He had five hours before the noon train was due from the north. He took off his orange raincoat and threw it on the Putt-Putt's seat. The Naugahyde cover was crisscrossed with strips of silver repair tape. He walked down a hiker's path until it intersected with a new logging road, which ran deep into the Algonquin. Logging operations had already begun here, and the forest was falling all along this road. Gabriel knew that by midmorning a nearly constant line of trucks would be moving up and down it, raising white dust. Mackenzie was eating the Algonquin from the inside out, as if to show as little cutting as possible to the people of Abenaki Junction until it was too late to protest.

Having left the tracks, Gabriel knew that if someone caught him now, he would never be able to hide the duffel bag, or to explain away its contents. There was nothing to do but get on with the job. He had done enough work of this type over the past year, and his mind was not clouded by fear, but he had never worked alone before, and this new feeling was strange and cold, like walking through patches of fog.

Rain found its way through the trees. The duffel was heavy and drew sweat from him in the humid air. Its thin canvas strap dug into his shoulder and he had to keep switching sides. Chain saws had started up in the distance. He was so used to the sound now that he barely noticed it except to gauge the distance of the loggers. When the wind changed direction, he could hear each creak, rustle and thump of the trees falling, and the howling of the chain saws as they sank into another trunk. The breeze was always playing tricks. The woods rustled with the rain. In the gloomy light, the colors were deep and slick like new paint. The only animals he saw were a couple of black-streaked, rust-colored chipmunks. They scuttled about on the path and vanished under fallen leaves when he came close. Red squirrels squawked and chuntered at him from above the path.

Gabriel moved parallel to the road, two hundred feet into the trees so that he would not be seen by passing trucks and his footprints would not show in the gravel, which had been darkened by the rain. The strip of road was like a constant patch of blindness in the corner of his left eye.

As he skirted past an area of clear-cut ground, he saw someone standing out in the middle of the devastated area. It was a woman. She was facing him, holding what looked like a pair of binoculars.

Gabriel ducked down and waited for some sign that he might have been spotted. But she seemed to take no notice. He could see that now. Out there by herself. He didn't recognize her. A stupid place to go birdwatching, thought Gabriel. After a while, the woman walked back to the logging road, climbed into a red Volkswagen and drove away.

Gabriel pushed on until he found an area staked out with white tape. This meant it was due to be cut in the next couple of days. Over the next seven hours, Gabriel spiked a hundred trees. With the blade of a penknife, he cut a round piece from each trunk. Then he took a ten-inch nail and drove it in at knee height, where the chain saws would cut. The hammer was a welder's hammer; the soft metal made less noise than an iron hammer, and its copper head would not draw sparks. He had also wrapped the head in a piece of cloth, so the metal would not ring when struck, a sound that carried a great distance in the woods. When the nail was almost all the way in, he took the bolt cutter from his duffle and clipped off the head of the nail so that it could not be pulled out. Then he used the point of another nail to drive it completely into the tree. After this, he replaced the circular piece of wood with a drop of glue on the inside so that the nail wouldn't show. He picked the nail head off the ground and put it in the duffel. Finally, he sprayed a band of red paint around the trunk, to mark that the tree had been spiked.

After every nail, he paused and listened for the drumming of a truck engine or the crunch of footsteps on the road. The rain fell harder and the woods grew misty. Puddles formed out on the gravel road. He was sweating and his arms were tired. Sometimes they cramped so badly that he dropped the hammer. When he unclenched his hands, they creaked like old hinges.

Gabriel drove his last fifty nails into trees at shoulder height, so that the chain saws might miss the nails, but the logging saw down at the mill would strike them and be ruined. He knew that each circular logging saw cost almost $3,000 to replace. These trees were also marked with red paint. With the last of his paint, he marked trees that had not been spiked, to increase the numbers that would not be cut.

He tore down the plastic tape that the loggers had used to mark the boundaries. The last thing Gabriel did before he headed back out to the tracks was to paint S-P-I-K-E-D in letters as large as he could make them on the trunks of trees that faced the road. This way there would be no mistake.

He ran back toward the Putt-Putt, feeling the air cool him. When he reached the tracks, he looked to make sure they were empty. It was warmer here than in the woods. The rain beaded into rainbowed pebbles on the creosoted ties. He climbed back into the Putt-Putt and rode two miles toward town. On the way, he stopped and buried the spray-paint cans in the mossy earth beside the tracks.

He reached the depot at noon. Ten minutes later, the VIA train roared past. Four engines. Fifty cars. The driver waved to him and blew the horn. Gabriel waved back, sweat clammy down his back. Then he sat down on the waiting bench outside and ate a peanut-butter-and-raspberry-jam sandwich for lunch. The raspberry seeds got stuck in his teeth.

Back into the woods again, sleepy now from the food. For the rest of the day, Gabriel walked the tracks, marking places in need of repair. He had easily enough time to do this job. New sweat replaced the old sweat. He thought about how everything was in motion now. Gabriel wondered how long it would take the police or the logging company to catch him. It seemed only a matter of time before they did, and he knew he stood a chance of being killed or badly hurt, depending on who caught him. At the very least, he would go to prison. Then the most he could hope for was to be like Swain and make a showcase of his trial.

Other times, he had always been sure to leave himself an escape route, but often that meant not doing as much work as needed to be done. By taking a job in Abenaki Junction, by renting an apartment and eating each day at the diner, he made his face familiar. If they ever found out who he really was, they would know long before he ever found out they were on to him. But he knew this was the only way to do more than just bother the Mackenzie Company. Bothering them would not slow them down enough or stop them altogether. He had to come back day after day into the woods and plant nails by the hundreds and thousands through the wilderness. When he started out in the west, it had been the hardest thing to do, to break the law. It took a while before he truly understood the line that he had crossed. More than just a line between doing something and just thinking about doing it. This was the line where his own safety became less important than carrying out the job. Strange, Gabriel thought, that I had to cross the line before I could see what it was.

When he reached home, he hung his heavy leather tool belt on the coat hook on the back of the door. He put on his leather-and-canvas work gloves and fetched a pad of paper and a pencil. He took a page from the middle of the pad, to be sure it would have no fingerprints on it. Then he sat down at the wobbly kitchen table. His hands were so raw and cramped from spiking the trees that he could barely grip the pencil.

He wrote a letter to Mackenzie, spelling out the words in capital letters. He told Mackenzie how much spiking had been done and asked him to stop all clear-cutting in the Algonquin, listing the reasons of old growth and the preserve that the Algonquin was to become. When Gabriel had finished the letter, he put it in an envelope, which he took from the middle of a box of fifty, and stuck a 32-cent stamp with an American flag on it onto the envelope. Then he posted the letter in a mailbox on the main street, next to the tourist information hut where campers signed for their fire permits. No one was in the hut, since it was after five, and he made sure no cars passed him as he dropped the letter in. Gabriel knew that the letter was probably a useless gesture, and that the other, harsher measures that he was prepared to carry out would most likely have to be done. But he felt he had to try.

Sometime that night, as Gabriel lay sleeping in his rusty-springed bed, the old nightmare came toward him, like wind across the water. He heard the thunder of the blazing oil spigots. The same gasps of dehydration rasped from his throat. His lips were so chapped that they felt like dried grass rustling together. He felt as if his teeth were coming loose. He wondered if he might be dying.

Suddenly, Gabriel had the sensation of standing up out of his body. He tried to prevent it, clenching his muscles as if to rein back with bands of physical strength something that was not physical at all. The shadowy image of himself set out across the sand, while his body stayed behind like the husk of a beetle on some old windowsill. He followed the chalky path of recent footsteps over the blackened earth.

I'm dead, he thought, as he reached a place where a man sat cross-legged by himself, while clouds of thick smoke billowed past. The man looked up. His face was painted half yellow and half black, the line drawn down the bridge of his nose. Shiny creosote black on the bottom, as if he had gouged tar from the soil and smeared it on his skin. The other side was an angry sulfur yellow, like the flames that rushed from the spigots until they vanished into smoke. At the man's feet was a drawing, made with a finger in the sand, of a circle divided into quarters by a cross inside. In the top right quarter was a crooked line, like a lightning bolt.

Before Gabriel could ask what this meant, he opened his eyes and found himself in the red house again. The Hudson's Bay blanket was pulled up to his throat. He smelled smoke and the sleep slithered out of his body, leaving him cold and wide awake. He swung out of bed and walked out onto his porch, catching sight of the clock in his kitchen as he walked by. It was five in the morning.

It was not the incense smell of burning pine or birch. Instead, this was the peppery-sweet stench of flaming oil. He knew then that this was what had led him to the dream. Smoke was rising from behind the gas station across the road. It muddied the sky like fountain-pen ink dropped into clear water. Gabriel ran over, feeling the jagged gravel against the pads of his bare feet. A breeze off the lake tousled the leaves of the sugar maple in his garden, green to white to green.

Gabriel couldn't see the owner in the station office. There was only the metal desk cluttered with pink receipts, the grubby candy-bar machine and calendars with beaming, long-toothed girls. Oliver Clemson, the owner, sat in the cold shadow of the back of his garage, wrestling with his German shepherd. The dog kept raising its paws and slapping at Clemson. Clemson had his fist in the dog's mouth and the dog clamped down without force, making soft growling noises that Clemson growled back, as if they had their own growly language.

The smoke was coming from a fifty-gallon oil drum. Ashes coughed into the air and scattered.

Gabriel looked around at the oil-patched earth, rusted machine parts and worn-out tires in a stack against the garage wall. "What are you burning there?"

Clemson and the dog stopped playing and looked at Gabriel. "Just some rags."

Turn away, said the voice of caution in Gabriel's head. Don't draw attention to yourself. Don't make enemies. Every rule of camouflage will be broken if you open your mouth. But Gabriel couldn't help himself. "You're messing up my clear blue sky," he said.

"I am?" Clemson asked. Even the dog looked puzzled.

"You just shouldn't be burning this stuff. It's a fire hazard. You could set your whole yard burning." Too late, said the voices. The damage is already done.

Clemson pushed his dog gently aside. The animal went to sit by its doghouse, dragging the chain leash. The chain jingled over the concrete. Clemson filled a tin bucket with water and poured it into the drum. Gray ash mushroomed out and Clemson stood back from the cloud. The water hissed.

Gabriel wished he could have explained to the stubbly-chinned gas-station owner why it was that he could not stand to see this funeral-pyre smoke, or breathe in this smell that he knew he would be coughing up for days.

"I got to get rid of them somehow," Clemson said, the bucket dangling in his hand, "and the garbage men won't take them."

"The town should recycle them."

"Yeah, but it doesn't." Clemson had no wish to offend this half-dressed man. He tried never to offend anyone, and putting out the fire was no great inconvenience. He knew this guy worked in Benny Mott's old job, so he could burn the stuff later, when the man was out on the tracks.

Gabriel thanked him and went back to his house. "Big mistake," he said quietly to himself, and wondered how many lives he had left.

Each night Coltrane lay in the hospital, he was woken by something that lunged at him out of the darkness. He would snap awake and lie staring at the pattern of rain on the ceiling, projected through the orange glow of streetlamps. At first, he didn't know what this thing could be, but in time he came to recognize it. The thing was Hazard, a memory of him at least, and the fraction of time that it took for Hazard to plunge the knife into Coltrane's stomach. It was all seen in a strange and reddish light, as if through a smear of his own blood. Night after night, Hazard lunged at him and the sleep was wrenched from Coltrane's mind as the blade flashed on a screen behind his eyes.

In time, the nightmare would grow dull with repetition, but for now he had no choice but to endure it.

After ten days, Coltrane returned from the hospital. His middle was wrapped in bandages, which made him walk with an unnaturally straight back. The expression on his face was one of nervous caution, as if he were treading on mirror-thin sheets of ice, which might at any second break and drag him under the ground. Coltrane had been in pain so long that he could no longer recall what it felt like not to be. The scar was purple and the marks of stitches showed like train tracks drawn by a child across his nipple and down toward his navel. He hoped he would never see another hospital again. It was the smell that stayed with him. A reek of dead things preserved. The stench kept reappearing in his nostrils, as if those people at the hospital had left something inside him and he was burping it up like a bad meal.

Clara had waited until her husband reached home before telling him about No Ears and what had happened to the dogs. As he listened, Coltrane hung his head. There was no sound except the quiet wheezing of his breath. First thing next morning, he climbed into his truck and drove to town. He stopped beside Mackenzie's house and got out and banged on the door.

After a minute, Mackenzie leaned out the window above him. "What the hell's the matter? It's six-thirty in the morning! Is that you, Victor?"

"No Ears is back!" he shouted.

"Who is it, Jonah?" Alicia looked up bleary-eyed from her pillow.

Mackenzie ducked inside. "It's Victor Coltrane. I think he's hysterical." Mackenzie stuck his head back out the window. "Who's back? What are you saying?"

"No Ears. The bear that mauled Gil Kobick. It killed my dogs."

"No Ears?" Mackenzie recalled the squads of men who had gone into the woods to hunt the bear. "But that was years ago."

"Ask him in," Alicia called behind him. "Tell him he must come in and sit down."

"He's back," said Coltrane again.

"Why don't you come inside, Victor?" Mackenzie glanced at the old paint on his windowsill. He reminded himself to get it repainted.

"Because it's your damn fault is why!"

"What the hell do you mean, it's my fault?" He stopped thinking about the windowsill.

"You can't cut down the Algonquin! That's where No Ears lives. You've gone and set him loose again." Coltrane clenched his hands against his stomach. It hurt to talk. He thought his stitches might tear out.

"It's not a ghost we're talking about, Victor. It's some ratty-furred old bear."

"I'm telling you, Jonah. You woke up that beast and now we're all going to pay for it."

Alicia appeared beside Mackenzie. "Will you come in for some breakfast, Victor?"

"No!" he shouted. Then he breathed out and seemed to have no energy left. "No, thank you." He climbed into his beaten-up truck. Mackenzie appeared at the door in his bathrobe and called to him, but Coltrane did not respond. He drove back into the hills. There was no sense in trying to make Mackenzie understand. He felt a fool for even trying.

Mackenzie watched the truck until it was out of sight.

Alicia appeared beside him. "Do you think it was No Ears that killed his dogs?"

He turned to Alicia. "It could have been any old bear."

"But any old bear doesn't come down from the woods this time of year and kill dogs."

"Not usually, I'll admit. I think Coltrane's just gone crazy is all." But then Mackenzie remembered seeing Harry Crowe at the police station the morning after Kobick's death. Crowe sat in a plastic chair while Dodge typed out a report. Crowe had pulled out his revolver and would not let it go. The gun was empty but Crowe would not put it down. It was his last useless and stubborn defense against the bear. All that lay between him and the madness of a person who has seen too much blood in one life.

Alicia was thinking to herself that the woods had always belonged to No Ears, and it did not matter whether the animal's heart was still beating or whether all that remained was a toothless skull patched with the stains of fallen leaves. "I think if that bear is still alive, it must have lived in agony."

Good, Mackenzie thought. Then let it live. Let the pain come down on it like rain.

Over the next few days, people stopped Coltrane in the street and in the stores and bought him beer he was not supposed to drink at the Loon's Watch and treated him like a hero. But Coltrane didn't feel like a hero. He had allowed a man to swat a loaded shotgun out of his hands. And he had hunted down a man who did not deserve to be hunted. He had kept silent about the tree spike, in the greatest act of cowardice of his life. I deserved to get that knife in my gut, he told himself. And now No Ears has come back. My dogs are gone. He took it as a warning from above. I ought to be dead instead of Hazard, he thought, and imagined setting the barrel of a rifle in his mouth, big toe of his right foot hooked against the trigger. The blued steel clunked against his teeth. The idea seemed so real that it shocked him, as if it were already done and all that remained was for him to go through the motions, whether he wanted to or not. Sweat beaded up on Coltrane's face. He wiped it away with the back of his hand.

He found himself wanting things to be as they were before. Back to normal. The unchanging objects that once had meant nothing to him, he now used like talismans against what his life had become. The badger-bristle shaving brush hanging upside down on its dulled copper stand in his bathroom cabinet. A stuffed bear with a brave but crumpled face, which he had bought at a flea market because he felt sorry for it, sitting among old lampshades and chipped crockery. His old aluminum coffeepot. Coltrane ran his fingers over these objects the way a blind person would, releasing the magic of the talismans they had become. One day he would let them return to what they were before. Just the coffeepot. Just the crumple-faced bear. Just the shaving brush. But until then he felt each day as if he were waking up in someone else's body. His own face seemed foreign to him now. Coltrane used to think he knew how much he could take. Until then, his life had run along the clear train-track lines of knowing where his limits stood. He never thought of what would happen if those limits were breached, like the tide coming over a breakwater. He assumed he would simply be dead.

Maybe I am already dead, he thought. Everything had the muffled feeling of being in a dream. In his frustration, Coltrane took his penknife from the desk drawer, opened the blade and slid the tip deep under his thumbnail, not trusting anything but pain to tell him this was not real. His nerves shrieked in long burning branches up his arm and into his shoulder, anchoring him to the world.

"I saw that," Clara said, "and all you had to do was ask me and I could have told you. This is where you really are, sweetie. In the land of flesh and bone."

"What the hell is that?" Barnegat sat behind the wheel of a Mackenzie Company truck as it bumped along the logging road. The truck was a two-ton Magirus, painted hunter green with a red stripe, the Mackenzie Company colors. It was dawn. The sun shined brassy through the mist.

Coltrane sat beside him. He looked up at the sound of Barnegat's voice. Coltrane had been studying a blueprint map of this section of the Algonquin, checking which wooded areas were to be cut over the next few days. He smoked a Lucky Strike. Every now and then, he held the cigarette out the window and let wind chip off ash that had gathered at the tip. "What the hell is what?" All he saw was mist and trees and the road.

Barnegat pointed at something up ahead. He wore his black wool watch cap pulled down over his ears and heavy-rimmed glasses, with fingerprint-smudged lenses. He had kept to himself lately, unsure whether to approach Mackenzie for the $10,000 reward, or to stay silent and hope that this whole business blew over. "There's writing on those trees."

Coltrane saw it now. "Stop the truck," he said quickly.

"What is it?" Barnegat's arms were slung across the giant steering wheel.

"I said stop the fucking truck!"

The truck shifted down, stopped and then backed up. The loggers sitting in the rear had also noticed the writing. They had parked their pickups and cars at the edge of the Algonquin and were hitching a ride in, not wanting to risk getting stuck in mud or smashing the undersides of their machines when their wheels sank into ruts. The loggers sat side by side on benches bolted to the floor. They wore T-shirts, hard hats and jeans. Some had flannel shirts tied around their waists. Their greasy-handled Kubota saws were locked in a rack at the front, chain blades pointing at the sky. When the truck came to a halt, they jumped off. In the grainy morning light, they walked past the huge letters and into the forest, silently treading by the banded trees, wide-eyed at the hostility that seemed to meet them.

"Back in the truck!" yelled Coltrane. Then again, when nobody moved, "Back in the goddamned truck!"

They piled onto the Magirus.

Coltrane climbed into the cab and slammed the door.

"Where to?" Barnegat asked. He did not look at Coltrane, but stared straight ahead. Barnegat would not have traded places with Coltrane when he brought this news to Mackenzie, not even for the $10,000.

"To the mill. Straight to the mill."

The truck turned around and drove out of the forest. It stopped at the main road to let the loggers get out and start up their own vehicles. Then they left for the mill in a convoy of over thirty cars and pickup trucks, kicking up dust like a cavalry charge.

Mackenzie heard the mass of engines long before they arrived. He looked up from his fax machine and then walked to the window. He saw the convoy, and felt something splinter inside him. Engines quit one after the other. The men gathered on the lot, reaching for cigarettes in the pockets of their vests or under their hard hats or bummed off friends. Lighters clicked open and burned. Nervous eyes flicked up

to where Mackenzie stood in the business office. Most of the loggers
never went inside except to buy a soda from the machine or collect
their paychecks.

Coltrane walked toward the business office, shoulders hunched like
a man walking into the rain.

Mackenzie started down the stairs. He stepped out into the lot as
Coltrane was about to enter the building. The two men began to talk.

Barnegat stood at the back of the crowd. The only movement
around him was the rising smoke of cigarettes. Coltrane and Mackenzie were standing very close together. He couldn't hear what they
said. Coltrane began wiping his hands on his chest. Barnegat had seen
him do this before, and knew it was a sign of nervousness. Mackenzie
listened, his head lowering slowly until he was staring at the ground.
Then Coltrane folded his arms and looked down at his boots.
Barnegat felt as if he were the one who had set all this in motion, in
that moment when the butt of his rifle connected with the back of
Hazard's head. Sooner or later, he told himself, you will pay for it.
Worry rushed through him like the onset of a fever, freezing and
burning and crawling all over his skin.

That afternoon teams of loggers moved through the woods carrying
metal detectors and cans of spray paint. They fanned the detectors
across tree trunks in the area where trees had been marked. In the first
three hours, they found twelve spikes. These they painted with two
broad yellow bands. The rest they painted with a single blue band, to
show the trees were safe for cutting.

Mackenzie shifted logging operations away from the spiked area.
Some loggers refused to cut in there, even if every tree was covered by
metal detectors and sprayed. They did not trust the detectors, and
most of them had seen what had happened to Pfeiffer, even though
Mackenzie assured them that the chance of actually being injured was
minimal. Rumors slithered through the lumberyard that it would be
only a matter of time before new trees were spiked.

Mackenzie sent for Coltrane. While he waited, he rolled a silver
dollar back and forth over his knuckles. His eyes stayed fixed on the
slowly turning coin. Except for the mechanical motion of one hand,

Mackenzie remained as still as a man who has rested his foot on a landmine and knows it, realizing that the slightest movement will trigger the device. He seemed to be collecting his thoughts, setting them in one last rank of order before the explosion. Then he heard Coltrane's boots in the hallway. "Come in and sit down," he said.

Coltrane was uneasy as he shut the door behind him, as if blocking an escape route he would need.

Mackenzie let his breath trail out. "Who's doing this to me?" he asked. "What have I done to deserve it?" He ran his hand across the dull, rough-edged steel of the tree spikes he had collected on his desk. "I have been honest, decent, kind and loyal to the people of this town." With the knife edge of his palm, Mackenzie chopped the thought where it hovered in front of his face. "I have done nothing to make people hate me. But how can I fight an enemy who won't show his face? I refuse to allow fifty dollars' worth of bridge spikes to ruin an operation worth millions. In years to come, Coltrane"—Mackenzie snatched up the nails and held them like daggers in the air—"it won't be this tree-spiking that people talk about. Instead, it will be how much I made these criminals pay for what they've done. And if the law won't make them pay, then I will."

Coltrane said nothing. He missed his wife and his dogs.

"Madeleine has something to do with it," continued Mackenzie. "She and all the fucking granola people who read that newspaper of hers. They're all too shit scared to do anything until somebody else does it first. And isn't it the biggest fucking irony that I'm the one who had the balls to start it?" He looked up at Coltrane, who had no answer. "You see, those people have no spine. They stick with something as long as it's trendy and then they drop it and move on to something else. I bet that as soon as they decided they were going to be environmentalists and protect our resources, as if they even knew what our resources are, I bet they all threw away their old clothes and went out and bought new ones with goddamned SAVE THE WORLD slogans on them. How's that for protecting our resources?" Mackenzie fell silent. He sat red-faced and out of breath, the nails still raised in the air.

"I ought to be going," said Coltrane.

When Mackenzie was alone again, he struggled to think of a plan.

The Algonquin was too big a place to patrol. Dodge couldn't handle it on his own and he couldn't spare his own loggers. They were working too hard as it was. It had to be something different. War against anyone who dared make war on him.

"Mackenzie's coming!" Martha the police switchboard operator yelled at Dodge over the row of rubber trolls arranged on her desk. She had been collecting them for years. They all had different uniforms and different-colored hair.

Mackenzie was talking even before he made it through the door. He swung his body in violent jerks toward them, the artificial leg dragging in the dirt and his cane jabbed so hard into the ground that the heavy wood bowed with the pressure. "What are you doing sitting here? Why aren't you out catching bad guys?"

Dodge stood. "I'm making patrols through there several times a night, Mr. Mackenzie."

"It's not enough."

"Well, you said you didn't want us bringing people up from Skowhegan, and seeing as it's your operation . . ."

"Damn right it is! And I got enough bad press with that *Forest Sentinel* dogging my ass. Bring Skowhegan people in and pretty soon the whole world is going to be in my face."

"We could try bringing in some US Forestry Service personnel. They might agree to patrol the woods on foot."

"No. For the same reason." He rapped his knuckles on Dodge's desk. "If they come, we'll all have more problems than before." There were other reasons Mackenzie did not want this. He was afraid the Forestry Service would have something to say about his clear-cutting methods, particularly the way he had been bulldozing some of the slopes of Seneca Mountain. The streams and lakes were silting up at a rate that surprised even him.

"There's only me here, Mr. Mackenzie. Victor Coltrane's been helping but . . ."

"It's not enough!" Mackenzie spat the words out, then spun on his heel and left.

Martha took off her headphones and set them gently on the desk in front of her. "What was he going on about? He knows you can't do more than you're already doing and he doesn't want you bringing in help from outside."

"I don't know what he's up to." Dodge leaned back and ran his fingers through his short-cropped hair. "It's like he was warning us or something."

Madeleine was in her darkroom, printing the pictures she had made of the clear-cut a few days before. She planned to release a special edition because of the spiked trees that had just been discovered. She knew people would draw a link between her paper and the spiking, and she wanted to make clear that she had nothing to do with it. The incident had sent a new tremor through the town, as if Abenaki Junction had just come under siege. Madeleine believed that Hazard had done the work, and wondered how many trees he had spiked before he died. But she wondered why. Hazard had never said anything to her about wanting to stop Mackenzie. She had never even seen him with a copy of the *Forest Sentinel*.

In the ghoulish red of the darkroom lights, she slid each 8x10 sheet of Ilford paper into a developing tray. Then with a pair of rubber-tipped tongs she tapped the paper back and forth in the liquid until the print began to appear. She bent down over the tray as the smoky images emerged. As soon as the picture was complete, she slid the paper into a stop bath to prevent overdeveloping.

The camera had captured it perfectly. The clear-cut ground looked like photos she had seen of battlefields in World War I. The landscape was so completely empty of life that the only things that could have survived the cutting had either fled or were hiding underground, the way the soldiers had done in their trenches, huddling from the shriek and blast of artillery fire.

While she printed another picture, she found herself thinking about what Jonah Mackenzie had told her—that she saw everything through the world of her camera lens, where everything was compacted and idealized. The lens did do that. She could not deny it. These neatly bordered pictures made the Algonquin seem more graspable, less overwhelming in its vastness.

A jagged barricade of torn-up tree stumps filled the picture. Behind it stood the uncut pines. Rising above them was the humped back of Seneca Mountain. She slid the print into the stop bath and at that moment she noticed a figure standing at the edge of the woods. She bent down, the fumes of the stop bath burning in her nostrils. Maybe it's just a tree, she thought. But she looked again and realized she had been right the first time.

A man stood watching her. He carried some kind of satchel. She could just make out the features of his face. It took her a few seconds to recognize him as the one she had seen in the Loon's Watch bar a while ago and since then each morning coming out of the Four Seasons while she was on her way to work. He was new in town, the one who had just taken Benny Mott's old job. Mott had called to cancel the want ad in her paper only a few days before. And Lazarus had called to say his house had been rented by a man named Adam Gabriel. This area of clear-cut was a long way from the tracks. It was close by the area that had been spiked. She had no doubt what he was doing there.

Her first reaction was to call the police. She walked out of the dark-room and into the harsh light of her office. She breathed out the acetic-acid fumes, which passed across her lips with the staleness of old tobacco smoke. She picked up the phone but then she paused and did not dial the number.

Madeleine was thinking of the way Wilbur Hazard had been treated in Abenaki Junction—always as a stranger. And now this new man had arrived in town and within a few days she was calling on the police to ransack his apartment and take him down to the station. It was not illegal to go walking in the woods. She realized she was think-ing with the same paranoia that she usually blamed on Mackenzie.

Madeleine decided she would talk to him herself. She waited until the end of the workday and then walked down to the old train station. She was sitting on the bench outside when the Putt-Putt rolled out of the woods, its burbling engine audible long before she could see the machine.

Gabriel recognized the woman. She was the one he had met in the bar. He knew she ran the *Forest Sentinel*. He had often seen her on her way to work, but he had stayed away from her, even if she was the person in town most likely to understand what he was doing. It was not a chance he could afford to take. He bottled up his worry and by the time he climbed from the Putt-Putt he was smiling. "That's a good place to catch the sun." Gabriel nodded at where she was sitting.

Madeleine looked at the bench as if she had never seen it before. Then she turned to face him. "I want to talk to you," she said.

He sat down on the bench with her. "All right," he said cautiously. She pulled the photo from her satchel.

It took a second for Gabriel to see the figure in the picture and a few more seconds before he recognized it as himself. Those weren't binoculars after all, he thought. Now he looked at her. "You said you wanted to talk to me."

"That's you." She did not take her eyes from him. Her face was grim.

He nodded. "I was on my lunch break."

"No you weren't. No that far into the woods. You were spiking those trees. Finishing off the work you started with your friend Wilbur Hazard."

"I never met that guy," said Gabriel quietly.

"All right. Even if that's true, why did you spike those trees?"

Gabriel looked at her and his gaze faltered. He could tell she already knew. He didn't want to insult her by lying. The photo was proof enough.

"Why?" she asked again.

He leaned back against the sun-warmed boards of the station building. The house of lies he had built for himself was coming apart already. Was it worth it? he asked himself. A hundred trees among millions? Was it worth what will happen to me now? He turned to face her, feeling the old paint on the walls crumble as he rolled the back of his head across the board. He felt a roughness in his throat. In all of the imagined endings to his struggle, he had never pictured himself sitting on a bench with a beautiful woman. "Have you already gone to the police?"

"No. I wanted to be sure it was you."

Gabriel sighed and stared at the scuffed toes of his boots. "Not with that photo you didn't. You were already sure. You just wanted to find out why."

She realized he was right. She took the photo from his lap and put it back in the satchel.

"What are you going to do?" Not since he had stood, oil-coated and delirious with his hands in the air, before the commandos in Kuwait did he feel his fate so much in someone else's hands.

"I don't know," she said. She could not tell whether this man and what he had done against Mackenzie was the embodiment of all the ideals for which she had worked or whether he was the worst thing that had ever happened to her. "I've never resorted to . . ."

Gabriel cut her off. "Violence?" He had suddenly stopped looking frightened, the way he had been only a second before.

"Exactly," she said.

He was staring out into the trees beyond the tracks, his face dirty with sweat and dust. "What are you trying to accomplish with your newspaper?" Then, before she could answer that question, he fired another at her. "Isn't it one of your main objectives to stop Mackenzie from cutting down the Algonquin? I mean, after all, if the Algonquin goes, you'll be writing an environmental newspaper in the middle of a wasteland."

"Of course." It was the first time she had ever heard someone in Abenaki Junction speak out passionately against the clear-cutting. "I'd give my front teeth to stop him."

"Is that all? Just a couple of teeth?"

Madeleine watched him closely. He did not have the wild-eyed look she would have painted on the face of a radical. He looked strangely calm, considering the things he was saying. It was as if he had worked out all avenues of possibility long ago. In that, he reminded Madeleine of herself. She wanted to tell him about about the gradual process that she had begun here years ago, about the tortoise and the hare, but she could sense just from the tone of his voice that his ideals had been fixed for a long time. There would be no room to convince him of anything except what he already believed. "Why this place?" she asked him. "Why here?"

Gabriel didn't answer immediately. Instead, he turned to her, head tilted to one side and eyes narrowed with curiosity. "Do I seem familiar to you?" he asked.

She looked at the slight upward curve of his upper lip and the russet in his hair. Slowly she shook her head. "No."

"I used to live here. A long time ago." Gabriel told her who he was. In the last few minutes, he had remembered Madeleine. He recalled how she had been on the fringe of groups at school, always so outspoken that few children her age felt comfortable with her. She seemed to have more patience for ideas than for people. Time has treated you well, he thought as he looked at her. Better than it treated me. "I could use your help," he said. "If you honestly want Mackenzie stopped, you'll see this is the only way it can be done. If we had all the time in the world, it would be different. But we have only a couple of months." Gabriel had lived for so many days in the intense loneliness of his forged identity that suddenly to be requesting help from this woman uncovered instincts he thought he had buried for good.

"You mean go into the woods and spike trees with you?"

"Well, you could start by not turning me in." He watched her closely. Even though she was a stranger, it was one of the few times in Gabriel's life that he had met someone with whom he had so much in common that there was almost no need to talk. His eyes were dry from staring.

Madeleine was surprised at herself that she did not immediately refuse his request. The softness of his voice was persuasive. He had a gentle face. He was not what she had expected.

"I respect what you do," said Gabriel. "It does a lot of good. It does all the good in the world, because from reading your paper and others like it, people will eventually understand how big the problem is. But it's not happening quickly enough. Mackenzie is out there in the Algonquin destroying life we don't even know exists yet. If you don't act against this clear-cutting, and I mean *act,* all you and your newspaper will be is the chronicler of the last days of the Algonquin Wilderness. I need you to help me." He paused for a moment. "To help me, please."

"I have to think about this," she said. She stood and heaved her satchel onto her shoulder. "I can't make you any promises."

Gabriel nodded. It was more than he had expected. He raised his hands a few inches from his lap and let them drop again.

Madeleine saw his gesture of helplessness. She realized how alone he seemed, but he was not a stranger to her either. What this man was doing now in the Algonquin, she herself had thought of doing many times before. And now she asked herself if the only reason she had stopped short of spiking the trees was fear or some high ideal of nonviolence. This man could not answer that for her. She would have to find it out for herself.

Madeleine walked away. In the light of sunset, shadows stretched across the road. TV aerials threw shapes like the branches of dead trees across the dust. She had gone only a few hundred feet when a metallic shriek came from the direction of the sawmill. It sent birds racing from the telephone wires.

Over the years, the people of Abenaki Junction had grown used to the whine of Mackenzie's band saws and the thump of the bark stripper as it bounced over uneven logs. They heard the constant humming of conveyor belts as wood was cut into planks and fed out to the lumberyard, where the planks were sorted by size and placed into different stalls. Forklift drivers carried the stacked planks into a storage house the size of a small airplane hangar. People set their watches by Mackenzie's noon lunch whistle. During the week, they no longer noticed the noise, the way a person stops hearing the tick of a clock in a room, but they would notice the silence if ever the band saws stopped running. They felt the rumble of logging trucks coasting down the hill that led to Skowhegan, scattering old wood chips like brown confetti, and the punched-out hiss of air brakes kicking in at the steepest part of the hill. By the time anyone from Abenaki Junction came to work at the mill, the sounds of its operation were so familiar that the only difference was a slight increase in volume as they set foot inside the logging compound.

But this shriek was like nothing anyone had heard before. One of the huge circular saws had bitten into a ten-inch nail, hammered by Gabriel into a tree above the line where the metal detectors had reached. Sparks sprayed like fireworks across the cutting room. The jagged edges of the saw bent sideways and the jolt threw the main piston of the saw's engine. The machine howled and crashed as its insides broke apart and gear wheels spun without connecting.

Coltrane was so shocked by the noise that at first he did not move. Then his senses returned and he ran to the greasy black ALL STOP button that cut power to the mill. Engines throughout the building hummed deeper and deeper until Coltrane could see the mangled shark-teeth cutting edge of the saw as it finally quit spinning. The conveyor belt stopped. The bark grinder stopped. All sound disappeared. Then came the clatter of workers running toward the cutting room.

Mackenzie had been in his office, on the phone to a trucking company in Bangor. When he heard the noise, he hunched over his desk, teeth bared, as if the blade of the saw were about to carve its way through his office wall. He replaced the receiver without saying another word and stamped down the main staircase into the logging yard. No one had to tell him what had happened. He walked from machine to machine. On a chalkboard in his head, he drew a series of numbers. It would cost $3,500 to replace the ruined parts.

Mill workers stood around, crowding doorways and blotting out the daylight. Coltrane waited with a shorn-off piece of the nail between his thumb and first two fingers. He prepared himself for the detonation of Mackenzie's rage. "We must have missed one of the spikes with our metal detector," he said quietly when Mackenzie reached him.

"Anybody hurt?" Mackenzie asked.

"No, sir. It's just the saw blade and the motor."

"Do we have a spare blade in stock?"

"There's one in the back." Coltrane jerked his chin in the direction of the storehouse.

"Well, replace it, and get the spare motor that's out there, too. Make sure to pass all the logs under a metal detector again. Get the place running."

Coltrane felt like a man in a bunker into which a grenade had been thrown. The time had passed for the explosion, and he was slowly beginning to realize that the bomb would not go off. Coltrane did not understand it. He did not trust the silence and the illusion of Mackenzie's calm. It seemed more threatening than the eruption he'd expected.

Mackenzie walked back to his office and shut the door. He sat with his hands neatly folded on the blotter in front of him. His lungs were filled with the sour lumberyard smell, like that of old beer left out after a party. It came from tons of woodchips dumped in a pile by the roadside. The pile steamed all year long, melting the snow that fell around it from October to late March. "Sal Ungaro," he said. "Sal Ungaro." He repeated the name as if it were an incantation, like summoning the devil from the letters on a Ouija board.

At the other end of town, Madeleine Cody stood in the middle of the street. She had been frozen by the noise, as if giant fingernails had scraped down a blackboard. What reached her next was not a sound but a lack of sound. Across the street, she saw Lazarus in the doorway of the Loon's Watch bar, a steel beer keg in his arms. He seemed to have forgotten about its weight. His mouth hung slightly open in his concentrated efforts to hear through this sudden stillness. There were others, waiting and listening. After a few minutes, they began to filter back inside.

Madeleine caught sight of Gabriel standing outside the station house. He was watching her. He did not look afraid, as if he had resigned himself to whatever choice she made. He just watched her, waiting to see what she'd do. Madeleine turned and walked on, finding her way home on instinct alone, swerving like a long-distance driver with each curve of the road, but miles away inside her head.

To hell with a clean fight, thought Mackenzie. To hell with all the gentlemanly rules of war. He paced back and forth in front of his fireplace. "What if it's one of those terrorist groups? The kind that set off bombs?" he asked Alicia.

"I'm sure Dodge has a handle on it." Alicia knew that nothing anybody said would make sense to him anymore. It was late at night, and he often talked wildly when he was tired.

"But Dodge is just one man. With a thousand of him, I could conquer the whole damn world, but I've only got one!"

"I don't think you're being fair."

"Fair? Why are you always waving that word in my face? Nothing in business is based on fairness! The only time people are fair is when it's profitable!"

"Don't shout at me. You can't win arguments just by making noise."

"I'm not shouting!" Mackenzie clenched his hands into fists. Then he began to speak more quietly. "I just don't think I can get this solved by relying on the law." Even though he sometimes pretended not to listen to her, Mackenzie balanced everything Alicia said, and thought carefully before proceeding. He considered her his equal in most things. And in the things in which they were not equal, he knew she far outclassed him. "I might have to hire some people."

"What kind of people?"

"People who will clear these bastards out of the woods. People who don't fancy-dance around." He breathed out violently. "You know."

"You mean you're going to be calling that old friend of yours. Ungaro. The one who does shady bits and pieces for foreign governments." She remembered Ungaro from their days at college. He was always at the parties, usually alone and standing with his back to the wall, shit-grinning at some joke inside his head.

"I might give old Sal a call. Might have to."

Don't use his first name to me, thought Alicia. Don't call him "old Sal." Don't try to humanize him. I've seen the man. I've seen the damage he does. She didn't have to say any of this to Mackenzie, because Mackenzie knew it well enough himself. Ungaro would get the job done, but it would be like unleashing a pack of dogs who wouldn't come back when you called them. "I can't believe you're considering this," she said.

"Jesus, Alicia! I can hardly believe it either. But extraordinary circumstances require extraordinary measures." The idea had walked into Mackenzie's head and now it wouldn't leave. It jabbered at him like the red-tailed squirrels in the trees.

"What if you try to contact these tree-spiking people and reach some kind of compromise?" Alicia thought of her talk with Madeleine. She didn't want to be the go-between, but they were both so stubborn that she knew it might be the only way.

"I refuse to negotiate with terrorists." Mackenzie's voice had reached an ugly calm.

"Well, maybe you should ask yourself why people might do this. Maybe you should think twice about clear-cutting the Algonquin. You have to remember that your father did things differently. He kept up a sustainable yield." It was always dangerous for her to bring up the topic of his father. Sometimes he would simply ignore her. Other times he would explode. There was never any telling what nerves would be struck. She had never known anyone so driven to succeed by the memory of a dead man. It was as if everything her husband did was somehow to gain the approval of his father. But since the man was long gone, the approval never came, and Jonah Mackenzie just kept working harder and harder, as if to bridge the gap between life and death itself.

Mackenzie avoided the topic of his father. "It has something to do with this damn *Forest Sentinel.* I know it does. If I could stop that little paper from spewing out all Madeleine's gossip, I know I'd stop the trouble. But she's not going to take my offer. If she were, she'd have done it already."

"So talk to Madeleine. Don't just try to buy her out and shut her up that way. Understand a little better what the environmental movement is all about. It's not just the Algonquin. And it's not just Madeleine, either. Your own loggers are afraid that you'll wipe out their jobs in a decade."

"That forest belongs to me, Alicia! I paid for it and it's mine. It's an investment. In order to get my money back, I have to cut down the trees."

She got up and stared down at him. "Ask yourself what it means that you're thinking of bringing Sal Ungaro into this. Are you just going to turn this forest into a combat zone? Your ability to hire someone to take care of your dirty work doesn't prove that you were right."

No, thought Mackenzie. But I'm the one left standing at the end.

The next day, in the space of fifteen minutes, even before the early-morning sun had untangled itself from the treeline, five out of seven circular blades at the mill struck nails and were put out of action.

The whole plant shut down.

Coltrane said nothing. When the fifth blade crashed, he just punched the grimed and sawdust-coated emergency ALL STOP button one more time. Then he took off his hard hat and kicked it like a football out into the mountains of logs that lay in the compound, still waiting to be cut and bleeding sap like honey. All of the logs that broke the saws had been checked in the forest for nails before they were cut, so he knew these had been double-spiked. The loggers must have checked each tree for just one nail. Either that, or they had been spiked after cutting.

The plank stackers and machine operators stood waiting, as if they were parts of the same broken machinery and their power had also been shut down. Everyone at the company, even the secretaries far above the cutting floor, weighed the possibility of anger slung in their direction.

For a few minutes, while the sawdust settled and curious eyes peered at the crippled teeth of the saw blades, Coltrane stood motionless on the loading ramp, as if waiting for his hard hat to come boomeranging back to him from its place among the logs. He was balancing in his mind whether to go on or to give up. He knew he might take the fall for this. Be the sacrificial goat. Then Coltrane caught sight of people watching him from the cutting floor and the administrative office. Eyes glinted softly from every shadow of the compound. All waiting.

"Get the metal detectors!" Coltrane called to them.

There was no hesitation. Loggers were almost fighting over who got to use the detectors, while the rest followed behind with pliers and chisels to dig out nails once they were found. Soon the lumberyard was humming with talk and the ear-grating bleep of detectors finding metal in the logs. Then came the whack of chisels digging into wood and the whispering *shush* of spray cans painting bright-orange splats over the spots where the nails had been. Soon the logs were polka-dotted with paint. No one stopped to think about the work that lay ahead of them.

On the other side of town, Dodge had heard the saw blades crash. He had been waiting at the old station depot for over an hour. He wanted to question the man who'd taken Mott's place, although no one he talked to said the man seemed suspicious, including Mott. Dodge knocked on the depot door, and because the place was not locked, he walked inside. The depot looked bare now and reminded him of when he was a little boy, catching the train west to Montreal with his mother. He remembered snow piled up so high that it blocked the light from the windows and the smell of hot cider spiced with cinnamon and cloves, stewing in a pot and given out free in tin mugs by the stationmaster, a man named Adler. And on the last day that the passenger train stopped in town, Mr. Adler got on that train with a suitcase, waved good-bye and never came back.

Gabriel was working on the tracks up by the Canadian border. Out there, he felt as if he had reached the end of the world, and that only a few miles away the polar ice was nudging against the land. He felt the strange seduction of routine. There was no sense of heroics as he set out each morning; there was only the fatigue of walking the tracks with the rolling stride he had adapted for moving along the ties. Automatically he reached into the pocket of his canvas Filson vest and pulled out a spray can of fluorescent paint to mark any place where a pin had come loose on the rails. All he had been thinking about was whether Madeleine would help him or whether this would be his last day under the open sky for years to come.

As Gabriel rode home, he listened to a portable radio that Mott had left behind. Its best reception was on a French-Canadian station that played cowboy songs in French. Gabriel sang along, inventing words to replace the lyrics, which he could not understand. Rounding the last bend in the tracks, the Putt-Putt's engine racing, he saw Dodge's police car parked at the depot. Bile tipped into his stomach. She brought in the police after all, he thought, and suddenly he knew how Swain had felt. That sense of being too tired to run. Of having no place to go. He was glad that he had spiked another hundred trees that day. It would be his parting shot. Swain had told him to expect rough treatment from the police, and even rougher if the loggers got to him first. The more he resisted, the more he would be beaten. If they caught him out in the woods after all the damage he'd done, there was a fair chance they would kill him, the way they had tried to kill Hazard. As soon as Gabriel stopped the engine, he climbed out with his hard hat in his hands, like a man come to ask for a job. "What can I do for you?"

Dodge walked out of the shadows. "I just wanted to know if you'd seen anybody walking on the tracks these past few days. You know, we've had a little trouble with some trees being spiked."

"I did hear about that," said Gabriel. It dawned on him that Madeleine had not gone to the police. He felt relief like nervous laughter in his throat and had to choke it back. He wanted to find Madeleine as soon as he could and thank her. Perhaps she had even decided to help him. The great cage of his loneliness was suddenly gone, even if he knew it would return.

Gabriel recognized Dodge. They had been in school together for a while, although they had barely known each other because they were two grades apart. They had crossed paths several times since Gabriel had returned to Abenaki Junction, and Gabriel had waited for the sharp stare of recognition to pass across Dodge's face. But there was none. It made Gabriel both relieved and sad to think that he had vanished from Dodge's thoughts.

"Where did you hear about the spikings?" Dodge walked to within a few feet of Gabriel, deliberately too close for comfort. He knew that to get answers from a person, he sometimes had to make them ill at ease.

"They practically have it on the menu at the Four Seasons."

Dodge smiled, but Gabriel's face stayed serious. Dodge sat down on the station-house bench, remembering how he had once sat here when his feet didn't touch the ground. "So you haven't seen anybody on the tracks lately?"

"It's only me out there."

"Personally, you know"—Dodge folded his hands on his lap—"I don't think they should be cutting down the Algonquin."

It seemed like a trap to Gabriel. Even a clumsy trap. "I only just arrived in town," he said, as if this would excuse him from anything.

Dodge knew he would be keeping his eye on this man for a while. He didn't want to make him too uncomfortable for now. Dodge slapped his knees and stood. "Well, if you see anything, give me a call."

"Yes, of course." Gabriel waited while Dodge climbed back into the patrol car and drove away. He was suspicious that Dodge asked no more questions. That man's not through with me yet, he thought.

A face loomed gruesomely against the window of the *Forest Sentinel* door. The pebbled glass seemed to make its flesh boil. The door opened and Jonah Mackenzie walked in. He wore a black-and-gray-check woolen vest, khaki trousers tucked into boots, and a plain blue wool tie that was frayed at the knot. He instantly became the center of the room. Even the walls appeared to back away. "May I talk with you?" he asked Madeleine and crumpled his face in an unenthusiastic smile.

Madeleine knew what this was about. Since her dinner with Mackenzie, she had tried not to think about his offer, but it was as if he had planted a tiny transmitter in her head that sent messages crackling through her brain. A constant and monotonous voice announced the reasons she should leave Abenaki Junction and begin again someplace else. It reminded her of when Barnegat had come back from Vietnam, out of his mind on heroin and the knowledge of

Black Ops atrocities, swearing that the Vietcong had captured him and replaced one of his fillings with a miniature radio that broadcast Radio Hanoi twenty-four hours a day.

Each time Madeleine wrote about Mackenzie in the *Forest Sentinel,* which was almost every issue, she had expected him to come storming into her office, but this was the first time she had seen him walk into the building. She saw the familiar smile knife through his waxy cheeks. It was his perfect camouflage. He was the most pokerfaced, unreadable man she had ever encountered.

"Have you been thinking about the money?" he asked.

"Yes," Madeleine told him. It felt like a confession. The voices were still there, hundreds of them like dirty sea-foam bubbles piled up in the corners of her mind.

"It serves us all in the end."

"I'm not going to sell the paper, Jonah. If I were in your shoes, I might be making the same kind of offer. But I think that if you were in my shoes, you would say the same thing I'm saying now, which is thank you, but no."

Mackenzie had prepared himself for this. He had even expected it and was glad Madeleine spoke so gracefully. People had come to him in years past and tried to buy him out, and he had sent them on their way far less politely than he was being sent now. He began to feel sorry for her, wishing he could explain that the alternative to selling the paper was a call to Sal Ungaro. Mackenzie decided to make one last effort, and came straight to the point. There had been enough slippery talk. "How much do you want?"

"Nothing. Really. It was a generous offer to begin with." Now that she had refused, the voices were suddenly gone.

"I'll increase the offer by five thousand dollars. That's my limit."

"It's not for sale. My business isn't worth even a third of that. You're making fools of us both."

"Please take the money. Let me worry about who looks a fool." For your own good, he wanted to say. Or I will scythe you down. I will clean the slate. "Look, I know, even if you don't, that your paper has something to do with whoever is spiking the trees."

Madeleine drummed her fingers once on the tabletop. "If you can find one paragraph in my paper that advocates tree-spiking, I'll *give* you the damn paper."

"Well, what about this?" He yanked a neatly folded page out of his pocket. "Your last issue had a whole segment on it."

"An explanation of what's going on. Nothing more."

"It's practically a battle cry! Look, this is my final offer. Instead of buying your paper, I will offer to leave a thousand acres of the Algonquin standing. And you don't even have to stop writing your paper. You don't even have to leave town."

"What do I have to do?"

"You have to stop the tree-spiking. Make it stop." He had the thousand acres already bracketed in his mind. It was bottomland, so swampy that few trees grew there and those that did were stunted and not worth the cutting. What he hated most of all about the offer was that it made him look like someone backing down from a fight.

It was at this moment that Madeleine decided for certain she would not call Dodge and tell him about Gabriel. The things that Gabriel said had sunk into her mind. Now was not the moment for the tortoise and the hare. With so little time left, there was no other way to fight Mackenzie except with the same ruthlessness that he himself employed. She could not see herself out in the woods spiking trees, but her silence made her just as guilty as if she had hammered in the nails herself. "I can't make it stop," she told Mackenzie.

"That's unfortunate," he said very quietly. Mackenzie felt old just then. Older than he was. He wished it hadn't come to this. He left without waiting for a nod or any words of confirmation, leaning heavily on the ball of his ivory-topped cane. On his way out he smiled at Madeleine, as if to show that there were no hard feelings. The truth was that there were no feelings at all. He had barged through the stages of anger—from migraine tension in the back of his neck to threats that would not be carried out, to threats that would, to the seeing-red rage, to violence, and suddenly through all the heat of those angers to a place that was cold, where all emotion seemed lost.

A minute after Mackenzie had left, Gabriel appeared at the door. "I came to thank you for not turning me in."

"I don't know if what you're doing is right." Madeleine walked to the window and drew down the blinds. "I just don't know anymore if it's wrong. I used to think that if we could gather together enough concerned people . . ."

"I used to think that," he said. "I believed it, too. But after a while

I realized that everyone's *concerned*. Nobody wants the wilderness destroyed. Of course, if it's their own dam they want built, or their own contract for a housing development, they don't give a shit about the wilderness. But as a general rule, as long as it doesn't cost them anything, they're all for the wilderness. As for the rest of the world, the truth is so bad, they can't even stand to hear about it. They throw a few bottles into a yellow garbage can every week and they think they're saving the world. But *concerned citizens* aren't going to save the wilderness. Radicals are. At least that's what they'll call us until they figure out we are right. So until then radicals are what we'll stay."

She heard the urgency in his words. It was the voice of someone who might do anything. "Who's 'we'?" she asked.

"Well, I thought . . . I thought you might help me."

"I don't want to break the law," Madeleine said. "Any more than I already have. That seems like taking a step backward instead of forward."

"In terms of technology and development, saving the wilderness *means* taking a step backward. People aren't used to doing that. They're only used to going forward."

"But the only law I've ever broken was to park illegally outside Mackenzie's mill!"

"Whose law are you talking about?" Gabriel leaned over the desk. He caught the faint smell of her soap. Her perfume. He didn't know what it was. It distracted him and he had to force his thoughts back on track. "Most great changes in the world have involved breaking laws that existed at the time. It's not just laws. It's reason. How we see things. How we see ourselves in the universe."

"This isn't the universe," she said. "It's just a little logging town in northern Maine."

"It doesn't matter where we are. What counts is that every leap forward in our civilization has come after we've been shaken out of the order that we've imposed on the world. Copernicus: that the earth isn't the center of the universe. Darwin: that we are descended from apes. Didn't their theories seem unthinkable at the time?"

"Tell that to Mackenzie." Madeleine shook her head at the hopelessness of it.

"Tell that to every major religion on the face of the earth! Tell it to all the laissez-faire individualists. Tell it to the American Dream. People have been tortured and crucified for saying less than what I've just said."

Madeleine shook her head. "Maybe he'll call me a witch and burn me at the stake."

"Don't laugh. He might be planning something even worse. You have to be careful. We have to be careful."

"Mackenzie offered to leave a thousand acres of the Algonquin standing if I could get the spiking to stop. He's made a real offer. Neither of us can just ignore it."

Gabriel sat in silence for a while. It was as if he saw before him the entire mechanism of his thoughts. A thousand acres. He looked across at Madeleine and voices inside begged him to reclaim his old life. Set the whole struggle aside. Sometimes it was too hard living out in the black-and-white world of the extremist, where identity was what a person did and nothing else mattered at all.

She was waiting for his answer.

"Not enough," Gabriel said, and was struck by the finality of his own words. "If I stopped now, it would only be proof that the *Forest Sentinel* was involved."

"This is all sacred to you, isn't it?" she asked.

"Of course it's sacred." For a moment he looked confused, as if he did not understand why she had asked the question. "I mean, I guess every cause is sacred."

"But it's also personal, isn't it? You grew up here. Your father was fired by Mackenzie."

"Every cause is personal. But what am I supposed to do? Nothing? Because I can find a personal reason for being involved in this struggle for the wilderness, does that mean I don't have the right to play a role in its defense? We're a part of the wild. When we defend the Algonquin, we're defending a part of ourselves. That's the most sacred cause there's ever been. Don't you see?" Gabriel was desperate for her to understand. Even if she wouldn't join him, he wanted her at least to understand.

"This is it," Mackenzie said to himself as he stepped into the Range Rover. It was morning and the mist was heavy in the tall grass. Soon the sun would burn it off, and the heat of the day would rise in blurry sails from the baked roads. Mackenzie held up a letter he had just pulled from his mailbox and waggled it. There would be no more trouble from Madeleine. She had finally come to her senses and accepted his offer.

While he drove, Mackenzie held the steering wheel in one hand and the letter in the other. He read it in a murmur that sounded like his stomach rumbling. It was not from Madeleine. It was the letter that Gabriel had written, stating that two thousand trees had been spiked in the Algonquin. The words reached him like shouts from the page.

Mackenzie did not go straight to work. He motored up the logging road to the Algonquin, swinging his body into the turns, bony fingers in a bloodless grip upon the wheel. He passed a work crew who stopped their chain-sawing to watch him hurtle by. They ducked away from the shower of pebbles that his Range Rover kicked up. Mackenzie drove into an area of woods where the logging had not yet begun. Then he stopped the car and jumped out.

The silence of the forest swept around him.

Mackenzie made his way over the drainage ditch, clawing out handfuls of tall grass as he dragged his artificial leg down and up the embankment. He needed to be alone and it had been a long time since he'd walked among the trees. He had grown used to seeing the forest as a single thing, a mass, but now suddenly the details of it made him dizzy. The vast complexity of each branch, the texture of the bark and the way, when he bent down and dug his hands into the soft earth, he could see how generations of pine needles had become the black soil. He felt the coolness of the air beneath the sheltering trees. He stumped back to the car. He did not want to see anymore. I'm becoming my own enemy, he thought.

Back inside the Range Rover, Mackenzie turned on the engine and then the air-conditioning and the radio. He looked at the letter again, staring so hard at the words that they seemed to scatter across the page. He felt so certain that it was Madeleine who had sent it, or who had caused it to be sent, that he decided he would not even bother handing it in to the police. In fact, he thought, considering what I am about to do, it's best if Dodge doesn't see this letter.

Mackenzie began to feel very tired. He didn't have the strength he used to have. Voices in his head asked if he shouldn't just give in. You could stand to lose just once, the voices told him. For every person who says publicly they do not like what you're doing to the Algonquin, there are fifty who think the same but do not speak. There's some sense to what the letter says—what use was a clear-cut wilderness? What right do you have to cut so far beyond the point of the forest's recovery? These forgiving, soft-voiced reasons bulged into his head like the ballooning veins of an aneurysm.

Mackenzie heaved them aside. He wiped away all thoughts of weakness. Nothing more would be left to chance. He picked up his car phone and put a call through to American Airlines. He booked himself on a plane to New York, leaving from Portland the next morning. As he spoke to the booking agent, the phone tucked under his chin, he tore Gabriel's letter into so many pieces that when he let them go out the window, the shreds slipped from his hands like the petals of a crushed white flower.

Half a mile up the road, Dodge and Coltrane stepped out from the canopy of trees. They had been patrolling the woods since well before sunrise. Their clothes were dusted white and the dust was in the corners of their eyes and the corners of their mouths and when they swallowed, they could taste it. Their canteens were empty. Pine needles had gone down their collars and were scratchy between their bare necks and their shirts. Everywhere they went in the Algonquin, through each dark stand of pine, they felt as if they were being watched.

Mackenzie's Range Rover came rumbling toward them, sending up dust so thick it seemed to erase everything it passed. The Range Rover drew alongside them. Mackenzie powered down his window and stuck his head out. The dust cloud billowed past him and filtered into the trees. "Gentlemen!" he called. "How goes the war?"

Dodge and Coltrane squinted at the man. The cheerfulness in Mackenzie's voice was something they had not heard since before Pfeiffer's death and not very often before that.

"We found another bunch of spiked trees, sir." Coltrane found it difficult to speak with all the dust clogged in his windpipe. He reached instinctively for his canteen, but then remembered it was empty. His fingers glanced off the metal.

"Well." Mackenzie grinned. "Can't get them all."

"We'll be continuing the patrol later this afternoon," Dodge said, to fend off the charge of inefficiency he felt sure was coming.

"Right." Mackenzie nodded. He barely seemed interested. "Truly, gentlemen"—he scanned them both with his pale-blue eyes—"you don't have a chance of finding these people, do you?"

Coltrane stepped forward, boots shuffling in the dirt. "They'll slip up sooner or later. Alls we got to do is catch one of them."

"How many of them do you think there are?"

"We don't know," Dodge said. "Do you?"

"No, and that's my point. We know nothing about them. The only suspect you had was that guy who took over from Benny Mott."

"We kept an eye on him." Dodge made his case. "He doesn't go out at night. He doesn't leave town. I talked to him and he didn't seem nervous. I even searched the depot when he wasn't there. There's nothing suspicious."

"Has he been doing his job?"

"According to the comptroller in St. Johns, he's been doing as good as Mott."

"Mott." Mackenzie curled his lips around the word as if it were an obscenity. It was nothing personal. At that moment, he just needed to insult someone. "Anyway," Mackenzie said, "that's a dead lead."

"We think it's more likely to be someone local. Someone who knows the woods." Coltrane needed to rest. It had been a long day. He wanted to sit down right where he was and let Dodge and Mackenzie carry on the conversation without him.

"What about Lazarus? He hates everybody." Mackenzie smiled at his own suggestion—the idea of Booker Lazarus running through the woods.

Dodge breathed out sharply through his nose. He knew Mackenzie was just making a joke of it. "Lazarus doesn't have the strength to hammer in even one of those nails."

Mackenzie nodded, grinning. "You want a ride back to your car?" Mackenzie made the offer because he felt he had to, and he let his voice show it.

"No, sir." Dodge shook his head.

When the Range Rover had gone and its dust was settling, Coltrane turned to Dodge. "How come you didn't take the ride? It's a mile and a half to the patrol car."

"I don't want to ride with him. Do you?"

"I guess not." The sun had gone behind a cloud. In the softer light, Coltrane let the muscles around his eyes relax. Sweat-fused dust crumbled from his crow's-feet wrinkles.

"I tell you, Victor, we're fighting on the wrong damn side this time." Dodge strode off down the road.

Coltrane shuffled after him through the dust. He had never heard such anger in Dodge's voice. He knew Dodge was right. He just didn't know what to do about it.

At two in the morning, Mackenzie lay restless on his bed. It was always at night that doubt would creep around him. He thought of what Alicia had said about Ungaro. Then he thought about his father, and wondered what the old man would have done.

Abraham Mackenzie had been a compact little man, creaky-boned in winter, looking half-dehydrated and oiling himself each night like the Tin Woodsman in *The Wizard of Oz* with the heavy cream he drank before he went to bed. The man had lived by codes that made no sense to anyone but him, harsh rules with penalties for breaking them. Abraham never taught these rules. He just pointed out when they had been broken. Years after Abraham's death, Mackenzie would hear one of these maxims and cringe.

Of all the symbols of his father's life, none had frightened Mackenzie more than the image of the blood eagle. Abraham invoked this image as a threat against himself, like someone drawing down a curse, whenever his business was failing. He said it came from the time of the Vikings. "They chose their leaders for many reasons," Abraham told Mackenzie, "but the greatest reason was for their luck. And when the luck ran out, they turned the old leaders into blood eagles." That was all he would say about it.

Mackenzie imagined a mythic red bird, painting the clouds scarlet as it flew by. How a man could be turned into this, he had no idea. This bird soared through Mackenzie's dreams, with the same cold eyes and hard, hooked nose as his father.

Years after Abraham's death, he had asked an old college friend who was teaching Norse history at the University of Minnesota to find out the meaning of the blood eagle. What the friend told him was far worse than Mackenzie had imagined. As a punishment for failure, the Vikings would carve two gashes into a man's back. Then his lungs were pulled through the gashes, to flap like red wings as his last breaths carried him off to death.

Mackenzie remembered the day his father handed over the company. It was one week before the old man died. He had walked into his father's study with a briefcase, ready to take the company's insurance documents away with him. It was Indian summer. The cold had come and the maple leaves had turned all shades of red and amber and marmalade and gold. Then the chill subsided for a day, the last gasp of warm air before hard winter set in. Abraham sat at his desk in the pale sunlight, which ran like water into the crystal decanters racked up on the mantelpiece. Small copper plates hung by chains around the necks of the bottles, listing the names of the drinks. The crystal contained the light, and compressed it and then threw it from the angled sides in rainbows. The square Seth Thomas clock standing alongside the decanters struck the half hour with delicate chimes, as if the crystal itself were ringing.

Mackenzie had never seen his father so tired. He had the white-faced look of an old golden retriever. Now that his work was over, age had flooded through and overtaken him. The years of work had ground him down until he was all foggy like a piece of sea glass. "Wealth dies," he said. "People die. But the only thing that never dies is the judgment on how a person has spent his life." The man's hair hung illuminated like some shabby halo around his skull. His hands rested on the blotter of the desk in front of him, fingers crooked with age. "So how do you judge me now?"

Mackenzie had no answer. He had never thought to judge his father. Mackenzie had always assumed it was himself who was being judged.

All night Mackenzie could not sleep. He lay there watching the lace curtains billow in the breeze that came down off the mountain, like the drifting veils of ghosts come to his window. He kept thinking of the blood eagle. The verdict on each person dead.

*O*n a humid July afternoon in New York City, Mackenzie walked into the air-conditioned chill of the Yale Club, across the street from Grand Central Station. He was there to meet Sal Ungaro. He went up a wide staircase, past a rail of the fence that used to ring the old Yale campus, to the large sitting room filled with the sound of rustling newspapers. The huge, yellow-curtained windows did not let in much light. The massive building opposite cut out the sun.

Mackenzie found himself a chair and sat down. He set his trenchcoat in the chair beside him. It was a deep leather chair with brass rivets and a smell of tobacco smoke sunk into the hide. After a few minutes, a man at the other end of the room stopped reading the pink pages of a *Wall Street Journal* and walked over to Mackenzie, not smiling, trenchcoat slung over his arm.

Mackenzie thought it was typical of Ungaro to have arrived early. It was all about having the edge. Mackenzie could not recall a meeting with Ungaro, not a conversation or a meal or a joke told or a glance by which Ungaro did not try to gain an edge. Salvatore Ungaro had been at Yale with Mackenzie. He was a thick-necked man with heavy hands. His face was round and made rounder by the fact that he was bald. His ears were small and set back against his head like those of an angry cat. He was perpetually tanned, which almost but not quite hid the dark smudges below his eyes. They gave him the look of a man who never slept. He wore spread-collar Turnbull & Asser shirts and Hermès ties and Lobb shoes. His suits were double-breasted Gieves custom-mades, so perfectly fitted that most men who approached him immediately began to feel uncomfortable in their own clothes. It was the way Ungaro walked that let him down. He loped about as awkwardly as the artificial-legged Mackenzie. Ungaro was not muscular or tall. He had been forced at an early age to compensate for his lack of physical strength by being vicious.

Mackenzie remembered Ungaro as someone who was always doing small favors for people that they didn't really need and didn't ask for. Then Ungaro would ask a favor in return that required a ridiculous amount of effort and seemed designed more for the pleasure Ungaro took in seeing people work for him than anything else.

Shortly after graduating, Ungaro had gone into a line of work that was never made clear, except that it was for the government. The rumor had reached Mackenzie that he was involved with smuggling German war criminals out of Europe into North or South America. During the Cold War, experts were needed to fight Communism; the only true experts were Nazis. So many deals were made that in the end the deal-makers themselves became criminals. Sal Ungaro disappeared, only to surface again two years later at the Yale Club, suntanned and half-starved and out of work. Nobody knew where he'd been.

From the start, Mackenzie did not like Ungaro. Nothing to trust—these three words became a catchphrase that people used when speaking about Sal, as if it had been the motto on a coat of arms assigned to him. Ungaro didn't expect to be trusted. He occupied a niche between people who wanted illegal jobs done but didn't want to get their hands dirty, and people who didn't mind getting their hands dirty but who had no way of getting in touch with the people who needed jobs done. He could acquire handguns, their serial numbers burnt off with acid, for acquaintances who thought they might need untraceable protection. He could produce passports, driver's licenses, license plates, immigration papers, green cards. Mackenzie had seen Ungaro arrange for second-term abortions, deliver unpleasant messages, make someone's life miserable. None of it was personal. That was why you could count on Ungaro to do the job. You didn't need to ask him how he did it. You just had to pay him a lot of money and then get as far away from him as you could.

Ungaro was there if you needed to fight dirty, and everyone Mackenzie ever knew who had survived had a deep and lasting knowledge of the methods of fighting dirty and had survived because they were prepared to use them. Ungaro was the button you could push when all honorable methods had failed.

"Thanks for coming, Sal." Mackenzie pulled his trenchcoat off the chair beside him so that Ungaro could sit down.

"It sounded serious." Ungaro threw his own trenchcoat onto the back of his chair. Its lining was the tan, red and black of a Burberry. Then he sat down, working his backside into the seat to be comfortable. "Did you come all the way here just to see me?"

"I did."

Ungaro folded his hands across his belly and flashed a smile. "Well, then it is serious. How's your family?"

Mackenzie ignored the question. He didn't want to make small talk. He leaned forward so he could lower his voice. Then he explained what had been happening. When Mackenzie was finished, he breathed deeply and sat back. "I need this done quietly. I need you to find me someone who will stop it."

"Stop it how? You mean with a court case? I'm not sure I'm the right—"

Mackenzie swept his hand in front of his face, cutting off Ungaro's words. "I don't have time for a court case. I'm working on a deadline. I don't want the press on my back. I want these people stopped completely and as soon as possible."

"Completely. I see." Ungaro sat forward and wiggled a finger in his ear, as if to make sure he had heard Mackenzie correctly. "That's the operative word, isn't it? You know, I'm not really involved in that sort of work anymore."

"But you can find someone who is," Mackenzie said with a fed-up voice, to show he had not come to play the game.

"No, you misunderstand me, Mac." Ungaro slowly pressed his thick-palmed hands together. "I'm just not involved anymore. Not at all. It's not even a question of money."

"It's always a question of money." Mackenzie hated asking Ungaro for help.

Ungaro swept his eyes over the pale yellowy walls and the ceiling far above them. The room was full of people now, all of them locked in conversation, heads bowed toward one another so that they could be heard above the mutter in the room. Nobody raised a voice here. They just leaned closer. Waiters in short blue uniform jackets delivered drinks, sidestepping the dozens of briefcases set down beside the chairs. Club numbers were muttered quietly to the waiters and the waiters walked back to the bar to start a tab. No money changed hands in this room.

Mackenzie knew full well that Ungaro had not left this line of work and would never leave it, because it was not in his nature to do so. Ungaro was just playing the game that all people like Ungaro loved to play, forcing Mackenzie to ask again and again for help. Making him beg. This was Ungaro's edge. He played it up like someone who hadn't felt the edge in a long time.

"I'm sure you can look up some of your old contacts, Sal." Mackenzie knew that now would be a good time to smile, but he could not bring himself to do it.

Ungaro wrapped his arms around his ribs, as if the room had grown suddenly cold. "Why don't you get us a couple of drinks? No, I'll tell you what. Why don't we have some champagne? Celebrate. We haven't seen each other in so long."

"Fine." He'll choose the Cristal Roederer, Mackenzie thought: $175 a bottle at this place.

Ungaro chose the Roederer.

The waiter opened the bottle, holding a towel over the mouth. At the dull pop, a few heads bobbed up from the huddles across the room. They knew that someone was either very happy or very desperate.

Ungaro inspected the bubbles before he drank the silvery liquid. "Why come to me, Mac? Can't you solve this by yourself?"

"No, I think I need some help at this point." Fucking Cristal Roederer, he was thinking.

"And your old friend Sal came to mind after all these years. Is that it?"

Mackenzie nodded solemnly. "That's it." Ungaro was sparing him nothing.

"You haven't been in touch, Mac." Ungaro rapped him on the knee in playful punishment. He was getting what he wanted.

"I know. I feel just terrible."

"It's a shame to neglect a friendship."

"Certainly it is, Sal."

"And now you need a favor." The politeness had gone suddenly and completely from his voice.

"No, Sal. Not a favor. Let's not call it that. I'm not asking you to do it for free."

"Oh, but it would be a favor. The kind of thing you're asking. No, I just don't think I—" Ungaro let his words disappear into the glittering champagne flute.

"Look, Sal"—Mackenzie measured a space in front of him, as if trying to cram his thoughts into a box—"you're the only one who can help me out of this." He's making me dance, Mackenzie thought. He looked at Ungaro and the words filed past behind his eyes—I hate you so fucking much I could kill you with one of my chain saws. But a different set of words unraveled from his mouth. "You really would be doing me a favor."

Ungaro helped himself to more champagne.

"Well, I really can't stay any longer." Mackenzie shifted in his chair, ready to stand. The idea flicked through his head, a sputtering candle flame of an idea, that perhaps he had misjudged Ungaro, and the man truly had a different life now. Mackenzie wondered if maybe he should stay and see this new man, see what was left of the grinning, slithering one he had known. He rose to his feet, frowning with uncertainty. "I'm sorry to have bothered you with this."

"Sit down for a second, Mac." Ungaro wafted his hand toward Mackenzie's chair.

Mackenzie slumped back, not quite gracefully, as if given a shove by Ungaro's words. There had been no misjudgment after all.

"Just how good friends are we?"

You bandy-legged fucker, thought Mackenzie. You're about to go too far. "You've always been a good friend of mine, Sal."

"I'm glad to hear it. I never really felt that, though. All through college. Always seemed as if you were trying to avoid me."

"I'm sorry you remember it that way, Sal."

"The truth is, Mac. I've fallen on hard times."

What's that mean? Mackenzie wanted to ask. You no longer have your $300 shirts made at Turnbull & Asser?

Ungaro kept talking, "If we weren't good friends, you and I, I'd never mention this. Of course I wouldn't."

Mackenzie felt a headache gathering at the base of his skull. "So you are interested?"

"Not really. I think you could say I am compelled."

Now Mackenzie sat back and drank some of the champagne that had been growing warm in his glass. The hard part was over, he knew. Now it would only be about money, and that he did not mind. Unlike with people, Mackenzie knew exactly how far he would go with money before a mental guillotine came down on his patience.

"This is a very delicate business," Ungaro muttered. "If it's not done properly, it puts us both at risk."

"I trust you completely, Sal." This is a day of Great Lies, Mackenzie announced to himself.

"But how much can I trust you, Mac? I'm asking myself how well I really know you. A thing like this—"

"Oh, I think you know me pretty well. And I hope you won't take this the wrong way, Sal." Mackenzie bowed his head toward the man. "But if you think I would have come all this way just to fucking buy you champagne, then you don't know me after all."

Ungaro's gaze seemed to soften a little, as if the two were finally speaking the same language. "All right, Mac."

Suddenly Mackenzie did not want to waste any more time on this fancy badminton with words. He told Ungaro he would pay thirty-five thousand dollars to have the job done. "I don't want a whole crew of people. I want one man. One woman, if you like. But one person to go into those woods and find whoever is hammering all those fucking nails into my trees. And then I want your employee to stop that person or those people. I really don't give a shit how."

"Give me five thousand to get it started." Ungaro's face was without expression. He had reached the part of bargaining that was sacred to him and not to be muddled with emotion.

Mackenzie pulled an envelope out of his breast pocket and from it he took fifty hundred-dollar bills, which were wrapped in bundles of ten with a yellow banker's band. There was more in the envelope, and Ungaro squinted to see how much.

"You shouldn't carry that much money in this city," Ungaro said.

Mackenzie stood, and for good this time. He put on his trenchcoat and tied the belt at his waist. "I always have to carry this kind of money when I talk to someone like you."

The two men paused for a moment outside the Yale Club. A humid wind was blowing down the street, making the whole city smell like the locker room in a gym. The blue-and-white Yale flag snapped in the breeze above them. "When you have your person," Mackenzie said, "call me. Send him to meet me, so that I can fill him in. You'll get half of the money up front and the rest when the work is done."

"Good to see you again, my old friend," Ungaro held out his hairy-knuckled hand.

Mackenzie just nodded good-bye, and kept his hands at his sides. This was a bigger insult than any parting words he could have heaved into Ungaro's face. It was payback for making him beg.

Ungaro's lips pursed slightly. Then his hand curled slowly in upon itself. "You know," he said slowly, his voice raised above the thundering engines of the city, "even if I can get this problem of yours stopped, it will probably come back. The conscience of the world is turning against the way you do your business. The days when you can just go in and clear out forests are numbered."

"What do you know about the conscience of the world?" You protector of Nazis, he wanted to say. You handshaker of butchers.

"I see the balance between what people say is justice and how far they are prepared to go to get that justice." There was no irony in his speech. "There's always a point when people have had enough. A line they refuse to cross. And from everything I know, you're a little too close to the line."

"You let me worry about that," Mackenzie said, but Ungaro had already turned away. He walked across the street with his loping stride, disappearing into the bowels of Grand Central Station.

When Ungaro had gone, Mackenzie stood still for a moment. He thought of a story Ungaro had told him about one of the Nazi doctors who had been smuggled to Brazil. The man had done experiments on

Polish prisoners of war. The experiments involved placing people in almost-freezing water and then trying to revive them again when they slipped into comas. They also put men in low-pressure chambers to see when their lungs collapsed. The information was used to treat pilots who had crash-landed in cold water, or whose pressurized cockpits had failed. The information was useful, Ungaro had explained, even if the results had been unethically obtained. Mackenzie thought to himself—if Ungaro had not found this reason to excuse himself, he would have found another. That's the kind of person I am dealing with. A destroyer of worlds. A zoot-suited Horseman of the Apocalypse.

Mackenzie raised his hand and flagged a cab. A trickle of sweat ran from between his fingers, across his palm and down the sleeve of his shirt. Six hours later, he was home, the constant rolling thunder of the city not yet faded from his bones.

ackenzie sat by himself at the Dutch Boy diner in Skowhegan. Ungaro had called that morning and told him to meet a man there. First, Mackenzie had to transfer the money into Ungaro's bank account. Now everything was in motion. Mackenzie had the feeling that events had slipped suddenly and completely beyond his control.

Mackenzie looked at the door whenever anyone walked in. Sometimes he kept his gaze on the person, hoping to make eye contact because he felt sure this was the one. Every time he raised his head, he caught sight of the sign out in front of the diner—a blond-haired boy in Dutch costume. The boy had a fat-lipped smile and stood with his arms folded and one wooden-shoed foot stuck out, as if frozen in the middle of a Cossack dance. The boy's clogs were outlined with glass bars of white neon. They lit up at night.

At last one man returned his stare. Mackenzie's hands clenched under the table. Despite all the mental preparation he had done, the face still caught Mackenzie by surprise. He looked like a college boy, square-chinned and heavy chested from bench-pressing weights. He wore hiking boots and slightly baggy khaki trousers tucked into his heavy wool socks. He walked with his hands in his pockets. His blue-jean jacket had a worn-out corduroy collar. The man walked over. He had rosy cheeks and dirty blond hair and eyes like old glacier ice.

"Hey," the boy said, and sat down. He moved confidently. "You are Mr. Mackenzie, right?"

Mackenzie nodded. Face-to-face with the person who would help him, he felt suddenly embarrassed to be needing the assistance.

The boy set his folded hands on the place mat. On the ring finger of his right hand he wore a gold college ring of the knuckle-duster type, with two lacrosse sticks in an X set into black enamel at the top. "Well, I hear you got some trouble, sir."

"A little." He listened to the boy's accent. South but not Deep South. Not Alabama south. Virginia maybe. Kentucky. The great-great-grandson of some Bowie-waving Rebel at Bull Run.

"Well, all we have to do here is find out who you think is causing your problem."

"How do you know Sal?" Mackenzie asked. Questions crammed Mackenzie's head. What on earth is a clean-cut boy like you doing in this job? Do your parents know? Do you do this for a living? Who the hell trained you? How much is Sal paying you? The questions jostled in his head, lining up to be asked.

"Friend of a friend. My name is Shelby." He extended his hand to MacKenzie.

Mackenzie shook the hand and felt its strength. He told Shelby how he thought Madeleine was either out there in the woods spiking the trees herself or was getting someone to do it for her. He mentioned Wilbur Hazard's death, but nothing more about it.

"Are the police still carrying out an investigation?"

"There's only one guy. He patrols the woods twice a day and once at night. It's not having any effect."

"And if it is who you think? Exactly how far are we going here?"

And here it is, thought Mackenzie. Of all the questions I have asked myself, this one I did not answer. "I just want them to stop."

"Good. Then that gives me some latitude."

"Take all the latitude you want, as long as you can make them quit." Just thinking about it made Mackenzie angry. "Have you been to Abenaki Junction before?"

"I've been there for the past four days. I passed your Range Rover on the way down here. I wanted to get a feel for the place before we met."

"I didn't see you around." Mackenzie felt old and slow. The boy was far ahead of him. The people who never play games, Mackenzie thought.

"No, I expect you didn't see me," said Shelby. The south twanged in his voice. "I'll see if this woman is spiking the trees. If she is, I will give her grief. But if it isn't her, we might have to meet again."

"Yes. I'll give you my number." Mackenzie fumbled for his notebook.

Before Mackenzie could write anything, Shelby rapped on the table with his knuckle-duster ring. "Good-bye, Mr. Mackenzie." He slipped out of the diner. No waitress had come to give him coffee. No one turned to watch him go.

Mackenzie looked out into the parking lot but did not see where Shelby had gone. Suddenly he knew who else Shelby reminded him of. It was the Dutch Boy. The one whose wooden shoes lit up after dark. Shelby the Dutch Boy. Mackenzie tried to laugh about it but only slumped further into quiet. He did not feel the cat's purr in his heart as control returned to his life, the way he had hoped he would. Instead, Mackenzie knew he had unleashed a wave of chaos into the neatly ordered streets of his town.

Shelby drove straight to Abenaki Junction. He parked his metallic-blue Honda Civic across the street from the *Forest Sentinel* office. For three hours, he watched who walked in and who came out. He thought it was a shame to be sitting in his car on a beautiful morning like this when he could have been out canoeing on the lake or climbing the mountain that rose up so steeply beyond the town.

Shelby thought how desperate Mackenzie had seemed, and how clumsily the man had tried to hide it. He wondered what kind of woman it was who could be running this paper and doing so much else on the side that she could send a man like Mackenzie out of control. Shelby had no doubt that the man was out of control, because that was when people like Mackenzie, who valued control above all other things, called for people like him. He knew the questions that Mackenzie had wanted to ask. Everyone thought the same thing when they met him. He was more surprised than anyone at how a bright Virginia boy like himself could end up in a job like this. At the University of Rhode Island, he had planned to study Ocean Sciences at the University's Bay Campus after his undergraduate work. The only way he could afford his time in school was to sign up for five years of military service after graduation.

Now, sitting in his car in the quiet Abenaki Junction street, Shelby wondered if, should his former self come walking down the street, that man would even recognize the person he became on the night he parachuted onto an airfield in Panama as a member of a Special Forces unit. He remembered how, on landing, he had become separated from the rest of his squad and run for the first piece of cover he could find, diving into a drainage ditch and feeling his bare hands sink into jellylike mud at the bottom. His eyes were stinging from the oil that filmed the ditch water. He could taste it in his spit. It raked at his throat like steel wool.

A Panamanian truck with a searchlight mounted on the back drove around the airfield. It seemed to plow up the ground with its harshly glaring beam. The truck stopped a hundred yards down the runway and began to play its light back and forth across the ditch water.

Shelby remembered taking the rounded bottle-shaped charge of a 40mm rocket-propelled grenade from his assault pack. He fitted it into the grenade tube under the barrel of his M-16.

His eyes felt as if they were on fire. They had never been the same since. Even now, as the memory returned, Shelby took his hands off the steering wheel of the Civic, closed his eyes and touched his fingertips against his lids to stop the pain.

When the Panamanian truck was fifteen yards away, Shelby had a strange feeling of standing outside himself, as if from a hundred feet up in the air, looking down without concern for the men in the truck or for the spidery shape that crouched in the ditch. He wondered at the time if this meant he was about to die, and already his soul was leaving his body, knowing what his heart did not yet know.

He undid the safety on his rifle and stood, the crumpled rainbows of oil making him slip. The truck was huge, almost on top of him. Shelby fired from the hip, and the round seemed to fly out slowly, hissing and wobbling through the air. The RPG splashed through the truck's windshield, and in the explosion that followed Shelby was thrown back by a wall of heat and concussion. Then he was under the ditch water. When he rose to the surface, the ditch was burning in patches of ignited oil. The truck was only the frame of a truck now. It roared with flames and sank down on the melting rubber of its tires. Ammunition exploded like a string of Chinese firecrackers.

Shelby felt his soul returning to his body. Suddenly he was whole again, and clinging to the earth. He lay there for a long time, watching the last yellow-orange flames burn out on the surface of the ditch water. He heard waves break and the clatter of seashells being dragged back down with the tide. When he raised his head from the ditch, he saw a pile of smoldering rags. One of the men who had been inside the truck. The body was whole, but shrunk into something almost baby size and leering like a gargoyle torn from the stonework of a church. The breath of its burning blew past him. He remembered the smell, and how for one disgusting moment it had reminded him of food.

The next thing he recalled clearly was standing in a chow line three days later, when all the fighting had finished, while army cooks slapped spoonfuls of scrambled egg and beans into the mess tin in his outstretched hand. In one of his pockets, he felt what he thought were dried apricots, which had been part of his rations when he landed at the airfield. But when he pulled them out into the light, he saw instead that they were human ears. He had no recollection of how they came to be there and felt none of the fury that would have driven him to take these gruesome souvenirs.

After coming back to the States, he received an early discharge from the service. He tried to make his way back into the ranks of old college friends, but it was as if a curtain had been drawn down between them. Too much had happened to him and, it seemed to Shelby, not enough to the friends he left behind. They helped him find jobs, but he didn't want to work and he didn't even want the kindness that went with their offerings. Time pushed past him. It was a simple fact, like the fact of dying, and he could not explain it to people who had planned out their lives around houses and cars and what vacations they would take. Shelby looked around and what he saw were people who were not dead but lifeless nonetheless. Wind just rustling the dried-out tongues in their mouths.

Then Shelby met Mr. Salvatore Ungaro. Or rather, Ungaro met Shelby. Tracked him down from God knows where, which, now that Shelby knew Ungaro well, did not surprise him at all. He had been working for Ungaro ever since. Some of the jobs were legal. Most weren't.

Sitting silently now in this car in the blue-sky Maine afternoon, Shelby felt as if his senses had been chiseled away until the only ones remaining were those that kept him alive. Shelby didn't know where the rest of him had gone. One day, perhaps, those lost fragments would belong to him again. Then he would go back to the world in which he used to live. But for now Shelby lived where he was comfortable—out in the dark, where things made sense to him.

At a quarter past five, a woman walked out of the *Forest Sentinel* office. Madeleine. Mackenzie had told him her name. She looked as if she had a lot on her mind. She was so far from the kind of person he had imagined would unhinge a man like Mackenzie that Shelby waited several minutes more, expecting someone else to emerge from the office. But no one did, and by now he had lost sight of the woman, so he could not follow her home.

There were instincts Shelby had come to trust since he began working for Ungaro. They told him when it was dangerous, who to trust and who not, and when he was on the right path. Now these instincts muttered to him. They told him that this woman was either very good at what she did, or she had nothing to do with Mackenzie's troubles. Shelby knew this job would take longer than he'd expected.

A bird shrieked in the trees above him.

Gabriel dropped down to his knees. His eyes struggled to refocus. Nothing. He had been spiking pines out in the woods near Coltrane's farm. Gabriel chose the areas at random, sometimes walking two or three miles into the woods and not following any trails so that he could lead people away from the idea that the railroad tracks were being used to deliver the spikes. Gabriel knew that these areas would be found eventually. It was not important that they be found all at once. In fact it was important that they weren't. He wanted to give the impression of many people working at the same time. He began to use the helix nails that Swain had left him. They were shorter than the bridge spikes, but twisted in such a way that once the heads were clipped off they could never be removed. They were harder to work into the wood, and the heads of his hammers were becoming badly dented. Even though he wore gloves, his hands were patched with calluses that bulged off the level of his palms.

Light filtered down through the trees, touching the ground only in places where white birches reached up their slim and bony trunks. There was no more sound. After a few minutes, Gabriel's breathing became regular again. He had come to rely on birdsong to warn him of anyone's approach. A great stillness had entered his body since he'd started working on the tracks. He could ride the rails now almost without thinking, his body swaying in and out of the turns. On clear mornings, his eyes narrowed automatically as he passed the sun-reflecting ponds. Now he knew the many shades of green, from the pale reeds beneath the Narrow River bridge to the dullness of the new pine needles. The green of wild strawberry leaves and the green of loganberry bushes. Green of mold on fallen trees and brassy green of the sky before it rained. And all these greens had facets of other greens in the different lights of day and shadow. He knew them all without thinking, as he moved through the wilderness without sound, relying as much on instincts that he didn't understand as on those he did, beyond all sight and smell and hearing.

He drank deeply from his canteen. It was a canvas-covered one that Mott had left. Printed on it was the pine-tree emblem of the US Forestry Service. The water was cold but metallic-tasting.

Then something moved.

It was not far away, perhaps thirty yards, at the edge of his vision before the trees became a solid wall. A large bear. The animal raised its head and sniffed the breeze, nose bobbing up and down. Its coat was shiny. The bear knew something was not right. It looked around, but couldn't see far through the trees. It kept sniffing the air. Then slowly it moved away in the direction of the farm.

Gabriel raised himself off the ground. He slapped the dust from his clothes. Then he sprayed the trees with red bands and was done for the day. He headed back toward the tracks and across the logging road. There was the sound of a logging truck in the distance. Just as he reached the sunlit part of the road, where the angle of the trees made no shadow, he saw the twin exhaust stacks of a truck jut like horns over a rise in the road. Then came the cab of the truck. The wind had played a trick on him. The truck was much closer than he thought. Gabriel had no time to think whether the driver of the truck had seen him. He sprinted across the road into the shadows.

The truck powered down a gear as it climbed the slope.

Gabriel hurdled the drainage ditch. Suddenly he slipped and felt a thump on the back of his skull as his head struck the ground. It blinded him for a second. Spoked wheels of sunlight glinted down through the trees.

The truck howled nearer, down another gear. Its chassis bounced on a pothole and the sound was like a gunshot.

Gabriel rolled, the thumping pain in his head shifting as he stood. He ran into the woods, not looking back. The truck seemed to be plowing after him into the woods. He moved with arms flailing like a drowning swimmer, swatting the branches away. At last exhaustion grabbed him and he dropped.

The truck was just visible. It rumbled in neutral. The cab was towing an empty flatbed.

Gabriel crawled behind a tree. He peered through the filter of branches as the cab's door opened and a man jumped down. He walked out in front of his truck and seemed to be staring directly at the place where Gabriel was hiding. The man had on a black watch cap. He wore his blue jeans tucked into tan leather work boots and his shirt was blue-and-black plaid, untucked and trailing down to his thighs. The man unzipped his fly and pissed into the drainage ditch. He sang a song that Gabriel either did not know or was being sung too badly for him to recognize. The man didn't sing the words. Instead, he made a noise like a guitar—*dar-nar-nar-nar-nar*—until he had finished his business. He bowed his legs slightly as he zipped up his fly. Then he fished a crumpled cigarette from his pocket.

Gabriel waited while the man smoked and picked his dirty nails. The smell of tobacco and pine sap drifted across the road and mixed in his lungs. Gabriel looked at his watch and realized that the VIA train was due down from the north in one hour, and would smash into his Putt-Putt if he didn't reach it in time. On the sharp bends that led into Abenaki Junction, even a small collision could derail the entire train. He broke out in a sweat that covered his whole body.

Five minutes later, the man stubbed out his cigarette and left. The dust from the truck had not even begun to settle before Gabriel was running for the tracks. As he ran, he pulled the liquid-filled compass from his pocket and took a bearing. He reached the tracks a hundred feet away from the Putt-Putt, ran to it, threw in his duffel bag and started the machine. He swiveled the seat around so that he was facing back toward town, took hold of the second set of gears and drove, leaning into the turns with the Putt-Putt's engine racing.

He heard it then. The train's whistle back in the woods. Depending on the wind's direction, it could have been ten minutes away or it could have been two.

The Putt-Putt wouldn't go any faster. Gabriel knew the train would never be able to slow down in time. Images ricocheted through his mind of what would be left of him and the Putt-Putt after the VIA train had struck.

He sped across the Narrow River bridge and heard the whistle again, a high moan echoing off the Pogansett. With the heel of his hand, Gabriel pushed the red handle of the accelerator hard against the control panel.

He passed the Booths' cabin, with its white walls and green trim, on his left. Some people were there now, but he didn't recognize them. He saw a tall woman with blond hair wearing shorts and a bikini top and a man in khakis and a dark-green shirt. Both waved at the Putt-Putt. Gabriel was too frantic to wave back and he saw the look of disappointment on their faces when he did not return their greeting. He could not think about that now. He craned around in his seat and saw the snub mountain of the VIA engine as it rounded a bend in the distance. The whistle blew again. Gabriel bent farther forward, like a sprinter leaning into the finish tape of a race, as if that might make the creaky-motored Putt-Putt go any faster.

The fallen-in shacks at the edge of town snapped past. The jabber of birds rose screeching into his ears and faded.

The whistle blew again. The driver had seen him now. The moan grew longer and more urgent. The train could be slowed down a little, but not much. Not with eighty freight cars.

The siding was close. Gabriel could see the tarpaper roof of the depot. The crossing-guard bell was clanging and the railroad lights flashed red. Cars stopped behind the tracks as the red-and-white boom lowered to let the train pass.

The whistle was a constant shriek in Gabriel's ears. He thought about jumping, but everywhere he looked there seemed to be broken bottles and old nails and stones.

The tracks were shaking with the force of the train's approach. Gabriel could feel it, like thunder channeled through the iron rails. He looked over his shoulder and saw the massive face of the engine, the mesh grille across the windows and the light on like a door open to a furnace. It was so close it seemed to him he could smell the engine. The whistle deafened him.

He careened onto the siding, switched off the ignition and jammed his foot on the brakes. They squealed and he smelled burning. He held his hands up over his head to stop the shock. For a moment, he imagined that the train had veered onto the siding as well. The brakes were burning out. Foul smoke billowed behind him.

The Putt-Putt slammed into the buffer, which was padded with layers of old tire rubber. Gabriel sprawled across the steering wheel, the air punched out of his lungs. Everything that was not strapped down flew forward and clattered around the Putt-Putt's cabin, raining down on him in small sharp things and broken things and splashes of lukewarm coffee from his smashed thermos flask, then jangling outside onto the ground. Gabriel looked up in time to see Alain Labouchere lean out of the side window of the engine. He was laughing. He and Benny Mott had raced this way before. They knew it was a dangerous game, but they played it anyway, and they laughed because their luck had always held. Gabriel felt too relieved to be angry. The train sped past. The clunking rhythm of its wagons. The door was open in one of them, and two hobos with scraggy beards and sunburned cheeks sat with their legs dangling down, their bundles dumped beside them. Then suddenly the train had gone. The sound of it faded away.

Gabriel felt sweat clammy as it cooled under his arms, down his sides and on his dirty face. He turned on the Putt-Putt's ignition and was surprised to hear it start. Gabriel eased his way out of the cab like an old man with arthritis, and walked around gathering up the wrenches and oilcans and screwdrivers that had come flying out of the Putt-Putt. He looked around to see if anyone had noticed him crash into the buffer, but if anyone had, he was no longer paying attention.

By the time he reached home that evening, it was pouring. Clouds shredded across the top of Seneca Mountain and hung their ripped bellies down over the lake. Gabriel pulled up the hood of his Grundig raincoat. The *pat-pat* of water on the rubberized canvas drowned out all other sounds except that of cars passing close by him on the road, their tires hissing over the blacktop. His wrists were cold in the downpour because the sleeves of his coat, which had once belonged to Mott, did not come down far enough.

Gabriel had almost reached his house before he realized that someone was standing by the door. He breathed in sharply and stepped back.

A person walked out of the shadows, across the creaking boards.

By the light of a streetlamp, Gabriel saw it was Madeleine. His shoulders slumped with relief. "You gave me a shock," he said and climbed up onto the porch.

"I have some bad news," she said. Her hair was wet and hung in ringlets across her face.

"Well, come in." Gabriel unlocked the door and swung it open. He felt the corkscrew of worry in his stomach. She wouldn't have come unless it was serious. Gabriel followed Madeleine into the house. Its smell was familiar to him now and he carried it in his lungs and in his clothing.

Madeleine didn't wait for him to ask. "Mackenzie has hired a man to track you down." She had just found this out from Alicia, who was close to panic when she had run into the *Forest Sentinel* office with the news. "He's some kind of professional. I don't know if he's coming or whether he's already here."

Gabriel said nothing. He unbuttoned his raincoat and hung it on a peg by the door. Then he knelt down and unlaced his boots, which he also set by the door. He walked over to the bed and sat down. He looked dazed by the news.

Madeleine sat down beside him. "Are you all right?" she asked.

"I don't know," he said. He smoothed wrinkles from the red-and-black Hudson's Bay blanket on the bed. Then he looked up suddenly. "Do you remember when they used to send up fireworks over the lake on the Fourth of July? I used to sit where I'm sitting now and watch them explode over the water." Just then he needed to find something in common with her that was not spoken in the war talk of what their lives had become. He wanted to fill in the huge blanks that still kept a part of them as strangers to each other. Gabriel didn't know how he would cope with this new danger. He didn't see how he could go on working in the forest while a man who made pain for a living was out there hunting him down. He wondered what he would have to do in order to survive the days ahead, and whether he would lose whatever remained of his humanity in the violence he felt sure was coming.

Madeleine remembered the fireworks. She had stood with the crowd at the edge of the lake and watched the great flowers of sparks spread and drop and disappear into the night sky. She understood why he would speak of something other than the danger. Madeleine recalled the way he had seemed before. All avenues of possibility mapped out. All reactions planned in advance. She was seeing him for the first time as he really was, without the mask of his ideals to shelter him.

"You could leave town," she said. "I doubt you would be followed."

"But this is my home." He lifted his hands, palms up. "It was before and now it is again."

"I think you're in a lot of danger."

Gabriel nodded, lower lip clamped between his teeth. Then he turned to face her. "But he's got to catch me first," he said, and smiled weakly.

She reached up and touched his cheek with the palm of her hand.

Gabriel felt the warmth of her brush through him, and it brought to the surface all that he had tried to hide away. She leaned toward him and he closed his arms around her, sweeping across the smoothness of her back.

Her arms were around him, too, and she felt the buckle of his belt press into her stomach and his breath across her neck and the sharpness of his unshaven chin along the delicate outline of her ear. She pressed her hands to his face and kissed him until she was dizzy behind her eyes. She ran her fingers through his hair, smelling the pine-tar soap he used, and pulled him down on top of her. The old bedsprings creaked. She had closed her eyes while she was kissing him and now she opened them again. His eyes were open, too, and so close that they were out of focus. It was then she remembered that she did not know Gabriel. All she knew was his ideals, and even if she was in love with them, it was not enough. She realized what she had not known before. She was in love with someone else.

Gabriel watched a glassiness come to her eyes. He understood what she was thinking and sat up.

Then they were both shy and looked away.

Gabriel lay down beside her on the too-small bed and she fell asleep with her head on his chest. He smelled her hair and ran his fingers through it and imagined how it might be to lie beside her more than just this once. He was not lonely anymore, even though he knew that when she woke she would walk out and this would never happen again. Sometimes, he was thinking, you run into people and after five minutes it is as if you've known them all your life. But that knowledge is fragile. Something always seems to come along to make them strangers again. As close as they were, too much still lay between them. Gabriel found himself wondering if she had ever been one of the voices to call back to him when he had sung out the Old Man Tucker song in the woods however many years ago it was.

Then Gabriel's thoughts turned to Mackenzie and the man who had been hired to track him down. It would not be long before the man found out who he was. He remembered what Swain had said about knowing when to quit, and until today he might have said the time was now. But in the moment he had raised his hands to Madeleine and said "This is my home," he realized he would not be leaving once his work was done here. Not if he could stay. Before, he had planned to move on and exorcise this place and all its memories from his mind. But he could not do that, could not start again somewhere else.

He left Madeleine sleeping on the bed, easing her head onto a pillow, and went over to where he kept the Webley revolver. He fetched out the gun from its hiding place beneath a floorboard where, as a young man in this house, he had kept a bottle of slivovitz plum brandy, knocking back the clear and burning liquid late at night while he sat on the windowsill, feeling the breeze off the lake on his alcohol-numbered face. He unwrapped the gun from its cloth and then unpacked the bullets from their waxed-paper case. With the cloth he wiped the thin gun oil from the barrel and the grip and then wiped the bullets in the oil. He opened the gun, which cracked the way a shotgun cracks to load. Then he filled the chambers, checking each bullet for rust as he slid it into the breech. He would carry that gun from now on and for the first time he knew he would use it. He stashed the gun in his boot by the door and went back to lie beside Madeleine.

The rain had stopped now. Stray drops plipped off the gutters.

When Madeleine woke, it was late in the night. Gabriel was asleep next to her. She did not need to wake him, or to say good-bye. They would see each other again. They had gone as far as they could go and turn back and still be friends. Madeleine was not filled with regret. She knew she might never have been sure about Dodge if it had not been for Gabriel and these past few hours spent beside him. All her life, Madeleine had been trying to find a balance between a love of people and a love of ideals, thinking that she could never have both. And what she realized now was that a worship of either extreme would reduce her life to misery. There had to be some middle ground, and now she had found it.

Madeleine slipped out into the dark and walked home through the empty streets. She thought how peaceful Gabriel had looked asleep, and then she wondered how long it would be before this town became a combat zone.

She was wrong about Gabriel. In his dreams he was not peaceful. He had gone to the place where he had often been before, hunted like an animal through the green and shadowed labyrinth of the forest. When he opened his eyes an hour later, it was still dark outside and he was covered in sweat. He had known that Madeleine would leave when she woke up and the worst thing he could do was try to make her stay. Still bleary-eyed, Gabriel pulled on his boots and stuffed the Webley in his coat pocket. Then he took up his duffel bag and headed back out into the forest.

*T*he Milky Way pushed back the other stars, spreading a blue-steel halo across the sky. Gabriel was moving through the woods. His joints ached from lack of sleep. As he passed through an area of clear-cut, he smelled the torn earth and sap on the tree trunks that lay uprooted on the ground, their roots like crooked fingers reaching up into the air. The soil was soft and clotted on his boots. Once he trod on an empty soda can. The metallic crackle dropped him to the earth in search of cover, the Webley yanked from his pocket and its hammer cocked before he realized where the noise had come from.

He had brought with him his angle-headed military flashlight with a red filter over the bulb, but he did not need it. The red filter would have kept his night vision and made the light harder to track, but the moon was bright enough to see by. He had stopped at the cache and picked up more supplies. They were heavy, and he was covered in sweat from the effort of carrying them. Mosquitoes whined in his ears. In the distance, he could hear cars on the road that ran past Coltrane's farm.

Gabriel reached the logging track and stopped. He was worried about leaving footprints on the road, so he pulled an old pair of socks over his boots. It was a trick he had learned out west. As Gabriel advanced through the trees, he could distinguish the silhouettes of flat-bed Magirus and Mercedes and Volvo trucks, Case, Komatsu and Mitsubishi bulldozers and a road grader made by CAT. He could smell the damp-oil reek of the machinery. The day had been warm, and now as the metal cooled, it clicked and muttered to itself. The machines were parked by the side of the logging road, all painted yellow with their company names in black on the side. The steel had rusted through dents in the wasp-colored paint. The huge tires had treads four inches deep. Gabriel ran his hand over the teeth of the bulldozer, worn shiny and blue in the moonlight. They looked like dinosaurs. Some of this road-building equipment, Gabriel guessed from his scouting trips, had been sitting here for weeks, unused. But the flatbeds were used every day, and the bulldozers too, skidding down the slopes with their shovels serving as brakes, peeling off the top layers of soil as they cleared the land.

Gabriel had brought with him a funnel, some heavy wire cutters and a loaded grease gun.

He knew that it would be possible to damage the vehicles just by pulling out or cutting any wires he could find, slashing tires and ripping the stuffing out of the driver's seat. This might keep them out of action for a number of days. But he only had one chance, so the damage he did was permanent. He moved from machine to machine, removing the oil-filler caps and pouring in handfuls of powder-fine graphite sand. Then he carefully wiped away any spilled grains from around the cap. After that, he took the grease gun from his bag and pumped grease into the lubrication zerk points at each joint in the machinery. Before he left home, he had emptied half of the grease from the gun and replaced it with the graphite. Now he pumped the grease and graphite mix into the lubrication points. After a few hours of use, the sand would have dispersed itself throughout the engine lubricating system and would begin to grind up the insides. The graphite-grease mixture would also do irreparable damage. Gabriel knew that by the time the engines showed signs of breaking down it would be too late. The vehicles would have to be towed away and their engines dismantled completely. Most would be beyond repair.

The work took him a little over an hour. Every few minutes, he crouched down and listened, but there was only the booming sound of wind gusting over Coltrane's fields, and the traffic on the road, becoming less frequent as the night grew deeper.

Coltrane sat in the Loon's Watch. It was almost closing time, but the bar was still crowded. There had been no work that day at the Mackenzie Company. The mill had completely closed down while each log was inspected for nails. There weren't enough detectors to keep everyone busy, and at least half the workforce had been given the day off, this time with no wages. Now the men talked about the bills they had to pay.

Coltrane would normally have been at home and asleep by now, but he had promised to help Dodge patrol the Algonquin that night. He lifted his mugful of the local north Maine beer called Gracey's, took a drink and felt the bubbles crackling against the insides of his cheeks. It was his first time in the woods at night since he'd been stabbed. These days, Coltrane could not look at a knife without feeling the cold pinch of being cut. He couldn't look up at the sky on a clear night without remembering how it was to lie in dirty water at the bottom of a canoe and have his life sputtering out like a candle with the wick burned down.

Half an hour later, Coltrane and Dodge stood at the yellow metal gate that marked the entrance to the Algonquin Wilderness. Martha had driven them to the head of the logging road and then taken the car away.

Dodge took a wine cork and burned it with Coltrane's lighter. Then he blew out the flame and spread the black across Coltrane's face. "Like war paint," he said. Dodge's face looked ghoulish in the light of the Zippo's reeking flame.

Coltrane tried to hold his breath so that the sour smell of beer would not reach Dodge. He wished he hadn't had the drink. It only made things worse on his nerves.

They jumped up and down on the spot to check that none of their gear was rattling. Each carried a flashlight, a canteen and their gun belts. It was the middle of the night when they headed into the Algonquin.

"We got no better chance of finding someone tonight than we did last time. And that was in daylight," Coltrane whispered.

"At least we're out here." Dodge was barely listening. The faces of centuries-dead Algonquin Indians shimmered from the pillared darkness. He wished he had not painted his own face, as if in invitation to the ghosts.

The rain was falling again and the woods seemed filled with footsteps. Water slithered through the chinks in their raingear and their bodies shrank away from the cold. They walked to the end of the logging road, where it disappeared into piles of gravel and cut tree branches.

"Why don't we just go to the Booths' cabin and sit on the porch all night?" Coltrane told himself that if Dodge quit, then it was all right for him to do the same. And even going to the Booths' cabin, where his blood was still dried into the wooden floorboards, was better than sitting in the woods.

"We have to do this, Victor, even if it is almost useless. We have to do it because it's all we can do."

They found the trailhead, took out their flashlights, and headed into the forest. Stones on the path glimmered like drops of spilled mercury. Now and then, Coltrane stopped and swung the beam of his light among the trees, but all they saw were the shuddering leaves of the white birches, and the darkness ready to lunge at them again as soon as the light swung away. Dodge kept his flashlight aimed at Coltrane's heels. He couldn't hear anything except the rain. Someone could have walked past ten feet away from him and he would not have seen.

There was a shriek. The dark came crashing into Dodge and he cried out. His flashlight went spinning into the trees. He hit the ground, hard rocks under him, and heard Coltrane howling in confusion. Dodge rolled into the forest, struggling through the layers of raingear for his gun. He felt his nose begin to bleed and his eyes fizzed full of painful tears. He spat the blood off his lips, and tasted the blood mixed with the gritty bitterness of burnt cork. Dodge crawled through the dead leaves. Coltrane was shouting something, but

Dodge did not know what. His hand closed on the gun butt and he pulled it from the holster. Dodge rolled onto his back and held the gun out at arm's length, his eyes useless in the night and the rain.

Coltrane stood on the path, looking hunchbacked in his rainclothes. He held the light toward something that blocked his way.

At first, Dodge thought it was a fallen tree. Then he saw it was a moose, nine feet tall at the tips of its fuzz-covered antlers. Coltrane and the animal stood frozen in the glare of the flashlight, each terrified of the other.

Dodge let the gun drop slowly down to his knee. His heartbeat was so out of control that he felt as if he were being slapped rhythmically in the face.

Coltrane switched off the light.

Blindness swam into Dodge's eyes.

When Coltrane switched the light on again, the path was clear. He aimed the beam into the woods, but the woods were empty. The huge animal had disappeared without a sound. Then Coltrane shined the light in Dodge's face.

Dodge waved his hand, as if to swat the beam away. He crawled around until he found his own flashlight, spitting the last trickles of blood from his lips.

They set off again, this time with Dodge in front. The two men had been walking for several hours when they heard the long wail of the night train coming down from Canada. The sound was muffled by the rain. The woods ended suddenly. The canopy of trees pulled back and they found themselves at the tracks. The rails flashed their lights back at them. The dull line of tracks converged into the forest. The wail came again, closer now, and then the first winking glare of the train's beams sparked in the distance.

Dodge and Coltrane turned off their flashlights and stood back from the tracks. Out in the open, the rain fell harder but not as noisily. They felt the clamminess of raingear against the bare skin of their arms.

The rails *pinged* as the train came close, the headlight not winking now but steady and growing. The sound of the engines made a single unchanging rumble through the Algonquin. All other sounds were lost to it. The huge snub face of the VIA engine grew and grew and was suddenly almost on top of them, booming in their ears. The wind was in their faces. One, two, three, four engines. All deafening giants.

The two men squinted from the force of it. The passing cars were like houses of coal and then suddenly cars that were not dark. They saw people walking about, or sitting or sleeping. A dry, calm bubble in the middle of this thunder, having no idea that eyes were on them from outside. Thinking it was only the great darkness of the woods. Then the cars were dark again. Cargo wagons clattered by. And then the caboose, with a light to fend off the darkness that came careening in after it.

It was in that light that both Coltrane and Dodge clearly saw a man standing on the other side of the tracks. He was dressed in black and his face was also blackened and the only thing to bounce back any light were his blue eyes.

"Jesus," Coltrane said quietly. Ever since Hazard's death and the discovery of more spiked trees, Coltrane had felt as if he and Dodge were not on the trail of anything human, but a supernatural presence, which at any moment could explode from the forest and kill them, the way No Ears had butchered his dogs. And now, staring at this figure only a few feet away, Coltrane didn't know whether he was in the presence of a man or Death himself, who had come up to finish the job.

The man was gone. They heard the thrashing of his footsteps as he ran away.

Dodge sprinted after him, leaping over the tracks made warm by the huge metal wheels, and then skidded down the slope onto the other side. Coltrane followed, the beam of his flashlight igniting the raindrops. Then the beam found the man in black and locked on him. He was following the path that led up the side of Seneca Mountain.

Dodge knew that when this man left the path, they would have only a few seconds before he lost himself in the maze of trees. He raced after the man with all his strength.

The ground was beginning to slope. Coltrane was already falling behind, exhausted by fear and the pain of his wound.

The man in black tried to evade the flashlight's beam, as if the light itself would bring him down. Then he swerved into the trees.

Dodge jumped off the path after him. The cold air raked at Dodge's throat. He didn't know how long he had been running now. He did not reach for his revolver, because he was afraid that if he took his eyes off the man even for a second, he would lose him. "Will you Goddamn slow down?" he called. "I'm not against what you're doing!"

The man's steps faltered, as if confused by what he had heard.

Dodge ran faster, gaining on him.

Then the figure in black stopped suddenly, hunched down as if prepared to take the impact of Dodge slamming into him.

Dodge ran faster, holding his arms up, ready to bring the man down.

Then the man turned and suddenly Dodge was staring at the squared-off barrel of a Glock pistol. He threw his arms up and tried to stop, but his momentum kept him going. Dodge tipped over and fell hard against the ground. He skidded on until he came to within a few feet of the man.

The figure stood his ground, keeping the gun level with Dodge's head.

Now the two of them were motionless except for their heaving chests. The beam of the flashlight in Dodge's hand shuddered up into the trees.

"I'm a police officer." Dodge choked back spit.

The words brought no movement from the man in black. The barrel of the gun stayed pointed at Dodge's face. His breathing changed pitch. He opened his mouth as if to speak. Then he stepped forward, gun held out.

Dodge closed his eyes tight and gritted his teeth.

The man in black kicked the flashlight from Dodge's right hand. It flew against a tree and smashed and went out. Then the man was running again, footsteps quickly fading.

Dodge did not try to follow. He clenched and unclenched his right hand to see if any bones were broken. He felt as if a couple of his fingernails might have been torn off. Blood trickled onto the heel of his palm, then down his wrist and into his sleeve. He let his head fall back and closed his eyes and let the rain touch his face.

"Marcus!" Coltrane called from somewhere down the slope. The beam of his flashlight stabbed holes in the dark. "Marcus!" He scrambled hand over foot to the place where Dodge lay. "Oh, Christ," Coltrane whispered, and dropped to his knees in front of Dodge. He tucked the flashlight under his arm so he could use his hands and still see. His hands hovered over Dodge, not daring to touch. "Oh, God, what did he do to you, Marcus?"

"I lost him." Dodge breathed out in a sigh.

"What happened to you? I couldn't keep up." Coltrane held his hands against his chest and moaned, rocking back and forth. "Oh, I knew we shouldn't have gone into the woods. I knew it the first time! This is all my fault."

Dodge cupped his right hand in his left and felt the pain in his bruised fingers. "I'm all right."

"No, you aren't. Oh, Jesus." Coltrane was crying. "Oh, what are we going to do?"

"We're going to get up and walk out of here, Victor." Dodge clambered to his feet and now stood looking down at Coltrane.

"You're standing!" Coltrane sat on the ground, looking up in awe at Dodge.

"Of course I'm standing."

"So you're all right?"

"I told you I was." Dodge held out his good hand and helped Coltrane to his feet. "He had a gun. He aimed it right at my head." Dodge's back hurt him where he had fallen.

"I thought you were dead!" Coltrane smeared tears and rain and burnt cork across his face with his fingers. "I'm a lousy friend to you. I can't even watch your back. Oh, I'm no fucking good!"

"What are you talking about?" Dodge scratched at his neck.

Coltrane said a few more times that he was no good, thinking of the silence he had kept and how he'd be paying for it the rest of his life unless he set things straight somehow.

Dodge stood there patiently, his nose plugged up with blood, waiting for Coltrane to finish cussing himself. When Coltrane was finished, they started walking down the slope. Dodge's ring finger and index finger were throbbing. Pain gnawed into the place where his little fingernail had been. "I wonder who he is," Dodge said. "I wanted to talk to him."

"And he wanted to shoot you." Coltrane gave him a tap on the arm with the flashlight.

The light went out.

Coltrane shook the flashlight and the batteries rattled inside. "Oh, shit." He aimed the thing at his face and switched it on and off and there was still no light, so he stuffed it in the pocket of his raincoat.

It was pitch-black. Rain pattered the leaves. The two men groped their way from tree to tree until they hit the tracks. Then they started walking toward town. The sun was coming up as they moved across the iron bridge. The sky was bands of purple, pink and blue. They started thinking about food. The Four Seasons would be open by now.

Coltrane was already scanning the menu in his head. "I wish I knew what it is about the Algonquin that's making him do all this. I mean, why wouldn't he pick some huge stand of redwoods out in the Pacific Northwest?"

"Because it's the Algonquin." For Dodge, nothing more needed to be said. It was all clear to him, and had been for a while.

Coltrane was silent. He threw his busted flashlight off the bridge. It plopped into the black river water.

They walked straight to Mackenzie's house and woke him up. "Dressed in black," Coltrane said, "and carrying a forty-five as well. It could have been a woman. I mean, it looked like the person had a chest, or something tucked under there."

Mackenzie stood in his doorway. He wore a gray dressing gown which had twisted black and yellow braid around its edges. The dressing gown was falling apart. Its lining hung down in tatters around Mackenzie's knees. "Is this true?" he barked at Dodge, as if he could not take Coltrane's word on anything.

"All of it," said Dodge. He kept his right hand in his pocket. Blood had gathered black and painful under the nails. "What surprised me is that there was only one person. If there were more, they would have been working together and we would have seen them."

It's Madeleine, thought Mackenzie. She's the kind who'd have a gun tucked away someplace, and who'd be in good enough shape to outrun Dodge and Coltrane. He wished he had been there, to use all the strength he had left in the world and catch her and sink his hands, purple-bruising, into her neck. He almost said her name out loud, it seemed so clear to him. But he kept silent. He no longer wanted Dodge to catch Madeleine. That job was Shelby's now, and Shelby would get the job done.

≡

Shelby ran halfway up Seneca Mountain before he stopped to see if he was being followed. Twice he had run smack into trees and now one of his teeth was chipped. He could feel it, ragged and stabbing pain up through his jaw. He estimated the cost of repair and deducted it from the money he'd be getting for this job. Rage skulked wild-eyed and rabid in the corners of his mind.

He had been drawn from his hiding place by the sound of the train, wanting to stand as close to the tracks as he dared and feel the force of the train hurtling by. And then those two men had appeared, and he had almost laughed out loud, it seemed like such bad luck. Shelby promised himself no more mistakes.

He knew he could have outrun that policeman much more easily if he had not been carrying so much gear. Strapped to his chest was a starlight scope, for viewing infrared. It could be used as a sniper scope, but he had brought it along to observe any movement along the track. The scope weighed almost twenty pounds. It had cost him over a thousand dollars and he could not afford to ditch it.

He did not know how close he had come to shooting the policeman. Probably closer than the policeman would ever want to know. He would have to be much more careful now, because these two men, possibly others as well, were searching for the same people he was. Shelby knew he had to get there first. Mr. Ungaro had been very clear on that. The only thing that had not been clear was exactly what should be done with the tree spikers when Shelby found them. Shelby knew from experience that Ungaro's lack of clarity meant he didn't care if these people ended up dead.

Now, with the rising sun, and the rain only leftover drops finding their way down from leaf to leaf to the ground, Shelby walked back toward town. He did not stick to the path, but kept inside the woods. Bands of sunlight burned and faded in the clearings, as clouds began to scatter overhead. Just as he reached the Narrow River bridge, he heard a noise, the awkward thrash of footsteps in the bushes. The silhouette of a man was already above him, flickering past the spacers of the bridge. Shelby slipped into the reeds, leaving barely a ripple behind. He let himself sink below the surface. The cold clamped against his chest and he felt his hands sink down into the mud. Shelby lay there like a drowned man, the air growing hot in his lungs.

It was Gabriel that Shelby heard. As he climbed up to the tracks and crossed the Narrow River bridge, he heard his footsteps echo off the steel. They bounced back from the water ten feet below. Suddenly Gabriel had a feeling that he was being watched. He stopped and looked out at the lake and the bushes near the water's edge. There was no sound except water lapping at the bridge pilings. It was not the first time he'd felt this. Sometimes even the trees seemed to have eyes. But this was different. He had a sense of being stared at by another person, and that this person was very close by, wearing the night and the fog. Gabriel waited for a moment longer, mouth half open to hear better, sweat cooling on his back. Nothing. He told himself his mind was playing tricks, and kept moving toward town.

In the predawn mist packed like clay between the trees, the reeds beneath the bridge began to shift. Then up from the mud and the tea-brown water rose a face. The body followed, slipping from the swampy ground, and then a figure waded to the bank. It was Shelby, dripping ooze like the first of his species coming to life. He eased himself down onto the gravel and rested his back against the stone foundation of the bridge.

He knew he had almost compromised his position again. Again he felt the anger. Now it was more like disgust. Shelby had no doubts that if he botched his job, Ungaro might send in someone else to clean up the mess. Then Shelby knew he might find himself being hunted, and he was unlikely to survive.

Shelby had come to see his jobs almost as things made of glass. If it was handled properly, the job might take place so quietly that no one would know it had happened until long after he'd disappeared. The strength of the operation would never be in question. But if even one thing went wrong, one chip to the crystal, the whole job might be ruined.

Shelby wondered who this person was who had tromped past overhead. It was a man. He had seen that much in the fragment of a second before he disappeared under the water. The silhouette, barred by the heavy tarred railroad beams, still replayed in his head, like a movie stuck on one frame. Shelby knew the man would be back, and sometime soon would walk across this bridge again. So what it became was a waiting job. The cold was in him now, clammy river cold, as if he really had been drowned. Shelby left the cover of the bridge. The sun was up, making rosewater of the clouds. He climbed to the tracks and then crossed them. On the rocks that padded the tracks, he saw a knife. It was a Gerber Mark II, dropped by some hunter, Shelby figured. He picked it up and saw old blood on the blade. Shelby had his own knife, a heavy-bladed sub-hilt with Micarta grips, custom made for him by a man named Engle out in Montana. He threw the Gerber into the river, and the last trace of Wilbur Hazard vanished under the water.

By the time the ripples had cleared, Shelby was gone, across the tracks and into the woods with barely a sound. Moving when the wind moved. When the water slapped at the shore.

Mackenzie stepped out of his car at the end of a hardscrabble road that wound up the side of Bald Mountain. It was noon. Shelby had called that morning and told him to meet him there. The bare rock at the summit was iron gray, run through with veins of glittering mica that caught the sun and winked like signal mirrors out across the Algonquin Wilderness. The wind sifted up from the valley, bringing with it the sound of chain saws.

Mackenzie heard a footstep behind him and turned.

Shelby was there, at the edge of the woods, only a few feet away. He had hiked up through the trees in case the police followed Mackenzie to the meeting place. It had taken him more than two hours to find his way through the forest. At one point, he came to the basin of a dried-up pond. At the edge of it was the wreckage of some kind of vehicle. Shelby scanned the woods for signs of an old road that might once have led down to the water's edge, but there was none. Then, as he approached the tangle of old metal, he realized it was an airplane. Looking at the struts, which pointed at an angle from the fuselage just ahead of the open cockpit, he could tell it had once been a biplane. Mud had painted the wreck. The wings had crumpled and one had torn off completely. Only a rotted stub was left of the propeller. All that remained of the cockpit windshield was still-jagged teeth jutting from the mud-crusted frame. Shelby stood up on the remains of the lower wing and looked down into the cockpit, which appeared to have been built for two people. It was filled with dirt and leaves. There was no sign of bodies. Shelby took out a jack-knife and scraped at the fuselage. As the layers of mud flaked away, he saw traces of white paint. He figured the aircraft must have landed on the pond. Engine trouble, maybe. Shelby wondered if the fliers had survived. He shuddered. It made him lonely to think of dying in a place like this. Then he moved on quickly, because he was still a long way from the road. It took him another hour before he came in sight of it. When Mackenzie arrived, Shelby crouched in the shadows. He watched the old man pacing nervously. Then Shelby stood and walked out to the road.

"I didn't hear you coming," said Mackenzie.

Shelby gave a nod. His eyes were glittery with fatigue.

"Any progress?" Mackenzie asked. "The police almost caught a person last night, but he got away. I'm hoping you had better luck."

Shelby did not tell Mackenzie that it was himself. "I saw somebody," Shelby said.

"Where? In the woods?"

"In the woods. Yes." Shelby studied his ring. "If he moves again, I should be able to get him."

"Well, what if this person doesn't move again?"

"Then presumably your troubles are over."

Mackenzie paused as the words sank in. "Yes. Of course." Prickly heat fanned across his forehead. He had been standing too long in the sun. "Can I ask you something? What exactly are you going to do when you find who you're looking for?"

Shelby picked up a stone and skipped it down the road. "The best thing for now, sir, is to leave it all to me. The less you know, the fewer lies you'll have to tell if people start asking questions."

"People are already asking questions."

Shelby wiped his hand slowly over his mouth, as if to brush dust from his lips. He moved away. Then he turned back suddenly. "You have to keep them out of it for as long as you can. I need things quiet until I can get the job done. Then I can get out of the way. Do you understand, Mr. Mackenzie?"

"Well, of course I do, but I can't hold them off forever."

"Mr. Ungaro will not stand to have his business compromised."

"Sal Ungaro is an old friend of mine." Mackenzie was not sure what good it did to say this.

"Mr. Ungaro has no friends."

Mackenzie thought about this for a moment and realized it was true.

"And if my job is compromised, you are in a lot more trouble than you were when you started. I expect to leave here without a trace. Don't make that difficult for me." Shelby's soft Virginia voice did not sound angry, but the threat was there in his words.

To Mackenzie, Shelby did not even seem human anymore. A nightmare flitted through his head of Shelby tearing off the rubbery flesh of his own face, revealing a bird's nest of circuitry. "Look, I told you I think I know one of the people who's doing the damage. It's Madeleine. That newspaper's involved in it somehow. Can't you get at them through that? Show that there are people on this side of the fence who are prepared to play hardball. Some kind of warning. Then they might see . . ." His words died out. "You're not going to kill anyone, are you?"

"You said you wanted them stopped."

"I didn't say I wanted them dead."

"Sometimes you have to be thorough. A job with loose ends can be traced. You need the slate wiped clean. Tabula rasa," said Shelby.

It was the first time Mackenzie had ever heard anyone use that phrase besides himself. Now, as as the words reached him like an echo from his own mouth, he saw the finality of their meaning in a different light. He was no longer the one who swept everything aside. Instead, he was one among the multitudes, scythed down and nameless in death.

Shelby stepped back into the shadow of the pines, his blue-jean jacket fading like a piece of turquoise dropped in muddy water, until he was gone.

"Oh God," Mackenzie said to himself and got back in his car and drove away.

As Shelby made his way along the pathless ground, he felt the same clenching of his stomach muscles and drying out of his saliva that he always felt when he was about to do something violent. He had a fear that one day he would become again what he had been in Panama, something so unspeakable that his mind had sheared all memory away, leaving him with only the leathery petals of human ears as reminders of what had happened. He knew that once a person had unleashed that part of himself, it could never be completely laid to rest.

After two hours' sleep, lying in the depot on an old bench with a dusty tarpaulin pulled over him for a blanket, Gabriel headed back into the forest for another day of rail repair with a crew that came down from St. Johns. At five P.M., he waved good-bye to them as they headed back into Canada. Then he turned to walk the half mile to the Putt-Putt, on which he would head back to town. Sun had baked the rails. Heat rose from the creosoted ties, blurring the air. As Gabriel walked, he thought of the St. Johns crew on their way home, deep in the shadows of the forest now. He knew they would be quiet with fatigue, smoking cigarettes and rooting for odd scraps of food in their lunch boxes. Gabriel felt thirsty and his canteen was empty. He touched the corners of his mouth and scraped away the dried spit. He decided he would head down to the lake and take a drink.

He was just stepping off the track when he heard the thump of a footstep on a railroad tie. A shadow swooped over him. Then a huge weight crashed onto his back and he fell down the slope into the ditch.

The assault had taken him so much by surprise that he still didn't know what had happened when he lifted himself from the oily, knee-deep ditch water. He felt pain between his shoulder blades. As he stood, he saw a man just the other side of the ditch, and the shock that jolted him inside was as hard as the one that had thrown him down the embankment.

Gabriel could see that the man was young. Maybe in his early twenties. He had short blond hair and wore a blue-jean jacket with a green canvas shirt. His trousers were tucked into socks and he wore a pair of hiking boots. He was wearing a shoulder holster and carried a large black automatic pictol under his left armpit. He had the level gaze of someone who was not afraid.

Plainclothes police, Gabriel thought. Maybe even FBI. He wondered if it might be the one Lazarus had described. This man is no logger, anyway, thought Gabriel. It seemed to him that he could already hear voices echoing off the glossy painted concrete walls of a prison cell. But it was the man speaking, and Gabriel realized he had been more stunned than he first thought by the kick that sent him down.

"I've been tracking you," the man said. "You were doing good there for a while."

Gabriel saw no sense in denying who he was. The canvas bag in which he kept the nails was on the seat of the Putt-Putt. He had left his gun there, too, so the St. Johns crew would not see it.

"Come here," the man said, pointing to the narrow patch of ground between the ditch water and himself.

"Who are you?" Gabriel took a step out of the ditch. "Am I under arrest?" Already, in the back of his mind, he was assessing everything he had done. Not the guilt or correctness of it, but whether he had been effective. Not whether it had been worth it, but how dearly he had sold them his captivity. Now would come a different kind of struggle. It would be the opposite of everything he had done so far. Whereas before he had kept his work a secret, now he would talk as much and show his face as much as he could, force Mackenzie and the loggers to defend themselves in public. He knew the names of the lawyers that Swain had told him to contact. Gabriel could feel things closing up on him, the helplessness of the prisoner.

The man reached across and grabbed Gabriel by the collar of his shirt and dragged him away from the ditch water. His grip was powerful. "I'm not arresting you," the man said. Then he punched Gabriel so hard in the stomach that he lifted Gabriel off the ground. Gabriel gasped, but drew in nothing and fell into the ditch and immediately the man had hold of him again and lifted him. Water coursed from Gabriel's clothes. The man set Gabriel upright, then spun around in the tall grass and kicked him in the chest just below the throat. Gabriel flew back against a tree and slid down to the ground. He rolled onto his hands and knees, groaning and sucking in air.

The man was walking steadily toward him, fists balled into knots of flesh and bone.

Gabriel understood that he was going to die. He forgot about pain and launched himself at the man, who took the force of Gabriel's head in his stomach. The man staggered backward and as soon as

Gabriel had regained his balance, he smashed his elbow into the man's nose, feeling the cartilage crunch with the impact.

The man's eyes closed and he doubled over, hands to his face. "You fuck!" he shouted through the bars of his fingers. Blood trickled out across his knuckles.

Gabriel's mind was racing so quickly that all movements seemed ridiculously slow. As the man raised himself up and drew back his fist, Gabriel kicked him in the balls with his heavy work boots and dropped him to his knees. Gabriel shoved him back and had him by the neck, reaching for the man's pistol, when the man jabbed the knife edge of his hand into Gabriel's throat.

Gabriel staggered back and his hands clamped onto the pain as if to choke the life out of himself. But he could barely feel it. All knowledge of pain had disappeared now that he was fighting for his life.

The man drew his gun. He pulled it in one fluid movement from its sweat-darkened holster and cocked it and aimed it at Gabriel. "You don't think I'll use this, do you?" The man walked forward, clumsy-footed from the nausea rising thick and congesting from his genitals. "Do you?"

Gabriel steadied himself. He raised his hands uncertainly to the level of his shoulders, showing the empty palms.

The man held the gun against Gabriel's forehead, dragging the steel through his sweat. "I was going easy on you, you stupid bastard." Blood from his nose had run down over his lips and now when the man spoke, he peppered Gabriel's face red.

"Get it over with." Gabriel could barely speak. The jab to his throat had injured his windpipe.

"You still don't understand!" In one fast movement, the man raked the side of his boot down Gabriel's shin.

Gabriel crumpled, feeling the blood bead up out of the torn flesh.

Then he took hold of Gabriel's collar and held the gun to the side of Gabriel's head.

Gabriel closed his eyes.

"Look at me!" The man shook Gabriel until he was watching him again. "You leave town. Do you understand? You don't wait for someone to take over your job. You don't pack up your stuff and take anything with you. You just leave. You do not go to the police. Go do whatever you do someplace else. I don't give a damn. But you leave

Mr. Mackenzie alone. Because you got no place to hide now. Not from me, you don't. And you aren't dumb enough to think I'd give you a second chance, are you?" He shook Gabriel again. "Are you?"

"No," Gabriel whispered. The adrenaline that had blunted all his nerves was fading now. He did not want to think about the pain he would be in when it wore off.

"If you're in town this time tomorrow, I'll kill you. You understand? The only reason I'm not doing it right now is because I know you're going to be smart, aren't you?"

Gabriel didn't answer. He concentrated on his breathing, slow and rasping along the laddered walls of his windpipe.

The man let go of Gabriel. "You aren't listening to me, are you?"

"I am," Gabriel said.

"You aren't taking me seriously."

"I am," Gabriel said again, and he saw that now the man was coming unhinged.

The man shoved Gabriel down to the ground. His hand passed behind his back and when it reappeared, he was holding a large fighting knife, the steel bead-blasted to an unreflecting grayness.

"No," Gabriel said and held out his hands.

The man slapped them away with the flat of the knife. "I said I wasn't going to kill you," said the man. His teeth were clenched. The man touched the blade against Gabriel's stomach, then jerked it up through the buttons, sending them flipping into the air.

Both men looked at the paleness of Gabriel's chest. The fear had given him goose bumps.

"Please," Gabriel said. He could smell the man's breath. He looked him in the eye and was surprised to find no anger there. The voice had been angry, but not the eyes. This man has killed people before, Gabriel thought.

Then quickly, almost as if to avoid pain, the man pinched the skin of Gabriel's right nipple and raised it and with one movement of his wrist sliced off the nipple, the blade passing through the flesh as if it had been nothing.

As the scream rose in Gabriel's throat, the man slapped his dirty palm down hard on Gabriel's mouth.

The man was out of his mind now. He was someplace else. He put the lump of flesh in his mouth and then he spat the meat into

Gabriel's face, the saliva rosy with blood. "That was easy," the man said. "Did you see how easy that was for me?"

Gabriel was deafened by pain. He shook his head from side to side, eyes clamped shut, and sucked in breath through his teeth.

"All your lives are used up, Mister. You think about that when you're driving out of town." The man splashed Gabriel with his own blood from the words spat into his face. Then he stood back, breathed in and punted Gabriel with the flat of his heel in the chin, bouncing Gabriel's head off the ground and knocking him out.

Shelby stood for a minute over Gabriel's unconscious body. He was shaking, trying to stop himself from carving Gabriel apart with the knife. Part of his mind shrieked an order to slaughter the man. Butcher him the way livestock is butchered. Then Shelby turned and ran, before he could no longer help himself.

When Gabriel opened his eyes, the man was gone. He may have been gone for some time. Gabriel hadn't heard him leave, and there was no sound of fading footsteps. His hand was pressed over the wound and blood ran out from between his fingers. He rolled onto his side. Pain spread across the branches of his ribs. Eventually, he stood, then stumbled and fell. He landed on one hand, tried to raise himself again but gave up and slumped to the ground. Gabriel found he could not walk. So many points of pain had blossomed on his back and chest that he did not know where he could put his hands to dull the hurt. He crawled back to the Putt-Putt, then started the motor and drove home. All this time, he kept his hand over the wound, as much because he could not bear to see it as to stop being bathed in his own blood. The wind cooled his face. It ran its fingers through his hair. He walked the backstreets home and then poured iodine on the deep red place where his nipple had been. Then he touched at the edges of the wound with a silver nitrate shaving-cut stick until the blood began to slow. The pinched nerves began to clear his head. He soaked a towel in a bowl of warm water and baking soda. Then he wrung it out. Water, gritty with soda, trickled across the table. He set the towel, still twisted in a cable, around his neck. The wound would take a long time to heal. The man had probably known that when he did it. The scar would be ugly and the pain would take up residence in him for many weeks. But Gabriel knew that if he kept the wound clean, he would not die from it. This had only been a warning. Gabriel thought about the blond man's threat. It was real. There would be no hesitation.

He imagined himself packing and leaving, his thumb stuck out to every truck and car that passed, taking him anyplace, it would not matter where, as long as he was gone from Abenaki Junction. There would be no one to call him a coward. No numbers or addresses by which he could be tracked. His job as a railway repairman would quickly be swallowed up by someone else. All trace of him would vanish, just as it had vanished once before. Gabriel could tell himself that he had done the best he could. He had risked his life until the odds grew far too strong against him. And if there was ever any doubt, he would only have to undo his shirt and look down at the scar across his chest. The course of his life had changed today, as totally and irretrievably as it had done when he parachuted out into the Arabian night. Suddenly Gabriel wanted very much to stay alive. It was a feeling he had lost and now regained. Even breathing was a pleasure to him. His world of absolutes seemed a hopeless place in which to live. He had taken on too great a task and he had failed and the challenge that lay before him now was to accept it. In his mind, he was already gone, the miles of road unraveling beneath him. He felt the lightness in his heart that comes from setting out on a great voyage.

Then a different idea barged through his head. You never know, Gabriel thought, whether you will stick to your brave words when the time comes to hold fast. You only know when you are there, and then the words don't count for much. All that counts is what you do.

The lightness left his heart. It was precisely the same feeling as when clouds come in front of the sun. That clamping down of gloom that was nowhere and suddenly was everywhere. It was only then that Gabriel knew he would not quit. There was no one to say he had been beaten except himself, and he could not bring himself to say it. In the past, he had imagined his greatest measure of sacrifice to be one final act which tapped out all his strength and took his life. In one sense, that was easy. It would surround and overwhelm him and he would be dead. Now Gabriel understood that his devotion would be tested not in this single moment, but in thousands of moments for the rest of his life. The sacrifice was to persevere, despite the threats and drudgery and loneliness that hollowed him out until he no longer knew who he was. Tomorrow he would go back into the woods and the day after and the day after. And he would bring the gun and use it if he had to. Gabriel knew that if Shelby was there waiting for him, he had slim chance of surviving. But he knew he could not quit and make himself believe the dream of his freedom and the preciousness of his life if he gave up what he had sworn to see through to the end.

Shelby stood in the shadow of the trees until Gabriel had gone from sight. He was still nauseated from the kick to his balls. Shelby felt along his nose to see if the bone was broken, but it wasn't. He would have two black eyes in the morning and this upset him more than pain because he knew he would stand out now, particularly to the police. Already Shelby was wondering if he had made a mistake in not killing Gabriel. He had hoped to avoid it, because killing always made for complications. Perhaps, he thought, I have misjudged that man's commitment. Now I'll have to kill him anyway.

Shelby walked toward town, along the line of the tracks but keeping to the trees so he would not be seen. As he passed the Booths' cabin, he saw a man and a woman sitting in chairs on the porch, looking out across the lake. They held hands. The woman's long blond hair trailed over the back of the chair. Shelby was close enough to see the silver feather earrings that dangled down to the shoulders of her white T-shirt. The man said something, and on the path of the breeze Shelby heard an English accent. In the rustle of the breeze, Shelby moved on, and they knew nothing of his passing. They seemed so peaceful sitting there. Shelby hoped he would be that peaceful himself one day. But not today, because this wasn't over yet. The warning not complete.

The *Forest Sentinel* burned to the ground that night.

The rear door to the office was forced open and a cylinder was placed in the wastebasket next to Madeleine's desk. The cylinder contained a mixture of potassium chlorate and sugar, and had inserted into it a time fuze made from a glass vial. In the glass vial was battery acid, potassium chlorate and gunpowder. Just before placing the cylinder into the wastebasket, Shelby had turned the glass vial upside down and set it into the bomb. He knew he had about twenty minutes before the battery acid would eat through the paper stopper between the acid and the gunpowder. He removed the small fire alarm from the ceiling. He took the battery out and then put it back in the wrong way round, so the battery might still be found by investigators, although it would probably explode in the heat of the fire.

Before Shelby left, he looked around the little office. The walls were covered with newspaper and magazine clippings—mostly about logging in the Pacific Northwest, but a few about saving endangered species like the greenback turtle and the Pacific spotted owl. Shelby didn't know what to think of these people who opposed the logging. More trees could always be planted. Neither did he understand why others spent their lives trying to stave off the inevitable disappearance of these obsolete creatures. He imagined them to be like the obsolete creatures themselves—they too would soon be extinct. Shelby turned away from the corkboard walls and slipped out into the dark.

Half an hour later, the explosion set off a fire that melted the glass from the office windows.

Everyone in town was woken by the coughing roar of the fire-station horn.

Men and women volunteers ran to their cars, still so asleep that only their memories knew what they were doing. They switched on the blue lights glued to their dashboards to mark them as volunteer fire personnel and drove to the fire station.

Dodge lived opposite the fire station. The siren pulled him from the dark pool of his sleep and swung his legs out of bed. He stumbled across the room to find his clothes. As he dressed, he watched the cars of the volunteer brigade come skidding into the fire station parking lot. Half-dressed and undressed people shambled on bare and painful feet across the scattered gravel. Some had bedsheets wrapped around them. To Dodge, they looked like dead people woken from the grave, hobbling on rigor-mortised joints. Dodge followed the fire truck in his police car. As he rode down Main Street, the fire truck's exhaust reached through his car's ventilation system and peppered his nose. The rising and then falling wail of the truck's siren was deafening. He flipped on the Crown Victoria's blue and red flashing lights. He prepared himself for the sight of a house reduced to shabby outlines, sketched black on a background of pumpkin-orange fire, and its owners either dead inside or crying naked on the sidewalk.

By the time Dodge arrived, the fire had eaten so much of the building that not even outlines remained. It was like something out of a cartoon, where a tree is struck by lightning and for a moment the skeleton balances in place. Then, to some tinkling music, the whole thing falls into what looks like a pile of black pencil shavings. Dodge opened his car door.

The fire crew held the leg-thick hose under their arms, ready to take the shock of rushing water. There was a great hiss as water struck the flames. The men and women lost their footing and then regained it. They looked like goblins under their yellow helmets and black coats.

People wandered out of the dark toward the fire. Dodge recognized Madeleine. She had a coat on over her nightgown. Madeleine walked straight up to him. "How did it happen?" she asked.

"I just got here," he told her. "I don't know." The stench of burning was all around him. He stood with his arm leaning on the car door, looking down at a thin trail of water that pushed its way across the dry and gritty ground

"It's arson, isn't it?" Madeleine dragged her heel through the stream of water. Its course changed to a dozen tiny rivulets.

"I wouldn't be surprised."

In twenty minutes, the fire was out. Smoke-bitter steam billowed around them. Loons made ghost calls on the lake.

"That place was my whole life," Madeleine said and turned away. Her hair brushed across Dodge's face.

"I know," said Dodge, and rested his hand on her shoulder. "But you can start it up again. Promise me you will."

"I promise," she said. "I was wrong about you."

"Wrong in what way?" he asked.

"Ways you don't even know about." She stood in silence for a moment, watching as the last shreds of fire were put out. Then Dodge drove her home.

She opened the chipped and blistered green paint of her screen door and asked him inside. She didn't want to be alone just then.

Dodge made them both cocoa from a packet of Carnation mix. They sat down on the carpet in the living room until the kettle whistled.

"Will the insurance cover the damage?" he asked.

"It should." Madeleine looked so pale, as if her skin had turned to rice paper.

"People will chip in." Dodge hunted for optimism. "They'll help you get started again." He fetched the cocoa from the kitchen, handed it to her in a white tin mug.

"I have something to tell you," she said, staring at Dodge through the steam over the rim of the mug, never letting her glance slip from his face. "I thought I was supposed to be with someone else," she said. "All this time, I—"

"You don't need to say it," he said.

"But I want to."

He leaned across the carpet and kissed her. Their teeth brushed together. Kissing for the first time. Her hand was on the back of his neck, still cold from outside. He heard the click of her fingernails as she undid the buttons of his shirt. Her warm hands swept across his chest. She pulled off her nightgown and he felt her breasts against him. He breathed in the warm dryness of her body. His short nails raked across her back and down the smooth curve of her thigh. Vertigo whirlpooled his mind. He kissed her, and her teeth were clamped together. Her face was so serious. He almost didn't dare to say her name; then before he could say it, her shut-tight eyes popped open. They stared into his and then slowly closed again. He followed the line of her neck in the dark and felt with his lips the deep noise in her throat. Her hair fanned out like seaweed in the tide. The smell of his sweat sifted through her body like smoke. The cold night air pushed through the screen door, but he could not feel it and he sensed himself falling, as if off the precipice of sleep, and he thought if he fell any deeper, he would never wake up. And then he was not falling anymore. The cold reached him again, except for where her hands pressed hot against his back. As Dodge held her to him, he felt a ringing emptiness and clarity and the room came back into focus. For the first time in a long while, he thought only of her and not about the work that lay ahead.

*C*oltrane had suspicions. They invaded his mind. He was thinking so hard that he barely saw the woods around him as he bumped along the logging road, driving a dirty yellow CAT backhoe. He reached a place that was out of sight of logging crews and slowed the engine to a stop. Then he engaged the backhoe and raised it up and down. The shovel operated, but not the way it should. Its movements were uneven and the controls felt watery in his hand. Coltrane wrapped his right hand around the black ball of the gearshift stick and put the engine in neutral. He climbed down and examined the joints of the hoe, but couldn't find anything wrong.

Then he climbed on again and put the engine in reverse. He backed up fast, and something was wrong here, too, in the high-pitched whine of the machine. The engine was not handling properly. It slipped. The gears were grinding.

Coltrane stopped the backhoe once more and got out. He stood before the machine, kneading the rough pads of his fingers deep into the bristle of his chin. An idea spread like wings behind his eyes and he breathed out slowly, hoping it wasn't true. He went to the oil-distributor cap and checked the oil level. The oil was fine, the amber color not yet turned coffee brown with dirt. He pulled the dipstick, wiped it on his sleeve and checked the oil again. This time the stick had picked up some flecks of white grit. Carefully, he put the rod back into the distributor and closed the cap. Then he took out a penknife and dug gently into one of the zerk points on the backhoe. He gouged out some of the joint-lubricating grease and rolled it in his fingers. He could feel the grit in there, too.

There was no expression on Coltrane's face. His eyes were unfocused. He wiped the grease onto his brown Carhart jacket and unclipped the walkie-talkie from his waist. He raised it to his mouth, then sighed and lowered it for a second. His lips moved without sound as he rehearsed what he was going to say. Then he began to speak. "Barnegat? Barnegat, can you hear me? This is Coltrane." He let go of the red TALK button and static purred in his ear.

"Go ahead."

"Are you with the road grader right now?" Coltrane could smell old smoke on the mouthpiece of the walkie-talkie.

"Ya."

"Well, tell the driver to quit working on it until I get there. All right? Tell them to quit now." Static punctuated his words.

"We already did."

"You did? Why?"

"Something wrong with it."

Coltrane's arm dropped to his side and he stared for a while without seeing at the wall of trees before him.

Barnegat's metallic-fuzzy voice came back to him. "What's going on?"

"They got us good this time, Barnegat."

"But I can't find anything wrong with the machine."

"Check the grease in the zerk points. Then check the oil a bunch of times. See what comes up."

"You're kidding me. Somebody silted the oil?"

"Worse than that. They used silicone grit. A real thorough job, by the look of it."

"Then I guess we're out of business, Mr. Coltrane."

Coltrane shut off his walkie-talkie. He clipped it back onto his belt.

It was hot now, so he took off his jacket and set it on the ground where the bulk of the machine formed shade on the road. Then he sat down in the shadows, with his back against the huge tire of the back-hoe. The rubber was warm and Coltrane felt the heat soak through his shirt. He knew that if a couple of machines had been damaged, then probably all of them had. If the grit had been in the engines for more than a few days, they would have to be junked. Coltrane doubted it would be possible to get hold of equipment from another logging company, not since Mackenzie had put all the local ones out of business. It would take months for any insurance claims to come through, and Mackenzie could not afford to buy new machines, not at such short notice and with so much money sunk into the Algon-quin deal. Maybe he could rent more stuff, Coltrane thought, but what company is going to rent its gear out to a mill whose operation is being sabotaged?

For the first time in his adult life, Coltrane was sure he would be fired from his job. It was not the nightmare he had once imagined. In fact, he felt relieved. With the burning down of the *Forest Sentinel,* the last arguments of support for Mackenzie among the loggers had begun to come apart. It wouldn't be long now before they called a general strike. Wind hissed through the tops of the trees. Coltrane folded his hands on his chest and closed his eyes, taking his last calm breaths before he faced Mackenzie again. It was only then he realized that, all through the forest, the sound of the chain saws had quit.

It took three days for flatbed trucks to tow away the last of the Mackenzie Company's machines. Mackenzie ordered the cutting to continue, saying the logs should lie where they fell.

The sawmill was down to one cutting blade, and new blades were on order.

First Mackenzie had told Coltrane he was fired. Then he called Coltrane back into the office and told him he was hired again. "It's got to be somebody's fault!"

"It would be the fault of whoever had the authority to post guards on the machinery." Coltrane spoke in a low and even tone.

"And who's that?"

"You, sir."

"Don't fuck with me, Coltrane."

"No, sir."

Mackenzie launched himself out of his chair and went to stand by the window. "People are starting to say I'm whipped, aren't they?"

"No."

"Well, what the hell are they saying? I never heard so much whispering in all my life."

"They're wondering if you had anything to do with the newspaper burning down." That's it, Coltrane thought to himself. I just went too far. I'm going down the pipe just like that other foreman did.

"And where's a piece of news like that come from?"

"Well, it's hard to say."

"Fucking wilderness people. Madeleine was just in there smoking marijuana and torched the fucking place. Of course they're going to blame me! Everybody always does!"

"But is it true, sir?" Coltrane waited for Mackenzie to turn around. He was tired of staring at the back of the old man's head.

"What?"

"About the fire?"

Mackenzie was staring at his hands, the way the veins zigzagged under his skin. "Let's just get hypothetical here for a moment. What if it was true, Coltrane? I always treated you right. I let you do your job and you let me do mine. Now, I always think of my employees first. That newspaper was getting in the way of our industry. It's jobs we're talking about here. Jobs and opportunity. Jesus Christ, we're living out the American Dream here, aren't we? It doesn't matter who burned that paper down. The only thing that matters now is that it's gone. So get out there and start cutting those trees. I don't care if they're lying on the ground six months. I don't care if we have to dig them out of the snow this winter. If we cut them, they're ours. Now tell everyone to get back to work." He walked over to Coltrane and gave him a slap on the shoulder. "We'll still show them. By the first snowfall, there won't be a single tree standing!"

Coltrane turned around and walked out.

"OK!" Mackenzie called after him, the way a coach calls out to a player going onto the field. Then he walked back to his window and looked down into the yard.

A small crowd had gathered there. Cigarette smoke rose from the jumble of khaki jackets and frayed work shirts and baseball hats.

Coltrane spoke to them, shaking his head. He stuffed his hands in his pockets and shrugged. Then, as a new thought occurred to him, he pulled his hands out and shook them to make his point. It looked as if he were shaking change from a piggy bank.

As Coltrane spoke, the mill workers looked up at Mackenzie's office.

Mackenzie's first instinct when he saw them look his way was to duck from their line of sight. But he stayed where he was, because he knew he couldn't hide.

Coltrane was shrugging again.

"Tell them it's about jobs," Mackenzie muttered. "Make them see."

Coltrane held up one finger and then another, listing off points.

"Tell them it's legal," Mackenzie whispered.

The men began walking toward the gates. They talked among themselves.

Mackenzie felt bile spill into the back of his throat. He stumped downstairs and out into the yard. From behind the tinted windows of his office, he had not realized how bright it was outside. Now he was almost blinded in the glare.

The men were walking to their trucks. Doors slammed and engines coughed into motion.

"Where the hell do you think you're going?" Mackenzie shouted at the workers. "You taking a fucking holiday?" Then he spun around to face Coltrane, walking stick raised as if to jab him with the nickel tip. "You better do something about this!"

The tough hide of Coltrane's face was red from all the talking he had done. "It isn't right, what you're doing in the Algonquin. Not with it being declared a preserve. And people feel you are responsible for the newspaper burning down. They just need some answers from you, sir."

"And who are you? The fucking pope all of a sudden? Eh? Are you afraid to go back in the woods?" He gave Coltrane a shove and then immediately wished he had not. It was one of those short shoves that start fights, and Mackenzie knew Coltrane would not fight him.

Coltrane stepped backward from the shove. Then he steadied himself. Now it's you who went too far, he thought.

But Mackenzie hadn't finished. "You've got enough wilderness in this state already. It would take you weeks even to hike through it all.

How much more do you want? And what the hell do you care about a beatnik who is trying to take away your jobs with her fucking newspaper?"

The lumbermen stood watching in silence, cigarettes burning unsmoked in their hands.

Mackenzie's voice rose to a howl. "One of these days, you'll realize that everything I did, I did for you! If this mill closes, I'm still set for life. I don't have what I don't need. But what about you? If you go out those gates, I don't want you coming back. You think hard about this. Because one way or another, those trees are coming down. I'll bring the Canadians down. I'll bring the Japanese in here if I have to. One way or another, gentlemen!"

They drove away in the dust.

Mackenzie turned to Coltrane, his face twisted with anger. "So what did you tell them?" Before Coltrane could reply, Mackenzie shouted, "I don't even want to know. Just get the fuck out of here."

"You're falling apart," Coltrane said quietly.

A memory returned to Mackenzie. It was a picture of his father. The thought came rolling like a bowling ball down the corridors of his mind until it seemed to crash into his skull behind the eyes. His father had told him never to explode in anger. To take it home and sleep on it and see in the morning if it was worth the trouble that explosions always cause. Mackenzie could not recall the exact words his father had used, but he remembered the lesson, and with it came a strange light that he knew belonged in his father's study, the sun glancing off the coffee-dark mission-oak furniture. Before the memory retreated again, Mackenzie saw his father at his desk, turned sideways and staring at the bookshelf, his eagle-beak nose profiled against the blurry diamond panes of his study window. His hands were raised, fingertips touching. That was the picture. Those were the words that came with it. Then it disappeared, and Mackenzie found himself gone from staring deep inside himself to staring outward, into the hard light of the lumberyard.

Coltrane was walking away, jacket slung over his shoulder. He clicked open his lighter and lit a Lucky Strike.

"Fuck all of you," Mackenzie said, without bothering to raise his voice. He walked across to his car and drove out into the wilderness down the empty logging roads. He drove until the road ended in a berm of dirt and stacked white birch trees, rotting in the sun. He climbed out and moved along the side of the car, hands sweeping through the film of dust, dragging the heel of his artificial leg. He fetched a chain saw from the trunk of the Range Rover and carried it into the woods. He jammed the blade against the ground, using the saw as a walking stick, until he was under the trees and the air was still and cooler than it was near the road. He pulled the cord and started up the chain saw, diving the blade into the nearest pine. Mackenzie had not cut down a tree since the night he lost his leg. Now he dared it to fall on him, the way the last had done. The tree began to creak and then it fell, swishing through the branches of other pines until it thumped against the earth. He didn't wait, but attacked another tree. His street shoes barely gripped the soil. The saw was heavy in his hands, drawing sweat from his palms and splashing down from his armpits across his ribs and soaking into the band of his underwear. The blond spray of sawdust blinded him, and he had to keep stopping to gouge it out of his eyes. The smell of spilled sap was all around him. He wore no ear protectors, and the roaring of the saw made him deaf. He watched another tree fall, the last pale splinters giving way and throwing pine needles into the air like green confetti. Tree after tree he dared to fall on him. He dared the chain saw to break and snake back and rip up his head as it had done to Pfeiffer. He challenged the one talisman that had shielded him through his life: that he had once gathered from somewhere inside him the strength to mutilate himself so horribly and crawl to safety, past all barriers of pain and shock, only to stay alive. Never far from his thoughts was the idea that he could do it all again if he had to, and if he'd been able to saw off his own leg, he did not need to fear anything. Not even death. Mackenzie had never spoken this aloud. Never dared to put it into words, because it was the last ditch of his power and to speak it would have been to diminish the great hold it had on him. Sweat was still running off him. It trickled out of his cuffs. He was powdered with sawdust. What frightened him now was that his talisman might fail him, that the great reservoir of strength in which he had believed had long ago dried up and left him weak. After the seventh tree, he swung around, not even bothering to watch the pine fall, and his smooth-soled shoes slid out from under him. He dropped and the saw bounced off the ground, its jagged chain still spinning, and when Mackenzie hit the ground he closed his eyes, because the last thing he saw was the blade and his hands stubbornly gripping the handle. He lay there for a second, the air thick with sawdust all around him, and he realized he was safe. The saw had bounced away from him and lay at the end of his arm, still clasped in his bloodless, knotted fingers.

Mackenzie rolled onto his back in time to see an eagle fly over, cast its shadow on the polished green hood of his car and then swerve suddenly, wide wings flexed, and swoop past where he lay. As it passed directly above him, Mackenzie swore it was no bird, but some man cloaked in wings—the unforgiving angel who had watched him all these years and judged him as harshly as he judged himself. He craned his neck to see where the bird had gone, but could see only the highway of blue sky in the path he had cut through the forest.

It was then that Jonah Mackenzie had a vision of his own death. Not one concrete image. Instead, it had a quality of light. White. Yellow. It dropped from the clear sky like crystalline splinters of sun, broken into the hard lasers of each primary color. It was a feeling of certainty. The experience was strangely familiar, as if this news had been brought to him long before but somehow he'd forgotten it. From the silence that followed, stilling even the breeze through the tops of the pines and the razzing hum of cicadas, it seemed to Mackenzie as if every living thing in the forest had felt the shock of this vision and was hushed by it. Even the forest itself, for which Mackenzie had shown no pity in his life, seemed to be pitying him. Death walked toward him at a steady pace, and as it drew closer Mackenzie felt the swirling emptiness that surrounded it.

"Wealth dies," Mackenzie found himself muttering, eyes tightly shut. "People die. The only thing that never dies is the verdict on each person dead."

The vision slowly faded, as if whatever it was had traveled through him and past him and carried away with it the savage waking-dream. Mackenzie climbed to his feet, one metal and one bone, and staggered back to his car. Then he drove home and got drunk by himself in his study on the smoky burn of Islay whiskey, staying up until late in the night. He offered no explanation to Alicia. If he did not mention it, the thing might not be real. But even if the promise of it had not been true, the vision itself would never leave him. Not even in the pendulum rocking of his skull as he raised the decanter to his mouth and drank the fiery liquid, blue night winking off the crystal.

Coltrane put in a call to New York. It was the first time he had used his phone in months. He had made up his mind what to do. Days had passed since he walked out of the Mackenzie mill. Each morning at five, he swung himself out of bed and got halfway to the sink to shave before he remembered that he didn't have a job. The perfectly rationed energy that had seen him through the days began to smolder in him. He sat confused in a chair in his kitchen, watching Clara go about her day and fuss over him, but he was beyond any help she could give. Slowly his confusion began to distill. He knew what had to be done, as much for himself as to put right some of what had happened.

He made an appointment to see Linda Church, producer of a television program called *Focus America*. Her assistant was clipped and rude on the phone, the way people are rude to door-to-door salespeople. On the day, Coltrane put on a pair of Florsheim shoes and a jacket and a tie, none of which he had worn in years. The shoes were so old and out of use that they had curled up at the toes and made him walk as if he were on rockers. He told Clara where he was going. He had expected that she might try to talk him out of it, but she did not. She seemed to have a better idea than he did about what he would accomplish with his trip. Coltrane took the bus to Portland and from Portland down to Boston. Then he boarded an Amtrak train and headed south.

Eight hours later, Coltrane left the train at Penn Station in New York. It was his first time in the city. He walked out through the low-roofed corridors, past a gift shop where mechanical toy dogs yipped and wandered around the dirty floor as if they were looking for something. Past one man wearing the pink plastic wristband of a hospital patient. The man was dressed in army-surplus clothes and stalked invisible enemies, shooting them down with a gun made from his fingers. Others stood beside closed shops, talking to themselves and swinging their heads from side to side. Coltrane rode up the escalator, past a flower seller and a legless Vietnam vet holding out a paper cup for change. "I suffered for you," the man said. "I suffered for all of you fuckers."

Before Coltrane stepped into the cab, he stood looking around at the chinks of blue sky above the buildings and the cars and the sky-reflecting windows. He was trying to figure out how he would explain this place to Clara. Not just describe it. Explain it. It would not be enough to talk about the legless man or the way he found himself taking shallow breaths so as not to cough on the fumes. There was something else. Some discord that he felt beyond all senses he could name. He realized it would be hard to explain to these people what was being lost in the place he had come from, because it was already gone from here. He understood then that this was the source of the discord, not all the things that were here but the things that were not. It would not make a difference if they drove out to a forest for a week or so each year. The thunder of the city would not have left their bones by the time it came to leave again. If Coltrane had known this in advance, he would not have come to the city. He would have lived out his life feeling like a coward for not having tried, but he had come this far and he had nothing left to lose.

Ten minutes later, Coltrane climbed out of a cab at the entrance to the *Focus America* studios on Forty-fourth Street and went inside. The guard at the front desk called his name upstairs. He was on time, but was made to wait in a little room with seafoam-green walls and magazines fanned out like playing cards on glass tables. Eventually, an assistant showed him in. She was petite and wore a short cherry-red dress. He followed her past many booths with papers stacked on desks and phones ringing, to a room with a view.

A bald man with an earring walked out carrying a file and Coltrane stepped back to let him pass. Then he found himself looking at a very tall, pale-skinned woman, whose silvery hair was parted severely down the middle. She wore a dark blue suit with gold buttons. This was Linda Church. *Focus America* uncovered scandals and schemes, people jailed unjustly and cases of political corruption. On the TV at the Loon's Watch, Coltrane had seen people run away from Linda Church as she and her camera crew ambushed them outside office buildings and chased them down streets in a flurry of trenchcoats and wiring, bawling out questions as she went.

"Mr. Coltrane." She cleared some papers off her desk, as if to find a place where she could rest her hands. She told him with her movements that she had no time for chat.

"Yes, that's right." He undid the front button on his jacket and sat down in the chair opposite her desk. The toes of his shoes were still curled up. He planted his feet hard on the floor.

"So you have a story for us." She talked almost without moving her lips.

"I believe so." For days, Coltrane had thought about little else but the moment when he would explain his story to her. Now that he was here, his words and everything around him seemed pillowed in an anesthetic fuzziness.

She tipped in her chair. It looked for a moment as if she was about to pitch backward out the window and into the crawling traffic ten floors below. "We normally have a policy about doing stories that involve personal vendettas."

"It's always personal," said Coltrane. He had become uneasy in the waiting room, but now he began to gather himself together. "If it weren't personal, I wouldn't be here. And if it weren't more than personal, you wouldn't be talking to me."

The black dots of her pupils seemed to freeze. "I suppose you could see it that way," she said.

Coltrane explained the Algonquin deal, and told her what would be left of the wilderness by the time Mackenzie had finished with it. She took some notes with a fat black Mont Blanc fountain pen on a yellow legal pad. Not looking up. Lips pressed bloodlessly together. Then she sat back and set the pen down on the desk. "I don't believe a person would put himself in danger just to save a bunch of trees."

"It's not just the trees." Coltrane allowed his voice to rise in the soundproofed white walls of the office. "It's the wilderness. It's where you come from," he said. "And when it's gone, even if you haven't ever seen the wilderness, a part of you goes with it."

"Really." She smiled at him. It was the kiss-off smile. "I just don't think it has the kind of appeal that we're looking for."

Coltrane nodded, to say thank you and good-bye. He stood and felt a hard pinch in his stomach where his scar was still healing. A quiet groan worked its way out of his throat. He pressed one hand to the scar and with the other he propped himself up against the desk. "Jesus," he whispered.

"Are you all right?" Linda Church stood. "Do you want me to call someone?"

"No." It hurt to talk. "I got stabbed a while ago and sometimes when I stand too fast, the hurt comes back." He looked up, straining his neck to meet her eye. "It goes away in a bit."

"My God, who stabbed you?"

"It was out in the forest. It was a guy some people thought was spiking trees. But it wasn't him."

"What happened to the man?"

"My best friend shot him in the face. After that, he got hit by a train, but by then I think he was already dead." Coltrane lowered himself back into the chair. "If I could just sit here for a minute."

Linda Church also sat. She unscrewed the cap of her pen and made another note. "And have there been any other deaths?"

"Ayuh. There was James Pfeiffer. That was what started it all."

"What happened to him?" She was writing it down.

"Chain saw."

The phone rang. Linda Church picked up the receiver, listened for a second and then said, "Not now." She hung up. "Chain saw, did you say?" Her eyes were narrowed almost shut.

Coltrane nodded. The pain was going now.

"Mr. Coltrane, I think maybe we could work with you on this. Now tell me again from the start."

One hour later, Coltrane walked out into the street. Linda Church had said she would be looking into it further. She had made him promise to go on camera with what he had said and Coltrane had agreed. He took the next train north. It was night when he left New York. For a long time, Coltrane looked out at streetlamps rushing past like fireflies. As he watched the lights go by, Coltrane thought back to when he watched the fireworks exploding over Pogansett Lake every Fourth of July. The glittering and falling stars always amazed him, as if he were witnessing the creation of another universe. He felt the same sense of wonder at being involved in something that was larger than he was, something he could never fully understand and was not meant to. He kept his face pressed to the window, not wanting to miss a single light, and the train carried him on into the dark.

≡

When Mackenzie arrived back from work at his office the next morning, Alicia had just finished writing him a message on a pink piece of While-You-Were-Out notepaper. She wore a white dress printed with tiny red roses.

Mackenzie smiled at her. "You look good," he said. He was feeling better today. Some of his workers had returned. He felt sure that the rest would follow soon. He would find someone to replace Coltrane, and when Shelby had finished his work, the mill could get back to business as usual. The mill would survive. The town would survive. It was one of those days when he felt sure that he had saved himself a place in heaven.

Alicia tore the piece of notepaper from the pad and stuck it on his chest. "I think you're about to be famous," she said.

"Why's that?" He tried to talk and read the note at the same time. It said that Linda Church had called. There was a number for him to call back. For one confused moment, Mackenzie felt pride balloon in his chest. First, he imagined himself in front of a camera outside the Mackenzie mill, walking with Linda Church down one of his logging roads, both of them wearing trenchcoats and deep in discussion, followed by the camera crew. More pictures lined up, like anxious students, arms raised and hands waving. Then suspicion snapped him out of it. "Did she say what she wanted?"

"To talk to you about the Algonquin." Alicia touched her dress, as if to pick the printed roses from the cloth. "Should I just call them back and say you don't want to talk?"

"No." The spit had dried up in his mouth. "They'd find someone else to talk to." Mackenzie walked upstairs to his study. He went in and kicked the study door shut as he dialed the number, calling Linda Church collect.

Linda Church was polite, in a way that threatened not to be polite. She told him who she was, with the springy voice of someone stating a fact that everyone should already know. "Mr. Mackenzie, we are just fact-checking for a story."

"Yes," Mackenzie said. His thoughts were roller-coastering.

"Is it true, sir, that you signed a deal for logging rights to an area of forested land called the Algonquin Wilderness?"

"Yes."

"Good." There was the sound of a phone ringing in the background. "What we also need to know is whether you were aware that the Algonquin Wilderness is scheduled to become a protected area one month after your logging rights expire? In effect, sir, that the area in which you have disrupted or destroyed all wildlife is to become a sanctuary for what no longer exists?"

Then Mackenzie went from having no plan to having the only plan there was. "The government called me and made the offer. They said it was to become protected, but they were the ones offering me clear-cut logging rights. I assumed they would have a good idea of what they were doing." Now he laughed. It was a deliberate and dreary chuckle. "I mean, if the wilderness-management people don't know how to handle the wilderness, who does? You see, ma'am, my job is to cut the trees down. I have all this on paper if you need to see it."

"Well, that's very kind." It was not a voice with any gratitude or trust. "Would you be prepared to talk with us about this on camera?"

"Of course. How soon can you get up here?"

"Well, perhaps within a few days. What we're interested in, Mr. Mackenzie, is whether you see any kind of unethical conduct here."

"I'm a businessman. I was made an offer by the government. Like I said, it was a good offer, and if I had turned it down, someone else would have picked it up. The only thing you can be sure of, ma'am, is that these trees will fall. There's too much money in it. Too many jobs. And no amount of terrorism is going to change that." He was angry now. The veins were thumping in his neck. "I'm the victim here!" Mackenzie shouted into the receiver. He realized in the silence that followed that she was still listening to him. He knew he might still be able to win her over to his side. Suddenly he was no longer worried. He saw the whole thing turning toward him, like a great ship coming about. "The law is being broken up here in the North Woods, Ms. Church," he said, his voice a conspirator's mumble, "but it's not me who's breaking it." The sweat was running down Mackenzie's face. He gripped the receiver hard. "I am grateful for the opportunity to bring this story to the American people."

When Linda Church hung up half an hour later, Mackenzie felt the breathless stun of someone living purely off instinct. Slowly he breathed out. Then he called Ungaro's answering service.

Ungaro called him back ten minutes later. "Hello, Jonah." Ungaro sounded impatient. An echoing voice in the background announced a flight departure. "I'm just getting on a plane. What do you need?"

"I was wondering if you had any way of getting in touch with our friend. I had some news for him, but he's a little hard to find."

"Well, that's what he's good at."

"So, ah, do you have a number or something?" Mackenzie scanned the racks of unread books along his study shelves.

"No. I wouldn't even know where to start, Jonah. That whole situation is kind of on autopilot right now. It's in motion. There isn't anything you or I can do to stop it. That's what you wanted, isn't it, Jonah?"

"I just had some information that I thought would be useful." Mackenzie sighed out the words. He wanted to call the whole thing off. He didn't mind losing the money. Not at this stage of the game.

"Don't you worry, Jonah. Don't you worry about a thing."

"No." Mackenzie sighed again, and in the pause that followed, he realized that Ungaro had already hung up. "No, indeed," he said, as the dial tone buzzed in his ear. If he could have cut his losses then and walked away, he would have done so. But the talk with Sal Ungaro had confirmed what Mackenzie feared—that it was all far beyond his control. He thought of the way Ungaro had said the word "autopilot," of how confident he had sounded. Mackenzie felt none of that confidence. To him, the Dutch Boy had become a vast wrecking force, like a train off the rails with no way to stop except to lose momentum in the path of its destruction.

Mackenzie walked downstairs and told his wife what had happened. "What the hell am I going to do?" he asked her.

"Perhaps you should wait and see how many people show up for work today."

"Once those TV people get through with me, it won't matter how many show up because I'll be finished. Besides, it was probably one of them that blew the whistle on me. What am I supposed to do? Go around to each of them and apologize? And for what? For getting them jobs they can keep? I am in the right, Alicia!"

"Are you?"

Mackenzie folded his arms. "You don't believe me, do you?"

"I think there might be a difference between being in the right and in doing the right thing."

"That's just talk, Alicia. I have legal papers that say I can cut that land, which is what I intend to do."

"By yourself?"

Mackenzie screwed up his face. "There'll be people to cut those trees, even if I have to drag them in from some no-name third-world country. I don't need this town. It's them who need me and even in your cynical mood today, Alicia, you know that's the truth."

"You could hold a town meeting. Give people a chance to air their views. Give you a chance to talk back to them and make your point. Get things straightened out one way or the other. At least you would know where you stood."

Mackenzie stayed silent for a while, trying to find something wrong with the suggestion. It would make me look good, he thought. Answer their questions before they have time to ask them. "Yes," he said eventually. "I think that's what I'll do."

The next day, he drove to the mill at his usual time. A crowd had gathered at the gates of the Mackenzie Company. Some of the people who had walked out were there, but they did not go inside the gates. Only a few lumbermen had gone to work. They moved uncertainly around the yard, as if no longer sure what jobs they were supposed to do.

A TV crew was there. Mackenzie saw two city cars. Continentals. As his Range Rover rumbled over the potholed company road, Mackenzie caught sight of the red-white-and-blue license plates on the Continentals. New York. The *Focus America* people had arrived even sooner than he'd thought they would. He saw a man with a camera lodged on his shoulder and a sound technician with a giant foam-covered hot-dog-shaped microphone. He was fiddling with dials on a box that he carried strapped to his waist. Then Mackenzie saw the reporter, coiled microphone line in one hand and the gray mike in the other. He recognized her. Linda Church. It was too late to panic.

The Range Rover pulled up and Mackenzie saw the crowd ooze

toward him through the dust. The soundman held his microphone in the air above the bobbing heads. Linda Church advanced toward the car as if she meant to pick it up in one hand and shake Mackenzie out of it like a cookie from a jar. To Mackenzie, she looked so completely out of place here, with her just-so-tousled hair and white turtleneck sweater and green skirt and trenchcoat. She was wearing too much clothing for this summer day. Probably, he thought, because she's one of those people who think that any place north of Boston is a permanent region of ice.

The car nudged a path through the people. Loggers peered in at Mackenzie as if they had never seen him before. He stared straight ahead and gunned the engine. Mackenzie could not hear what the people were saying, but he could hear their talking. It was a constant, beehive hum.

Linda Church came into view. Mackenzie expected her to lunge at the glass and he braced himself for the shock. But she just stood there and watched him go by. Mackenzie had the feeling he was being scanned by some machine, drinking in each thought he could no longer hold inside the bone box of his skull.

Mackenzie didn't bother to park the Range Rover. Instead he just cut the engine once he was inside the lumberyard. He opened the door and stepped outside. The ground crunched under his feet. Then he closed the gate to keep out the crowd. It made him angry at the ones who'd walked away, leaving him to do a job he wasn't strong enough to carry out, especially with his leg. He blamed them for making him tug at the dull gray latch, inching the rusty wheels along their dirt-filled runners.

The crowd had cleared a space for Linda Church. She stood at the gate, flanked by her TV crew. The air seemed about to explode. "Mr. Mackenzie." Her voice had a ring like struck bronze. "You really should talk to us."

"And I will, ma'am."

Linda Church muttered to her camera operator. A red light winked on the camera.

Mackenzie watched the cyclops eye of the lens twist as it focused on him. "You can all talk to me and I'll hear your questions and you can hear what I have to say. Tomorrow night at the Woodcutter's Lodge." He grinned at them with his best worry-less smile until he thought his jaw would crack from the strain. Mackenzie had no idea what he would say to them. He had a sense of digging in, like a soldier gouging a foxhole in the soil before an artillery barrage. It was an old and familiar feeling—of not giving in or giving any ground. Mackenzie told himself he would stonewall them until he was dead. He did not know where he would find the strength to do it, but this was the only way he knew.

Some loggers turned to leave, as if they had been waiting for any excuse to go home but needed one before they could depart. Others looked at Mackenzie as if this whole thing had gone far beyond what words could set straight.

Linda Church hauled in a length of her black microphone line like someone coiling a bullwhip. "Mr. Mackenzie!" she called out in a louder voice, above the murmur of the crowd.

"I said tomorrow tonight, ma'am." Mackenzie gave one last tug at the muscles of his jaw and then let the smile collapse.

When he reached home, he walked straight up to his study. The great silence of the place rushed in to meet him. He had lost count of the nights he spent here in his office. His father had died in this room after giving up the company. It was as if the act had somehow torn some vital organ from his father's body, like a bee that had spent its stinger. He wished his father were here now to give him advice. Just as he reached his study, Mackenzie heard a half-choked sound coming from the other side. When he opened the door, he found Alicia sitting at his desk. Her face was blotchy with tears.

"Why are you crying?" Mackenzie asked.

She shrugged and shook her head. "I've just been thinking all this over. Everything you've done, Jonah. You used to say you would never do anything to hurt this town and that everything you did was for the good of this town. But I don't know if that's true anymore. You always talk about the clean sweep you like to make of things. Your tabula whatever it is."

Mackenzie stared at her. "Rasa," he said in a soft, choked voice. "Tabula rasa." It hurt him to see her cry and know he was the cause of it.

"Whatever it is," she continued. "You only ever think about

knocking things down and then you build what you want in the space that's left behind. Only first, you've got to destroy everything. I don't want to be in your new world. I'd rather be swept aside with the old one. I feel as if I've waited half my life to tell you that, but before I didn't know how to say it. So go ahead. You and people like you can knock the whole planet down and build it back up the way you want it to be. But it won't be worth living in, because you and all the Sal Ungaros of this world aren't smart enough to see what you're destroying."

Mackenzie continued to stare. He saw in Alicia's words a thing he never dreamed he would see. She was pulling away from him. She no longer trusted him, and he realized suddenly that she had not trusted him for a long time.

All that night, Mackenzie sat alone in his study with the lights turned off. When Alicia asked him if he was going to bed, he was so lost in thought he couldn't even answer her or move his dried-out, staring eyes from the blotter on his desk. He had no sense of time passing, except the pale sweep of moonlight across his bookshelf and the books he never read. Alicia had said the one truth that made a mockery of all the truths he had invented for himself. He realized it with perfect clarity, and he despised himself. He remembered lying in the woods a few days earlier, struck dumb by the certainty of his own fast-approaching death. He remembered the words he had chanted. The verdict on each person dead. Now he knew what that verdict would be, because the person he loved most had called it out. There would be only one way out of the chaos he had created. There was no time for pride or stubbornness or careful thought to covering his fast-retreating tracks. No time for strategy worked out in the smoky war room of his brain with the blind-obedient generals he had invented over the years.

He had not known until that moment what it was he would say to the town when he stood before them. But now the words unraveled in his mind more quickly than he could have spoken them. He would halt all cutting in the Algonquin. He would return to an industry of sustainable yield. He would call back Coltrane. He would start everything over again. Mackenzie found himself filled with the same sweeping energy that had accompanied all the great adventures of his life. He was filled with optimism. This would be his triumph after all. Mackenzie turned on the lamp that perched crooked-necked like a vulture on his desk. He pulled out a sheet of paper and began to write, his dry lips forming the words.

Shelby sat down on the bed in Gabriel's house. He had broken in through a back window after he saw Gabriel leave for work. Now Shelby took out his gun from its shoulder holster. He had not owned it long and found that it had a tendency to jam. He was not used to the Glock's squared-off barrel, but had practiced with it at a firing range until he knew he could use it. He had practiced so much that he had worn the skin off his trigger finger and had to use a synthetic substance over the blister. It was a rubber compound made for burn victims, and he dabbed it on each day so he could keep shooting. Shelby checked the magazine and then cocked the slide to put a bullet in the chamber. Then from his other pocket he took a silencer and screwed it onto the end of the Glock's barrel. The added weight of the silencer made the balance of the gun feel strange in his hand.

He made a point of not looking through Gabriel's drawers, or familiarizing himself with the tiny details of Gabriel's life—the way he hung his clothes, the food in his cupboard and the titles of a stack of books piled neatly on a shelf beside his bed. The way the black-on-faded-red lines of the Hudson Bay blanket wrapped like bands around the mattress. His little alarm clock still perched on his bedside table. His spare boots still standing by the closet, heels against the wall. Shelby kept his distance from these things. It made his job easier and afterward more simple to forget.

All day, he sat in the room. He watched the shadows stretch across the wall. By six o'clock that evening, Shelby realized that Gabriel wasn't coming home. Now things would be more messy and more complicated. Shelby slipped out the back, the same way he'd come in. As he made the dash to the forest, he noticed that the streets were filled with people. They moved in a shuffling stream toward the Woodcutter's Lodge with its clock tower and illuminated clock face, like a full moon lodged against the meeting hall. Then he knew where Gabriel had gone. He wondered what was happening.

Shelby wiped sweat off his forehead on the sleeve of his jean jacket. Then he jogged out to the road, hands in pockets. His eyes had blackened from the fight with Gabriel, so he had dabbed base makeup on the areas to hide the purple stain on his skin. He hoped that would be enough. It was too late now to care. He spread a smile like grease-paint camouflage across his face and slipped into the walking crowd, heading for the hall. He grinned at children who laughed with excitement and slalomed around the adults. With an easy motion, he brushed a hand across the fabric of his jean jacket, feeling the pistol snug against his rib cage.

Dodge stood in the road, wearing an ankle-length, signal-orange duster jacket. He directed traffic into the gravel parking lot of the Woodcutter's Lodge. When the headlights fanned across him, the orange jacket made him look as if he had burst into flames. The hall itself was blinding bright from lights that had been set up by the television crew.

Mary the Clock walked past Dodge into the hall. She sat down next to Paul, the caretaker of the Woodcutter's Lodge, who sat patiently and alone on a chair in the corner. Then Madeleine came up to Dodge and kissed him and smiled. "I'll see you afterward," she said. A few minutes later, Gabriel entered the hall, still wearing his work clothes and carrying his lunch box under his arm. He nodded hello to Dodge, who nodded back and smiled.

A man Dodge did not recognize slipped past him. He did not see the man's face. All Dodge saw was the short-cropped blond hair and broad shoulders beneath a blue jean jacket and a heavy knuckle-duster college ring on the ring finger of his right hand. The man stayed at the back of the hall, hands in pockets, head turned away from the fish-eyed camera lenses.

The TV crew were checking their sound system. A man with black jeans and a black T-shirt climbed onto the stage. The logo on his T-shirt said STEPHANIE'S BONES—SANTA FE, NEW MEXICO. He leaned toward the microphone attached to the podium and said "Pop, pop, pop." The steel chairs creaked as people sat in them. Eels of black cable slithered across the floor. Talk was constant in the room, spiked with laughter that rose and fell back into the mumble of the crowd.

Shelby sat down next to Mary the Clock. "What's going on here?" he asked her. As he spoke, he kept his eye on Gabriel.

"Mr. Mackenzie is going to give a speech," she said. Then she wound up her clock.

"What about?" Shelby felt suddenly panicked. The old man's buckled on me, he thought. He's going to turn this into a confession. He got up and moved toward the side door, where he knew Mackenzie would be waiting. Just as he approached the door, Mackenzie himself walked out. "What are you doing?" asked Shelby. "What the hell are you doing?"

"I'm just going to check the speaker system," replied Mackenzie. "Is everything all right?"

"No, it is not." Shelby's voice was low and angry. "What exactly are you going to tell these people?"

"I'm going to tell them I made a mistake." Mackenzie's heart was beating fast as he thought of addressing the crowd. The formality of it made him nervous. "I'm going to stop the logging."

"You're going to blow everything!" Shelby couldn't help raising his voice.

"I'm going to undo what I've done," said Mackenzie. "It's all right," he said. "You get to keep your money."

"It's not about money anymore," snapped Shelby, still trying to keep his voice low. "It's about timing, and what I'm telling you is that you left this too late." The doors of the hall closed with a thump. Shelby turned to see Dodge taking his place in front of them.

"Will you take your seat, please?" Dodge called to him.

Shelby looked around wide-eyed for an escape route. He knew he was about to be compromised. His worst fear was coming to life. He could not allow it.

"Sit down!" Dodge called to him.

"Yes, do sit down," Mackenzie said.

Slowly Shelby took his place. His face was blank with shock.

Alicia opened the side door and motioned to Mackenzie.

Mackenzie walked over and kissed her.

"Good luck," she told him. "I'll wait for you in the back room. I wish you'd let me see that speech. You know how you hate formal speaking."

Mackenzie held it away from her and smiled. He wanted her to be as surprised as everyone else. He turned away and walked over to the podium. He cleared his throat into the microphone and the rumble of the crowd immediately fell to a murmur. The lights were in his face and he couldn't see anyone, but he could hear the size of the crowd. Hear their breathing. Hear the soft rustle of clothing as people settled down into their chairs.

Alicia closed the door behind her. Just before it clunked shut, she looked out at Mackenzie. He seemed very alone out there by himself on the stage, squinting into the lights, which showed up the creases around his mouth and eyes. They looked like a spiderweb spun across his face. Alicia dragged a chair to the keyhole and spied through it. She thought of the dances she had seen out in that hall when the Woodcutter's Lodge was not just Jonah's private club—swing bands staffed by old men in glitter-encrusted jackets who played as if their lives depended on it while the windows sweated condensation. She remembered weddings and raffles and jumble sales and memorial services. These pictures charged so fast and clearly through her mind that Alicia wondered if this was how it might be to drown, her life flashing before her eyes.

Mackenzie felt the heat of the floodlights. They sealed him off from the crowd. The stage seemed so vast. Everyone had stopped talking. Now there was only the rustling of clothes and the occasional cough.

There had been no opening applause. No introduction. He set his walking stick against the podium, checked that all the pages of his speech were there and in order, and then raised his head to meet the stares of the audience. He tapped at the silver-webbed ball of the microphone. "Can everyone hear me in the back?" No one answered him. "Good!" he said and laughed nervously. He stared for a second at his speech. For a moment, the words all clumped together and his mind could not pull them apart. Slowly they drifted into meaning. "Thank you for coming!" His words sealed the silence of the hall. "I know we have been living in a time of trouble lately."

In the front row, Shelby stood up. Mary the Clock, in the next seat over, reached out to touch his arm, but Shelby pushed her hand away. Then Shelby pointed at Mackenzie, as if to single him out from a dozen others on the stage.

"Please," Mackenzie said, and held up his hand. "If you'll please just listen to what I have to say?" Then everything stopped making sense. His hand slapped back against his shoulder. He couldn't understand how it happened. A jolting hum washed through him. He couldn't hear properly. The hall was filled with noise. He could not move. Could not speak. He felt impossibly weak. He just stood there, trying to go on with his speech, but he could no longer read the words. The page was all messy. It was blotchy with something, and at first he thought these blotches were in his eyes and then he saw they were coming from his hand, which hovered over the paper, still ready to turn to the next page when he had finished reading. Almost all the words had vanished now, and the blotches spread and mingled, filling the pencil-ledge of the lectern, spilling onto his shoes and the floor. Then Mackenzie held up his hand and he could see right through it to the crowd. There was a huge hole in the middle, with red and blue veins hanging down like jungle vines across his palm and the flesh was titanium white. It was blood on his speech. He had been shot. He understood that now. His breath slopped like scalding porridge into his lungs.

He took one step backward. Nausea rushed up to meet him. He did not feel himself falling or the moment when he hit the floor, but he knew he had fallen because he was staring at the ceiling. The pages of his speech slipped through the air above him, flitting first one way and then the other and then skimming across the stage.

Everyone seemed to be screaming. Chairs tipped over. He heard the clang of metal as they hit the floor. Please, he wanted to tell them, give me time to finish my speech. He wanted to gather the fallen pages and continue reading. But slowly the knowledge was reaching him. There would be no speech. He realized now that Shelby had not just been pointing. He had been aiming a gun. Faces crowded around. I've been shot, he thought. So this is how it feels.

Mackenzie wanted desperately to get to his feet. Not to need help. To walk home and for everyone to stop staring all slack-jawed with horror. But he couldn't get up. He couldn't even remember how to get up. It seemed as if his mind had forgotten which nerves connected to his legs and his arms. His brain sent out signals but none of them went to the right places. Instead they sent back messages of pain, which scattered like embers through his body.

Then Mackenzie saw Shelby standing over him. He was still holding the gun. He's going to finish me off, thought Mackenzie. He imagined it would be the same as in the old film footage he had seen of Frenchmen who had collaborated with the Germans being shot at the end of World War II. The firing squads let loose a volley and then an officer walked past the bodies, putting a bullet into the head of each one to make sure the job was complete. He felt strangely calm about it. Shelby set the gun against Mackenzie's forehead, but it did not go off. Shelby swore and tried to cock the slide but it was jammed. Then he was gone, out through the little side door.

Dodge waded through the crowd, which poured past him and out into the street. He swept them aside with the motion of a swimmer. He kept moving forward until he found the crumpled-up body of Madeleine. She was lying under a chair. He picked her up, searching in panic for the wound.

She opened her eyes and her hands grasped his arms and then he knew she had only been taking cover. "Stay," he shouted, and even with the shout, his words barely reached her over the chaos in the hall.

Dodge jumped onto the stage and saw Mackenzie. The old man was gasping in a way that reminded Dodge of a landed fish. Alicia Mackenzie crouched over him, hands pressed down on his wrists as if they were wrestling and she had won. Dodge began telling people to step aside. But they did not hear him, so he pushed them away, gently at first, but using force when they did nothing more than totter and return to their hypnotized staring.

Then a vicious, clattering bell sounded through the hall. It shocked Dodge so much that he ducked down behind the podium and was going for his gun before he realized that the sound came from an alarm clock and that he was crouching in a puddle of Mackenzie's blood. It soaked through the fabric of his trousers at the knee.

It was Mary the Clock, and the Big Ben that rested against the ledge of her breasts was already dying as the spring wound down. She was just sitting there in the front row, hands resting on her lap, crying.

Mackenzie had heard the bell, too. He looked across at Mary's tearstained face and thought how hard he had tried to keep secret what had happened between them. Too late, he thought, to put things right. The clock's bell rattled to a stop.

Alicia's face appeared over him again.

"I was going to make it all better," Mackenzie said. "You would have been so proud of me." Then he closed his eyes, and for the second time in his life he began to pray. He prayed to the angel who had watched him all these years, always flying just above the trees. He prayed not even with words, but with one half-formed idea that he might find his way back from this chaos that war-danced all around him, so he could have another chance to put things right.

"Please, Mrs. Mackenzie." Dodge took hold of Alicia's forearm, the bones so thin he felt as if he would break them if he gripped with any force. "Call an ambulance!" he shouted into the crowd. He took off his jacket, balled it up and rested it beneath Mackenzie's head. Then he loosened the old man's tie, took a handkerchief from his pocket and wrapped it around the tatters of Mackenzie's hand. Luminous white sticks of bone jutted from the skin and the delicate trenches of his handprints disappeared into the crater where the basin of his palm had been. The white cloth covered it up. Blood dyed it red. Dodge knotted the bandage, then unbuttoned Mackenzie's shirt to see where the bullet had entered.

Alicia sat on the floor. "Get up!" she told her husband. "Jonah! Get up!" Then she held her hand to her ears, as if she could no longer stand the sound of her own voice.

Dodge pulled back the soggy red mess of cloth that had been Mackenzie's shirt. The bullet had gone in high on the right side of the chest. He slid his hand under Mackenzie's shoulder, feeling for the torn skin of an exit wound, but there was none.

Mackenzie breathed in shallow gasps. His skin was green, as if a layer of jade lay just beneath the flesh and glimmered through. His pupils were great black disks. "Save my speech," he croaked at Dodge. He waved his arm toward the scattered sheets of paper. "You read it to them."

Dodge did not understand Mackenzie's slurred words. He kept his hand pressed against the thumbnail-sized wound. Blood had seeped across Mackenzie's stomach and stained his white chest hair and the band of his boxer shorts. Dodge could feel the blood welding his hand to Mackenzie's chest. He did not feel sick about this now, but had a prickling sensation along his scalp that told him he would be sick about it later and probably for a long time.

The pain had left Mackenzie now. His head was filled with the gibberish of fever dreams. For a moment, he forgot why he was lying there. Then he recalled that he had been shot. This knowledge, reappearing suddenly as if for the first time, did not frighten him. Mackenzie felt so far removed from himself that it was as if the shock of the bullet had jolted his soul half out of his body. Now Mackenzie saw himself the way people see images through a pair of broken binoculars: two identical but slightly overlapping images. Mackenzie recalled something his father had told him just before he passed away. The man had said he just wanted to sleep for a long time, as if it were not death that he approached, but dreams.

Dodge sat on the floor with Mackenzie's gray-topped head in his lap. Looking at him, a man who had seemed at all times indestructible, Dodge was struck by how flimsily the old man's life was anchored to his body. He marked Mackenzie's breathing as if it were the ticking of a clock. Sweat collected on Dodge's forehead and leaked into his eyes. He tried to move his hand to reach for a handkerchief, but his fingers had blood-bonded to Mackenzie's wound.

The paramedic team arrived from the fire station in their wide-axle ambulance, flashing red and yellow and blue lights like giant Christmas-tree baubles racked up on its roof. A moment later, Twitch Duvall burst from the little room onto the stage, swinging the steel suitcases containing his medical equipment.

Dodge stood back while Twitch measured Mackenzie's blood pressure. He wrapped the band around Mackenzie's arm. The short gasps of the blood-pressure gauge were like Mackenzie's own breaths as Twitch pumped air into the armband. He shined a penlight in the old man's eyes, then hooked an IV into Mackenzie's arm with a long needle that slid into his flesh as if it had no more substance than smoke. Twitch and Dodge lifted Mackenzie onto a stretcher and carried him out to the ambulance. As soon as it was gone, Dodge went back inside the hall to find Madeleine. A few people remained, sitting stunned in their chairs, as if they expected the meeting to continue. The television crew was also there. They sat in a huddle, smoking cigarettes. But Madeleine was gone. Dodge heard someone calling him. It was Linda Church.

"Is Mr. Mackenzie dead?" she called to him.

"I don't know." Dodge started walking out of the hall.

"Can we interview you for a moment?"

The huddle of TV crewpeople began to stir, throwing their cigarettes on the floor and stepping on them.

"Not at the moment," Dodge said. "I'm going to be closing up the hall now. So you've got fifteen minutes to pack the stuff or I'll have to leave it locked in here until after the investigation. All right?"

Linda Church breathed out sharply through her nose and dropped her hands to her side. The crew began packing up.

Outside, people moved through the streets like sleepwalkers. Their voices filled the air with muttering. Dodge looked from face to face, searching for Madeleine.

Shelby sprinted to his car and jammed the key in the ignition. Then he stopped. He turned off the ignition and felt the car shake and be still. There was still one job to finish. Gabriel. In Shelby's mind, the man's time had come and gone. His death and shallow grave in some nameless muddy place were overdue.

t was morning. Shelby lay in the shadow of the trees, in sight of the steel railroad bridge. The only things he carried with him now were the Glock and a hunting rifle with a telescopic sight. He knew Gabriel had gone in with the Putt-Putt that morning, and that the VIA train was due to pass by at twilight, so Gabriel had to come out before then.

Shelby lay there all day. By midafternoon his eyes felt dried out from staring across the swampy ground that led down to the river. He had already memorized each girder of the bridge, the color of the metal and the way the reeds at the base of the structure all seemed to bow toward the water. He watched a dragonfly making right-angle turns in the air above the tall grass. The movements were hypnotic. He felt himself drifting off to sleep, so from a small plastic bottle he took a capsule filled with powdered guarana and swallowed it. A few minutes later, the concentrated caffeine crashed through his body. He knew he wouldn't be sleeping for a long time now.

Crickets chirped by the tracks, which clicked and sighed in the heat haze. Sun caught on the green-glass insulator caps of the old telegraph poles. Shelby lined them up in his gunsights. On any other day, he would have used them all for target practice. As the afternoon went by, forest shadows stretched across the water and into the woods on the other bank. The air quickly lost its warmth. Shelby rolled onto his back and buttoned up his jacket. He flexed his hands to make sure his fingers did not grow numb.

Fading sunlight purpled the river. All around him, the colors became muddied and gray. Shelby sat up and cradled the gun on his lap. His joints were sore from lying on the ground. He propped up the gun, elbow balanced on one knee to steady himself, and twisted his arm around the sling. It was twilight now. The time window for his target had been reduced to a few seconds. Shelby stretched his legs out and began to rub the blood back into them.

Something crashed close by in the forest. Shelby froze. The crash came again. It was moving toward him. Something large and not caring how much noise it made. Shelby jumped to his feet. The carbonated sleep rushed through his legs. He could see nothing among the jumbled branches. The crashing was closer now. The fine swish and snap of undergrowth giving way. He heard the sound of breathing.

Shelby leveled the gun at the darkness, but he was as good as blind. He knew he couldn't risk a shot without sending a warning to Gabriel, if this wasn't the man himself come stumbling into his own trap. He would have to be quieter. Shelby was just putting down the rifle and reaching for his fighting knife when the blackness hurled itself against him. He sprawled on the ground. The rifle fell from his grasp and his knife slipped from its sheath. Shelby struggled to find it in the grass. Then a shape rose up, as if the darkness itself had taken form. Shelby felt the presence of something in the air in front of him. He reached slowly inside his jacket, until his hand was on the butt of the pistol. The pads of his fingers squeezed into the handle's gridded grip. He pulled out the heavy gun, smelling the sweat of his fear.

Shadows plowed into his face. They hooked into his brain and his entire head seemed scattered about him like broken pottery. Something huge stood over him. He could no longer feel the gun in his hand and when he held his other hand to his face, his fingers dug through ripped flesh and scratched against the bone of his cheek. The huge thing lunged down on him. It had a smell, a rank mustiness that Shelby began to piece together in his frantic mind. It clamped down on his head and Shelby felt as if his skull had been screwed into a vise. It was some kind of animal that had grabbed hold of him. He raised his hands and sank them into the rough tangle of fur, groping for its eyes. He reached the stubs of its torn-off ears, fingers slipping through the animal's saliva and only then knew for certain that it was a bear. Shelby started to scream. Then all the screws of the vise turned on him at once. Shelby felt the crunch of bone giving way. His throat filled with blood and the pressure behind his eyes was huge and suddenly gone. His thoughts grew vague. This darkness had become a part of him. There would be no coming back into the light.

No Ears dragged Shelby out toward the tracks, jaws still clamped into the man's skull. Then it heard a noise and flattened itself in the undergrowth, resting on the body of the man.

Gabriel crossed the bridge in his Putt-Putt, the wobbling beam of his flashlight held out in front of him because the Putt-Putt had no lights of its own. He sang to keep himself company and did not turn to see the darkness riding the rails close behind. Gabriel was still in shock from the night before. He was unused to the silence that had met him as he worked on the tracks that day. No chain saws unzipped the air. Without Mackenzie, not only the company but the whole town had come clattering to a stop.

When Gabriel had gone, No Ears dragged the body a little farther and had just reached the railway embankment when it heard another noise, this one much louder than the first.

The three-engine, fifty-wagon VIA train appeared in the distance, the blaze of its headlight carving a path through the woods. The driver was Alain Labouchere. The last periwinkle glint of twilight always brought him peace of mind and he never tired of it, even on the lonely winter runs between St. Johns and Montreal, when ice packed up so thick on the iron grille across the train windows that he could barely see where he was going. As he crossed the bridge, he saw a shape at the side of the tracks. He couldn't yet tell what it was.

He grabbed above his head for the train whistle. His fingers slid through the greasy red-painted iron loop and he pulled. The whistle rattled his bones and fanned out across the Algonquin. Now he could see it. A bear, balanced on its hind legs, reared above a carcass that lay hidden in the undergrowth. It looked to Labouchere as if the animal was baring its teeth at the oncoming train. He pulled the whistle again.

The bear dropped on all fours, sank its snarling face into the meat of its kill and dragged the body back into the trees. The dead thing left a sheet of blood over the green raspberry leaves.

The train drew level with the bear. Labouchere gaped down at the animal, and saw that its head was disfigured. He realized it had not been snarling, only staring at him. One of its jowls had pulled back from some old wound and never properly healed. Its eyes were not raging, the way he had imagined them to be. Only scraps of fur remained where its ears had been. Labouchere watched the bear's curved black bayonet claws, chafed white at the tips. The animal's chest was covered with blood. The kill lay partly buried in the muddy ground, its belly torn wide open and an orange-gray tangle of stomach half in and half out of the body. Labouchere had no idea what it could have been.

As the train passed by, Labouchere stuck his head out the window. He watched the bear until the train had rounded a corner. The black woods converged around the tracks and it was gone. Labouchere slumped back into his seat. He gunned up the massive engine and rode faster on the polished iron rails. He roared through Abenaki Junction, glancing out at the winter-beaten houses and beyond them to the sawtooth ridge of Seneca Mountain, on whose granite peak the sunlight and the moonlight were always beautiful and changing.

Dodge opened his eyes. It was dawn. Madeleine lay sleeping beside him. He felt her warm breath on his skin. In the strange honeyed light of his dreams, he had seen the Abenaki Indians with their black-and-yellow-painted faces, silent as they shadow-walked among the trees. He wondered why they had appeared to him again. Perhaps the dream was never meant to come clear. It was a secret, caught in the path of its own revelation and not containable within the bony brackets of the mind.

"Are you scared?" she asked him.

Dodge was surprised to hear her voice. He had not known she was awake. "Scared about what?"

"About waking up here next to me?"

"No." Then he laughed. "God, no." One day he would tell her how many times he had imagined it. He got up and dressed and headed down to the Four Seasons. The owner had called and said there was a car with Virginia plates in the parking lot that had been there a couple of days and they wanted it removed. Dodge figured it belonged to the man who had shot Mackenzie. There were manhunts all over the state for him, but so far nothing had turned up. Dodge took the license number of the car and then walked into the restaurant. He called out, "Does anybody know who that blue Honda belongs to? I'm fixing to tow it away."

People looked up and around. When no one stood or raised a hand, they went back to their food, and the Quebecois who had not understood put their heads together and muttered their translations to each other.

Coltrane was there, on one of the round stools at the counter. He raised his hand in greeting, eyes deep-set with fatigue but smiling. He had not slept the night before, but had driven back from Portland, where he went to see Mackenzie and Alicia. Mackenzie was still unconscious, but seeing him had reminded Coltrane so much of himself in the hospital that his voice grew thin with shock when he tried to speak with Alicia. Even his own experience did not dull the impact of seeing the old man under an oxygen tent, with one tube up his nose and another down his throat. The IV drip was like a bag of diamonds in the sunlight. In the hospital room, Alicia took from her purse the pages of Mackenzie's speech. She had peeled them from the stage of the Woodcutter's Lodge and read through the footprints and bloodstains that obscured the words. "I had hoped he could explain this to you," she said to Coltrane. "But now you will have to read it yourself."

Coltrane sat down on the floor because there were no extra chairs in the room. He read what he could through the brown-black splatters. Then he folded up the speech and handed it back. Dried blood fell in dust to the floor.

"Can you do what he wanted to be done?" asked Alicia. She had never looked so pale. "Can you see that it's carried out?"

"Yes, I could," said Coltrane. "I could begin tomorrow."

"I want Madeleine to help you. She will know how to get some of these measures started. We have to go back to the way things were before, at least for now."

"Yes, ma'am."

"I'm staying here for a few days. You can head back now." Alicia smiled at him weakly. "There's a lot of work to do."

Coltrane was just grabbing some breakfast before his interview with Linda Church. After that, he would head over to find Madeleine. They would talk about the work that lay ahead.

Dodge took off his cap and sat down next to Coltrane. The waitress filled his mug from the black goldfish bowl of her coffeepot.

Gabriel walked in and sat beside them on his usual stool. He set his tool belt on the floor.

" 'Morning, Mr. Gabriel," said Coltrane.

Gabriel smiled. He was lost in thought. As he had set out into the silence of the forest these past few days, there was no sense of having won. Instead, he felt only the vastness of the work in which he was involved. It spread beyond the boundaries of the Algonquin. It spread across the world. The struggle was so much larger than he was that he knew he might never be able to grasp it in his mind, but that did not matter. The vastness was what made it sacred.

"The leaves are changing in the Algonquin," Dodge said to Gabriel. "Must be pretty out there now."

Gabriel was jolted from his thoughts. "I always did like the Algonquin at this time of year," he said, tipping milk from a pitcher into his coffee. It was only then, as he watched the white swirl into the black, that he realized what he had said. Now they would guess he was no stranger to this town. For an instant, the mask of Adam Gabriel slipped away.

"Yes," said Coltrane absentmindedly. He was thinking about the interview. He didn't know what he would say.

But Dodge was looking hard at Gabriel. He had seen the mask slip, and now he understood. A moment passed and Dodge said nothing. He nodded slowly, as if greeting Gabriel for the first time. Then he turned away.

Gabriel knew the gift that Dodge had made him, but there was no way to thank him for it. Both men knew that. There was only the quiet that followed. And in that silence the mask returned to the face of Adam Gabriel. It would stay there the rest of his life. The ghost of his old self shuffled past and through the wall and away. The sound it made was like the sweeping of a broom.

Linda Church walked down the logging road. Her trenchcoat snapped in the breeze. Coltrane walked beside her. He kept his head down against the wind. The camera operator struggled in front of them, walking backward. He moved in a waddling shuffle to keep the camera steady on his shoulder. His right eye was squashed against the rubber lens-protector and his left remained crunched shut against the sunlight.

Linda Church talked as rapidly as she walked, almost choking herself at the end of her sentences because she did not pause to breathe. "It appears that your time is running out for logging the Algonquin," she said. "Why don't you send crews back in here to continue the cutting?"

"Because there will be no more logging in the Algonquin, or clear-cutting anywhere else on Mackenzie Company land."

"So what will happen to the logging industry in this town?"

"I don't know, but if we don't change the way things are being run now, in fifty years there won't be a logging industry here at all. We are going back to the old methods for a while. It was a less destructive way. Then we'll decide what to do."

"Do you think Jonah Mackenzie will recover?"

"I don't know."

Linda Church stopped walking. She tightened the belt of her trenchcoat. "There seems to be a lot you don't know, Mr. Coltrane."

He looked her up and down, his old confidence returning. "That's the best place to start, don't you think?"

When Coltrane reached home after the interview, Clara ran up the driveway to meet him. Her hair was corncobbed with curlers. He could tell from the look on her face that something was wrong.

"That bear is back!" she shouted and opened the door and climbed into the truck. "It's out in the cornfield again. But, Victor, I've been thinking. Before you go getting angry—"

"Goddamnit!" Coltrane roared. He jammed the accelerator to the floor and roared down the drive.

"Why don't we just leave the bear alone? Just let it go." Clara was pleading with him.

Coltrane skidded into the farmyard, cut the engine and ran into the house. When he ran out, he was carrying his Springfield rifle. He climbed up the ladder that led to the top of the barn.

"Please, Victor!" Clara called to him.

"Get in the house!" he shouted down. He sat on the roof of his barn, thirty feet above the ground. It was evening, but heat from the day still rippled off the roof. He peered across the purple-topped cornfields. All he could think about was killing the bear. For weeks now, thoughts of vengeance had filled his imagination. In his dreams, Coltrane had slaughtered the bear so many times that if he did not kill it now he knew the animal would haunt him the rest of his life.

Clara raised her arms and let them drop against her blue-and-white checked apron. "Please," she said again, knowing it would do no good. Then she walked back inside the house.

The corn shuddered as something large moved through the rows. "I got you now, you big fucker," Coltrane said. He unslung the Springfield from his shoulder. The tall cornstalks moved again. Coltrane fired a round into the middle of the rustling. The roar of the explosion turned to a high-pitched shriek in his ears and then there was only a single ringing note, like the sound on a television when the channel has signed off for the night. He popped out the empty case and chambered a new one. The empty finger of brass bounced off the roof and flickered down into the barnyard.

He fired again at the same place, and again and again, his lungs full of cordite and his eyelashes flicking off sweat. In his mind, each bullet plowed into the black shag of the bear. He had begun to think that No Ears might never be killed. He saw himself in a fight against all that was evil, and all that was evil was balled into that monster's black hide. When his bullets were gone, Coltrane lowered the gun and set it down on the copper strip. He shielded his eyes with the flat of his hand and squinted into the cornfield.

The screen door creaked open and banged shut on its spring hinge. Clara was back in the farmyard. "Will you stop this?" she yelled up. "I am tired of you making war on that poor bear!"

"I don't even know anymore if he is a bear," Coltrane shouted down. He scanned the field. A breeze tousled the corn tops and the whole field seemed to be moving. He reached into his pockets and grabbed a handful of loose ammunition. The brass cartridges rattled together.

"You're crazy! You know that? You're obsessed!"

"I got him this time. I swear I did." Coltrane was talking to himself.

Then the corn exploded at the edge of the field. Coltrane saw the huge bear loping toward the trees.

"Goddamnit!" screamed Coltrane. "Ain't we even yet? How much more do you want from me? Didn't I do enough to put things right?" Coltrane grabbed for his rifle. He jammed a round into the breech, half-aimed and pulled the trigger. He slid back the bolt and the empty cartridge flew up into his face. It was hot and still smoking and he cried out as the brass hit his cheek. By the time he realized he was losing his balance, it was gone. He slid backward down the roof, without even time to cry out. Then he hit the rain gutter and flipped. The rifle flew out of his hands. He heard Clara scream. The back of his barn swung up and past, and now he was falling although he had no sense of falling. It was everything else rising up to meet him. He saw the mountain of his hayrick and the cornfield, right-side up now and from the other side of the barn Clara was hollering. Then he vanished into the hay, a great rustling crunching sound all around him. Yellow dust kicked up. The sun-warmed stalks caught him softly and held him and suddenly he was not moving anymore. His brain sent out its cautious messengers down the long paths of his bones to see if they were broken. Slowly, he opened his eyes. He studied the tangled threads of straw close to his face.

Coltrane knew he had almost been killed. The knowledge reached him in a strange, tingling warmth through his body. For a moment longer, he sat there breathing, enjoying the smooth rustle of air into his lungs. Then Clara climbed up the hayrick to find him. She was crying as she dug through the hay, and when she did, he looked up grinning, the way he had not grinned since he was a child. "Will you give it up at last?" She reached down to embrace him. "Some fights you aren't supposed to win. That bear is just being a bear, and killing it won't give you what you need."

Coltrane still sat where he had fallen, listening to the heavy-boot plod of his heart. At first, he did not understand what Clara meant. The bear just being a bear. The animal had been wrapped up in all his ideas of what he had done in keeping silent about Mackenzie's spiking of the tree and the payment he had to make to live with himself again. Only the spilling of blood had allowed him to see what was real and what existed in the shadowy parallel world of his imagination. But now it was clear to him. The rage that had stockpiled itself inside him began to diffuse, and suddenly it made no sense to him. For Coltrane, it was like waking from a dream in which he did not recognize himself.

Victor and Clara Coltrane thought back to the times just after their marriage when they had come here to lie in the hay, and how much had changed since then beyond the quiet valley of their farm. The quality of light had altered in their memories, and their surroundings seemed to fade, as if into the watery brown of an old sepia print. They saw themselves fading as well, and held on tightly to each other as they vanished into the past.

Jonah Mackenzie lay in a coma under the clear plastic hood of an oxygen tent, looking like a man entombed in ice. The green line of his heart-rate monitor drew shark fins in the black. Where the color had been on his face, there was now only a slick and waxy sheen. In the cellophane clinging of flesh to his bones, the places that were once light had turned to gray. Mackenzie had become like a photographic negative of his old self. He was not dying with the fireball swiftness that he once imagined. Instead, death wandered slowly and patiently through his veins. It took his strength fragment by fragment, until at last nothing remained.

Now he was moving away. The room and the hospital and the tiny bunched-together houses of the city faded quickly from his view. He forgot he had ever been born.

Jonah Mackenzie set out into the ancient forests of an undiscovered land. He was filled with fear and wonder. Distant voices called to him, speaking the words of his prayers. They reached him in the depths of stillness, where even his heart made no sound.